THE SCORPION'S STING

J.D. Masterson

THE SCORPION'S STING

A Magdalena LaSige Novel

TATE PUBLISHING & Enterprises

Published by Tate Publishing & Enterprises, LLC
127 E. Trade Center Terrace | Mustang, Oklahoma 73064 USA
1.888.361.9473 | www.tatepublishing.com

Tate Publishing is committed to excellence in the publishing industry. The company reflects the philosophy established by the founders, based on Psalm 68:11,
"The Lord gave the word and great was the company of those who published it."

Book design copyright © 2010 by Tate Publishing, LLC. All rights reserved.
Cover design by Scott Parrish
Interior design by Stephanie Woloszyn

Published in the United States of America

ISBN: 978-1-61663-652-4
1. Fiction / Suspense   2. Fiction / Occult & Supernatural
10.09.22

DEDICATION

Dedicated to my eternal Father for making me look with my heart and not my eyes and for keeping the promise that through You all things *are* possible.

ACKNOWLEDGMENTS

In loving memory of my mother who shared her perpetual quest for knowledge; my father for keeping life grounded and subsidized growing up; my sibling, spouse, and friends who have filled my life with travel, music, theater, art, education, and some astounding adventures on this unbelievable ride we call life!

Many thanks to my primary editor, Carolyn Abbott, for her keen attention to detail, mutual interest in etymology of words, and the fortitude to keep me updated on so many crucial topics. Leo, for the continual input and excitement about the project. And most importantly, my publisher for giving this series a home, with special thanks to Kalyn McAlister for edits, Marianne for graphics, Scott Parrish for cover design, Stephanie Woloszyn for layout, and the hard working staff that makes a project like this possible.

PREFACE

John F. Kennedy proclaimed, on November 21, 1963, "We seek a free flow of information...We are not afraid to entrust the American people with unpleasant facts, foreign ideas, alien philosophies, and competitive values. For a nation that is afraid to let its people judge the truth and falsehood in an open market is a nation that is afraid of its people." John F. Kennedy was assassinated the next day, November 22, 1963.

> Behold, I am sending you out like sheep in the midst of wolves; be wary and wise as serpents, and be innocent (harmless, guileless, and without falsity) as doves.
>
> Matthew 10:16, Amplified Bible

PROLOGUE

To everything there is a season, and a time for every matter or purpose under heaven ... a time to kill and a time to heal, a time to break down and a time to build up ...

Ecclesiastes 3:1–3, Amplified Bible

JULY 29

 *ump*, I'm holding on for dear life. *Bump*, blood is bursting in all directions and voices are yelling frantically, "She's been shot. Is she dead?" *Bump*, only partially aware. *Am I in a wheelbarrow, am I hallucinating?*

Boom, an explosion. The earth trembles. Darkness.

The sweat's dripping from me as I awake with a gasp. It's been like this the last few nights. I know what post-traumatic stress disorder is, and I'm in its throes. You don't survive a bullet wound and not have some aftershock, especially when you're a peace-conscious, former child psychologist like me. I wasn't in a war after all…I was just a semi-intellectual trying to help a friend.

After the dream started to wear off and my heartbeat returned to normal, I thought about how blissfully innocent I'd been that July 9th morning, when I thought my only purpose that month was to unwind from the crazy days of work, seeing if I could regain some perspective in my life. It had been forever since I'd decelerated. As it turned out, I'd barely had time to step on the brakes.

If destiny has a direction for people, I certainly had no idea that day, and the joke has been on me. I had awakened calmly pre-dawn that morning, anticipating the kaleidoscope of colors sneaking up from behind the efferent pines. Silent music. The sun, conductor of all, stretching endlessly over the horizon, regally announcing itself while emanating its universal, unspoken words, "A new day has begun." If only I could have foretold the future, I might have been better prepared.

Today, I force myself to move from bed. I had some computer research I wanted to do before the sunrise, so had set the alarm for 4:00 a.m., but the dream woke me instead.

The searching occupies my mind, and upon finishing, I'm bound and determined to enjoy the sunrise. I hope getting outside will make the claustrophobic pressure in my body release.

As I shut down the computer, I stare through the large window overlooking Lake Memphremagog, located directly on the Canadian and Vermont border, praying for serenity. I tell myself to shake the nerves off. I'm safe.

Physically, the bullet wound is healing nicely. Mentally, there are so many thoughts running through my mind. I don't know where to begin. I envision a puzzle with a myriad of pieces floating around and wonder if I'll ever be able to complete the picture again … to say nothing about feeling at peace. I fear that even if I can put the puzzle together, some evil manufacturer or higher power has broken or chipped a piece, or even worse, mischievously neglected to pack the final one, so that I'll never experience the complete picture.

I wander onto the deck of the boathouse. Scantily clad, I settle into a vinyl car seat—a 1972 Spitfire I'd been told, not just any car seat—that the owners use for outdoor furniture. I take a deep breath in and watch expectantly.

I gaze out past the mountains at Munsell's universal color atlas for artists, blending burnt sienna into umber, adding bright yellows and oranges and hues that, to the untrained eye, are nothing short of miraculous. Experiencing the sunrise: Painted oils reflecting off the horizon, a moment caught in time. Success.

Nature lifts my mood and a flicker of excitement hits. *I actually figured it out. After the fact, but I did it!* New life comes flooding in, and I force myself to sit quietly with this revelation and enjoy it. Perhaps this time I'll be able to take the month off as planned and not have it get cut short just four days in.

Listening to the sounds around me triggers thoughts of how that fateful day began. Total silence, broken only by an occasional bird chirping and faint sounds of squirrels rustling in the woods. I ingest the magnificent views, specifically the mountains stretched across the two-mile wide lake. To the right, Owl's Head; in front, the elephant etched by nature lying down in the dirt but called Bear Mountain; to the left, a small island awaiting its next group of corporate pheasant hunters. The lake that day was "barefoot" calm, a water skier's heaven.

I'm not much of a water skier, though I am extremely athletic and have worked to keep my figure strong with weight training and sports—sports that used to be known as "boy sports": down-

hill skiing, ice hockey, speed skating. I'm a little over five foot ten, weigh 135 pounds, and have that odd mix of freckles; thick red, wavy hair; and green eyes.

The hair color has grown on me through the years, but as a child, I can assure you I wasn't interested in being a redhead. Children never like to be the oddball. I was told that, at the age of four, I used to get angry at my parents and say they "shouldn't a never planned to give me red hair and to change that emimitly."

"Ever, my dear Magdalena LaSige; should not have *ever* given you." My mother would gently correct my poor grammar, regardless of my age, and when she used our last name, I knew she was serious. I wanted to be blond, "immediately" that is, and believed that, since they were my parents, they could control everything.

It's amazing how the older we get, the less our parents seem to control, much less know. I considered dyeing my hair in my teens, but somehow I got used to and liked the special attention. I finally decided that if God had given me red hair and He knew every hair on my head, well then, that's what I'd live with. I only wish I could have such resolution in other matters today.

Now sitting here my brief excitement wanes as the residue from the dream sneaks back in, and the fear takes over without my approval. Somehow it's as if the water senses my turmoil. Suddenly it's as choppy and turbulent as my soul, with white-caps rapidly surfacing. The barefoot calm of the past few weeks, even hours, is now an inner storm, and I am a bundle of questions. Who am I really? What do I want from life? How had I been so blind? With all my degrees and knowledge, how could I have lived with my head in the sand for so long? I think of nicknaming myself "Ostrich." Head in the sand, backside flopping around in the air, going around in circles, tripping over my own long legs and awkward feet, never getting anywhere at all. It certainly seems an appropriate label for me, especially after the latest mess I'm now working my way through.

I've not yet absorbed all that has transpired, but every second I'm gaining more appreciation for those struggling with PTSD (post-traumatic stress disorder). My emotions are cycling and few are really making any sense.

The one clear emotion I have is longing. I ache to have that sense of wonder back: the wonder in the world, the unexpected sensation of anxious anticipation for new adventures, the consuming joy of watching perfectly geometrical snowflakes fall like glass specks in winter. I ache to hear the sounds of woodpeckers as their vibrations echo through trees, the buzz of bees fervently protecting and working for their queen, and all things natural we take for granted—that is, until they are gone.

I want the feeling back of believing people at their core are all good. I want even more to retrieve the illusion I once had in my twenties when I believed I had life in my hands and was using the reins to my advantage, vigilantly controlling my destiny. I used to have that confidence, that deep belief; yet despite my still relatively young age, it feels like I lost it long ago. I ache, truly *ache,* to have it back.

Speaking of aching, I can't believe how a small hole through the shoulder can sting and burn the way a bullet wound does. I'm told it is healing nicely and that I'm lucky it went clear through my muscle without causing any further complications. *Lucky,* I think, bemused. Luck is winning the lottery; luck is missing the train that crashes; luck is being born beautiful with all the riches in the world. I can assure you this feels nothing like "luck." I could never have imagined me hanging out, recuperating from a bullet hole in my shoulder. I guess the saying is true. "What a difference a day makes."

I wince as I try to readjust my body in the car seat while reprimanding myself for being such a wimp. I am no pain hero. I prep myself for a form of self-hypnosis to work my way through the surfacing feelings and stinging shoulder. I have become

somewhat anti-meds, another new facet of my life since it has taken such a dramatic turn these last few weeks.

I close my eyes and start the technique I've used with children fighting pain from cancer or preparing for the ultimately excruciating bone marrow syringe or spinal tap. At first, all I envision are flashbacks—my body bouncing around in a wheelbarrow with legs dangling everywhere.

I take a deep breath and push those thoughts aside. *Close your eyes and take a deep breath in. Now breathe out. Pretend you are in your favorite place feeling happy and safe. There is peace surrounding you, and you feel a beautiful, white, vibrant light, like the sun shining over you on a summer's day. Your body is starting to feel heavier and heavier. You are going deeper and deeper.* My mind slips back to that glorious early July day. The sun was shining. I was soaking in the rays. *One, your muscles are relaxing; you are melting into the chair.* I feel the warmth on my face and body. *Two, you are getting heavier and going deeper as your fingertips and toes begin to tingle.* I think about how I felt that day when I forced myself to put my anxieties and fears behind me and managed to feel at peace. *Three, you are content, quiet, and relaxed. A wonderful warm sensation has come over you as you evaporate into the skies, becoming lighter. Floating up, up, and away...*

Then, it happens—the thing that snaps me out of any sense of comfort.

The phone rings. And it all starts again, full circle, the ring, the past events, replaying again in my mind in the most unnatural and annoying way. From the end, then starting back at the beginning, with no resolution. Like a CD stuck on replay. The phone ring is permanently ingrained in my mind, as it pulls me back to the day that started it all, July 9, 2008.

chapter
1

*It is extremely sad to think that while nature
is talking, humankind is not listening.*

Victor Hugo

JULY 9

-D-D-D-*Dring.* Like an electric shock
through me. This phone is obviously set
up for a deaf person. I wonder who could
be so rude to call this early in the morning. *Is it even 5:30 a.m. yet?*

D-D-D-D-*Dring.* Vibrating so deeply
in my heart I think I might lose a beat or need to be zapped for
atrial fibrillation. *The nerve of some. Don't they know nature's working
its morning phenomenon and that to truly honor it, silence is necessary?*

Annoyed that no one else picks up the phone since it's not my house, I start to move toward it, tripping on a twenty-five foot extension cord that serves no practical purpose. The phone is only a couple of feet away, and anything more than about ten feet would be surrounded by water, or, quite frankly, leave one in the water.

"Oui? Bonjour?" My weak attempt at using high school French. After all, I'm on the Canadian side, so imitating the Québécois guttural tone seems appropriate. Unlike the phone, it's a sound that, quite frankly, I find sexy and calming.

A gush of French words comes back in my mind so quickly I hesitate and say, "Sorry, I only speak English."

"Is this Dr. Magdalena LaSige?"

"Yes?"

"Please hold," and then the voice I least expected, this sexy, deep, velvety timbre, comes on the line trumpeting, "Ma-G-Dal-Ena, is that you?"

At this moment, I know my life will never be the same.

Nine years had passed since I had heard that voice. But like a rubber band in a makeshift slingshot, I was snapped back to the past as if it was just yesterday. My graduate professor from Columbia University in New York City; one who, I admit, was twenty-some years my senior and to whom I was extremely attracted in an indescribable way. He was my biochemistry and pharmacology teacher whose classes, along with physics and statistics, were less than shining moments for me since I nearly failed them.

Education: Some hierarchical bureaucracy setting restrictions they call guidelines that make those courses a ridiculous and necessary evil for a doctoral degree in child clinical psychology. In sardonic moments, I have wondered if it was just another way for the universities to line their pockets. The proud students graduate from Ivy League schools with nothing but debt and shockingly little practical experience, while the large lending institutions amass fortunes from outrageously high interest rates.

Control: Get them while they're young and make them believe "we" are doing them a great service. Without an education, what can one do, anyway?

Child Clinical Psychology: One of those professions I now know doesn't pay so well, and if I'd had the stomach for autopsies and medical school, I would have become a psychiatrist. The pay is about 60 percent better. No exaggeration. I could've been retired by now. But the truth is, I don't have the ego or the constitution to be a psychiatrist, and in the end, I don't believe an overdosed pharmaceutical patient is the answer to most problems anyway.

"Dr. Janus, is that you? I can't believe it! Wow, how did you ever find me? Silly question, yes, you do have your ways. What can I do for you? How are you, your sister, the university?"

He quickly stomps out my rush of questions and is down to business. "Are you still practicing criminal archepsychology?" Well, that's a *new* term for my latest career. I kind of like the ring of it. "I heard through the grapevine you were a prominent success on the NYU student case."

Oh, yes, the New York University case. I'd been struggling existentially and financially for three years in all sorts of professions when I was asked to consult on the death of a young NYU student and some questionable satanic rituals. I was successful in figuring out what had happened and in catching the murderer, but in the end, it was somewhat by chance, so the accolades felt partly empty.

Since then, I'd been wondering if I needed to find a new profession … again. I wasn't sure a situation like that would ever develop again, nor, for the victim's sake, did I hope it would.

"Well, I'm flattered. I thought you'd forgotten all about me with my practically failing grades," I say, flirting shamelessly in a playful voice.

"A mysterious and intriguing woman like you, piercing green eyes and red hair to go along with the never-ending fire stream of questions? I would doubt so!"

A compliment from the professor? My heart thumps.

"Magdalena, I need your help. I can't discuss it over the phone, but would you allow me to send the family jet to pick you up?"

"Are you kidding? Do you know where I am?"

"I'm the one who called you, didn't I?"

Ah, pedantic, I think.

"You know this is important, or I would never have bothered you."

"When do you need me?"

"In ten hours. I need you here by 3:30 this afternoon. It's urgent, and I don't trust too many people."

Odd, I think, *but hey, if you want to pick me up in the family jet, who am I to say no?*

I always thought it must be great to come from old family money and have all the luxuries of the world accessible to you, versus struggling for every dollar, trying to plan for retirement, and then breaking all your retirement funds prior to age thirty-three, like I'd done.

"All right, I'll drive over the Canadian Border to the Newport Airport. The weather appears clear and calm. Do I need to bring anything in particular?"

"Nothing but you. I'll brief you in when you arrive."

Brief me in? What is this, an episode of CSI?

"I have nothing but summer casuals here, so do forgive my appearance when I arrive."

"This will not be an issue," he says flatly and firmly, which is not like him at all and a certain sign of internalized stress. "The limo will be there to pick you up. It will not bring you to the mansion in Dobbs Ferry but to an undisclosed location, so don't be alarmed. I'll expect you this afternoon. Please do not let family and friends know the nature of our business."

I don't even know the nature of our business. Not let family and friends know? I'd just arrived four days ago, said I was staying a month, and now I'd be heading out.

This would be gossip for the summer.

Gossip: The poison ivy that spreads in every community. Idle chatter. Babble, originating from the word *Babel,* the work of the devil, some would say. Even people who don't realize they were touched by it become the carriers as it spreads like avian flu. This beautiful piece of heaven was not immune.

I start planning my getaway story. A lecturer at NYU falls ill, they're paying $6,000, and I need the cash badly. I'm a consultant now, work on and off, and since giving up my psychology profession and others to stay out of the sick political arena of certain "professions" with their required "professional associations," everyone knows I can't retire any time soon. I digress about the dues, the politics, the brown-nosing needed to move up in stature. Like any other scavenger, hundreds fought their way in, eating their way to the largest part of meat while fighting off any other competitors who might get the goods before they did. And this is what we aspire to after graduation?

After watching the sunrise from the boathouse and attempting to process the phone call, I prepare to head up to where the owners are—no easy task since the water is well below the cabin and the cliff above has numerous, treacherous steps that leave even the fittest panting for breath.

The ascent. Careful footing, as dew-stained leaves and rotted wood slip beneath my sneakers, forcing me to grab the nearest tree branch for stability. I could swear a chipmunk, watching my every move, is chattering at me with amusement. Stones force me to contort my ankles and balance my body in unusual ways, while hidden moss makes for an unexpected skating glide. Putting my hands down as I slip backwards, the large stone I'm risking my life on unwedges and bounces one, two, three, four times until the

eventual splash. I don't want that to be me. Managing to make it up in seventy-two steps, which sounds like nothing, I'm shamefully out of breath. At last, I make it to the cabin, open the screen door, and enter.

The squeak of the door should've awakened those inside, but most are dead to the world. The hours-old smell of *Labatt Bleue,* Glenlivet Single Malt Scotch, and cigars lingers in the air. Poker chips, cards, and stragglers are sprawled everywhere. It had been a night that elapsed into day for most, but I had retired by midnight, not wanting to miss nature's wake-up call. Relieved no one is moving, I decide a note will do. No coherent conversations will transpire. Vacation is in full swing.

I stick with the lecturer story. I hate lying and secrecy, but there are times you do it for the good of those you love. A huge rationalization, of course, since this is the excuse given by military, governmental agencies, and large conglomerates who lead you to believe the lives of a few are worth sacrificing for the good of the many, when really they are sacrificing the many for a couple of their own power-hungry few. Every now and then, over a stiff scotch or a few too many glasses of wine, I think I'll break down and blurt it all out, but I know the stakes are high, and the damage it would cause would never be worth it. So, a few less scotches and a few less glasses of wine are required to stay in check.

Now, when totally on my own, I occasionally release and escape into oblivion, put on music as loud as it can go, prance around, and sing at the top of my lungs. Letting loose to kill the pain for a couple of hours, but never letting go so far that I can't function for days. Not that I haven't ever had a hangover! But work needs to be done now, and my mind needs to function like perfectly greased cogs in the wheel of a clock. The party's over. I'm leaving the nature I was supposed to be listening to.

chapter

2

*The easiest way to gain control of the population is
to carry out acts of terror. The public will clamor for
such laws if the personal security is threatened.*

Joseph Stalin

 arrive at the airport on time. A relative
unknown in the area, I hope to incon-
spicuously board the "room-service" jet.
Crossing the border back into the U.S.
from Canada is becoming more and more
of a hassle. My passport has stamps from
the United Kingdom, Holland, Belgium, France, Italy, Africa,
Spain, and a multitude of other locations that tend to raise eyebrows with the Border Patrol. Also, so many new patrols are

being trained since the Homeland Security Act was implemented that one has to expect longer delays.

Driving down the winding, empty roads, I almost miss the left
turn to the airport. Planted off in the woods somewhere is a sign
with an airplane on it that can't be seen coming from this direction.

Newport, Vermont: No real need to point new visitors to their
destination, most likely because if headed to that airport, they're
familiar with the area. That's what I love about the hidden gems
of towns and, specifically, Vermont. No huge billboards messing
with the scenery and convincing you to buy or eat something you
don't need. No desire to please those other than the leaf peepers
who make their annual voyage north to see the changing of the
seasons, or the winter snowmobilers who enjoy the best V.A.S.T.
(Vermont Association of Snow Travelers) trails in the world. No
state does it better.

It was the quiet and unobtrusive back roads oozing "rural,"
not "suburbia," that drew me to the area. The magnificent Roman
Catholic Church on the hill announced that a civilization did
exist, with houses lined high up into the hills overlooking that
inspiring lake. It was a place I dreamed of retiring to one day.
Part of me hoped it would always remain a secret, secluded from
the rest of the world. The other part of me who empathizes with
the plight of small business owners wanted it to be a booming
town where all could flourish.

I make the sharp left turn abruptly because I'm too busy
checking out the views and almost miss it. I pass the Sanitation
Department on the right and, coming down the final stretch,
spot the airplane immediately. It stands out among the rest, and
not just because of its value and stature.

I often drive to this isolated airport to sit and watch planes
take off and land and have gotten to know most of them. Watching planes makes me realize how little I know about the mechan-
ics of things. In this case, the bold lettering spelling what looks

like *T. Janus,* my mentor's family name, on the side of the plane tells me this will be my flight.

Even from a distance, it's clearly a Learjet 60. Sleek, about seventeen feet long; white on the upper part, a red stripe along the middle, and blue on the belly. I wonder if Newport has ever seen such a large jet before. I know they have single engine planes and maybe a couple of twin engines, but a Learjet? That will make people talk!

As big as this jet is, I guess there'll be no transoceanic flight today unless Dr. Janus is sneaking me to the British Isles via Newfoundland. The plane isn't made for longer flights. I know this because I'd seen some TV show on the rich and famous that announced this model, launched in 1993, was an improvement to the 55 and had "inboard sections of the 'Longhorn' wing and an all new wing-to-body fairing to reduce the interference drag between the wing and the fuselage for improved handling. I have no clue why the show shared this information or what it even meant; it was just more jumbled information stuck in my head.

Only worth about $11 million dollars new, but could probably still command $7 million, a drop in the bucket for the ultra wealthy, I guess. I'm impressed.

I look around the parking lot to see if anyone I know is here. I'm not in the mood to explain. The coast is clear, so I park my famous little Mazda Miata convertible that has been through life with me and put up the vinyl rooftop. My parents had purchased it for themselves in 1990, secretly plotting its eventual liberation to me. The car was a hit the first year it was released, and the red shiny exterior with black interior made even the most unaffected turn their necks.

It was amusing to see my parents' heads and bodies towering above the roof because the car looks small when an average person is in it, never mind a sixty-two-year-old, five-feet-eleven-

and-a-half-inches tall mother and a sixty-three-year-old, six-foot-three-inches father. When they first shocked me by pulling into the driveway at our house in New Jersey, I burst out laughing because all I could think of was *The Flintstones.*

Watching them get out of the car was like watching a daddy longlegs spider stretching its legs out almost flat to get enough inertia to leverage itself to the next step, even though it was only a small drop down, but needing a certain boost to force itself out and then up. My parents were nowhere near as elegant in this case. But the grins on their faces wiped all previous antics away.

The Miata: A history of its own. Mostly true, but in time, stories of its travels have come back to me slightly exaggerated as the lines between truth and fiction have blurred. Like most of history, its story has fallen victim to alterations. After 340,000 miles and a couple of accidents, it's still my baby and running like a dream.

Top up, car locked. I grab my belongings and head to the jet.

Although the sunrise had been perfect, the weather is changing with every minute. The mugginess hangs thick, and my lungs need an extra gasp to feel comfortably filled. Unusual for this time of year, which is usually still warm, yet dry. It had been a rainy summer, I'd been told, so I feel lucky to have gotten the beautiful days I had. Even if a storm blows in, the Learjet will have no problem getting us out.

Absorbing every step to the cabin, I smell the new leather wafting outside the plane door; not one of those fake, purposeless, hanging scented decorations emitting chemicals, but the real thing. And then I'm jiggered by the most heavenly, gloriously attired and handsome captain in full uniform, who greets and escorts me to my seat as if I'm royalty.

"The stewardess will be with you momentarily," he oozes. I take a picture in my mind.

Freeze frame. My life could have ended at that moment and been complete!

The beautiful interior: No hints of 1997 décor here. Matching light beige leather, brass fixtures, mirrored cabinets, and glass everywhere with royal blue and gold detailed carpeting. The jet looks as though it could fit six to eight people comfortably. The captain has to tilt his neck forward. I'd put him at about six foot two inches and the plane at around five foot eight. Even I have to tilt my head and be aware of the ceiling.

All these purposeful observations drift into my head in an obvious effort to distract myself from staring hopelessly at the pilot.

I pick the first seat on the left with extra legroom and a table in front. I feel compelled to quickly settle into the splendidly puffy leather seat that's seemingly custom-made for me because the neck fits well. Not like commercial planes, where your head juts forward uncomfortably and you have no room to stretch. Then you either get the seat next to the gabbiest person on earth or the one who has some severe cough so you can't get a wink of rest. I've been on the flights to Africa with screaming babies, tired stewardesses, and cranky people.

The masses: Transported from one part of the world to another, all with the ever-present hope of finding a better life. Whatever that means. With so many on the move, and with so many tired and more hostile passengers, I'm surprised the controlling powers don't pipe in some anti-anxiety vapors of medicine to keep people calm while circulating air and oxygen in the cabin. After this last episode in my life, some standardized governmental control combined with a pharmaceutical company profiting by doing just that would not surprise me.

Eyes back to the pilot. *Shucks, can't you just sit here with me for a bit?* I think I blush slightly as the pilot develops a hint of a smirk and then stands up from where he had been elegantly leaning on a chair arm, excuses himself, and heads toward the "cockpit."

Cockpit: The word originated from vicious fights between truculent chickens in China as a sick gambling venture. It then was used as a metaphor referring to any place of combat. Eventually in World War I, it became a term for the small, constrained space in the front of the fighter pilot's plane. I blush at the thought of the word and can't believe what comes to mind. Obviously sexual tension is in the air today.

I do find etymology fascinating. How words and terms come about and their development through the centuries is extraordinary, but at this moment, all I can focus on is this man who is going to take my life in his hands and get me to another part of the earth.

"Ten minutes, Dr. LaSige, and we'll be off. Weather's great, so should be a beautiful ride to our destination."

If going near Dr. Janus's other mansion, we'll be headed north of New York City. I wonder if private jets can fly over the city where the World Trade Centers had once been. I assume not. Ground Zero. Still little progress in uncovering the truth behind the attack, and although an agreement has been reached for plans for the Freedom Tower and World Trade Center Memorial, building has not yet started. Sad. I'd had friends and coworkers there, and it seemed like months of funerals, one after another. Not that I wasn't prepared; I had, after all, been a psychologist who worked with dying kids.

Homeland security, I think. *Was it really* secure, *or was it just another distraction pretending to make us feel safe?* It was Stalin who favored control of the population through acts of terror. Was something this delusive going on underneath the radar in my own country?

chapter
3

"What a Wonderful World" was written in 1968 for Louis Armstrong as an "antidote" to our politically charged nation.

"What a Wonderful World"
written by George David Weiss and Bob Thiele

 hear the pilot speaking to the control tower, which is only one man in a tiny room at the back of a portable building just a few feet longer than the plane itself. The plane moves into take-off position on the runway, and in no time, we're airborne and heading over the vast miles of empty, breathtaking landscape. It seems so rare to find such natural, untouched beauty today, which is the reason I keep returning to Vermont.

I've always found solace in trees, and they were the reason I finally moved out of New York City's pavement jungle. There was so much noise and so much chatter there, my body needed a break from it all. Spending at least fourteen hours a day as a therapist and a teacher and battling traffic left me exhausted.

I'm gifted at the interactive and healing process, while also being an extrovert, the life of the party, displaying proper amounts of humor and wit at the right time (and that is precisely what it is, a display). I'm really an introvert at heart who cherishes every moment of entrenchment in the intellect, philosophy, and esoteric truths. Being adopted at six months and raised as an only child by older parents, thinkers themselves, most likely influenced this. However, even if they hadn't raised me, I believe something much deeper has tickled my interest in the unconscious and kept it alive.

No matter how you slice me, I am *not* your normal, average psychologist or person. Some days I think about how perverse it is to have intimately known more dead people than people alive today, as my circle has purposefully become smaller. I wonder at times if that is why my intuition is so strong. Wouldn't that be a kick if angels were filtering information to me? Trained as a "clinical" psychologist, the diagnosis for this thought process is "297.1 Delusional Disorder," under "Schizophrenia and Other Psychotic Disorders," according to the psychologist's bible, the DSM-IV, the *Diagnostic and Statistical Manual, Fourth Edition.* I, however, know I'm not delusional.

In my practice, I made a point of encouraging patients to trust their intuition and to allow their sleeping minds to guide them through dreams, even when it was unfashionable. I was surprised to see how often a problem at night presented itself with a solution by dawn. The phrase "sleep on it" was coined for a reason.

These intense dreams with morning revelations happen to me repeatedly, which is why I believe I've had an eternal fascination with dreams and even drawings. The unconscious comes through more than most would ever want to know. For me, it is extremely strong when a patient or person approaches death. It may also be why I attract such odd situations.

I look around the cabin feeling content. My stomach speaks up reminding me I haven't eaten anything yet, and I hope there will be something other than peanuts served.

To distract myself from the hunger pains, I continue to reflect on my early fascination with the unconscious mind and how it led me to an exploration of religion and spirituality. I'm captivated by all the hidden and unspoken things that go on in life around us. Some spiritual, some physical.

The spiritual: Necromancy, or the communication with the dead; seeing spirits; analyzing dreams that foretell the future; reading people's emotions and neuroses by looking at their drawings; Jungian psychology; Cayce's healing under hypnotic trances; psychic phenomenon; astrology; witchcraft; and all that New Age stuff has fascinated me for years.

The geophysical: The signs and wonders on this earth and in the universe that we just don't bother to pay attention to or are forced to draw the wrong conclusion about because we were strongly encouraged to add up the clues incorrectly.

For example, in our skies, I'm fascinated by the way the three stars line up to create the belt of Orion, the brightest of all the constellations, while on earth, the pyramids at Giza in Egypt mirror and match this exact formation, and for that matter, so do the pyramid configurations on Mars discovered in 1985 by NASA (with pictures to prove it), but the public is not supposed to know about that. I mean, how it is that a giant spider configuration etched in Peru at the Nazca plains thousands of years ago is an exact repre-

sentation of the constellation Orion as well? With clues this enormous, don't you think someone wants us to pay a little attention to their meaning? Who is stopping us today from really getting to the truth of why these things exist in this way?

The Mayan calendar that dates back to around the sixth century BC has calculated, through looking up to the stars, the movement of time on earth perfectly. Yet we civilized people just started to define the precession of the equinoxes and earth's wobble through the discovery of "torque" in physics by Sir Isaac Newton, who lived from 1643–1727. At least this is what certain school systems would have you believe. Not that I don't give Newton huge amounts of credit, but this information is just plain delayed. There is a 2,200-year information gap, to say nothing about all those great people who understood the wobble of the earth's axis well before Newton. How could anyone in school get away with teaching such crap and call it education?

I know I'm jaded, but come on, how about this crazy story that Christopher Columbus "discovered" America? He set sail in 1492, so how is it the Chinese have sketches of America from centuries before drawn on their elaborate maps? How is it Native Americans were already here?

And then there are our famous Americans, like Thomas Edison. Was he really the first one to create the light bulb? Wrong. In the Denderah pyramids of Egypt, there are clear hand-painted pictures around 50 BC of the light bulb—remember, pictures don't lie; words do—that can be rebuilt from the drawings and would work today. Why do you think in the pyramids there is no residue, no soot overhead from burning torches to be found anywhere? Because they did not light with torches, nor could they possibly have done so, because, get a clue, that deep into some of these pyramids there is not enough oxygen to keep those flames lit. So they created a form of a light bulb. Who is teaching us the true information? No one in my history or science classes.

Now, Thomas Edison was a Freemason, and they were known to pass down some of the most elaborate and technical information and secrets of the world. Masons were skilled and knowledgeable people, and whether or not one believes they were infiltrated and corrupted, taken over by the evil groups, this is most likely how they were able to invent so quickly and in such mass quantities. They had access to past information. Why keep this quiet? Why not share the materials with the world for the betterment of mankind?

It is truly amazing that we spend hours learning false facts in school and getting ridiculous grades on outdated information versus learning the real truths in life and thus furthering our scientific and spiritual nature and all the possibilities they hold. Somehow, knowledge is being held back, and through the years, we are being taught to blank out real wisdom and truth. But why, and who would want to do this?

The eternal truth is from centuries before Christ, perhaps from our initial birth as man. Truth was embedded somewhere in our psyche, and huge symbols are left in the universe to remind us. We, in our ultimate *wisdom*, stopped paying attention to those symbols both "under the sun" and beyond our world as we focus on immediate gratification and become one with the "idiot tube." We are being brainwashed and manipulated daily and are so distracted we don't take the time to find the truth. In centuries past, by looking above, the summer and winter solstices were predicted and worshiped in every culture. Monuments, like the pyramids, Stonehenge, and others that we claim to serve other purposes, show us their complete understanding of the universe, and we call those civilizations primitive! Why is it that they all designate twelve major constellations in our immediate universe, no matter what religion, time, or civilization, whether Egyptian, Chinese, Tibetan, Asian, Greek, European, American, Indian, Peruvian?

Twelve. Why not fifteen or twenty? Why do all civilizations chose twelve? How do they all see the same thing in the sky when there are no words that spell out Virgo, Sagittarius, etc., and with each constellation containing numerous stars? The pictograms were duplicated through the centuries, but this was before civilizations even knew others existed across the oceans. That intrigues me.

My mind never stops analyzing. Why my hair is still red versus gray is probably surprising to some. It was times like these when I used to blurt things out to my parents as my mind raced, and I could hear my mother say, "*Ah, ma petite, avec la tête dans le ciel.*"

The unspoken and the mystery—in the end, isn't that what adventure and hope in life are all about? It's not about the known, the money, the bling, the things to impress the outside world, but about the unknown, the hidden, the miraculous things that are not flaunted but quietly experienced. The minute we lose our internal sense of adventure, getting trapped by the needs of the ego and the demands of society, is the minute we lose our *joie de vivre.* So few today can sit alone with themselves, instead needing to talk about nonsense, judgment, comparing every petty little thing they deem wrong in someone else's life to inflate and feel comfortable with their own. They are missing precious moments in the beauty of life, never to be regained again. Our soul, our spirit, our psyche needs to break free of all these illusions and entrapments in the material, controlled world and see beyond. We need to break this shield, this veil of distortion, manipulation, and control and rejoin with our essence. Will we ever be able to achieve this, or will those crazy doomsday prophecies get us first?

Current day life: Negativity and futility replace precious hours of productivity and happiness, which spurs depression. The futility of one's situation, working for items you can't take to heaven to impress those you don't even care about. The self-imposed stress as people become overachievers in the early years and burn out by their thirties, wanting to "escape" life. It's a sick and narcissistic system that breeds illness, but one that pays the pharmaceutical company by adding one medicine on top of another. No wonder people burn out, kill others, commit suicide, or simply just stop paying attention and end up dead, accidentally.

But since I learned these are all things out of my control, rather than finding answers to them, I chose to spend hours lost in Jungian psychology, the collective unconscious, dreams, symbols, and escaping into the translation of words, not planning to solve the mysteries of the world, just trying to experience and honor them. I have tried to help as many people as possible but have learned few are willing to listen or to change.

Out of nowhere, a stewardess quietly emerges, perfectly attired in red, white, and blue. *So American,* I think as I smile. That's my country and I love it! I suppose I should say flight attendant to be "politically correct," but friends of my parents were stewardesses, and they had such pride attached to their jobs, I can't bear to change the title. So *my* personal stewardess effervescently offers, "May I get you a drink, Dr. LaSige?"

Nine a.m., too early for a real drink. "Water would be great," I say.

"Spring, distilled, Perrier, mineral, or Evian?"

"Hmm, Perrier please."

"Lemon, lime?"

Wow, the choices, and just for water. No wonder the world is so overwhelmed with daily choices.

"Perrier with lime … please."

"Ice, or no ice?"

I'm starting to laugh. "Ice"—*Filtered or unfiltered, flavored or unflavored,* I think—"would be great. Wow, how the civilized world lives," then slips out, shocking myself.

Her bubble bursting, the now somewhat overly professional, tight-lipped stewardess faintly smiles. She takes her job seriously, and perhaps I'm coming across as pompous. She tries to brush the comment off, but she quickly rushes off.

I was always extremely sensitive to the feelings and thoughts of others, even as a child. I tuned in to every movement, every word, and even thoughts that weren't said out loud. Unfortunately, this is a negative trait in a society where one needs to be hardened to the daily grind of life. Intuitives, sensitives, and those types of people are considered oddities; perhaps less today, but still true. Hard-core lifers, non-feelers, that is what is needed to survive in this world. The introverts are eaten alive and discredited, if not careful.

Minutes later she returns with a small bottle of Perrier, a sublime water glass thin enough to think one could crush it by picking it up too roughly, with a slice of lime on the rim and chipped ice within, a rose in a crystal vase, a hand-dipped white chocolate biscotti, and a huge red strawberry enveloped in dark chocolate. She places a white linen napkin on my lap after strategically centering the tray perfectly in front of me.

I'm speechless. It all looks so perfect. I hadn't had breakfast yet, so I'm salivating. *Okay, I'm glad I didn't die with the entrance of the captain because this is getting good. Somewhat surreal, but good!*

Insignia start appearing more often with the *T. Janus* in beautiful but uncharacteristic lettering. Not only had it been painted on the side of the plane, woven into the carpet in the aisle, but now it's imprinted on the napkins and etched on the water glass. Is it a form of a family crest or hidden symbols disguised as letters? I'd never seen anything like it.

This triggers a thought about my favorite symbol, the oroborous; some call it the serpent, the snake biting its tail, the dragon, or even the scorpion in the same wrapped-up position.

It's a sign of individuation, of death and rebirth, and I have had experiences, some even in the same day, where therapy patients, a dying five-year-old and an elderly lady saying good-bye to her huge family, all saw the oroborous in a dream or put it in a drawing in some form. Not one of them had ever been exposed to this symbol, and yet each of them experienced the same internal revelation because of their situation. That universal symbol allowed me to help move their process of growth and/or death along in a healthy manner and proved to me just how anachronistic and awesome are the world, the mind, and nature.

I think about Dr. Janus and the fact that he is still in the same profession, still teaching graduate courses at the same university all these years later. A better man than I. I think over all the different careers I've had since my "unconventional" doctoral degree that combined Jungian and analytical psychology, spirituality, thanatology, mythology, and various cultural belief systems into a strange dissertation. It left professors unsure as to what to do with me. They opted for letting me do the independent research, overseeing the technical parts of the projects, while I consulted with the leading professionals in the field to put my thesis and dissertation together. I've never been able to do things the way everyone else seems to do them, and still can't, to this day!

I wonder how I'll ever be able to fill Dr. Janus in on all that has happened since college. It seems like lifetimes have passed, to say nothing about careers!

I had taught classes at NYU and used to get the most interesting responses from students when I explained that different cultures over different centuries, without even knowing the others existed, all had similar symbols in their dreams or drawings and that, somehow, universally they meant the same thing.

A class on analyzing dreams, drawings and symbols was new to the university the year I taught it, but so popular they had to max out the class at 150 students a semester. I loved to perplex my students by comparing humans to our primates, who seemed to communicate across the lands using their collective unconscious as a given, while we are still struggling with trying to figure out if intuition and telepathy are even real.

I'd explain "The Hundredth Monkey Effect," which proves a monkey trained to wash a sweet potato in one place of the world starts the behavior, others nearby join in, then soon all over the world most monkeys start to perform the same behavior. This is not because they were exposed to each other, but somehow telepathically they have transmitted the thought to another same-specied mammal in a totally isolated part of the world and they now all mimic the behavior. Imagine if we uncondition-ally accepted the existence of this telepathy! Our rate of growth, intelligence, and advancement would be nowhere near as stunted as it is today, using only about 9 percent of our brain capacity.

My first few years of "prof"ing were exciting. Sharing and con-vincing students, watching their eyes light up, or in reverse, watch-ing their minds close down in utter disbelief, fighting to get to the truth. Arguing, laughing, trying to disprove these theories as little by little they were left feeling they knew less than they had known when they had cockily arrived for their first day of class.

Then the teaching experience became dull, a bore, like pull-ing teeth. I felt trapped explaining the same things over and over again, arguing about grades, giving exams the university over-seers required us to use, despising especially the ones the text-book authors wrote in multiple choice style, which I have always felt were useless. I tried to maintain my enthusiasm, but seeing students lose their energy by the end of the semester, know-ing that some ridiculous exam, perhaps from the three to seven other courses they were taking, would beat them down enough to no longer care about the content and excitement of my course, clinched it. Just get those three credits per course and get on, they were told. That is what life requires. Get that degree.

How my parents ever managed, both Ivy League professors, no less, I'll never know.

The result of my teaching experience? One day I was reviewed by the Psych Department Chairperson and reprimanded for adding too many interactive experiences as learning tools, like stories, pictures, cases, and props. My students loved those and commented on it being the best course they had ever taken. They felt they'd learned something that would stick with them. I ended up in "Who's Who of America's Teachers," so I had to have done something right. But because I didn't stick 100 percent to the course material, I was reprimanded and treated like a five-year-old. The entire situation was so absurd, I couldn't think of teaching another course if I was going to be forced to operate under those demented rules. Thus ended my next potentially fulfilling profession.

Coming back from my musings, I look out the window at the clouds, creating pictures in their images and wondering what it is all about; the world, the universe, not just the Janus issue.

I sit there enjoying myself immensely. I'm in a private jet with personal service, after all. I'm feeling slightly guilty that some possibly terrible secret thing is the reason this journey has started. I've been trying to learn that the time to be happy is now, so I'm soaking it all in! I start to hear in my head:

"I see trees of green, red roses too.
I see them bloom, for me and you.
And I think to myself, *What a wonderful world.*

I see skies of blue, and clouds of white.
The bright blessed day, the dark sacred night,
And I think to myself, *What a wonderful world...*"

A certain sadness seeps in as I think about how this song had been written for Louis Armstrong and released in 1968. Its purpose was to serve as a certain antidote, which of course means to counteract a poison, for the extremely disturbing and rapidly changing political environment in the United States. People were looking for respite because of Vietnam, Kennedy's assassination, racial tensions, riots, and international and national tension. *Has anything really changed in all these years?* I wondered. It seems today we are just as politically charged and angry as we were then.

This song was written to bring hope about our future to those who sang it and heard it. To me, it was a beautiful song that left a somewhat double-edged pain in my heart. *Maybe there has been positive change,* I think. Optimistically I reflect back to a couple of days ago and the July Fourth Independence Day fireworks luminously displayed across the lake, proclaiming the continued freedom of the United States with the groups of partiers that celebrated the occasion. It was a joyous day.

Little did I think beyond my myopic world to know how dark that day actually was elsewhere. Dr. Janus is waiting for me, and from his tone, not with good news. This I know in my heart, but the specifics are something I could never have prepared for.

chapter
4

*One must keep hands folded under the scapular, and so
as not to be immodest, "custody of the eyes" was a rule
intended to prevent provocative or indulgent gazes.*

Rule in 1917 Code of Canon Law

JULY 4
A convent in Lisieux, France

he awoke seconds before the clang as she always did. *How is it one awakes every night or early morning at the same time?* she wondered. *Is it communion with God or is it simply one's own internal body clock?* The clang hit on the third hour, reverberating differently from the other ones. In two and a half hours her day would officially begin exactly as all her other ones did. She felt safe at the convent; she felt content. She liked her routine.

Her structured life began with two hours in the chapel of formalized prayer, the Mass, then chores, work, meditation, and praying the rosary. She felt her stomach growl with pain. Although meals were served in between prayers and chores, they were scant and really nothing exciting to think about. The emphasis was on self-denial and submission of one's will to the authority figure under whose charge one was. She thought fondly about her training period.

There was the formation period that began with postulancy, where one tested one's calling. That lasted nine months, after which she received the Carmelite habit. Then two years as a novitiate, at which time she made Profession of the vows of chastity, obedience, and poverty. Then from the first or temporary vows there was the final formation period as she studied church history, canon law, the Rule of Saint Benedict, the lives of the saints and Jesuit casuistry, the belief that the end justifies the means.

And then one day, five, not the normal ten, years later, it was time for the crowning glory, the Solemn Profession, receiving the black veil, which marked the definitive, life-long consecration as a Carmelite nun.

She contemplated the privilege of coming from such a special order, the strictly enclosed Order of the Carmelites, a penitential order, but one that could talk in between prayer times, unlike stricter convents. She honored the rigid rules and was glad they necessitated the habit and the scapular itself, worn to by-pass Purgatory. This was better than the weaker, less conventional orders that gave up the need to wear the habits since the Roman Catholic Church had lightened the rules. The Catholic Canon Law now only required one be "identifiably" serving as a witness to the values of the gospel. The simplicity of her order, signified by the habits, continued to be a sign of detachment from the greed, vanity, and possessions of the outside world.

Her stomach growled again as she thought of herself as stronger than the other nuns. At times the "weak ones" would complain of the discomfort, the humiliation, the self-imposed suffering that were the tools for training in sanctification. They were thirsty, hungry, at times sick, and yet this is what one did to be the Bride of Christ, to please the Lord. She was an excellent disciple and could take all this for His glory. *A little discomfort is an easy sacrifice for my Savior,* she thought.

Oh how she loved her God and her Mother Mary. She had devoted years of her life to contemplation and prayer. Finally, at fifty years of age, she had found peace ... or so she thought. Her routine later that day would be broken, perhaps permanently.

She was not ready, but the universe had another calling on her life, because just as one becomes comfortable, fate steps in and pushes life to an unexpected Y in the road. One would never have chosen such change voluntarily.

She fell back asleep comfortably folding her hands as if under the scapular and thinking of the safety in following rules, like the one of the custody of the eyes so as not to be immodest.

chapter
5

Fifty men have run America and that's a high figure.

Joseph P. Kennedy, the father of J.F.K.,
in the July 26th, 1936 issue of The New York Times.

 must have dozed off because the next thing I remember is the captain coming on over the loudspeaker, "Would you like to have dinner with me, Dr. LaSige?" The firm but petite hand shaking my shoulder makes me hear more clearly, and the voice is really saying, "Please fasten your seat belt, Dr. LaSige. We've been asked to circle a couple of minutes but then will be coming in to land."

It takes time to open my eyes, register his words, and fumble with the seat belt. I foggily look out over the pulchritudinous land and wipe the half-dried drool from my face, knowing the stewardess has seen it. Charming impression for the captain!

Acres and acres. Developments cropping up everywhere, too many for my liking. I've never much liked the McMansions, each trying to be bigger and better. The "owners" display the gas guzzling SUVs prominently at the front of the house versus hidden in their four-car garages. Little did people know that these houses had little furniture and no more than one car because it was all about appearances, not the wealth you had really acquired. Big house … no furniture within. To me, it was just another symbol of people's preoccupation with looks. Everything going to make the outside look perfect, keeping up with society's ideas of beauty, and nothing going on within. Empty.

What appeared to be the Hudson River came into view, and I could see the train, Metro North, making its way up the tracks. We must be near Tarrytown. I wonder, with the open acreage still visible around the developments, if it's the Rockefeller three thousand acres, their Kyuit estate and the surrounding towns. Did Dr. Janus know the Rockefellers?

Perhaps we're going to Pocantico Hills, a little hamlet around Mount Pleasant, complete with state park preserve and trails. Last I heard, the Rockefellers still owned about 60 percent of the land and have the right of first refusal to most purchasers. The rest has been deeded to conservation. It's touted that this area could be all subdivisions, but due to charity work, the care of the non-profit organizations founded by John D. Rockefeller, Jr. and due diligence, land is being preserved. The area is also known for its non-denominational Union Church, boasting stained glass windows by Henri Matisse and Marc Chagall. And, of course, it

would not be complete without the Roman Catholic Church of the Magdalene. Nice name!

I had lived in the lush Westchester County area while going to university in New York City, so became well versed in the Rockefeller rumor mill and supposed histories. No one can deny their active contributions to the growth of New York City and Westchester County. It had always irked me how hard I had worked to try to get a degree and make a buck while these rich families just eased through.

For me, every morning started with a quick, fifteen-minute jaunt down a steep and winding hill to the station. I would be half running, head down, only noticing the white sneakers and white socks piled on top of the nylons or under the business pants running next to me. I could never seem to get myself together first thing in the morning to take my time and enjoy the scenery.

When you start your day galloping, who has time to look at the glorious view? Those were good days, full of hope and expectation. It didn't matter that you were shoved into a train, rushed, fighting to get on and into the city the quickest because you were going to make a difference. You were going to be the one to change the world. So what if you only ever had enough to pay for rent, the train, and lived on coffee, macaroni and cheese, and baked beans? You told yourself it was only temporary, and somehow at that time, you believed it. The steep hill you had gone down so easily in the morning had to be mounted in the dark at night and at the end of every sixteen-hour day, including Saturday, which should have been indication enough of the futility of it all. But hope and expectation makes one do things that later don't seem humanly possible. It still does.

The plane's descent is under way. Getting closer to the ground unearths so many stories about the Rockefellers in my mind. It's as if as the ground coming into focus is whispering its secrets about their true history.

The Rockefeller name: Grandeur and charity. What it must be like to be a legend. John D. Rockefeller, Jr.—such a royal sounding name. Born in 1874; died in 1960. The only son of America's most famous billionaire in turn had six kids of his own. I was fascinated by philanthropists in my early years and studied how he had lost his first million with a bad Wall Street speculation, a decision he had made on his own. Having to face his failure and inexperience early, from that point on he consulted his father for business advice. Most people will never make a million dollars in a lifetime; forget about losing it in one deal!

The Rockefellers have an interesting history. When the grandsons were alive, John D. III ran the Rockefeller Foundation and Lincoln Center in New York City, but he died at the age of seventy on July 10, 1979. He died in an automobile accident near the Pocantico estate.

Each grandson's story is more interesting than the next. Laurence built resorts, was supposedly a conservationist, and spent time getting information disseminated about UFOs. He died in 2004. Nelson died in 1979 "in flagrante" under mysterious circumstances that still have not been clarified today. Initially, it was announced he had perished due to a heart attack in his Rockefeller Center office. Seemed appropriate, I thought, slaving over his work, amassing indeterminable wealth behind the desk. Then come to find out he was found dead in his 54th street apartment and his dear twenty-six-year-old female aide, a beneficiary no doubt, was there. If there was nothing to hide, why change the story as to where he died? I guess that is what's done for those who pursue life in politics and get appointed, not even elected, Vice President of the United States. Then, of course, there's David, the head of Chase Manhattan and Chairman of the Board

of the Council on Foreign Relations, probably the most famous of them all, with grandiose memoirs to prove it. He is still alive.

And then there were the homosexual Winthrop and his black friend, who owned the largest porn collection ever and died in 1973; Winifred Rockefeller Emeny, Nelson's cousin, who murdered her two daughters and committed suicide; and Michael Rockefeller, who died when he tried to bribe New Guinea tribesmen with large sums of money to go head hunting and make shrunken heads for him. Had all their legacies died with them? Were all their past secrets put to rest in their graves?

You would think this was make-believe, but truth really can be stranger than fiction.

All families have scandals; think of the "beloved" Kennedys. The Rockefellers are not exempt. When families are shrouded in secrecy, we should worry. I wondered if Dr. Janus's family was anything like these great thirteen to fifty families that supposedly control the world. He'd always fascinated me. Was he like a Rockefeller, rumored to be part of some great secret society, like the Skull and Bones? Was he part of some conspiracy controlling the monetary flow, both domestically and internationally? Was he like the Rockefellers with over one hundred homes all over the world, a couple thousand servants, and believed to be America's top Illuminati family, as the Rothchilds are purportedly England's? It's known that the Rockefellers have frequently built many hidden tunnels and rooms into their buildings. They even paid to have the railroad tracks moved so as not to interfere with their property, yet still provide access to it! They succeeded.

They were recorded as having hosted a meeting at Pocantico Hills in July 1972, with the support and blessings of the Bilderbergers. Was the Janus family in attendance? Still to this day, no reporters are allowed to get near the attendees to get comments, and mainstream media pretend the group doesn't exist, but that meeting in particular, along with those of the CFR and the Trilateral Commission, suddenly birthed the great *tax-exempt* Rockefeller Brother's Fund. Could this be how Dr. Janus made his money as well?

I've always been intrigued by how large groups move their money around and get richer. It's something I aspire to. Some interesting foundations were formed during that Pocantico Hills meeting, like GM, Time, Exxon, Wells Fargo, Texas Instruments, etc. Perhaps the Janus's owned stock in these companies early on and thus the reason for their fortune.

I've not yet figured out how these corporate conglomerates have any connection to being tax-exempt. We the little people have to pay our taxes, so how do they get this benefit?

Rumor has it the Rockefellers have developed their occult and worldly powers to the point they consider themselves sole rulers, maybe even gods. Was I going to some huge estate with hidden passageways and secret meetings? Who knew? Or was it more like the Kennedy's, plagued by evil and scandal and heartache, who, despite their strange luck, had a few who seemed to try to create change for the good of the people. So what if it was amidst sordid affairs, alcoholism, and tragedies?

Some years ago I read an article from a foreign newspaper that had a haunting statement from David Rockefeller's June 1991 speech at the Baden-Baden, Germany Bilderberg meeting, where he boasted about the One World Order and the Council on Foreign Relations' "secret agenda." Sometimes in foreign countries these meetings aren't as secret, and what happens takes years to trickle into the U.S. It went like this: As the Founder of the Trilateral Commission, David Rockefeller says,

> We are grateful to *The Washington Post, The New York Times, Time Magazine,* and other great publications whose directors have attended our meetings and respected their

promises of discretion for almost forty years. It would have been impossible for us to develop our plan for the world if we had been subjected to the lights of publicity during those years. But, the world is now more sophisticated and prepared to march toward a World Government. The supranational sovereignty of an intellectual elite and World Bankers is surely preferable to the national auto-determination practiced in past centuries.

Such eloquence, but when broken down, it simply meant that they, the powerful, knowledgeable, elite, controlling ones need to make a move for a one world order secretly because the masses are too stupid to be involved. Funny, wasn't that what Hitler believed before he started exterminating our beloved Jews?

If that was not enough, in his *Memoirs,* published in 2002, he says:

> For more than a century, ideological extremists at either end of the political spectrum have seized upon well-publicized incidents to attack the Rockefeller family for the inordinate influence they claim we wield over American political and economic institutions. Some even believe we are part of a secret cabal working against the best interests of the United States, characterizing my family and me as 'internationalists' and of conspiring with others around the world to build a more integrated global political and economic structure—one world, if you will. If that's the charge, I stand guilty, and I am proud of it.

How scary.

Then there was information I had read that said, "As strong as the Rockefellers are in the U.S., they have nowhere near the power the Rothschilds yield in England." It warned the American people to look into the Rockefellers' thousands of trusts and explain why Nelson, who was one of the richest men in America, did not pay one penny in taxes in 1970. How is it the Senate Committee was told by Nelson one day that his personal fortune was $33 million and then later admitted it was $218 million? One newspaper article warned:

> The more money you appear to give away, the more you can move into safe zones. The richer you then become. Look into the largest corporate holdings of *Exxon, the new name for Standard Oil of New Jersey, one of the companies formed when John D. Rockefeller, Sr., was ordered to de-monopolize the Standard Oil Company.* The stock directly owned by the family (not counting that held by such family controlled entities as banks and foundations) amounts to $1.5 billion plus dollars.

This was in the seventies!

When I started researching that, I found an article from the *Los Angeles Times* dated September 30, 1974. It listed $85 million of stock in Standard Oil in California, $72.6 million in IBM, which in turn held over $10 million or more in stock in Chase Manhattan Bank, Mobil Oil Corp, Eastman Kodak, General Electric, Texas Instruments, and Minnesota, Mining and Manufacturing (3M). The article states that they owned significant portions in over fifty American companies and one hundred international companies and were growing rapidly. Could this be even worse today?

Could something so evil and sinister really be going on behind the scenes, a one-world government that wants to control all monetary flow, that count themselves as elite and the population as flunkies, so they can make these rules in secrecy, without the people knowing? Was Joseph P. Kennedy correct

that fewer than fifty people have controlled America? If this is true, are we a "democracy"? I could hear my parents' voices correcting my limited knowledge of American politics, since I spent my life devoted to psychology: "Mags, dear, the U.S. is not a pure democracy; we are a constitutional republic. There's a big difference, and it's important not to perpetuate this misperception." *Truly forgive me,* but those insinuations about the top thirteen people internationally controlling our constitutional republic, doesn't that make puppets out of us? Could organizations really be working on sinister ways to depopulate the world, or is it all some crazy story made up to confuse the population even more? The more confused Americans are, the less likely they are empowered to make change.

Too many questions are piling up. My hands are tightly interlocked. I take a deep breath. Coming back to this area is so overwhelming, I feel like this short plane ride is taking an eternity. I've started to stress myself out about the unknown. My own fault, I've been told, totally unaware of the seriousness of what is about to be revealed to me.

chapter
6

*The advantage of a classical education is that it enables you
to despise the wealth which it prevents you from achieving.*

Russell Green

he glare from the sun quickly blinds
any chance of comfort in seeing the air-
strip, and I have butterflies for a second,
wondering if the pilot can see what he
is doing. The man does have my life in
his hands, after all. No matter how many
times the technical aspects of aviation are explained to me, I
still can't grasp them. My dad used to sit patiently and explain,
"You see, the air lifts under the wings and over … until we're air-

borne." He always ended with, "You know, Mags," in his gentle and warm tone, "the most dangerous part of flying is riding to the airport. Hmph." *Chuckle, chuckle.*

I've heard this speech so many times, you'd think I'd ask him to be quiet, but it's the pride in his voice, the reminiscing over his old pilot and flying days that makes me feel so secure and comfortable. I can hear his words over and over again like the best bedtime story ever told. I can envision myself as a child, Mom patiently smiling, me between the two of them when flying, as she just let him ramble on! That's my parents. You don't see too many couples after that many years together still so patient with each other.

A sudden dip grabs my stomach first, and we're on the runway in no time, truly the softest and smoothest landing I've experienced. It's good to have money. This pilot is certainly worth his salary. Or perhaps the phrase from the rich and famous show announcing the leading edge droop, wing cuff, and wing to body faring really means something!

I hear, "You may now unfasten your seatbelt," clearly coming over the intercom system from the cockpit.

Thanks for that tip! I grab my carry-on bag with the necessities from underneath my seat: computer, cell phone, purse with toothbrush, toothpaste, hair brush, a small plastic bag of cosmetics, a few clean pairs of underwear, and, of course, the Echinacea. Never leave home without it. It's the only thing that seems to fight off those nasty airborne illnesses when I fly.

The captain and stewardess are already positioned by the open cabin door. What a shame. I like my dream dinner invitation with the captain better! I thank the stewardess, and just then the captain leans down close to my right ear and says, "Come fly again with us … soon, Dr. LaSige."

"I hope to! Have a nice day and thanks for the perfect flight!" I gush, hoping I will indeed see him again. Then, in perfect Magdalena style, I trip over my own foot, practically falling down the stairs, not paying attention because I'm flushed and my eyes are already focused on a huge, black, stretch limo pulling up on the small runway parallel to the Learjet. I take a couple of seconds to rebalance and sheepishly look back. "Ostrich legs," I say, laughing. All are polite and professional, as if they have not noticed. Please!

The limo is practically the length of the plane and, sure enough, has the same insignia in gold on the side. It's now parked impressively before me, and at the rear passenger door as if from some old movie, is the most impeccably dressed, perfectly austere driver outfitted in gray, black, and white. My eyes move from the shiny shoes, slowly on up. I do a double take the moment they make it to the face.

"James?" I squeal with delight. "Is that really you?"

And in one second all that professional class stops oozing from his presence as he opens his mouth and the thickest half-Brooklyn, half-fabricated drawl, "Well ya!" emerges. "I heard I'd be getting a special guest, just never 'spected it would be you! How's it hangin'?" he asks as he picks me up in his arms with a bear hug strong enough to make you think your insides would be left splattered on the road like entrails.

"I see you're still with Dr. Janus."

"Right on! It would take a crowbar to pry the two of us apart. We're the best in welding tools."

Not sure exactly what he meant, but James has always been known for inverting phrases and doesn't need any help correcting them because he truly "just doesn't give a cow's petunia," or some mixed phrase like that.

They don't come more loyal than James. The irony, his true name is Joseph. J-oseph, A-lberto M-ariviano, the third, which somehow got translated years later to *J-A-MES*. If there is something in a name and limo drivers are referred to in jest as James, perhaps there is something to the custom. I've heard that Jewish

tradition is to claim a name that reflects the person's nature or status and that nuns chose a saint's name upon consecration. Joseph, consecrated as James—I've heard stranger things!

A Hebrew scholar friend once informed me that in the Bible, God changed Abram's name, meaning "exalted father," to Abraham, meaning "father of a multitude" because, in Hebrew, *h*, the fifth letter of the Hebrew alphabet, denotes grace. God also did this with Sarai, meaning "princely," although some define it as "contentious," when He renamed her Sarah, which means "princess" and "mother of nations" in Genesis 17:15.

I admired James, a man who had no expectations and no dreams outside of his daily routine, who just seemed content to do his job. I wish I could be like that.

He opens the door with elaborate style, and I crawl in. His large and powerful hands close the door with purpose as he professionally announces, "Enjoy the ride, ma'am." I feel an "abysmal" warmth—meaning immeasurably deep or great, versus the way most people understand the word to mean "extremely or hopelessly bad or severe,"—and profound comfort in seeing him again. I really should be better about keeping in touch with people from my past, but we all have busy lives, and that doesn't seem to be my forte.

Legs stretched out with room to spare, I take in the expansiveness of the limo and am just lifting up a shelf to sneak a peek at the submerged bar to my right when the window in front starts to automatically come down, and like a kid with her hands stuck in the candy jar, I pull my hand back. The clunk makes me jolt back in my seat.

"Go ahead! Don't be a lamb's foal. I was just gonna say, help yourself to whatever," he states.

"Actually I'm fine; I was just curious as to what was in there."

"That's my Mags, curious Georgetta!" And he puts the window back up.

He knows me well.

I feel a little claustrophobic since the windows are so dark and I can't see where we're going. Dr. Janus's plan, I suppose. I again take in the fresh leather smell and start to look more carefully at the Janus insignia. Like a coat of arms, most people who create these put great thought into them, and they carry deep significance. This one is strange. The *J* has an odd loop to the bottom part and is almost triangular at the upper point. The *T,* which I assume is for Theodore Janus, Dr. Peter Janus's father, has an extra vertical leg-line. It's artistic, but I can't come up with any meaning for it.

I'm back thinking about symbols again and how in an odd way my life is like the oroborous. I reflect on how many turns it has taken, meanderings that used to appear so unrelated, but the older I get, the more they seem to have some strange, interconnected weave. After years of distraction, they seem to bring me back to the same place again: the collective unconscious at work, yet my persona has changed somewhat because I seem to have lost my ability to be such a good listener.

To loosely paraphrase Alice Miller explaining psychoanalysts in *The Drama of the Gifted Child,* who else would spend that many hours a day listening to other people's problems unless they had experienced similar pain? I think about the psychotherapy process and how initially I was so devoted to it. It was such an intense experience. I'd had days with patients when we were sailing along, moving at a good pace, nicely making progress, then boom, dead stop, like dropping anchor while in motion and getting jolted out of one's seat.

And then, nothing. Paralysis. Unable to move beyond it.

At that juncture, the patient would either stop therapy because it was too painful and return to the old comfortable behaviors or leap into the ocean of what the profession deemed "appropriate" attitudes.

Those tumultuous, often fearful, new reactions all transpired for the long-awaited but worthwhile catharsis. Carl Jung called our journey of life the process of individuation. Unfortunately, even the best therapists can't force change unless the patients want it themselves, so we wade through years of latent memories and hurt feelings all to get to a point where people are healthy enough to cope with daily life.

For the patients, those trips are often full of countless mistakes and heartbreaking recollections; for the therapist, it's a constant battle to give them enough coping mechanisms and strength to move forward. For both, it's a continual, eye-opening experience as we try to learn from past mistakes—assuming, of course, that we even realize we're in the midst of the biggest one of our lives.

Since then, that professional endeavor has been replaced numerous times throughout the years while trying to "find" myself, and my current purpose in life has been replaced with my current job, one I inadvertently fell into, as a type of consulting criminal symbologist. *Criminal archepsychologist,* I smile as I hear Dr. Janus's words in my head. I don't have a definition for it exactly, as it's a combination of tracking history, myth, symbols, and religion to build a psychological profile for individuals, thereby coming up with those who have committed crimes and studying those likely to do so, depending on personal background, behavior, nature versus nurture, etc.

Sometimes at a party or event, if I'm bored, I'll call myself the criminal archetype hunter. It leaves people silent. They have no clue what that means, often no interest in asking more, and so I walk away.

Take the red hair, green eyes, and the nature of my analytic mind, which never stops me from thinking, blending intuition and problem solving skills together, and I suppose that adds up to the unique consultant I am today. I've been told I'm one of those very rare people who is perfectly balanced on both the left and right hemispheric sides of the brain's visual versus auditory and sensory learning abilities. This gives one the talent to be a great problem solver while bringing intuition into language and getting across ideas and concepts others don't grasp as easily. Few can see the whole picture and keep the essential and minute details in order in their brain. Most would find much of my work tedious and pointless.

Getting the overall picture is like looking for a needle in a haystack. Since I have administered—and been administered to—practically every IQ, psychological, and cognitive test in existence, I continue to be amazed at how accurate some of them are. So, on a good day with my IQ of about 145, I'm able to solve problems and think on my feet quicker than most. On a bad day, I'm an overly-analytical female who is controlled by her emotions and heart and just wants everyone in the world to be happy, which in some form, I believe, can still happen if only they knew the truth.

What that truth is exactly: a gift given by grace waiting to be opened by each of us, if only we would take the time to see it or even recognize it sitting there directly in front of us.

Since "psychologist" has lost the pride once associated with it, I now hold no stock in a name or a profession, and people can call me whatever they like. In a strange way, my work is only now starting to pay off. When I'm not actively on a case, I'm a highly sought after lecturer on symbols, unconscious dreams, and drawings, and other pseudo-psychological, non-scientific studies such as psychic phenomenon, unexplained spiritual events, and other anomalies that baffle the human scientific mind. Things may finally be starting to come together for me, or that's what I was hoping to discover with my planned month off before receiving the unexpected call.

My mind drifts again as I think about Dr. Janus and what could possibly have made him this upset and secret.

At this point, the small TV on the left comes on automatically, surprising me. I'm not used to such up-to-date technology. James appears on the screen ready to chat, just as I always remember him. A welcome interruption. We banter back and forth for what seems to be a thirty-minute ride. I stopped wearing watches about a year ago, both in defiance and as a reminder to work on my own time schedule. I no longer want to be totally controlled by the world's systems. If absolutely necessary, I'll turn on the cell phone occasionally to see the time, and I've become really good at using the position of the sun to get an idea of the time of day. I respect being "on" time. I just don't like having my life controlled "by" time. However, the technology of this funky TV is a welcome invention, accompanied by James.

Eventually James stops talking and the limo starts to slow. The screen goes blank. I can hear him speaking to someone and assume it's security.

When he's done and we start to move, I say, "This seems awfully *secure*. Overkill, don't you think, James?"

"No I-de-ar," he says. "I don't ask, I just *Nike!* Keeps my life simple. I get paid well, and it assures a life away from poverty and pain."

"So you truly have no idea why I'm here?"

"No-ne." A combination of "not" and of "one" slur together. "But you'll know as quick as the twinkle in a bobcat's eye."

I guess this meant soon? This time I had no i-dea-r! I venture, "Not even the least bit curious, James?"

"We-l-l," as his intonation progresses upward, he pauses briefly. "No!" his intonation dropping back down. The all-Brooklyn guttural "coi-ffee" tone emerges.

I think I ask just to hear his most repeated phrase. I know the answer. I smile. Sometimes it's so good to be back around the people you knew years before. There's something to be said for familiarity.

James and I had met at a party at college in our freshman year. We were total opposites. I the polished, prudish student with a hint of underlying rebel, the product of two Princeton professors, and James, the guy from the hood, or as close to it as I've known. Back then, he oozed gold jewelry, Italian descent, and was as boisterous and uncouth as they come, but he always had a hint of compassion or genuineness underneath.

At times it was like watching an "animal house" party when he and the boys got together. How he ever got into Columbia University was beyond me. It wasn't until our reintroduction, when I was working on the NYU case and needed help scouring the unsavory neighborhoods of New York City, that we became reacquainted. I had only seen him one time since then, at his dad's funeral, the result of a terrible tragedy: a barber shot down in Brooklyn for no known reason.

The limo starts to move again. My stomach jiggles as I feel us take a series of turns. The smooth road feels as though it changes to gravel or stone; then the limo slows to a stop. I can hear the driver's car door opening, and then to my surprise, mine opens. That's what limo drivers do, but a fully uniformed, fully loaded security agent leans in, assesses me, and then motions me out. I look tentatively at James, and he gives me the big reassuring, "It's D-ucky." Not "It's Kosher," not "Thumbs up," but a Brooklyn guy with, "It's Ducky." I can't help but grin.

I step out of the left side door next to the security agent and feel a flutter in my heart. This is really quite a strange situation. With my feet firmly planted, I turn around and take a panoramic scan. I'm awestruck.

The place is immense. I check back toward the huge iron gate—with insignia, of course—as it automatically closes. There are stone pillars on each side that mark the end of a road tightly entwined by trees. The circular drive of cobblestone looks as though it had been laid by hand in the fifteenth century. The "cob" of the cobblestone is the true rounded lump of stone that gave a horse a good grip and could allow the road to be used heavily without sinking due to muddy conditions or getting too dusty from alternate dry conditions in the old days. I have not seen a true cobblestone road since my tours abroad; as friendly as they are to horses, they are not so kind to the human ankle.

As I get my bearings, I turn back to see this magnificently massive mansion that reminds me of a Crusades, if not a some-what Gothic, structure transplanted from another era. A little spooky, but certainly private enough. Built of what looks like huge blocks of granite versus stone and other materials, the building is astounding. The large wooden doors with brass bolts open, and out comes a little, old, pudgy Italian maid type. No taller than five feet, if that, she looks miniature due to the height of the immense doors.

"A *mia bella*, you must be Dr. LaSige-*a*. Dr. Janus, he *a*-wait-*a* for you inside in the study. You need-*a* something, you-*a* call me Ana. I everybody's N-ana!" Cackling laugh. I can't remember if that's the word for grandma in some language.

The closer she gets to me, the more that Italian smell emanates from her. It reminds me of when my family used to visit the old Italian homes where food was already cooking first thing in the morning, and it would take hours for the smell to leave their auras after the "mamas" were in public. This was no different. I have a love/hate relation with this smell, just like Pakistani cumin, cori-ander, and curry. When I'm starving, it's great. When I'm tired or my stomach is off due to nerves, I want to vomit! Some call this a psychological issue, but I have learned that our five senses can trigger things much deeper than just physical reactions.

I'm always amused by the characters that Dr. J., as James refers to him, surrounds himself with. I've only met a few of them at the annual, year-end college parties he threw in Dobbs Ferry, but they were like Dickens characters transported out of time and dropped into the middle of New York City, clashing like atoms ready to spontaneously combust at any moment.

Ana starts yelling some Italian phrases at James, who swiftly responds, grabs my bags, dumps them at the door, kisses my hand, says "*Ciao, bella,*" hurriedly gets into the limo, and speeds off before I even have a chance to ask if I'll get to see him again.

After I follow Ana through the large doors, watching as she fights to push them closed, she leaves me in the center of the entrance, and my mind transports me into some movie set, leaving the Dickens characters far behind. So much for my belief in not wanting things that impress the outside world. I want this as my daily entrance! I have never, in my entire life, experienced anything so grand, so colorful, so truly magnificent and inexplicable.

Perhaps I've been wrong. Perhaps absurd amounts of wealth would be a good thing. It's impressing me. Too bad an education that I thought would provide a prosperous life hadn't yet done it for me, perhaps it never would.

chapter

7

*Often the doorway to success is entered
through the hallway of failure.*

Erwin W. Lutzer

hat a masterpiece! I look around and am overwhelmed by the sheer uniqueness and beauty of the Vaticanesque entrance. The immediate inner shell is the shape of a circle, or turreted type structure, supported by huge columns separated by at least fifteen feet from each other. Beyond the columns are hallways leading to other parts of the house. If I'm standing with my back to the door and noon is straight ahead, the outer shell

starts to my right, at about five o'clock, and is outlined by an enormous circular staircase that moves counter-clockwise to the second floor. By about ten, it disappears into the next levels. Light shines in from the very top dome above, brightening the dark mahogany walls with prism colors reflecting everywhere.

As I move to the middle, Ana scurries in the direction of ten o'clock. My eyes focus above, and I move counter-clockwise, taking it all in, but the texture I feel through my shoes makes me glance at my feet. It's an entire mosaic that measures about fifty feet in diameter, and with the ceiling height of well over seventy-five feet, it makes this space appear more like the dome of a Basilica than an entrance to a home.

Taking one last glance up, I notice an incredible reproduction of the celestial heavens with the signs breaking it into twelve sections. I know it's the zodiac. I wonder what century or culture this originates from. I'll need time to review. I look from the heavens back to the ground, where there are colorful and perfectly placed stones and tiles. I notice they say something, and I need to move in a clockwise direction to read them:

BLESS THOSE WHO ENTER,
FOR WITHIN ALL PEOPLE UNVEIL THEIR TRUE
NATURE, AND ALL THINGS HAVE BEEN FORETOLD.
BEWARE OF THE … and the phrase ends.

I can make out the circle, and after reading the words, I realize they are enveloped in what looks like a snake, or perhaps a scorpion, as I notice what might be legs coming from the creature. Its head is reaching all the way around to its own end of the tail, which in turn is inserted into the mouth. I smile to myself. *There you go, the sign of the ever-present oroborous symbol at work in my life again.*

I check out every detail, look back up above, and face toward twelve o'clock, with the front doors behind me. I can tell the sign is Aries, the vernal equinox. That's the direction of the largest opening to a main hallway that stretches pretty much from Pisces to Taurus, or from eleven to one o'clock. From what I see, the serpent's head starts in Taurus, and I wonder if there's any significance to that. No doubt someone had put great thought into this, and I begin to wonder what it is we're to beware of, since the sentence never finishes. I relook at the words as Ana sneaks up on me and announces that Dr. Janus will see me now. I'm not sure what I'm more excited about: figuring out the entrance or seeing Dr. Janus again.

I feel a mix of emotions between anxious and aflutter. How would it be seeing him after all this time? An overwhelming, yet strange, déjà vu feeling fills my body as if I have been here before at some other point in my life.

Impossible, I think, and quickly dismiss that idea. I can't stop thinking about how, in Jungian dream analysis, the levels in the houses signify the conscious, unconscious, and suвconscious, and the entrance in the dream foretells what to expect in the future.

It's like I have received a blessing and a warning at the same time, and all before I even enter deeper into the house. But there's no time to think on that now because Ana is knocking on one of two huge wooden double doors that will lead to the study and my professor, Dr. Janus, at last.

chapter

8

Three may keep a secret if two of them are dead.

Benjamin Franklin

 y heart is pounding, and there he stands. Earth shattering, handsome of all handsomes. He welcomes me with, "Ah, Doctor Magdalena LaSige." And with those words, I think I'll pass out.

Weak-kneed and wide-eyed, "Dr. Peter Janus," I echo, trying to steady my voice.

"Right on time," he teases.

"Well, it's not exactly difficult with private jets, limos, drivers, door-to-door service, etcetera." I walk over and give him a big hug.

He greets me in his arms, steps back, and just stares, taking me all in. "It is so great, so great to see you."

In his arms, I feel the familiar pang. I can never determine if it's admiration, a childhood crush, or just pure goo-goo eyes over his incredible good looks. My head fits perfectly on his chest, his warm arms enveloping me, his beard gently rubbing on the top of my head, and that wonderful smell of Old Spice! Not exactly what I think a multi-millionaire should smell like, but one that has always brought feelings of great safety and fondness through my olfactory senses. Oh, how I've missed this man.

Ana pipes in with, "I-*a* bring you some espressos with steamed milk; is good-*a* with you?" not worrying about interrupting my special moment.

"Great," I say, mustering up enthusiasm, wanting to hold onto him and be left alone.

Dr. Janus steps back and gives some instruction in Italian as she hurries off.

The room is magnificently dressed with the most ornate mahogany paneling, teak floors, and beautiful trim. Huge oak chairs with golden fabric and some beautiful prints sit regally awaiting their next visitors. There is a fireplace, numerous unique clocks, archeometres, and so many things I could get lost in the detail for days. Dr. Janus could not possibly exist in an environment not perfectly or properly put together. No, not a man like him, at least not in my mind!

Always impeccably and fashionably dressed when teaching––I guess it helps to be wealthy, intelligent, and handsome—his looks alone could engage any female and was the sole reason that every year he taught his wretched courses, they were filled with hundreds of students, 98 percent of them females! When it comes to mandatory classes of no interest, but which one is required to spend hours and hours listening to, I assure you that a good-looking, good-sounding prof is never a bad thing!

"Nine years and you haven't changed a bit, Magdalena."

"You either," I say, except there is a secret sadness in his eyes, deep beneath, almost a resignation that has aged him. Another heart pang. Wow, can this man ever evoke emotions and physical reactions from me.

Very quickly he moves behind the desk and becomes all business, just as if he were once again that prof back at Columbia teaching the intricacies of biochemical structures or psychopharmacology.

"It is under seriously grave circumstances that I have called you here today, and I can't stress enough the need for total secrecy in your involvement in this matter. There are few people in this world I feel I can still trust, Magdalena." My name rolls off his tongue like bells tinkling on angel's wings. *Snap out of it, this man is sharing something serious.*

"You remember my sister, Tess, the nun of whom you heard me speak several times at the year-end parties for students?"

Yes, I nod.

"She has been kidnapped and is being held for ransom."

"What?" I gasp. "When?"

"On Sunday, July 6, at around 10:00 p.m. I received a call from what sounded like a male voice that said, *'We have your sister. If you ever want her back alive, you will need to collect fifty million dollars. Speak to no one. You have twenty-four hours.'* I dismissed the entire call as some childish college prank. Who has ever heard of a fifty-million-dollar ransom, and how many people really know I have a sister?

"I was so involved in the research and review I was putting together that I didn't really worry about it."

His hand moves to loosen his necktie. "Then on Monday, July 7, at 10:00 p.m., I was having my scotch…"

"Aberfeldy. A balanced and woody twenty-one-year-old single malt?"

"You remember that?"

"Sure do," I say, as if we were having a little jovial *soirée* and I was reminding him how he defined his scotch. *What am I thinking, interrupting like this?*

"Well, again to my great surprise, the phone rang with the same voice, same message. But this time, instead of just hanging up, I paused. I thought to myself, who would leave the same message and not say another twelve hours, or some lesser amount of time? Who uses the same twenty-four hours? I asked some questions, but there was no response, and then in the background I heard four bells and thought that was odd. Where would it be four o'clock when it's 10:00 p.m. here? And, again, although the voice sounded mechanical, the call sounded live. I also noticed a certain added resonance or clank to the bell on the third *dong* as if it was slightly misaligned. This jogged my memory. Tess used to tell me about this because of the bell at the convent. She used to joke, when she heard the clank, she knew she only had two and a half more hours before she had to get up. She also used to say how often she awoke right before 3:00 a.m. as if she was waiting to see if the bell had corrected itself yet. I'm sure I heard the clank on three and not on one, two, or four. This sound has to be the abbey near Lisieux, France, where my sister is in the convent. But that still didn't convince me they had her or that the call was real."

He pauses for a minute while running his hand down his beard.

"So, I thought if this is not coincidence, why was I being given another twenty-four hours? This piqued my interest but in no way concerned me. I just thought it was a more elaborate hoax and gave the pranksters some credit for creativity. I was intrigued by the attempt of these faux kidnappers and was vaguely amused that they would go to such trouble, but I knew there was no way to contact my sister other than by snail mail or a visit on Sunday from 7:00 a.m. until noon. She's in one of the few remaining cloistered convents, and no contact is allowed with family, even upon death of a parent or sibling, unless the visit is held there and the family member is Catholic."

He looks to the door to see if anyone is coming, then continues.

"However, it wasn't until last night when I got the third call, same message, same money, same twenty-four hours, the bells in the background, but this time I heard, 'Pedro, don't worry about me. I am in God's hands. I do not know what they are asking of you, but under no circumstances should you be forced to do anything sinister on my behalf. *Vaya con Dios, mi amor.*' And then the voice, '*This is not a recording, this is not a joke; we will call you tomorrow at 10:00 p.m. with more details. No investigators. No police. No media. Money in return for your sister's life. No exceptions.*' And they hang up."

His hand vibrates a bit as he points to the phone for emphasis. He's obviously shaken.

"Since then I have been beside myself. You know she is the only family I have left, and I am the elder brother by six years. I promised my parents before they passed away that I would always care for her. I can't help but feel alarmed and guilty that there must have been something I've done to attract this attention. She does not have a mean bone in her body. What would someone want from a nun other than to get to me, and what do they really want? Fifty million dollars is preposterous. I don't have *that* kind of money. Why not just ask for a billion?" He slaps his hand on the desk.

I snap back into reality. This is all really happening. Thoughts collide in my head. *How dreadful, but what does this have to do with me? What can I do to help?* I look blankly at Dr. Janus, and as if reading my mind, he says, "I guess you'd like to know how you fit into all of this?"

"Hmmm." I nod my head, as if the entire English language has fallen out of my brain onto the floor like Cheerios accidentally tipped out of the box, falling one by one into a huge pile, *ping, ping, ping, whoosh.* I just sit there, blinking.

"I have no one I can trust, Mags."

There was a creak as the door is pushed open by Ana. "Espressos for *tutti?*"

We both turn to look.

"Sorry to interrupt-*a*, but you need some energy and *mange* to carry on these intellectual conversations. *Si*, Magdalena?"

I see we're on familiar terms, no more Dr., which I like.

"Oh, yes ..." Dr. Janus eyes me.

I fill in, "Ugh ... these university projects just never seem to end." Faint smile. Obviously she knows nothing.

Not only were there coffees, but all of these lovely little treats and pastries sat there perfectly designed on the plate. How will I ever remember these incredible moments, despite the precariousness of the situation?

"*Buona degustazione!*"

"*Grazie,*" the only Italian I can remember.

"Thank you. That will be all for now." Dr. Janus excuses her.

Waiting for Ana to close the door, I venture, "So, as you were saying ..."

"I have gone over and over this in my mind, once I started taking it seriously, and I truly can't imagine who would pull such a prank or who would need something from me. I am pretty much past my prime as far as teaching, research, and any other endeavors. It would have made sense to me when all the new biotech issues arose in the eighties and I was so involved. Someone then might have wanted something from me, but now? What on earth could I have that would mean anything to them now?"

Still really confused, I blurt out, "So what is it you think I can do to *help?*"

"Ah, my Mags, getting to the point with her emotions on her shoulder."

"I'm just afraid I don't know what I can do for you, and we're wasting valuable time instead of bringing in real professionals, like the police. I can't bear to have anything happen to you and your sister simply because I might have cracked one case, and that was partially by accident!"

Ana had slid the perfect arrangement of goodies onto the desk. Dr. Janus picks up the espresso and starts to sip it, black. I follow by picking mine up but adding sugar and a small amount of the frothed milk. He takes another long sip, and then I take my first one. It was just like I remembered coffee from Italy. Divine. I look back at him, waiting to hear more but savoring the taste.

"About a month ago, I received a strange document, one I set aside more as an anonymous artist's gift than anything else. I am now beginning to wonder if there was something else meant by it. It came on July 4, Independence Day, and was left at the front door of the house in Dobbs Ferry. The envelope was intriguing because instead of it being addressed to me, it had the words, *Your Savior or Your Death.* When you come from family money, all sorts of things happen through the years and there are all kinds of kooks trying to relieve you of your money."

He picks up what looks like a mini *milles-feuilles,* and I follow by choosing a double-layered butterfly pastry stuck together with chocolate mousse filling and partially dipped in dark chocolate—my favorite since childhood.

"I thought if I could show you this picture and you could be here when the call came in, you might be able to determine if they are related and what this is about. There are symbols and words and things I don't have a clue about. So, after you have reviewed the artwork, and, if after this next call we feel there is nothing we can do on our own, then I will decide who else to call and you will have only been here for moral support and

trust since there are so few left I feel I can share this with. Any amount of money you need, just let me know."

"Dr. Janus, the money is *not* the point. Your sister could be *killed.*"

"I know, I know." He gasps for a full breath. "I just can't think in those terms at the moment. Let us sit here quietly, sip our espressos, have some pastries, and think on the next move."

Sit here quietly, I think? *What?*

I try. I really try. All I can hear around me is *tick, tock, tick, tock, tick.* My head is reeling. I'm about to have a cuckoo bird spit out of my mouth and have my head spin. How can he sit there quietly? But that's Dr. Janus, sipping coffees while his sister could be being murdered somewhere. The thought, *Only a man,* comes to mind.

chapter

9

Quality is never an accident.
It represents the wise choice of many alternatives.

Willa Foster

he clock strikes 3:45. It has to have been a good fifteen minutes that we've sat here in silence. Dr. Janus abruptly stands up and says, "Well, I will have Ana show you to your room so you have time to get adjusted, rested, and settled. Let us know what you need. We will have dinner at 7:30 p.m. precisely, thus leaving us enough time to eat and then get to the library for the 10:00 p.m. call, if there will even be a call." He walks around the desk and starts to lead me out.

I stand up, but a lump in my throat and unease in my stomach puts me off kilter. Dr. Janus steadies me and whispers, "It will all be fine, Magdalena. Of this I am certain."

But for the first time in my life, I just don't believe him.

"May I see the envelope and contents before then?" I ask.

"I will bring them to dinner. They are currently in my safe, and I did not want to remove them until necessary. To my knowledge, only my fingerprints are on them, and they are now in plastic to keep safe. I will also bring you the only close-up picture I seem to have of my sister, of Tess. Most of our photos are in black and white, and this one, although in color, appears black and white because of her habit."

"Excellent idea," I say.

Just then, as if psychically called, Ana comes in and motions for me to follow her. "*Ze* bags-*a* are upstairs; there is intercomm-*a*, and you call if you need-*a* me or anything. Dinner is seven thirty, *pronto*, so if you need bath or sleep, you have *pocco* time," she says as her forefinger and thumbs measure her statement for me.

I nod my head to Dr. Janus so as not to rudely leave without acknowledgment.

"A shower would be nice." She lets me know I'll have to go down the hall, but she will show me when we get up there.

We walk back to the entrance area, headed toward Virgo, or five o'clock, and start up the grand staircase. Stepping quietly, I notice there's not one picture of family or a regular wall hanging to be found anywhere. Most people adorn their houses with mementos of their time together as family, but instead of such family snapshots, a group of some strange form of hole-punched metal with the most incredible designs I have ever seen present themselves. They're not framed, but the type of metal reflects the sunlight, and the mahogany of the walls does the framing for them. I want to ask all about them, but the words *Curious Georgetta* fly through my mind, and I think it might be a bit too soon to interrogate Ana. I opt to make a mental notation. As I briefly glance up to see the towering constellations, we arrive at my floor. We go straight, but the stairs continue and look like they go up another two stories to the incredible glass dome that leads right to the stars.

We walk down the hallway past a closed door on the left and a huge grandfather clock surrounded by some beautiful oil paintings on the right, and then she opens the next door on the left, announcing, "Ze guest-*a* room-*a*. Was Tess-*a* room-*a*." Again feeling like I'm in some foreign film, I enter what is obviously a bedroom and look around. It's as if I'm entering a Victorian Rose greeting card. Lace and pink and gold are everywhere, angels peeking over bed stands and lamps, as if overlooking the visitor's every movement. Roses in vases on lampshades are partially in bloom, as if stuck in time. So many details and colors. I love it but can't take it all in. I would put this décor in my house, even though it would be overly decadent and perhaps gaudy to some. I could just see the shock on peoples' faces if I decorated a room like this in my place, considering most of my furniture is so staid!

Ana informs me that the bath, bidet, and toilet are in the next room, and I'm to use the closets and fresh towels on the bed. She motions me to follow her to the "shower room."

She's not kidding. The shower room, which should have been called the shower house, is just that, a twenty-by-twenty-foot room with at least a four-foot open shower and the virulent smell of cedar emanating from what looks like a fully enclosed sauna next to it. I could have escaped here for hours! And the decorative hanging towels, surprise, surprise, are initialed. But this time an odd sensation overtakes me. They read, *M. L. S.,* my initials. How could they already be here? Was Dr. Janus expecting me?

Trying not to get too spooked, I put it from my mind as Ana says, "I go-*a*, make-*a* dinner," and hustles off.

"Ana," I hesitantly yelled down the hall, jaunting out of the shower room, "I don't have any formal dinner clothes. I had mentioned this to Dr. Janus before I came."

"No problem-*a*. You have long pair of pants, no jeans?"

"Yes, a pair of black pants, almost khakis though."

"This is good. He be fin-*a* with this. No jeans-*a*, he an ol' fashion man. You stay longer, we order-*a* in the tailor for the clothes."

Okay, I think. *They don't go shopping. They order in the tailor for clothes. That's a new one!*

"Excellent. It was a pleasure meeting you. Thanks for the help," finally manages to emerge from my mouth as she disappears beneath the stairs.

When she's out of sight, I have a brief moment of sheer excitement where I just want to burst out and run up and down the hallways checking out the rooms, opening the doors, and yelling at the top of my lungs, "I'm rich, with money to burn, a billionaire no less!" I control myself, however, and instead opt for jumping up and down a second and then going back to the bedroom and sinking into the softest bed I think I have ever experienced, thinking I'll rest a minute then look around, but instead I fall asleep.

Forty-five minutes disappear, and I awaken a little confused as to my surroundings. Remembering where I am and why, I put my feet out over the side of the bed and head to my luxurious spa.

I sit in the sauna trying to clear my mind, mentally recapping everything that's happened, then head to the extraordinary shower, where there's every type of sample and herbal scent one could want for the hair and body. Lavender, eucalyptus, mint, rosemary. I chose the eucalyptus and mint combo, as I always find them refreshing. Feeling somewhat rejuvenated, I wrap myself up in the towels from the bedroom, smile over the *M. L. S.* initials on the decorative ones in the bathroom, and go dress for dinner. I splash on some nice scent left on the table—presumably there for guests—smear on some lip-gloss and a hint of makeup, and realize as I head out the door that I have no idea where the dining room is.

After reaching the bottom of the stairs, the place extends in so many directions I feel I need one of those hotel maps with pictures pointing to the ice machine, soda machines, emergency exits, and dining facilities. I can smell the food wafting down the hall from the opposite side of the entrance where we had gone to the study. Slowly I sneak toward the direction of the food, and sure enough, to the right I spot Dr. Janus already in the dining room, looking as handsome as ever.

"You found the dining room, I see."

"I did, thank you."

His yellow ascot with vibrant blue paisleys wraps his neck with dignity, defining his stature and height. The dark blue, perfectly tailored suit oozes Italian tailoring, and the black leather shoes have the same Italian softness. I am in the presence of greatness.

He has just poured what I assume is his scotch. A crystal decanter sits on an exquisitely detailed, carved serving table on the left; the magnificent dining table is set as if dignitaries are coming. The table is huge, stretching at least thirty feet long, with eight high-backed, oak chairs on both the left and right; those at each end have wooden arm rests.

He asks if I would like a scotch, but I see an enticing bottle of Cabernet Sauvignon on the table and decide I'll wait to enjoy the wine. He motions for me to sit way down at the other end of the table. Formally, my back straightened, my legs moving slowly but with precision, I eventually make it to the end of the table, dislodge a huge seat from its position, even though it feels glued to the floor, and proceed to disappear in the chair. Doing this makes me feel as though I'm in some fairytale like *Goldilocks* or *Alice in Wonderland.* To my astonishment, my feet don't touch

the floor, and I'm just over five foot ten inches! Dangling away, like a kid on a swing, I burst out laughing, not sure if this is due to stress, nerves, or true humor, which takes Dr. Janus utterly by surprise and makes Ana run in as if something is terribly wrong.

The two stare for a minute as I regain my composure. I say through my laughter, "I'm sorry, it's just that I feel like I'm at a table in a childhood fairytale where my feet can't touch the ground and I'll have to yell down to the other side of the table to talk!" Grasping my hands around my mouth, I bellow, "Ohoy matie, and how was your day today?" as if into a huge megaphone. They smile.

Dr. Janus says, "Point taken," laughs, and exclaims, "Ana, move the setting down next to me, on the right. I suppose it's a little too grand for just the two of us."

I'm relieved. *Good to find humor in things.* This eases the uncomfortable tension that has been in the air since I arrived. It's the formality juxtaposed with a feeling of some obvious gloom over the situation that mixes in the air, creating odd tensions and reactions, but this manages to lessen some of it.

Dr. Janus does the honors of uncorking the bottle of wine, samples it, and then pours a glass for me. *No sommelier,* I think.

Sommelier: I love that word and the history behind it. In past centuries, their profession not only chose and served the wine, but tasted it for poison, that being a favorite way to kill kings, queens, high-level officials, and even popes when wanting to force a power shift. I guess we've made some progress in the world since that no longer happens. Dr. Janus obviously does not feel the need for that level of protection.

The aroma and flavor of the wine is superb, intoxicating. Deep, buttery, and oaken, with a hint of cherry or perhaps blackberry, just as I like it. Dr. Janus proceeds to give a lovely lesson on its origin and the vineyards. I barely hear a word though; I'm too focused on just being with him, at last. I revel in his company. I could just sit here for hours and listen.

Ana comes in with the food, which almost exceeds the company. As she rolls in a silver cart with our first dish, I notice the detail on the dining table. Pure gold candlesticks about three feet tall, with ornate ivy detailing wrapped around them, flowering at the top. The two settings are blue plates with gold trim and inlay, with gold display plates underneath. Gold silverware completes the table settings. The color of the gold makes it obvious this is not gold plate, but pure gold. The setting itself could have paid for a semester at college for me.

The flowers in the middle of the table are an exquisite arrangement of exotic birds of paradise, white lilies, and all sorts of extraordinary bulb-type flowers I have never seen before. The crystal is Waterford, not sure what pattern, but heavy and beautiful. And above all this, an ornate crystal and gold chandelier, with arms that hold five light bulbs each, magnificently stretches over the table, shining its light without being too bright, but appearing as huge tentacles ready to snatch the guest at any moment. A huge fireplace at the back of the room, in summertime no less, roars and spits out a spark as if putting a final exclamation point to the perfection of the room.

The cart stops by Dr. Janus, and Ana carefully places on the plate in front of him a small, white, frail-looking, jug-shaped bowl with two handles and a huge gold spoon, the size of the ones I remember from Europe. She then does the same for me, leaves the tray, and disappears. I realize I'm beyond famished and can't wait to taste the beautiful, light-green, creamed soup in front of me.

Dr. Janus looks at me, raises his spoon with a *"Bon Appetite,"* and carefully places the spoon in his bowl. I follow, afraid if I eat too aggressively, I'll crack the dish with the heavy spoon. The first bite pleasantly entices me when I realize it's cold, creamed avocado soup, perfectly blended with a lovely flavor, garnished with an edible squash flower stuffed and baked with cream cheese and floating perfectly on top. So this is what life is like when you're born with a "golden" spoon in your mouth! It's all so elite.

The second course is rack of lamb, nicely roasted in a graham cracker-type crust with hints of spicy mustard and rosemary sprigs that made me salivate before even tasting. I'm now sure this is the smell that had led me in the direction of the dining room. Perfectly cooked, pink in the middle, crispy on the outside, absolutely delicious. The veggies are baby carrots in a mild garlic and honey sauce. The small green, feathery fronds at the top remain, proving they've been pulled fresh. The colors light up the warmed plate that's a simple white square; they're perfectly assembled and almost too beautiful to eat. Ana carefully puts the masterpiece on the decorative gold setting after removing the soup bowl and placing the remaining smaller plate to the left.

I remark on how heavenly the food and tastes are, and Dr. Janus fills me in on the fresh herb garden his mother planted years ago that he has kept up through the years. *Quite princely,* I think! *All fresh food and herbs grown on the property. They could be a kingdom of their own, perhaps I could be the queen!*

Dr. Janus elaborates, "The meat is all fresh, hormone and antibiotic free, and grown at a nearby local farm. My mother was especially into fresh food, natural cooking, and herbs. You will have to check out the gardens one day. They are quite brilliant."

Ana comes in, removes the plates, and brings in a colorful mixed-green salad with fresh mozzarella and tomatoes and a lovely hint of fresh lemon, salt, and pepper. Her Italian influence is everywhere, even down to serving salad last, just as it's done in Italy.

Dr. Janus and I busy ourselves with light conversation about my parents, who he used to know because they were all teachers at Princeton before he transferred to Columbia University; the ongoing changes at the universities; my studies that led me to my current position; and how the quality of education has changed. He is supportive and cordial, and we both attempt to make the best of the evening, despite the pressure of the impending call.

Then I finally brave the question that had been on my mind since this afternoon. "Did you bring the artwork from the safe?"

"I did," he replies as he walks over to a chair by the fireplace, lifts the cushion, and pulls the piece out of a large plastic bag and brings it to me. An odd place to hide it. I guess he doesn't want Ana to see it.

The envelope reads, "Your Savior or Your Death," as he had said. Inside is a beautiful and colorful drawing on a 15" x 15" paper that looks like old parchment, or perhaps even more like a light bark. There are four letters in the middle that spell *ZOAD* and what looks like a compass guide in the middle showing NSWE; east points to some sketched pyramids and sphinx. All of this is encircled by a scorpion-like creature, snake, or dragon. There are also other scenes around the circle, like the Eye of Horus, churches, pinecones, and various other symbols. *What no obelisks?* At quick glance, I think it's a trip through history, but the order and dates don't add up. The center has a picture that looks like hieroglyphic drawings around the time of the Egyptian kings and some wording that might be Hebrew.

I start talking and pointing, explaining the meaning of the scorpion wrapped in a circle: That due east references the sphinx in Giza, which faces east; that perhaps the pinecones are an indication of where Rome is; and I point out as much as I was familiar with off the top of my head. Nothing resonates with Dr. Janus other than that his father seemed interested in Egyptology, and their gardens had replica miniature sphinx, pyramids, and some other statues, like the Virgin Mary.

I make a mental note of that, but Ana returns, so I shuffle the work under the table, pick up my wine, and take a sip as if to say, "Nothing else is going on here."

She moves around the table, clears the plates, and says, "Dessert-*a?*"

I ask if we can wait a bit. I'm so full and pleased with the meal and the drink, and I need my head together for the call. I know quality is something only a few can define, but I have enjoyed the day because of it. How something so sinister could underlie such beauty is a dichotomy difficult to absorb.

What I really want to do is dive into another luscious bottle of extreme wine, curl up next to a fireplace, and have Dr. Janus talk to me for hours about what he's been doing all these years. But that's not going to happen, not tonight at least.

chapter
10

Imagination is more important than knowledge.
Knowledge is limited. Imagination encircles the world.

Albert Einstein

t's 9:45 p.m. when he tells Ana to hold dessert, and I'm amazed at how the time has flown by. I remember nice family meals like this growing up and have missed them being on my own. It's also such a hurried world these days; few of my friends participate in this art any more.

"We will retire to the library," Dr. Janus informs Ana. "I am expecting a call, so I will pick up."

"*Si. Si comprende… cappuccino o espresso?*"

"Not for me," I say, and Dr. Janus nods his head in agreement. "But thank you. It was a delicious meal."

Indelicately, trying to push the heavy chair back, I stand and follow Dr. Janus down the hall toward the back of the house. Stuffed from the meal and feeling tired, I think I should have had a shot of caffeine. We make a left, walk a ways, and there stand two French doors with beautiful etched glass. Dr. Janus opens them, and we enter.

Each room is becoming more astounding than the next. This is the most distinguished room I have ever seen in my life. A room I've pictured in my own dreams, library cases stuffed with books, not all in perfect order, which is nice to see for a change. It's as if they've been perused and then shoved back in the midst of Einstein madness and genius moments combined in the search for one answer. Taking a quick peek, I see Shakespeare and literature, philosophy, history, science, gardening, herbs, alchemy, pharmacology, and all sorts of combinations of materials.

A huge desk in the middle faces the doors, while the bookshelves keep silent vigil behind. On top of the desk are all the regular writing utensils and matching stationary sets and a large, white desktop computer sitting there looking totally out of place; as old as it appears, it's nowhere near as antique as the rest of the items in the room. At the right-hand side of the elongated room is a magnificent glass wall that looks out on an atrium of numerous plants and flowers. The stars sparkle far above and somehow reflect enough light into the room for us to enter and see around. I couldn't have dreamed up this part of the design. It's enchanting.

Dr. Janus settles in behind the desk, turns on a desk lamp that lights up the room, and motions for me to sit across from him. I halfway expect him to put on a smoking robe, pull out a pipe, and talk to me endlessly about analytical psychology. So, I'm projecting my vision of Jung on him.

At 10:00 p.m. promptly, the Bavarian clock nesting another beautiful bird begins to cuckoo more gently than the one in the other room, one, two, three, four, five, and in unison on the tenth cuckoo, the phone rings, completely contradicting the bird song. After two deafening rings, Dr. Janus picks up.

As if my ingrained hate for phones isn't bad enough, I know this one will ruin me for life. Why people keep their phones turned up so loud is beyond me. I muse to myself that I'll need to see a hypnotist to remove what is becoming a terrible phone phobia!

Dr. Janus puts the caller on speakerphone and, just as transpired before, a mechanical voice, using the exact words Dr. Janus has described, repeats the phrase about the money and his sister. I hear the extra trill to the bell and then Tess's phrase. This time a new phrase is added: "In two week's time, I will make you pay for what you are letting 'La Compagnia' do, or as planned, she will die. You are required to gather fifty percent in silver, twenty-five percent in unmarked bills, and twenty-five percent in bearer bonds if you ever hope to see your sister alive. In the meantime, on Monday you are required to attend the upcoming event at the Metropolitan Opera. There is a $100,000 donation per plate. Buy three tickets, on hold for you in your name, and you shall get your next clue and set of details then."

Buy tickets to an opera? That's a threat? was what I was thinking when Dr. Janus angrily yelled, "What did we do? What did I do? What do you want? Who is—"

But I put my finger to my mouth to shush him, in fear he will give away something. What exactly, I have no idea. I've probably seen too many cop shows. This is no movie though.

He abruptly stops speaking, and we hear a *click* that ends the call. We look at each other for a minute, and then, to our shock, the doorbell rings.

I duck.

I suddenly feel the urge to own a gun and call the police to see what's up. I jump out of my chair, yell to Ana not to open the door, and ask if security is still there at night. Dr. Janus nods assent and looks confused. Suddenly, I want a camera security system inside to view the surroundings; against my better judgment, I run to the door. The bell rings again. I jump again. There's no place to look out through the solid doors, no place to hide. Could a bullet come through them? Wow, I needed to lose my imagination for a couple of minutes. And then ... another knock.

"Hell-o? Anyone home?"

It was James. I throw the door open and jump in his arms. "It's *you!*"

"Well, who in the world did you think it was? The boogeyman?"

I compose myself and say, "Oh, no one," trying to act like a reasonable, composed adult. "This large place must spook me out!"

"Where are Ana and Dr. J.?"

Casually now, as if nothing just happened, "Oh, Dr. Janus is in the library, and I told Ana I would get the door."

"This is stranger than an orange duck in a goose pond," he says. He then explains he was off duty at the other house having a bite to eat when a package arrived. The envelope was marked "Urgent" and was delivered at such an unusual time, he thought he'd better get it to Dr. J. immediately. If the package hadn't been in his hand and the size of a large, soft, sealed, flat Fed-Ex envelope, with my imagination working overtime, I'd have assumed it was a bomb! But, to my relief, it looks like it might contain another piece of artwork. Dr. Janus comes out to the entrance. James explains and passes over the envelope.

"That will be all, James. Thank you for the extra effort."

"No prob, Dr. J. See ya in the morning. I'm goin' home." He pauses, then says, "Sure everything is okay around here?"

I fill in, "Fine, thank you. Like I said, I think the size of this house has given me the willies."

"*Willies!* That's a term I haven't heard for a while. If you need, I can stick to you like spit on tobacco. I don't *have* to go home now."

I, again, assure him everything is fine, although his analogy grosses me out a bit.

He smiles and turns. "Night."

"Good night, James."

I close the door and turn around to face Dr. Janus, who looks somewhat amused at my recent reactions. I immediately and defensively pipe up, "This is not acceptable. What kind of security do you have? What time do they leave? What about cameras? Who do you trust? If these threats are true, you need to do something. We need to call the police."

"Calma, calma, my dear," he says in a Pavarotti tone. "Let's see what is in the package; then, let's see what we need to do next."

I'm a big *help,* I think. *My nerves are fried, and nothing has even happened yet!*

The package has a single piece of artwork, again 15" x 15," on the same type of parchment. This one says "Divine Providence" on top; there's a set of scales, a mirror that reflects some words to both edges, and symbols on each side of the scale, and although I know some of them, most are unfamiliar.

I show Dr. Janus, and again nothing strikes a chord with him. I point out the top, which seems to indicate by the infinity sign and the angel's wings that Mika-el, or Michael as we call him, is holding the scales and doing the weighing. It's most definitely a fight between good and evil, and it seems, according to this drawing, that evil is winning because the scales on the left are weighted down with the words *evil* and *mortis* versus the ones on the right with the words *good* and *libertas*. But some of the signs throw me off track. What appears to be one horizontal slash with three vertical slashes intersecting, which I believe means poison, is on the side of good. It's confusing, but I'm tired.

Dr. Janus gently removes the artwork from my hands. "It has been an extremely long day for both of us. Why don't we go to bed? I'll put the two pieces back in the safe, and we'll get a fresh start in the morning."

I reluctantly agree but am not sure what else I can do tonight anyway. My brain's foggy and I'm exhausted. I know I need to ask more questions about "La Compagnia," about who might be after him, about this crazy request to go to the Met and so much more, but I'm really too tired to listen.

We say good night, and I head up to bed. My imagination is running wild, yet I know I need to get some rest. I enter the missing nun's room. Then safe and comfy in her bed, I wonder where she is, if she is hurt, how scared she must be, and what these odd pieces of artwork are all about.

chapter
11

And about the ninth hour Jesus cried with a loud voice,
saying "Eli, Eli lama sabachthani?" that is to say,
"My God, My God, why has Thou forsaken Me?"

Matthew 27:46, KJV

he stench of the musty, dirt-laden bare floor made even the thought of greenery and life outside hard to muster in her mind. It had been days, if not weeks, that she had been stuck, shackled, unable to move more than about four feet in any direction in an eight-by-eight-foot dungeon of all dungeons.

However much time it had been, she couldn't even think of what the captors wanted from her. Where was she? No window to the outside, no sound, just a mattress and dirt floor and this small trap door inside a larger door where food and buckets for water and waste appeared and disappeared. Then there were these constricting shackles burning marks in her wrists. Even when she lay still, the light from the single 100-watt light bulb in the sole, unadorned socket burned her eyes.

Have I been drugged? she wondered. Would she rot away like a dead body, eaten by larvae, and returned to the dust she once was, and no one would know? She had not even seen the person behind the voice that had briefly come through the speakerphones in an electronic-sounding way. Had she really heard it, or was she dreaming? What would happen now that it seemed even the electronic voice was gone?

She had been used to small rooms, damp and cold rooms, desolate rooms; after all, she had taken the vows of poverty and chastity, and that life meant a life that was to deny all material and personal convenience. But this, *this* felt so wrong, so dirty, so different.

Her thoughts in the first few days were positive and God-bound, but things seemed to be getting desperate and bleak. Trying to think through her circumstances, it had to have been close to a week since the perpetrator's last visit to leave her some food through the steel hole, and all she had left was some hard stale breadcrumbs and murky water. She continued to pray, "Hail Mary, full of Grace, pray for us sinners now and in the hours of our ...," but her faith seemed to wax and wane.

Her scapular and habit dangled on her as her only friend, the clothes she was wearing when she was taken. She remembered feeling drowsy and nauseous after evening vespers, and next thing she knew, she had awakened in this sick place. Her thoughts turned darker and darker, and in all her life, she had never felt so afraid and so attacked. Not even past events that had led her to the convent in the first place. She missed her devotions, her vespers, and her tiny room at the convent. She even missed the required silences because then, at least, she knew that, in time, she would be able to interact and to speak.

How, God, how could you have left me here like this? Have I not repented enough? Do I die here alone, not even knowing why I have been kidnapped? Is this how my life will end due to my sin of the past . . . my unpardonable sin? she thought to herself.

She sat there barely able to move, aching from head to toe, knowing the saints and martyrs she prayed to had been through so much worse. Her Immaculate Mother Mary and her Savior Christ had suffered for the world. How could she be so weak? Her habit stunk. She stunk, and if this was any indication of hell, she knew she needed to repent again, but for what this time? She tried again to focus on her Hail Marys and the prayers she had learned through the years at the convent, but they were offering her no comfort, and she was weakening.

She tried to picture the statues of the Blessed Virgin and other saints she would pray to for intercession. She didn't even have her devotional book, and then with great fear she realized her rosary was missing. Panic took over, not even her rosary? Her hands started shaking. How would she make it through the rosary—each step the devotion of some mystery in the life of Our Lord and to His Blessed Mother? How would she keep track of the fifteen decades, each decade consisting of the Our Father, ten Hail Marys, and the Glory Be to the Father? It was the last and only piece she owned—a gift from her father— before entering the convent with his words, "Guard this with all your life. This will be your Savior or your Death." He was refer- ring, she was sure, to her past indiscretions and the need to find absolution from those sins through worship.

She thought back to the little blue Catholic devotional she kept in her room or by her side and tried to envision it in her head. She was already forgetting the Glory Be, the meal prayers, and the Ten Commandments. Oh no, she couldn't remember the Ten Commandments. She had looked at that book over and over through the years, and this was the best she could do? Had she not ever really paid attention but simply said the words by rote, some memorized, some she peeked at in the book even after thirty years to get through the verses? She would have to work on that the moment she got out. "Hail Mary," she told herself.

She pretended she was holding the rosary and came to Part 2, Number Five, the Crucifixion where God gave His only begotten Son and the pain of knowing people had tortured Him to death surfaced. To sacrifice your own child for others. Who could be so strong? She couldn't imagine sacrificing her own child for mankind; she couldn't imagine "sacrificing" any human or animal for that matter. Could she do it for the Almighty One?

She started to think of some of the saints who had martyred themselves through the years and how she had nothing to complain about. She thought of her favorite one, "The Little Flower," who had experienced a miraculous healing when she was younger while seeing a vision of Mary. She was the epitome of martyrdom who vowed the day she died that roses would fall from heaven and, reportedly, they miraculously did. After her death, she became famous for a section in her journal called "Story of a Soul." Ironically, the girl's name was Thérèse Martin.

She paused to remember that while it was customary to take a saint's name when taking the final vows, she herself had not. Her birth name was Thérèse, and her family called her Tess for short. She liked this name and, therefore, kept it as her Virgin consecrated name.

Tess rubbed the area around her wrists and took a few minutes to ponder about the beautiful and pure girl who had given up everything for her Savior. How had the Little Flower been able to make a commitment at such a young age, eight years old?

It had taken Tess another nine years after that to make the decision. But then, St. Thérèse Martin of Lisieux died when twenty-four years old. Tess had many more years invested in the church.

Tess herself hadn't always been such an example of purity in her younger years, which is what had partially led her to the convent in the first place. In her spare time, Tess would wander over from her small, cloistered convent in France to St. Thérèse's in Lisieux to pray over the relics of the Little Flower. They brought her strength and hope. *Roses falling from heaven,* Tess thought, *what an honor.* She feared she would never make a contribution to her Lord if life ended for her here.

Tess tried to change her negative thoughts. If that pure child could be so strong and so good, she could do the same. But how? She was violating God's laws because she wasn't attending Mass or morning oblations, and she knew from what she had been taught at the convent that this wasn't good. Suddenly she felt a chill, and the room filled with the masculine voice of Mother Superior, a cold-hearted and harsh woman who always sounded as though she was reprimanding and chastising those around her, the voice echoing in her head: *The Tremendous Value of Mass… At the hour of death, the Masses you have heard will be your great consolation. Every Mass will go with you to judgment as a plea for pardon.* Had she attended enough masses? Fear crept in.

At every Mass you can diminish the temporal punishment due to your sins, more or less according to your fervor. Assisting devoutly at Mass, you render to the Sacred Humanity of Our Lord the greatest homage. This is something she knew she had *nailed,* poor terminology, she giggled like a child and then felt guilty, but fervor she had, and she was always first to help out.

He supplies for many of your negligences and omissions. He forgives you all the venial sins that you never confessed. Tess couldn't imagine if He didn't forgive inadvertently omitting trespasses.

The power of Satan over you is diminished. Any help she could get on this was appreciated. It confused her why all people didn't want the Roman Catholic Church as their only protectorate since Mother Superior had stressed that outside Christian brethren were not afforded such protection.

You afford the souls in Purgatory the greatest possible relief. She was pleased to know she was serving some purpose in her prayers to care for those in Purgatory. Purgatory was defined to her as the intermediate state in which those who have died in *grace* waited, atoning for their sins before being allowed entrance into heaven. She didn't want her prayers to go unnoticed, and she knew this life wasn't about herself but about God and His chosen church.

One Mass heard during your life will be of more benefit to you than many heard for you after your death. You are preserved from many dangers and misfortunes, which would otherwise have befallen you. At this thought, the desolate room, the shackles, devoid of all human contact, she wondered if she could survive like this. As if hearing Mother Superior's voice, she welcomed the chastising; she would work on her attitude and remember what the saints had suffered.

You shorten your Purgatory by every Mass. An unfamiliar feeling crept over her. Surely, she would not have long in Purgatory? She had never been confused before, and yet here she was feeling agitated and upset. Not finding the comfort she was hoping for, she considered stopping. How could some of these rules make sense? Discomfited with these foreign thoughts, she told herself, "This is the devil taking over my carnal mind." The last couple of reasons were better—she hoped.

Every Mass wins a higher degree of glory in heaven. You receive the priest's blessing, which Our Lord ratifies in heaven. She wanted the higher degree, and as long as the priest blessed her, this blessing would be rewarded. She started to get nervous. What happened if she never got to see a priest again? Were enough blessings given? Would they diminish in time and be forgotten? Would Jesus and Mother Mary understand? Would they know her situation and be merciful?

You kneel amidst a multitude of holy angels. You kneel amidst a multitude of holy angels. Tess repeated the phrase over and over, hoping her thoughts would somehow get to someone "out there" who could help her. She pictured the safety and comfort of her childhood room, so colorful, so covered with cherubs. She finished the phrase, "You kneel amidst a multitude of holy angels who are present at the adorable sacrifice with reverential awe." What a beautiful day that would be. She hoped it would be later rather than sooner.

You are blessed in your temporal goods and affairs. She had been blessed in the past, perhaps that was all she was entitled to. She was tired. Her head ached. A sick feeling started to overwhelm her. Was it hunger or, more dangerous yet, doubt? She knew time was passing, but with no window to look out to the outside world, no clock to tell her the time, no misaligned bell to ring its partial trill, she could not tell how much time had actually passed.

When you hear Mass and offer the Holy Sacrifice in honor of any particular saint or angel, thanking God for favors He bestowed on them, you afford Him a great degree of honor, joy, and happiness and win His special love and protection. She was thrilled she had just offered her blessings to the Little Flower. She now added Saint Christopher for travel, Saint Anthony for lost articles, and Saint Jude for hopeless cases.

Every time you assist at Mass you should, besides other intentions, offer it in honor of the saint of the day. She didn't know what day it was. She had been taken so suddenly and unexpectedly that she'd never had a chance to plan. How could she honor the correct saint? She had failed. Would this extend her time in Purgatory? She tried to add up her plenary indulgences credited

to her account, the "nine first Fridays," the one-phrase prayers called Ejaculations, the Advent prayers said every day of Advent, which carried at least one plenary indulgence, Mass, novenas. She wasn't sure how the counting added up so had always assumed if she did more than seemed to be required of her, God would see it and love her by forgiving her shortcomings and sins.

Uncomfortable questions were surfacing. Had the verses and teachings become nothing more than thoughtless mechanical words? She was hungry and now confused for her soul. The Mother Superior's condemning voice rang through her head. *You have failed.*

She placed the end of her scapular over her eyes as she lay there. At least she had this and her veil to cover her sins since she didn't have her rosary to help her repent.

She was burning up, as if on fire, from the lack of food and water and terrible revolving thoughts. The last thought she remembered before she blacked out was Jesus's cry on the cross, "My God, My God, why has Thou forsaken me?"

chapter
12

That which may be kindled into a flame, or into action.

Definition of a spark.

 manage to sleep. The bed is soft as feathers, and the sheets are that special Egyptian eight hundred thread count that's velvety to the skin. I've heard that people pay $100.00 per sheet. That seems crazy, but I enjoy them. Waking up slowly, I smile at the cute little angels peaking over the bedposts, and while communing with them, I hear a strange phrase in my head, almost as if a woman is speaking to me, *You kneel amidst a multitude of holy angels.*

I look around expecting to see a person, or at least a ghost. I am spooked. "Okay, thanks for that tip," comes out of my mouth in case someone can actually hear me. I'm trying to calm my nerves, still looking for where the voice came from. I had enjoyed the cherubs, but now they are freaking me out a bit. Good thing I don't hear voices too often or I may need to rethink hallucinations and delusions as they relate to me!

An old Victorian clock gently chimes seven times. It has such a perfect meditative tone it calms me down a bit; however, with an hour and a half left to get up and get ready for breakfast, I'm ready to move on with my day. I do some stretches, a couple of Pilates moves, and head for another luxurious sauna and shower. I want to go for a walk but don't want to ask where to go. It feels too early to bother anyone.

Heading down to breakfast around eight fifteen, I get there first. Coffee is on the side table; it smells wonderful, and I help myself. The breakfast table is set for three, and I wonder who's joining us.

Dr. Janus walks in, gives me a big "Good morning" greeting, and explains that he called James because he trusts him well enough to let him in on the strange artwork, and he lets me know the jury is still out on telling him the entire kidnapping story. I pipe in, "Any help we can get is great. I'm so glad you called him."

Since the NYU case, I've known James has some connections with people in the police department. I specifically remember one of his friends in the Bureau who had started as a cop and moved into the more covert operations area. James trusts these people completely and got their help when his father was killed.

Dr. Janus dutifully sits at the head of the table, and I ask if I can get him some coffee. "Oh, yes, that would be great."

"Black?"

"Yes."

"What time is James coming?"

"I asked him to be here at 9:00 a.m."

I serve Dr. Janus the coffee, and he jingles a bell in front of his plate to let Ana know he's ready for breakfast. In she comes, pushing her silver cart all prepped with the first course. She looks exactly as she did yesterday when she served food: the black and white uniform, the knee-high nylons below the skirt, the worn black shoes, and the dark blue-gray hair in a net.

Again, it's the loveliest presentation. Figs stuffed with soft, warm goat cheese, a leaf of basil, all lightly drizzled with balsamic vinegar. Not the cheap balsamic vinegar either, the thick, syrupy, sweet stuff that can almost be mistaken for good Port wine. Luscious. I explain to Dr. Janus that fresh figs are my absolute favorite, not the Fig Newton or dried type, but the actual fresh fruit. He remarks that they are his sister's favorites as well!

"She loves them so much that trees were planted in the back just to have the fruit fresh for her."

Bringing up her name leaves us both a little somber, as it solidifies the reason I'm here.

James enters on cue, and I tease, "Good thing you got here when you did; your figs were about to be history!"

He looks a little puzzled until he sees the breakfast plate and its contents. He grabs some coffee and sits down. Dr. Janus sternly starts with how the information he is about to share is of the utmost confidentiality while filling him in on the artwork but neglecting to tell him about the kidnapping. He somehow weaves in the fact that more security may be prudent due to changing times.

Ana comes in with part two of the breakfast: poached eggs on homemade biscuits, lightly grilled tomatoes with spinach nestled within, gobs of Hollandaise poured and topped with a black olive. This is no packaged Hollandaise! I savor the taste of the real egg yolks, the hint of Worcestershire sauce, and drops of fresh lemon and pepper to give it a little bite. I get lost in the food for a couple of minutes while Dr. Janus and James discuss details. James devours his eggs in a couple of bites. I carefully cut, chew, and slowly work my way through mine.

I get up and pour us each more coffee.

"So, any luck with the symbols on that artwork, Doc?" James asks, emphasizing the *Doc*.

"Not yet, James. It's a hodgepodge from numerous centuries and eras and doesn't seem to have a common theme yet. I want to scan them into the computer before you take them to be analyzed so I can do more research."

"There's a scanner and more modern technological conveniences upstairs," Dr. Janus offers. "I'll have Ana show you to the office when we are through."

Ana clears the plates and brings in the perfect finale: little finger pastries to finish the meal off. We make our plans, and then out of the blue, James says, looking directly at me, "Are you sure there's nothing else, Mags?"

Quite disarmed, I manage to say, "Nothing," relatively nonchalantly as a dagger goes through my heart, concerned that I'll have a death hanging over my head if we don't get the police and professionals on our case.

A limo driver, a professor, a maid, and a symbologist, I think. *Boy, are we ever well armed against terrorism and prepared to handle a kidnapping!*

The thought makes me inhale a pastry, and I start to cough. They both look at me. I grab some water and drink. "I'm fine. I'm fine. I really shouldn't speak and eat at the same time!"

Ana comes in again, and Dr. Janus asks her to take me to the office. He says he has some calls and things to attend to, and James says he'll be back in a couple of hours to pick up the "objects."

After James leaves, I ask Dr. Janus if he minds if I let my parents know that I'm with him, not up north.

"That's fine. Don't give any details though, please," Dr. Janus says firmly, heading out of the room.

"I won't. I just don't want them to worry unnecessarily." I have an overwhelming need to call my mom and dad; Ana directs me to the phone by the fireplace, saying, "No need ask-a. You *familia*; you help yourself. I be in *cucina*. You ring-*a* bell when you want me."

"I will, and thank you for that superb breakfast!"

"*Prego, Prego!*" she says over her shoulder as she rushes off.

The call is to France, since my parents spend summer holidays traveling and renting a place on the Mediterranean for the remainder of their summer. I wonder if I should remind Ana it's a long distance call, but then figure I can reimburse Dr. Janus if needed.

I sit in the chair by the fireplace, dial, and my mother picks up after the first few rings. "Well, hello dear! This is a pleasant surprise!"

It's so good to hear my mother's voice. "How is your vacation in Canada?"

"Actually, that's why I'm calling. It was cut short. You'll never believe who called me!" The conversation ensues.

"Really, you're with Dr. Janus? Where?" Her voice has an odd tone to it.

"Oh, at one of his secret undisclosed locations, somewhere in New York near Tarrytown because I recognized the Metro North train."

I don't fill her in about exactly why I'm there, other than to make some quick cash analyzing some symbols for him.

"How long?"

"Well, I don't know. I'll keep you posted though."

My father gets on the phone, and we catch up a bit on their vacation. They're doing well and sound nice and relaxed about the vacation, but both have an odd twinge to their voices when I mention Dr. Janus. Perhaps it's their excellent intuition, picking up that I was nervous about something and not telling the whole truth as to why I was there. I don't want to stay on the phone too long, so end with, "You have my cell number if you need it; just didn't want you to call Canada and get concerned! Love you and have fun!"

For some reason after hanging up, just having heard their voices, I feel a little more relaxed. I sit back in the chair for a few minutes, relieved that James knows something is going on. The food is starting to digest, so I take a few more moments to relax and review things in my head. I watch the tiny sputtering fire and hope something in me will be sparked too.

Nothing is.

I get up, ring the bell, and on cue, Ana runs in to take me up to the office.

chapter
13

Often the hands will solve a mystery that the
intellect has struggled with in vain.

Carl G. Jung

he office is the next room over from the bedroom and private bath I've been using. It's quite a ways down the hall on the left, and when I step into it, it feels as though I've entered a space ship. It's very high up, fully windowed, and obviously the room above the library, overlooking the same windowed gardens.

It has everything one could possibly need: a couple of computers, scanners, photocopiers, some kind of X-ray-type machine, phones, high-speed Internet, power cords, and a huge work desk that wraps from the left-hand wall to across the windows and faces out over the conservatory or atrium. If you aren't too distracted by the view, it offers a great work area. Plenty of desktop and a nice layout of the equipment that's all so recent. Nothing like the old-looking computer in the library.

I immediately go to work, scanning, setting my computer up, getting online, and starting to analyze and enter the symbols in the computer. My head starts working as symbols and ideas to research start to flow. I know a couple of hours won't be enough, so I work on a game plan.

I pull out my paper and pen, my true "think pad." Somehow, the creative process works better for me the old-fashioned way. I jot down a list:

1) Sister missing, 2) Gobs of money at stake, 3) Nun kidnapped, is she target or Dr. J.? 4) Something he's done or known? 5) Family revenge, or business revenge? 6) Why kidnapper using riddles and symbols? 7) Something only Dr. J. knows? 8) Vast family fortune still in tact? 9) What other players? 10) The Met? Strange! 11) And again, who would ever want to hurt a nun? I certainly wouldn't want harming a person "of the cloth" on my conscience.

Then it dawns on me; in a sense, it will be on my conscience if I don't figure this out. How naïve I've been to think I can even help. What am I doing here?

The part of the pictures I need immediate assistance with are what look like Hebrew words. I have a great friend, a Hebrew scholar, so I'll scan, e-mail, and send portions of the picture to him. I know he'll be discreet. I follow through on this, thrilled that technology has come so far this is even possible. Done. Sent. Marked "Urgent."

Three hours go by in a flash, and so I put the final touches on my organized materials, carefully replace the pictures in the plastic, and head downstairs with my list to find Dr. Janus.

I'm relieved to find him back in the study. The room is smaller, more intimate, and we, or rather I, will be able to focus better. The library is overwhelming to me because I want to sit for hours, pull out the books, and peruse every single piece of work on the shelves! This is why computer information will never replace those old, smelly, leafed-through pages of books all lined up. I still get great appreciation from having my Jungian collection and other books sitting there, exemplifying their hidden value, knowing the hours of enjoyment I've received from them.

Dr. Janus's back is turned to me. He's sitting in a chair, totally still. In front of him is a phonograph, an actual phonograph that works, with a plate of goodies and cappuccinos already waiting to the side. He's listening to classical music.

I softly announce myself. He smiles, gets up, and explains the music. His father had put a group of songs by Mozart, Debussy, Bach, Beethoven, Haydn, and others on a vinyl record well before things like CDs and recorders were invented. He titled it *Druid Music,* but Dr. Janus isn't sure why. We listen for a few minutes. It's beautiful. He explains that it calms him down, but then announces there's work to be done, so he stops the record.

We start with quick details about the Met event. Then more formally, he directs me to sit as he does and starts with, "Well, today is Thursday, July 10, and we can't get into Tess's room until Sunday morning. I have ordered a larger jet to take us outside of Paris. We will leave tomorrow, Friday the eleventh, around 3:00 p.m. With travel time, weather issues, customs and such, we should make it there no later than 11:00 a.m. France time on Saturday, July 12." I am relieved I have my passport with me.

He continues. "A car will pick us up, and we will head to l' Horologe, a family friend's inn. It is a lovely bed and breakfast.

All arrangements have been made. We will then be driven to the convent the next morning, Sunday the thirteenth, leaving around 5:00 a.m. and arriving at 7:00 a.m. Vespers are open to occasional public for three hours and close at 10:00 a.m. We can make our inquiries then. Since there are no phones and no other way to contact people, this will be our only option. This leaves us all day today to research and come up with any questions or ideas that might be beneficial for the trip. In order to avoid jet lag, we will sleep when we arrive and stick to our U.S. schedule of breakfast and meals."

As we're discussing the details, James arrives with a telegram from the convent. It's marked "Urgent" on the outside, and I'm beginning to wonder if anything is not urgent. The paper is a light tissue-type of stationary folded over and sealed. Dr. Janus takes it and then passes it to me.

"*We are hesitant but find it necessary to inform you Thérèse Marie Janus has not been here since July 4, 2008. Although she has been known in the past to disappear for a week and then reappear, this time all her belongings remain except the habit she was wearing and her rosary which are missing; even her devotional book, which she never leaves behind, is here, and no one has seen her. Please come immediately.*"

With this, I see a brief quiver on the side of Dr. Janus's lips that almost makes me want to break down, but I hold it together. The truth that this is really happening has just hit him. He shifts his weight, rubs his scalp, and says to me, "Go ahead and fill him in completely. I must go pack and finish making arrangements. We must leave for the airport tomorrow at three, James," and he quickly excuses himself.

Quietly, a subdued James replies, "Yes, sir," and then looks at me inquisitively. I sit him down in Dr. Janus's chair and explain everything. It feels like I'm confessing, and in a sense, it takes some of the burden off of me. I end by reiterating that we need to call the police. "I mean, what do you or I know about kidnappings? Nothing! What are we going to do?"

After some thought, he replies, "You go to France with him, Mags. I'll stay and work on security and start planning how to handle any further calls. Then I'll make a plan for a more secure trip to New York City for the performance. Tickets to the Met? That's odder than a pig on the top of the Empire State Building. What do you make of *that?*"

"I have no idea, and the worst part is, I don't really have any idea of what the symbols are saying yet. I'm hoping to do some more work today and that I'll hear from a Jewish scholar friend to help with some translations."

"All right, go to work and get packed," he replies. "I'll be here tomorrow to load you both up. I'll let you know if I can think of anything else. I'll drop the originals off to the agent for fingerprint and document analysis and ask him to do some preliminary work for us off the record."

"Sounds good. They're scanned into my computer. Eventually I'll want to know the type of parchment paper, what it's made of, the year it was done, and to have some analysis done on the ink. I don't get the feeling these were recently painted."

"All right, anything else?"

"I don't think so."

"Take care, Mags; it will be okay."

"Yeah, that's what Dr. Janus said, but I have a deep ache in my heart that just doesn't agree."

James comes up to the office with me, and I hand him the two pieces. He leaves, and I go back to work. The day goes by quickly, and since Dr. Janus decides to have dinner in his room, Ana serves me in the office. It's already 1:00 a.m. when I decide I'd better get some sleep. I feel like I've gotten nowhere. My head

swirls with symbols and unconscious material, and I go to bed
blissfully unaware that one day soon it will be my hands and not
my brain that will uncover some truth.

chapter
14

Waiting: When you can do nothing, rest assured God is at work.

Anonymous inspirational quote

itting around waiting the next day, packed and ready, is not easy for me. I go to the entrance of the humongous kitchen and am amazed by the copper kettles, pots, and pans hanging from the ceiling and walls, the fresh herbs growing on the counters under a special light, a large wooden table that doubles as a chopping board, and it's the first time I see any of the help other than Ana. There are three other people there. One per-

son is cutting and slicing slabs of fresh meat, another is cutting vegetables, and the other is putting potted sunflowers around the room and organizing other flesh flowers. It's quite a production. The shelves are full of glass canning jars containing various foods. Spices are lined up in rows, while others are hanging to complete their drying out process. There are enough appliances, mostly stainless steel, to my surprise, to cook for an army.

I make a sound, and everyone abruptly turns around, almost appearing to stand at attention. Ana is packaging food, lunches and meals for the trip; shocked, she says, "*Problema?*"

"Oh no, I was just wondering if I could take a stroll in the gardens before we leave."

"*Si, Signorina, Si!* It is tightly locked up, but you-*a* go through servants' house, you get-*a* to the main gardens. You must look at the herbs, the flowers, and the veggies. All things his *mama* set up. It is *bellisimo.*"

"Thank you."

I follow her advice, get to the gardens, and wander in silence, taking in the incredible smells. It relaxes me so much. I understand why floral therapy and essences have made such a comeback through the years.

Every step I take is a new experience. There are little walkways with herbs growing in bunches and little labels for clarification. I know plants like rosemary, lavender, basil, and oregano, but I have never seen so many different types. Their official names and classifications are by each one, appearing to be in Latin. There is so much to learn about nature. I really had never considered it before.

I come upon a sundial in the center of one walkway and see it's exactly 2:45 p.m. What an amazing invention. How had people known so much centuries ago? I can't believe that many minutes had evaporated. I had gotten lost in the beauty of it all. How time can fly. Why can't life be this simple?

The sun is warm on my body, and little gnats are just starting to invade my space, so I figure it is time to leave. I go back the way I came so I won't get lost.

James is there loading the limo. Dr. Janus is nowhere to be seen. Quietly James ushers me, whispering, "Listen, I just found out there may have been some strange meetings with Dr. J. over a month ago. Has he said anything about it to you?"

"No, not to my recollection, but again, we haven't been able to chat about all his work and acquaintances yet."

"All right. Keep this between us for now, but let's lock tentacles when you get back."

"Okay. Do you have my e-mail in case you want to quietly send me any information?"

"What, me? No way, man. I don't want to get trapped in the whole techie game. Call me if you need me, and we'll meet in person!"

"You're too funny, James!"

"Columbia University was enough bookworming for me. Remember classes. I ain't no noggins surgeon!"

Dr. Janus comes down, and James finishes loading. We get into the limo with a handful of goodies from Ana, as if we'll starve without her there to care for us!

"We'll be back Sunday for dinner," Dr. Janus informs Ana.

"You no be here in time, you call-*a*. I no want-*a* pasta overcooked."

"Sunday is homemade pasta day," Dr. Janus clarifies, looking at me.

"I need-*a* put butcher order in. You want lamb roast or venison for extra guest Tuesday?"

"Extra guest?" Dr. Janus says, completely surprised.

"Why, your brother. What-*a*? You forgot?"

"Oh no, perhaps I should cancel."

James and I don't think that would be a good idea. We should make things seem as normal as possible. Dr. Janus also clarifies that "brother" is a friend, as he'd seen the quizzical look on my face.

He agrees with us and turns to me, asking if I eat deer meat. I haven't ever had it, but am not opposed as long as the picture of Bambi doesn't come to mind while eating.

"Venison it is!"

Ana's hands indicate she's pleased with that answer. James waves to her, saying, "*Vaya con Dios!*" and she scurries back to work.

"Isn't that Spanish?" I test.

"Well ya!"

chapter

15

To turn $100 into $110 is work, but to turn $100
million into $110 million is inevitable.

Edgar Bronfman

e ride in the darkened limo on the way
to the private airstrip. It feels a little
like a funeral procession. Mozart's "Don
Giovanni" is playing, and there's some
tension in the air. I displace it by talking
about Mozart and the summer festivals
I've attended through the years at the Lincoln Center. It's a long
time since I've been to one, and I'm looking forward to getting
some culture at our Met night.

Dr. Janus and I start reviewing the people in his life and my outline.

Dr. Janus responds thoughtfully, "I have been thinking and thinking, and I just can't get an idea as to who would benefit from this. I mean, I have had competition and rivalry, but that ended years ago after I did my last stint in biotech. There's no sibling rivalry. Tess has no real friends outside of the convent. As you know, my father was a scientist; my mother was a devoted wife and mother who loved to garden. They started out poor, and everyone knows he made his fortune in the 1950s when he helped analyze information relating to the newly discovered DNA. He made a significant amount of money, and his investments just soared in that great era. He then carried extremely large life insurance policies on both of them. So between the growth in the value of properties, a good stock market, smart cash assets, excellent insurance, there it is, you have amassed great wealth."

I knew stories of the large families, and this made me think of Sam Bronfman's son, Edgar, who headed up the main New York City Seagram operation and stated, "To turn $100 into $110 is work, but to turn $100 million into $110 million is inevitable." Money attracts money.

Dr. Janus continues. "I have a financial advisor I call who gives updates as needed, but I really don't have a spreadsheet of my net worth. I'll never spend it all, so it grows." He seems pensive for a couple of minutes, then goes on, "Since Tess rejected all of it for devotion to God, and being much younger and requiring nothing from the estate other than the substantial yearly donations to the convent and the immense initial donation, or her "dowry" upon entrance, she uses little of the money. I spend little other than on housing, salaries, travel, and work. Since I have no family, it just grows and grows. I mean, if people are jealous about the money, that would be strange, as most of my acquaintances now are well off in their own right. Other than that, I think I have a loyal staff who are well compensated for their work."

He explains that Ana has been with the family since his parents were in their forties and is very loyal. Her husband had worked for them as well, but he died in 2001, which is when he hired James. He has never felt a need to have more security than the one guard at that house, and that's only because his father had set up a lifetime contract with a company that supplies the service for that house only. No other property has security coverage.

"We have never had a problem with security or any issues with staff. Ana has pretty much hired everyone through the years, so I can't imagine it's any of them." Dr. Janus looks perplexed.

I venture on, "I must ask, why all the secrecy on this house, even with me?"

"This was our family summer house. No one knew we owned it. They thought we went off to our home in the south of France."

Oh, just another home, in France no less. I manage to keep that thought to myself.

"As a matter of fact, it was so secret that, to ensure even the kids didn't slip up, we believed this was the south of France for some time. With a 144-acre parcel, you could believe you were in a country of your own. When we figured out we weren't flying to our destination, we told our parents we had caught on to them and demanded an explanation. They sat us down and explained Dad was working on secret research and, if anyone found out where it was stored, we could all be hurt. We certainly didn't want that, and we loved the house anyway, so we kept our mouths shut. I have asked James to pull the plans together of the house and property for you to see."

"Good idea. So who built the house?"

"Dad designed every inch of it and hired the builders. It was mostly completed by 1965, and we have needed to do little work on it since then."

"It appears your father was extremely detail oriented."

"He was."

"I mean the entrance with the precise mosaics and constellations is beyond impressive."

"He loved the constellations and the stars and spent hours studying them. My mother and he loved all things nature."

"The hangings on the wall up the circular staircase are unique. Did you hang them or did he?"

"I have not touched a thing in the house except for moving a couple of pieces of furniture in the master bedroom, purchasing some new sheets and comforters as theirs were getting old, and obviously updating the office equipment and kitchen appliances. So he had the pictures hung. He used to say, 'These are the truths and steps to our nature, son, the way our Creator really made us to be.' I always thought I'd get to them one day and figure out what he meant. However, when you see something so often, you stop paying attention. Come to think of it, I had practically forgotten about them and his comment."

"So you have no idea what the designs are."

"None."

"I've also noticed that, unlike most people's homes, yours has no family snapshots."

"No, there really aren't. We have a few albums in black and white from the early years, and that's it. My mother especially hated to have her picture taken, so that could be part of it. And, I'm not much of a sentimentalist either, so really have not found the need to change."

"What about friends growing up?"

"We were pretty isolated. Tess and I spent a lot of time together, but there was the age gap, and otherwise we did things as a family or read and played on our own. I guess this made me a bit of a social outcast; to this day, I find it hard to make the effort to make close friends."

I want to ask about women, lovers, but know it's too personal, and I'm not sure I really want to know. I'm enjoying my time alone with him.

"I will put together a list of people for you from personal to professional to associations I belong to. I'm not sure what good it will do, but it's something."

I ask again if he has any idea about the two pieces of artwork and their meanings, and he says no. "They're colorful and creative, but again I have a scientific mind, not an imaginative one. They mean nothing to me."

We pull up to the jet, James loads our bags, and we're off to France.

Imagine all that money. For me, it's as Bronfman says, turning $100 into $110 seems impossible. I wonder if I'll ever get to the point I can even afford a house, forget about a private jet.

chapter
16

*But He turned and said unto Peter, "Get thee behind Me,
Satan: thou art an offence unto Me: for thou savourest not
the things that be of God, but those that be of men."*

Matthew 16:23 (What Jesus said when
Satan assaulted Him through Peter.)

t was much later that, finally, as if a voice
from God, she heard, "Hey, wake up;
wake up! Can you hear me?"

It was the electronic voice! *Oh, I am
alive! Someone knows I am here. God heard
my prayers!*

It then dawned on her that it was her captor, but at this point
she was just happy to have someone near her.

It clarified, as only a monster could do this to another human,
"The shackles have been electronically unlatched. There's fresh

food and water, soap, a brush, and clean clothes. I was unavoid-ably delayed and didn't mean to leave you for five days."

Some compassion? Wow, it has been that long?

"Nourish yourself," it said. "We have some things we must speak about."

She wanted to be angry and yell, "You eat the food! Let me die!" but she was too weak and at this point just wanted to have these aches in her stomach go away and comply with its demands. She noted the instructions were in English. She won-dered where she physically was.

After she had guzzled down her food, she noticed the gar-ments it had brought her were civilian clothes. How could she wear those? She had spent years working up to her habit with the tunic, the scapular, the cowl, and her black veil, the one for professed nuns, not the white veil of the novice. She revered this outfit. She did not want to jeopardize her vows.

Also, like an amputee, she still felt the missing rosary was there, hanging from the right side even though it had been taken from her. She couldn't imagine what it would feel like to be in a pair of pants, jeans no less, and a T-shirt. What type of repen-tance would be required? Is there a patron saint to pray to? Would God rather she sit there dirty? She thought she could hold off from cleaning up, but after minutes of debating, the desire to be fresh and clean and get out of her smelly, sweat-infested habit had temporarily overcome her desire to follow her vows. *Please Mother Mary, forgive me.* She slowly disrobed and, little by little, experienced every moment of the freedom of her arms and wrists from the shackles, and this gave her strength. The feel of the water against her skin, the scent of the soap, the feel of a brush against her growing hair. She had not shaved her head in days. She paid particular attention to how quickly it had grown back in and how it glistened in the light of the single bulb. She could

tell because she now had bangs. It was all miraculous. After many minutes, when she was clothed, she said, "I'm ready to talk now."

"Have you any idea of why you are here?" the electronic voice responded.

"None. Do you even know who I am?"

"You are Sister Thérèse; your brother is Dr. Peter Janus."

"Yes? Is this about him? Is he okay?"

"At the moment he is," said the electronic voice with what appeared to be edginess, if electronic voices can sound edgy.

"Does he know I am here, against my will?"

"He does. No one knows of your location, not even those I take orders from."

Ah, *it* is not the one in control. Maybe there will be a chance to play on *its* sympathies and get out of this. "What do you want from us?"

"In time, you will know. In due time."

"How much time?"

"That, my dear sister, depends on you both. For this, I've no control and no time limit."

"Will you let me go when this is over?" She waited anxiously for the answer but then wondered if she wanted to know it.

"That remains to be seen, but likely not."

Likely not. Her heart started pounding; now she wanted to cry, to throw a tantrum, to scream. *How could my life be reduced to this? Why? Again, what have I ever done to anyone? Oh Jesus, Mary, saints, anyone; please, you must help me, please.* And then slowly and precisely she stated, "Well, if you are going to kill me, why don't you just do it now? Why make me suffer ... or perhaps I shall just take my own life!" The person she had been before, straightforward and headstrong, started to override the qualities she had learned as a nun, and like a virus, they were gaining ground in every core of her being.

"You would not do so as you have taken a vow to the Holy Father, God, and the pope, and suicide is not a transgression you would wish on your soul, as you will go to hell."

It was right. How did it have this knowledge?

Then it remained silent. No words from it. Counting quietly to herself and using her fingers to determine how many minutes, then hours, had gone by, she was shocked that it could remain silent that long. With all her training, she could do this better than it could, but within another hour, she was beside herself and said humbly, "Hello?"

No answer. She waited. No answer. She was getting upset. No answer. Now scared. No answer. What, had she been left alone again? How long would it be this time? No answer.

Then finally and to her great relief, "I am here."

"Well, why didn't you just say so?" she gasped in exasperation. *Forgive me, Father, for my impatience,* automatically ran through her thoughts. "I would like to know what you want from me and how I can be of assistance to my brother. It might help if I knew who you were and what you wanted so we can just get this over with."

"First, the ground rules," he said. "I will not disclose any information to you until I am ready. You will do as I say, and you will follow my directions. There will be no more silent games, no more outbursts, and no tricks. You can't win. You are my hostage, and if you want to eat and breathe, you will do as I say. You can make this hard or easy. Understand?"

A few moments passed, and finally Tess said, "I do," although in her heart she wasn't sure she would be able to follow these rules. She could in the convent because she followed her Holy Father, and you never questioned authority even if it felt wrong because it was all for a better good, the glory of God. But, since she wasn't sure that God wanted her to sacrifice herself and, perhaps, her brother until she knew why, she agreed.

"I will be passing you some reading materials. I expect you to read them."

"Reading materials?" she burst out in astonishment and then tried to contain herself. *Great, this will be* great, she thought. *What prisoner is handed reading materials? This isn't so bad.*

"When you have gotten through them, we will discuss them."

Shaking her head in utter amazement, "I can do that!" she yelled, excited.

The little food trap opened, and she could see something called the *Amplified Bible* coming in. Just as she was about to touch it, she realized what it was and pulled her hand back as if it were evil.

"This is a book for an evangelical, a Protestant or divided brethren, a non-approved Bible. What am I going to do with that? I'm Catholic. We don't read the Bible; we read from the devotional book. We go to vespers, confession, and Mass; we memorize our Hail Marys, and we don't read anything unless the Papal Supremacy has approved it. It would be a sin for me to read this unless I know it has been approved by the pope." Her hand just sat there paralyzed, unsure as to what it was to do because of the mixed messages from the brain.

With a huge gust of pressure, the book was vacuumed back through the hole and taken away.

She was stunned.

Then as she started to work through her thoughts, she mentally reiterated, *It's not the devil's Bible. It's a Bible. It does have Christ in it. How bad could that be? It's not some piece of science fiction or the numerous other books out there that deceive those lost souls who have not found the sanctity of the Roman Catholic religion.*

"No, no wait," she said. "I'm sorry; I was too hasty."

No response.

"Please, I apologized to you. It was just a shock to me. I'm sorry. Truly sorry."

"We have rules. What would be an appropriate punishment for breaking such a rule?"

"You could bring a priest in, and I could confess," she said hesitantly but pleased with her rediscovered spunk, knowing it could see right through her intentions. If a priest knew she was there, then surely she would be saved.

"A Bible is better than no reading at all, I suppose. I'm just not sure why you would want me to read that of all things. You are obviously not a religious man who wants to spend hours discussing the word of St. Peter, the first pope."

"You know nothing about me. How do you know if I am a religious man or not? Who are you to judge me?"

The slowness and directness of the electronic voice, even without recognizable intonation, made her realize she had angered the perpetrator, who she was now quite certain was a male. He had slipped! He said religious man, not woman. This was no guarantee, but she felt she was making progress.

She responded, "Correct, it's just that an individual who rips someone out of their home, leaves them with no food or water for days, and then forces a false religion on them would not necessarily give one the impression of being a holy or good person."

"Things are often not what they seem."

True, she thought to herself. Now she longed just to have a book in her hands, something to hold on to and read. How bad could that amplified version really be anyway?

"Please, I apologize; I will try harder. Please let me have the book back."

"You will read it?"

"I will."

Slowly the book entered through the hole and attached to the front was a piece of paper that read "Syllabus" on top.

Syllabus, she thought. *That is an outline for a college course.* Why did she need an outline? What was this all about? Never in her life had she heard of anything so strange!

"You want me to follow this outline, and that is what we will discuss?" She almost laughed.

"Correct," it said. "I will be back tomorrow."

The flap door shut. It had forgotten to reshackle her, which was exciting. She set the Bible in front of her, not quite ready to commit, but certainly curious. Now, at least, being left alone in the dirt-filled prison with one light seemed to have some odd purpose, some reason for living. *There are worse forms of torture,* she thought … until a certain thought popped into her mind.

Was this one of Satan's children trying to deceive her? "Get thee behind me!" she yelled. But no one answered.

She waited, but still nothing happened. So with nothing else to do, she read the next part of the Syllabus debating on what she was actually going to do with the Bible.

> Then you will seek Me, inquire for, and require Me [as a vital necessity] and find me when you search for Me with all your heart. (13) I will be found by you, says the Lord and I will release you from captivity and gather you from all the nations and all the places to which I have driven you, says the Lord, and I will bring you back to the place from which I caused you to be carried away captive. (14)
>
> Jeremiah 29:13–14, Amplified Bible

It had been years since she had held a Bible. She knew her family, although Catholic, referred to the King James Version on a regular basis, but they handled it as if it were a violation to the church. She wasn't taught from a Bible in the convent, and she obeyed what was taught there. She had heard of people who were told to burn the kjv before entering the convent.

At first she was afraid to really touch it. New thoughts flooded her mind. She didn't want to be corrupted, even worse, brainwashed. As if too much gas had flooded her engine, she sputtered and jerked, and then as if from second nature, she yelled, "I will not be corrupted," grabbed the evil book, and threw it across the floor.

After minutes of silence and praying, she got up and went over to pick it up.

When she glanced down, it had fallen open to the fourth chapter of the book of Hosea. She had never heard of that book before. She started to read and at verse six:

My people are destroyed for lack of knowledge; because you [the priestly nation] have rejected knowledge, I will also reject you that you shall be no priest to Me; seeing you have forgotten the law of your God, I will also forget your children.

Relieved she was one of the blessed ones, she knew she had knowledge. But this statement of *priest* stuck in her throat. Could it be saying that the priestly nation, the Catholics, had rejected knowledge and forgotten the law of God? It couldn't mean that.

She prayed out loud, "God, show me the truth." Her heart fluttered with anxiety for a moment and then, as if hit by lightening, she realized this was the work of the devil. This wasn't a "translation"; this was a manipulation of words to make you think against the one church.

Then it dawned on her. *This book is a test. I have been captured by the church to see how devout and devoted I am to its teachings. This is a set up. How could I not have seen this before! I must have done something to upset Mother Superior.*

She stood up and yelled at the top of her lungs, "I get it! You didn't tempt me! I am Catholic and will always be!"

She waited anxiously. "You can let me out now. I learned my lesson!"

Nothing. "Hello? Did you hear me? I won. I wasn't tempted. I got it!"

Still nothing. She waited. She started to fold up her habit because it would need to be cleaned. She put her scapular back on over the civilian clothes and then her veil so they could not see how long her hair had grown. She would be out soon and had to look respectable.

But still nothing.

So she began to think some more about being set up. In all honesty, why would the Roman Catholic Church go to such lengths to kidnap her, to test her faith, and what would her brother have to do with that? It didn't make sense.

After a few deep breaths, she realized she may not be on the right track. She thought she should make use of whatever time she had before they came to release her, and if by some crazy chance she wasn't being set up by the church and they were not involved, then the perpetrator would be angry at her for not having done the work she had promised to do. She decided to at least fake it, just to be on the safe side. If Satan were behind this, she would remain aware because she would not under any circumstance succumb. She prayed to the Father to be released from captivity, making sure to keep Satan behind her.

chapter
17

"The Martha Mitchell Effect"

Term for False Accusations of Delusional Disorder

r. Janus and I are settled in and the long plane ride has begun. He is sitting opposite me and it is apparently his turn to ask me questions.

Starting in his direct way he says, "So, Magdalena, what made you switch from being a psychologist to a symbologist? It's not the most common career change."

"You're correct about that. It was really a combination of money, politics, and having to deal with the insurance companies, who cared much more about the paperwork, which inevitably delayed payments, and about getting the sessions shortened than the patients and what they needed. Psychology became so entwined with greedy management companies that it conveniently forgot the purpose of therapy is to help our fellow human beings through suffering, hardship, and, for my clientele, often death. Do you really want to hear more about it?"

"We have a long ride and I could use anything to keep my mind off Tess."

"When I started out in the field, the therapist was there throughout the dying process, whether it was one hour, seven days, or weeks. One was not dictated to by a managed-care company that a patient was to cope with his or her own death in a thirty-to-forty-minute session once a week! You weren't told you couldn't deal with a parent's grief because insurance didn't cover it. You weren't forced to send family members back into their lives as if nothing had happened, as if their child never existed, forcing them to cope with more hardship, more loss, and more of life's cruel twists until they were the ones so broken down they also needed therapy.

"At that critical point, the managed-care company could suddenly enter as 'hero,' offering relief, but now with hundreds and hundreds of dollars of pharmaceuticals to go along with the mix. Quite a production, quite a well-greased machine that frustrated me to no end. In my mind, those care-giving systems should have just euthanized all the caretakers and therapists involved because the pain of the injustices related to fighting the medical and psychological systems during the process sometimes stung more than when the patient died."

I take a sip of water as Dr. Janus listens.

"Still interested?"

"Fire away!" Dr. Janus was always good at allowing me my dissertations.

"Then,"—I elongate the word for emphasis—"as if the managed care corruption is not enough, there is the interference of organizations that pretend to be established to help the poor but instead keeping them where they are versus giving them the tools they need to move out of their situation. Power-driven, controlling families surface as saviors to the masses, but end by hurting the poor and middle class. If they can keep us down and busy, dangling a few carrots of two-week vacations and $600.00 economic stimulus checks, then they can keep us in debt because we are stupid enough to spend the money to push away our pain or to keep up with the Joneses, thus falling perfectly into their trap. We continue to encourage their dirty work. What is worse is we seem to do it freely. So in turn, some of the wealthy get wealthier, the general population is left in a state of confusion, and no one seems to have the energy to find the answers. I seem to have become one of them. Lost."

I take a deep breath and look out the window for a minute.

"I can appreciate that. Sometimes I forget how fortunate I've been. Then something like this happens, and it makes one look at oneself, one's life, and the relationships created and nurtured—or not nurtured, through the years."

Then completely out of left field, he says, "And you Magdalena, any male relationships for you?" awkwardly placing me on the spot.

"Oh, that painful question," I joke. "Truthfully not lately, but I have a great story of my, then ten-year-old, dying cancer patient more concerned with helping me understand why I wasn't married than with his own impending death."

Duplicating my patient's tone, in a stern voice I say, "You spend all your time with us. If I was your husband, I'd want you to care more about me than us kids."

Dr. Janus smiles in appreciation, and I fall deep into thought about my dear Shakeem.

At age eleven, he died from a brain tumor, Neuroblastoma. He was alert the entire time until the night he fell asleep, moved into unconsciousness, and then death. He was my hero, but so were all of them. His mom was left to raise her little one-year-old mulatto girl, a "surprise" pregnancy with the "surprise" of her white husband leaving her to deal with a new child and a newly diagnosed son. She was trying to work a full-time job to keep benefits and support her family with no relatives to help. She could have been a welfare mom but wanted nothing to do with that *stigma*. I did my best to spend as much time as I could with her son at the hospital. He informed me that his sister's skin was lighter than his because they had different fathers. I had nice skin, he told me, but I needed to be careful not to get cancer from the rays of the sun since it was so white. He let me know he didn't have to worry about getting sunburned. The entire conversation ensued as if he was relieved skin cancer would not be his downfall.

I enjoyed many moments with him advising me about life and me helping him deal with his anger over the fact that the treatment he was receiving made him feel worse and he didn't want it because the doctors would not allow him to make his own choice and to die. He knew it was going to happen, and so did everyone else. The cancer was incurable and growing rapidly.

I was his advocate. To their horror, I told the doctors his thoughts and that if it were up to me, I'd have let him be in control. But, as if I was putting him up to this, they told me I had better treat his "suicidal ideation," and quickly. It was nothing like that. Children know when they're dying, so to the professionals' chagrin, I noted the boy's feelings in his chart, telling the truth, proud the child could voice his own opinion and be heard, documenting there was no suicidal ideation, and he was "oriented times three" (psychological jargon). For this honesty, I was "quickly" sent to the ethics board for a reprimand!

It could have ended in my termination when they discovered I had shared with the boy the fact that I had stood up for him, wanted his needs heard, and got in trouble by protecting him. I wanted him to know I cared and that I'd risk everything for him to be heard. He loved that and thought it would be great if I was fired so I could go get a husband who would care for me. He never put the pieces together, that, like his father or stepfather, not all men support their loved ones financially or even emotionally.

He died just as the hospital administration was getting ready to "deal" with me. So they let it slide, too fed up to add one more issue to their overloaded schedules, and why lose the only psychologist on staff for over two hundred children and families, one who worked fourteen-hour days, seven days a week?

The oncology nurses had ganged up on me in this case, as did the head psychiatrist. He was a young man in his thirties; I was nineteen with a master's degree while just starting on my doctorate. Looking back now, it's hard for me to even believe I was fifteen, a June baby, sent to my first year of college. I was the brunt of numerous jokes. I managed to get a B.A. in three years instead of four working like crazy; then I worked fulltime, went to school at night, and got my M.A. at NYU in one and a half years. With this degree, I was hired at the leading children's hospital in New Jersey as the psychologist to cover all of pediatric hematology-oncology—and I was nineteen. It blew people away, and often the nurses had to tell the parents, "We know she's young, but the minute you sit down with her, you'll see why she's here." There were never complaints after the initial shock. When I was twenty-four, I got my doctorate, but the running joke at the hospital to meet with the nineteen-year-old never dissipated.

The psychiatrist, who was the polar opposite of me, advised that I was to follow the DSM-III to the letter, and he would prescribe anti-depressants for the boy. I said the only ones who needed the drugs were the people who weren't accepting and dealing with the fact that the boy knew his death was coming and was coping with it. He informed me that prescribing drugs was his job and I was not to do what I had done with the *other* patient, a girl who was going through a severe pain crisis due to sickle-cell anemia.

"Oh yes," I say aloud as if Dr. Janus can hear my thoughts, "and speaking of patients, here's a perfect example of what happened at the hospital. I had shared with a teen girl that 'oobies' do exist and validated her experience. She was in great pain, and what she experienced was not a drug-induced hallucination; it was an actual out-of-body experience, and she had had them before. She was afraid of them, but after we spoke, we both realized they seemed to change her in some way, and the pain would dissipate. They were odd occurrences but more of a blessing. I helped her to understand she was not mentally ill, as the psychiatrist had *actually* told her, while he was convincing her that mental health problems were common, and she should not feel bad about the diagnosis."

"I explained it differently, that she was by no means mentally ill and that some people were closed-minded about these things and too afraid to move out of the textbook and into real life. I'd have fired the psychiatrist, but instead I was the one who was wrong, according to the staff and administration."

I see Dr. Janus's eyebrow raise.

"The parents loved me because it was the quickest she had ever recovered. She never had an incident again while I was there, and years later she had "miraculously" gotten healthy and more focused, turned into an A student, and was admitted into college with a scholarship. She wanted to become a psychologist or doctor to help people the way she had been helped. Poor girl, I still hope to this day she chose to become a physician because the battles psychologists have are all uphill. What happened during those episodes, I have no idea and will never know. That something did happen and was not delusional, I can say as a fact."

"I'm sure you are correct," Dr. Janus affirms.

The pilot comes over the loudspeaker to announce the weather and travel report.

I think to myself how it scares me to think of the number of people who have been convinced they're insane when it's really the limited knowledge of the professionals that's at fault. The perfect example is what is now called the "Martha Mitchell Effect." Martha was the wife of the U.S. Attorney General during the Nixon administration; she alleged that illegal activity was taking place in the White House during the Watergate period. She was labeled delusional by the psychiatrists who were asked to testify about her accusations. The professionals asserted that what she claimed wasn't possible and that she was making it up due to her illness.

When the scandal was finally revealed, they had to take back their diagnosis because, to their amazement, she was totally sane and had been telling the truth the entire time. Years of her life were lost, all because some so-called professionals couldn't accept what was going on in their own country! Harsh, I know, since many people were shocked and in disbelief. However, for a psychologist or psychiatrist to diagnose a delusional disorder a person can't be oriented times three, which means she could not have known her name, the time frame she was living in, and where she physically was. In court, Martha was able to answer all these questions accurately. The professionals could have called her a liar, but delusional was an outright misdiagnosis, and they should have been reprimanded or, even worse, had their licenses revoked. The professionals' authority and method of diagnosis were never even questioned.

In my mind, something heinous had to have been going on for the diagnosis of delusional disorder to stick, and that is what scares me.

With our sanity in other people's hands, how do any of us get by? Taken to the next degree, when you think about it, when one's own sanity, like Martha Mitchell's, lies in the hands of people who are setting out to deceive the world, how can the little person survive?

The unconscious tells the truth, whether you want it to or not. That's why I love working with it through dreams, drawings, and even free association. Children with cancer operate in the truth. They seem to understand time is precious and are, therefore, bluntly honest. Too bad the rest of the world is so closed-minded and so "unconscious."

chapter
18

Laughter heals what the mind fails to understand.

Jocelyn Soriano

ours later we can see the red and green lights of the landing strip planted smack in the middle of what looked like a farm, where a silver limo awaits us. There are very few other planes around. The weather is warm and beautiful. It's 3:00 a.m. our time. Twelve hours and *poof* we're in Europe. Such luxury.

Our driver is a leathery-skinned, obviously heavy French brand cigarette smoker, whose leftover tobacco smell infiltrates my body with a simple shake of his hand. He's a jovial little chatterbox, about nothing, really. Sharply attired too. His nose moves as he makes points, with a general demeanor that gives him that indescribable "European charm." I'm able to understand his French relatively easily, and Dr. Janus is quiet as we speak back and forth.

We take some old, fairly empty back roads with twists and eventually end up at a small T intersection with a gas station on the right and an inn on the left. A huge sign with the word *l'Horologe,* which means timepiece or clock, hangs over the entrance. Running out to meet us is an older couple, perhaps in their seventies. The man, only about five foot five inches with a mop of thick white hair, is holding a cleaver and obviously excited to see Dr. Janus. The Mrs. is wiping her hands on an apron, while obviously reprimanding the spouse for brandishing the knife. Dr. Janus had mentioned what good friends of the family they were. They kiss me on each cheek, as the French do, and then start hugging and holding me so hard you would've thought I was one of their own.

The inn is a classic Bavarian-style A-frame with a little country flower bed marking the entrance. It looks like a house transported from Holland but missing the tulips. We're shuffled in the entrance. The first room is a bar for both alcoholic and coffee beverages, with a dining room to the right that's partially set, awaiting the next culinary delights. Snacks are perfectly lined up on the bar. There's fresh melted Brie cheese, homemade baked bread, pastries, and coffee. I indulge slightly, then ask if anyone minds if I go to bed while they catch up. No one does. I actually want to give Dr. Janus time alone with them.

The gentleman shows me to my room and leaves quickly. The room is simple: a small bed with a white lace comforter, lace curtains, a small brown and beige woven woolen rug, a table with a handmade brown clay pitcher containing water, a glass, and some wooden shelves holding some trinkets.

After a snooze, I head to the bathroom to clean up. No luxurious shower here. I step into the old-fashioned tub, turn on the water, which is a hose with a shower head, and let it trickle over me … a reminder of how lucky we are in the United States. After a couple more trickles, some harsh soap, and lots of hand scrubbing, I at least feel clean and more alert. I finish getting ready and start down the stairs to see who's around. Voices are floating up, laughter is shaking the floors, and the inn feels alive. When I get downstairs to the dining room, which appears to seat about sixty people shoulder to shoulder at two extremely long tables, I can see that it's packed and booming. The owners provide lunches and dinners for set prices, and people obviously come from all over to get organic, fresh, home-cooked food daily.

People are laughing and eating and drinking, and I can understand most of the French. I'm immediately encouraged to sit amidst a group of good-looking young men as they push themselves aside and quickly make space for me. Three fine men, hands on different parts of my body, all generously help me sit. I decide, hey, I might as well. They're cordial and cute and help me along with my *Français Parisienne.* The banter is everywhere as everyone speaks above and on top of each other. Numerous conversations from all directions in the room ensue, and my neck is moving in all directions, like following a mosquito in flight, as I try to respond and look to each individual talking to me. I'm enjoying myself immensely.

I can see the owners keeping their eye on me; they keep coming over to see if I need anything. They may have known the young men better than I did. There's food everywhere, but I only feel like fresh bread and cheese at the moment. On one trip over, I ask the Mrs. if she'd seen Dr. Janus. She laughs, saying he

had only gone to bed an hour ago because they had been talking.
Good for him, I think. I'm glad he has company and someone to
bond with during this stressful time. I feel bad for the owners
because they probably had no down time.

After the luncheon crowd trickles out at about four, I pitch
in and help clean up. I'm having a blast, and these two are so
funny. They have one of those love/hate relationships and could
have been on some comedy show. They speak some words in
French, some English, out of politeness for me. The wife is the
verbal and controlling one, but the husband gets his two cents
in. Despite their jousting, there's no doubt they are still in love
and love what they do.

I wonder if I'll ever be so fortunate. I had, however, been
allowed to participate in a day of laughter, and for that I'm grateful.

chapter

19

Keep the Rule and the Rule will keep you.

1917 Code of Canon Law

r. Janus and I are in the limo at 5:00 a.m., and by 7:00 a.m. we arrive. There are no signs or directions pointing to the convent, and other than a small entrance with open gates, the Sisters are certainly not encouraging the public to come worship with them.

The limo driver drops us off at an archway that leads to the "inner sanctum," the chapel and the other buildings. The Mother Superior is coming down a path in the center to greet us. She's an older lady, about my height, heavy set with round glasses and an extremely deep voice. When she speaks to thank us for coming, her voice is more of a growl than a welcome. "You got my note? I wasn't worried at first, but then after this time frame, I knew I had to let you know. We're not in the habit…" I chuckle, she's not amused, it's my nervous tension laugh, "…of calling the police or even family unless absolutely necessary."

I feel my back straightening and my demeanor changing as one does this ridiculous thing of trying to act more pious around those we think are pure themselves. Why, I've no idea.

She continues. "You know the church; we like to keep our business to ourselves. Well, I assume that is how your family still is. I was deeply saddened to hear of your parents' deaths. Sister Thérèse took it hard, but she has been doing so well here that it's a shock to have something such as this transpire. Do you know anything at all about what's going on?" Her tone is so terse, it sounds as if she's blaming us.

"Not at this point." A big lie, and I feel guilt for Dr. Janus. "But we'll let you know if we find anything out."

Secrecy, I guess.

She asks if Dr. Janus will accompany her to the office, and all I can think of is being sent to the principal's office. We go through the garden courtyard as she explains that she needs him to sign in and do some paperwork. He obliges, and I say I'll stay and wander around the lovely gardens.

I can see why people are drawn to the contemplative life, away from the craziness of the world. As I head over to a bench by some roses, I spot a door slightly ajar with a brass sign that reads "Relics Room." I look around, and no one is there, so my curiosity gets the best of me. I carefully try to peek around the door but have to push it open to see more. The door lets out a huge moan, and I step back in embarrassment for a minute. Sure no one has seen me, I decide to enter. How much trouble could I get into in a convent anyway?

The sunlight sneaks in from the outside and lights up what look like souvenirs belonging to some nun hanging on three sections of a dark burgundy wall. I think it's supposed to represent looking into her room. It's unequivocally one of the oddest things I've ever seen. There are what appear to be a nun's red, curly, and extremely long hair hanging on the wall with an old pair of shoes, a shovel, some embroidered piece that must have hung around the habit, a rosary, a simple wooden cross, and some books. This is all blocked off with a single golden colored rope. The hair thing, old shoes, and shovel spook me out a bit. It looks like someone had been scalped. I turn around and leave.

I stop exploring and head back to the bench. I've never seen a relics room before, and this is all a little weird. Sitting on the bench, I see a plaque that explains that this area has been dedicated in honor of St. Thérèse, the Little Flower, who lived nearby. It explains she was also a Carmelite nun and that every year on the last Sunday in September, her relics are brought out for public adoration and a procession through Lisieux, France. It sounds like quite an event. The description elaborates that some of her remains have been inserted into a figure that represents her on her deathbed, which are kept in the Chapel of the Reliquary in the actual St. Thérèse convent in Lisieux with most of her relics enclosed underneath her there. I've never heard of such a thing, but to each his own. Raised as a Protestant, this act of placing body parts into a statue verges on the macabre!

I am relieved when I see Dr. Janus and the Mother Superior coming toward me.

"Please let me show you to her room. You have until ten this morning. I'm afraid I can't change the rules, not even for you."

"That will be fine," Dr. Janus kindly responds.

She whisks us away, leading us to Tess's room. It's a beautiful walkway with white, dark brown, and reddish bricks. My feet click on the floor, which I find a bit annoying. It's as if the Mother Superior is floating above the stones and I'm clunking along making the noise. I'm afraid she's going to be like a librarian and *shush* me, telling me to walk more quietly. She doesn't. Instead she starts to speak, "You realize we're one of the few remaining cloistered convents. We still call ourselves "Nuns" versus "Sisters" because we practice contemplation, and every task, no matter how minute, is approved through me. We are not like the more liberal "Sisters" who work in a church, a school, or even a hospital in their community. There are so few new nuns who enter the convents now, and thanks to the generous gifting of your father, Dr. Theodore Janus, we will always be well provided for." She continues, obviously feeling the need to educate us. "Other aging nuns are struggling to get money together to eat, and in the United States in 1971, Congress took pity and allowed for Social Security. Glory be to God, this will never be one of the things we need worry about."

Two thoughts are running through my head simultaneously. One is, I'm appalled to think the Roman Catholic Church, with its vast amount of money and resources, could leave its devoted children to starve, and how human it is of the Americans to step in and support their nuns. The second thought is regarding the "gifting" from Dr. Janus, which doesn't surprise me, but makes me wonder what would happen to their funding if Tess is no longer there.

Watching the Mother Superior walk briskly with her hands clasped under the scapular makes me wonder how anyone can walk so precisely and look so comfortable. We follow her for a couple hundred more yards, and then I decide to bravely ask, "So, I take it you're not in favor of the Vatican II?"

I knew very little, but enough to know that from 1962–65, Pope John XXIII and 2,500 bishops, known as "The Council" met to rewrite the Roman Catholic Church's constitution. I would not be surprised if Mother Superior is against it because, from what I understood, it took power away from her position and gave individual nuns more freedom to make decisions on their own. The Vatican II Council even removed the mandatory need to wear a habit. This group obviously didn't change that!

"A travesty." She shakes her head so vehemently I think she's about to take off like a bird in flight. Then her head stops, she stops, and, with utter sadness, she starts with a whisper that gradually crescendos. "A travesty, my dear. We are a dying breed. To think our Lord would be honored less and less in all countries. Terrible."

Her voice is getting even louder, and her eyes are now piercing mine. "This idea, declaring that *all* Catholics are to pursue holiness, thereby downgrading the stature of a devoted nun, is nonsense. Utter nonsense." I do everything I can to stand still and look her in the eyes. She finally starts to move, and I can take a breath.

Finally, Dr. Janus and I dare to glance at each other, and we're both mildly amused by her candor, not because the situation is remotely funny, but because it sounds so strange coming from this deep voiced, fully habited Mother Superior.

"Rules are made to be kept," she starts again. "We didn't create the almost two thousand rules and regulations in the 1917 Code of Canon Law for the fun of it. This is why *we* still hold Mass in Latin, the way it should be. We distinguish charity of the eyes, proper dress, and acting for a reason. How else is one to keep novices in line and teach them proper discipline? We pride ourselves on our devotion and stick to the strict belief that one should not even go home at a parent's death. Well, you are aware of that, Dr. Janus, and it didn't 'hurt' Sister Thérèse. She managed. We honor little contact with the family because it means little outside negative influence. Pardon me, not your wonderful family, but you know the loose morals of our Christian brethren. The rules are there for a reason, and if you break them for one sister, you might as well break them for all sisters, and *we* do *not* break rules here!"

A second later, like a judge declaring a life sentence, "Keep the Rule and the Rule will keep you." With that, her final words, "That is why your father was so insistent on your sister coming here."

I watch carefully where we're going while she's lecturing us. We've now passed two archways, and we're at the third one when she turns to the left. It's so abrupt, I'm in her way, and we almost collide. Her hand shoos me away … the pest. I move. We go down yet another hall, which are all beginning to look alike. At last we arrive at Tess's room.

I'm feeling a little attacked by this lady's strong presence, and as a past practicing psychologist, although I want to hear more about her thinking and why she's become this way, I want to stick to the job at hand. Find Tess. Find her alive and unharmed.

It's a simple room, and Tess does not miraculously appear, to my chagrin. I'd have no problem with a miracle, as long as it gets me off the hook! I note the small single bed pushed against the wall, covered by a dark brown wool blanket. A white pillow and linen sheet precisely folded over the blanket await their owner. Looking around, I see a basic desk with a lamp; a well-used, religious-looking book; a small open closet with a habit and some shoes; and a dresser with a glass and pitcher of water. *No shovel.* I smirk,

"Didn't she have her habit on?" I ask naively

"We all have two habits, my dear." The Mother Superior walks to the closet. "This one is her second one. It was just cleaned."

"I see." Looking around, I say, "And this is her Bible?"

"Devotional book. Yes, and she would never purposefully leave without it."

I start flipping through the crinkled pages, but there are no notes, no messages, and no clues as to where she is. I see it has a bunch of prayers in it, some I'm familiar with, most I'm not.

"Everything looks in order," Dr. Janus states, looking dismayed. "So you have no idea what might have gone on either?"

"None. Sorry." Her tone softens for a brief moment.

We all just stand there for a couple of minutes looking around, and then the Mother Superior announces she has to get back to chapel for silent prayer. She excuses herself and floats out of the room.

We stay until 9:45 a.m. so we don't overstay our allotted time, and just as we're about to leave, a nun whispers by the door, "Peter, Peter," and as she peeks her head in, it becomes apparent she has a smashing similarity to the black and white picture of Tess that Dr. Janus had shown me. Even he does a double take. She softly says, "Please follow me, secretly."

Of course, with habits, all you have to go on is height, weight in the face, eyes, basic bone structure, and how the habit falls. You can't even tell hair color or body type, unless someone is pudgy. She's not in the least; she's tall and elegant.

"Peter, I'm Sister Sophia Marguerite, a dear friend of Tess. Something is seriously wrong. She would not have left on her own. I snuck in and grabbed all the old letters from you and your parents because we look so similar in stature and from a distance people think we're sisters—you know, blood sisters. She wouldn't want anyone else to have them."

Dr. Janus asks her some basic questions while taking the items.

"She seemed fine. I saw nothing out of the ordinary. She was following through on her regular duties. At times she was starting to get fidgety, as if there were more out in the world for

her. She had questioned some things about the Roman Catholic faith and fate, but she bounced through it, and we went on with our normal daily lives. She seemed content."

Sister Sophia Marguerite then went on in a rush. "I can't stay. I'm missing morning duties, and I don't want the others to talk. Please take care and *promise* you will let me know how she is and if there is anything I can do. When all turns out well, come visit me." She then reaches out and, to my surprise, cups my face with her baby-soft hands. "What is your name?"

"Magdalena, Magdalena LaSige."

"Hmm, Magdalena. 'The silent one.' You are beautiful."

I thought to myself, *She knew French,* and then it dawned on me, we're in France. However, if only she knew the irony of such a name for me.

"Something is so familiar about you, so pure," she says.

"That's what everyone says to me! Well, perhaps not the *pure* part!"

It always makes me laugh. Whether I'm in a Wal-Mart or the Waldorf, people think I work there. If someone needs help or sees me on the street in a town I've never been to before, I'm asked for directions. Everybody always seems to think they know me. I, in return, am terrible with faces and never remember anyone. My parents say it's my sensitive, yet confident, demeanor that make people open up to me and trust me right away. Now I look familiar to a nun. That's a new one!

Just as the sister is getting ready to leave the room, another nun spots her. Without missing a beat, Sister Sophia Marguerite says she has been asked to bring us to the chapel to pray and light a candle for Sister Thérèse.

Pretty quick and a good liar, for a nun. I guess she knows that some consequences are worth a white lie. It makes me feel better about keeping certain truths from people, so as to not hurt them.

The other sister nods in understanding and moves along. To keep up appearances, Sister Sophia Marguerite leads us back to the chapel, lights a candle on the eternal way, and excuses herself. I'm not that religious, but I whisper a prayer to Our Heavenly Father to let us find Tess alive and safe, and I'm sure Dr. Janus is doing the same thing.

We head solemnly back to the limo, the tapping of my feet on the hallway floor the only sound. We don't see or hear anyone else.

Seeing us coming, the driver flicks his cigarette onto the ground and opens the door for us on cue. I slide in first. After sitting silently a few more minutes, I can't control myself. Putting my hands together, a stern look on my face, I say in a deep voice, "And we do not break the rules here. No, sir," ad libbing and exaggerating. "No, sir, not *us!*"

Despite the pressure, Dr. Janus cracks a huge smile and says, "Always the jokester!"

"Well, didn't you find that a bit extreme?"

He agrees.

"I could never be a nun," I say, then ask, "Did your sister want to go or was she sent?"

"That is an odd question," he says quizzically.

"I just mean, it seems awfully strict for someone these days, even for thirty-some years ago."

"I suppose. I never really got involved. It was her life, her decision, and my parents supported it, so I went along with their wishes."

"Hmm," I say, leaning back and shaking my head again, unable to control myself. "Rules, my dear, we have rules. Keep the Rule and the Rule will keep you!"

chapter
20

Lean on, trust in, and be confident in the Lord with all your heart
and mind and do not rely on your own insight or understanding.
In all your ways know, recognize, and acknowledge Him,
and He will direct and make straight and plain your paths.

Proverbs 3:5–6, Amplified Bible

he fought the Mother Superior's voice in her head saying, "Keep the Rule and the Rule will keep you," as she stared at the floor and thought about her next move. But how bad could this book really be? Millions of people owned an *Amplified*
Bible, and millions found guidance and faith in it. Her perpetrator could have given her a book on Satanism or some other sick, sexually perverse publication after all.

What did this electronic voice really want? She just wanted to get out, but she could find no way to escape. She had haphazardly tried to dig down a couple inches in the dirt with her plate and found a steel floor. It was as if she was truly being stored in one of those pods someone from the outside had told her about, made to look and feel like an old dungeon. She could be hanging out fifty pods up in the air in the middle of China and wouldn't even know it. What an odd thought.

She would take a crack at the syllabus. It stated, "The purpose of this course is to get a better understanding of the religion we have chosen, begin to discern errors in thinking, which may be our own or may be that of a specific religion itself, and make a determination as to whether or not we know what and who we worship. Is it a false Christ, money, idols, hubris, greed, lust? Who do *you* really worship?"

This interested her and seemed relatively easy. She knew the Roman Catholics would win hands down, and she would make a point of proving it to the poor, misguided soul keeping her hostage.

You will start in Proverbs. Find Proverbs 3:5–6, 4:20–22, and Proverbs 5:10.

She picked up the hard-backed book titled *Amplified Bible,* which had a beautiful picture of the sun shining through the trees and a cross with four equal appendages, to her surprise, similar to the rosary her father had given her. However, instead of what looked like three flowering leaves at the end of each stem on the book, hers had three stones on each stem but was flat at the edges. She missed her rosary, her brother ... her life!

She opened the book, prayed to Mary not to be deceived, and suddenly realized she had no idea where Proverbs was. She knew there was the Old Testament, life before Christ, and the New Testament, life after Christ, but other than that, she was rather ashamed to realize she could not place the other parts of

the Bible like she could some of the prayers in her devotional. That was okay. It was for the pope to know the reading material.

After a bit of flipping around, past Job, past Psalms, she decided she had better start at the beginning of the book and see whether or not there was a Table of Contents.

She became intrigued by the Preface. It explained how this edition had been compiled and placed great emphasis on the fact that many translations of the Bible had lost the true meaning through the centuries because words in English translated from Greek and Hebrew lost their importance, value, and even accuracy. Words that have been "updated" to the common language of our day have stopped readers from getting the real meaning of *The Word.*

The introduction was even more interesting and shocking because it was a *woman* who did years of research and devoted her *life* to getting this out. In the convent, women were forbidden by church policy to study theology of any kind. Women were thought to lack sufficient reasoning power and were disqualified from the "Magisterium," the church's teaching and theological authority. *Wow,* she thought, *how they must feel about this lady!*

This woman's name was Frances Siewert. According to the Introduction, Frances, along with the help of numerous other scholars, was able to pull the Aramaic, Greek, and Hebrew languages together with some archeological discoveries of the time to prove some biblical history by placing it alongside cultural remains. By doing this, Frances was able to put the picture together more completely, without changing the meaning of the "inspired" and uncorrupted "word" of God, as some of the newer and looser writings have purportedly done.

Tess was now intrigued. *What hubris that took,* she thought, *and in the 1880's no less.* She was becoming interested and inspired herself just by the fact this had been done by a woman. Although she respected the Roman Catholic view, secretly she had never really believed women were lesser scholars or preachers.

She turned a few pages forward to the Table of Contents and learned that the book of Proverbs was in the Old Testament and started on page 905. The book itself had 1,942 pages; no wonder they had priests to weed out the important information!

As she flipped to Proverbs, it brought her back to the days with her parents, when her dad would read to her and explain that the Bible had been well studied and documented through the years, every word, every page, every phrase.

She thought of an odd time when he had warned her that one day she would need not only to understand the *words* better but also to remember the significance of the *numbers*. She had passed it off all these years as simply one day, as a nun, she would obtain this knowledge. She hadn't though. Could he have meant something else?

She got lost in memories for a while thinking about her childhood, the houses, the incredible meals, and interesting debates. How long it had been since she had thought about them and her parents' deaths. She thought about people around the world who never even had a chance to experience that lifestyle and family love. She missed them. Had she made the right decision over thirty years ago? She missed all that time with them, and now they were dead, gone forever.

She went back to the task at hand. She made it to Proverbs and found the sayings mildly interesting. Unsure as to whether she wanted to continue with the syllabus, and still considering if this was morally allowed, she decided to close the book and let it reopen to where it may fall. Understanding this was completely non-scientific and probably a little crazy, she tried it. She ended up in Matthew 6:6, or, chapter 6, verse 6, "But when you pray, go into your [most] private room, and, closing the door, pray to your Father, Who is in secret; and your Father, Who sees in secret, will reward you *in the open*."

This was easy enough for her; she was in a dungeon! One couldn't get more secret than this. Even at the convent, she had heard about sinful preachers who would yell prayers out loud and get people excited and chant certain phrases. Then the congregation would spend hours afterwards socializing and talking about what they had prayed and what they had heard from the Lord on their own during the week, boasting about their success in communion with Him. She realized that, according to this verse, people were to pray in their own space and not share the prayer aloud. And to prove it was answered, God would answer it in the open.

That was a good reason to be in a convent, so perhaps this Bible wasn't evil after all. Perhaps it was a more proper translation, as the "Introduction" pronounced.

So, she moved along to Matthew 6:7–8,

> And when you pray, do not heap up phrases (multiply words, repeating the same ones over and over) as the Gentiles do, for they think they will be heard for their much speaking. Do not be like them, for your Father knows what you need before you ask Him.

That verse struck a nerve. Was she being referred to as one of those terrible Gentiles? She certainly repeated the same lines in prayer day after day. Is this not what God demanded of her? Could she have been given the wrong way to pray? Was she being chastised for doing a lot of speaking but not enough thinking?

She flipped the page on that one. She didn't want to think that her intensive prayer life had been a mistake. She moved on; she did not want to open herself up to thoughts from the devil.

Tess decided to go back to the beginning, where she learned that *The Septuagint* was the third century BC Greek translation of the Old Testament, and it all started with Genesis, which, translated, means "origin" or "beginning." She read on about separating fact from fiction and how archeology had proven some of the recorded events in more recent years. This was starting to really intrigue her. Imagine all the people who looked at the Bible and the story of Jesus as a myth. She realized that there was proof for some of these stories, and yet it seemed, from what she was told, that people glossed over that. Perhaps they needed to think of it as a myth because believing in something so powerful, so strong, could overwhelm them. The Introduction even clarified that most scholars agree that the stories of the patriarchs reflect information they have found in the Near East dating back to the second millennium BC That means 2000 to 1500 years *before* the birth of Christ! She had not learned or heard there was actual proof now. Not, of course, that *she* needed that.

She diligently read each word of the Introduction and how translations could have changed the meaning. The more she read, the more she got drawn in. She felt like something in her soul that had been dead a long time was being stirred. Was this okay? It was like an aphrodisiac, like perfect wine that made one's head woozy and comfortable but not drunk...never drunk. She couldn't put it down. She wanted some direction, a guideline to the meat of the book, the answers to life.

She decided she would work through the syllabus. It was a guide, a direction after all, and didn't God say in Proverbs 3:5–6 to trust in Him with all your heart, in all ways to acknowledge Him, and He would make your crooked paths straight? She was starting to like this thing called the *Amplified Bible*.

The next reading recommendation was Amos, and the following excerpt in the syllabus floored her.

> I hate, I despise your feasts, and I will not smell a savor or take delight in your solemn assemblies. (21) [No] but [instead of bringing me the appointed sacrifices] you carried about the tent of your king Sakkuth and Kaiwan

[names for the gods of the planet Saturn], your images of
your star-god which you made for yourselves [and you will
do so again.](26)

Amos 5:21, 26, Amplified Bible

She was so engulfed by what she was reading, she jumped when
she heard, "I am back." Could twenty-four hours have evaporated like so many of the years of her life? She couldn't remember a time since childhood when she had stayed up all night
reading and enjoying every minute of it.

She said excitedly, "I am reading, and it is interesting," but
with an edge as if it, *he,* was bothering her or interrupting her.
She wanted to tell him all about her feelings, but he cut her off.

"I will do most of the speaking," his voice droned, "but if you
have some basic questions or needs, I may try to address them, as
it could be weeks before we resolve this. Should your brother not
do as I request, you will ultimately die. Other than that, I will
not harm you. Do not think of escaping, do not think of trying
to get away, and yelling will serve no purpose other than to harm
your voice. You are in the middle of nowhere. You are also in an
electronically secure place that is set to explode, killing both of
us should you find a way to exit without approval."

Suddenly she was somber again. A terrorist, a suicide
bomber, willing to give his life for the cause? For the life of her,
she still could not imagine what was going on. A Jihadist would
not necessarily be interested in the truth behind the Bible, or
would he? Was this a clever rouse to change her to yet another
religion like Islam? She was embarrassed she couldn't remember
if any of them was Christian. This led her back to the thought
that perhaps she had been kidnapped as a test to the Roman
Catholic Church.

Hesitantly and softly, she said, "May I please ask one question? I know you are in control and I am not allowed, but I think

it will help me focus better and answer more honestly if I have this one answer."

"One question." A staccato response.

"Am I here as a hostage, a test by the Roman Catholic Church?"

A sick electronic, "Ha, ha, ha!" came through. "The Roman Catholic Church? Hold you hostage here? Oh, my naïve and blinded sister. The irony of it all. No, the church, to my knowledge, has nothing to do with this."

She felt a little relieved because if the church was not involved, then this newfound information and decision to accept or reject it was now between her and God. It might even take a little pressure off her because she would not have to answer to her church. She was learning that things really may not have been what she was led to believe, like her perpetrator had said, but how much more difficult would it be to answer directly to God?

Her running thoughts were broken by, "I have some gifts for you here if you are able to answer some basic questions and have done your homework well."

"Oh, I have," she said, more anxious for his approval over the correct answers than for the unknown gifts.

"First, what are the basic parts of the Bible?"

"There is the Old Testament that starts in Genesis and ends in Malachi and the New Testament that starts in Matthew and ends in Revelation. The Old Testament is from the prophets and is before Christ, when Moses handed down the law through the Ten Commandments; the New Testament includes the apostles and the birth and crucifixion of Christ."

"Very good. I am sending you a gift."

She was relieved. Her nature had always predisposed her to please those around her.

The small steel trapdoor opened, and slowly a plate came in with a delicious-looking chocolate truffle, a partially dipped dark chocolate biscotti, and a cup of tea. Her mouth was watering; she was so excited. She took the plate and carefully placed it on the mattress on the floor. She told him she would eat them slowly, as she wanted to cherish every moment. She felt like a kid again. She did take the time to have some tea though.

He let her enjoy a few moments before asking, "Where is the Apostle's Creed?"

She thought long and hard and then said, "Well, I don't know; it wasn't a question on the syllabus. No wait, it can be found in my devotional book of course!" Her smart attitude slipping out again.

"Wrong answer. Work on getting it right next time. Where is the Lord's Prayer, and how does God ask you to pray?"

Again she was stumped. "Why are you asking me questions that weren't on the syllabus?" She was frustrated because she was so proud of all she had learned and wanted to show off. "Again, I know the Lord's Prayer is in the Devotional, but what do you mean by *how* we are to pray? You mean like not heaping up repetitious phrases like the Gentiles?"

"Very good, that is part of it. The point is, have you ever thought for yourself? Done something outside the boundary of the task you were given, even question on whose authority it came?"

"Not for years," she said proudly, because that went against every grain of what she had been taught at the convent.

"Explain the difference between the Father, the Son, and the Holy Spirit."

She sat there silent and devastated. She had failed. She couldn't answer that question specifically, but she was still stuck on his last statement. She said softly, "I did do some thinking for myself. I read who put this book together, reviewed the general set-up of the Bible, read parts of Genesis and about the *The Septuagint*, and even pondered some verses in Acts, Matthew, and John. I read all night."

"Well, that deserves a gift."

She felt better now; she had not totally disappointed him. The slot opened and in came a drawing pad, colored pencils, markers, and tape. She was thrilled. She would have something to take notes with and to draw with. She had loved to draw when she was young. She had not done that for years. *Child's play,* she thought, and yet she couldn't wait to start.

"Now I don't have much time, so I want you to spend time thinking about what made you go to the convent in the first place and why that one in particular. Then, think about this: if you could get answers to your deepest questions, the ones they would not answer when you tried to leave, what would they be?"

She sat there stunned. This person knew her. Was he from the church? How much did he really know about her past?

Am I here because I tried to leave? Did I sin, so they want to kill me? She reverted to her original hypothesis, even though he had told her the church was not involved.

"Did you pick the convent or did your parents?"

"My father encouraged that one in particular. I agreed with him."

"Speaking of your father, I need to know what he was working on before he died and where he kept his most valuable research papers. I also need to know what type of research your brother is doing."

She thought about it for several minutes and thought she could lie, but the fact was, she truly had no idea. "I don't know. I am so sorry. I am not hiding anything from you. I just don't know."

"Have you ever been in love?" There was no prelude, no edging into this question.

Odd, she thought.

"Yes, once, but I guess most people would call it 'puppy love.' He was my dad's assistant, older than me, but so brilliant, so reserved, so kind to me." Her hands shook. She was nervous about confessing to a complete stranger.

There was silence for a while. "What happened to him?"

"I am not sure what happened to him after my father's death, but up until then, he worked steadily by Dad's side." Then after a minute, "Perhaps you should try to contact him. I don't mean kidnap him. I mean contact him to see if he knows anything about what this is in reference to. He would know better than any of us what Dad was working on."

"No outsiders are allowed to be contacted. What did this 'older boy' think when you decided to go to the convent?"

"I don't know. It was all so quick, and I was only sixteen, turning seventeen. I am sure he thought little of it."

"I can't imagine that." She knew it was a "he" for sure now. A woman would never have said that. "I need you to think, really think, where your father would have hidden his research or something valuable. This will not be over until it is found."

"I will," she said. "I promise, but at the moment, I can't recall any hidden places. I was not even aware he had something to hide."

"You are doing your homework and are trying. For that I am going to now send you some more questions for you to work on and the gift I promised. I will be back every few days and at worst, no longer than a week."

"A week? That is a long time."

"It is. Everything has now been electronically set up to serve you three full meals a day and change the basins once a day. I will be sending through a remote control that will handle all of that, but remember, the place is set to explode should you try to escape. Let's clean up the buckets, and I will be off."

They did all the swapping through the hole, she learned the remote, the new syllabus came in, and last, next to it, were five beautiful sunflowers, followed by a vase to put them in.

"These are beautiful," she said with excitement. "Just beautiful. They are my favorite! My fav-or-ite! Thank you! I don't even remember the last time I received flowers. Well, now that I think of it, it was before the convent. The boy I was speaking of brought me the most beautiful Iris. Dark purplish blue and dark yellow are my favorite colors. How did you know I loved sunflowers?"

He did not answer but simply shut the door, and there was silence. She spent the longest time holding, touching, and looking at the flowers. A flood of memories came back to her of childhood, of her brief romance with Saul, and of her life that led her to the convent. She allowed herself to go to a place she had tried to block out long ago.

How had the perpetrator known that sunflowers were her favorite and that her father always gave them to her from their garden? Did he know, or was this coincidence? Her father had even written a children's book about sunflowers and given it to her on her tenth birthday. It was beautiful and fun, and although she never understood all the words, she had enjoyed reading it almost every night for years to come. She started to repeat it in her head. She could see the written lines of the verses she had memorized years ago:

> Look to the sun, my little flower,
> Look to the sun, I say.
> Rise in the East,
> Set in the West,
> Look to the sun, I say.
>
> What one calls a flower
> is truly a head.
> Beware of the lies
> that you are force-fed.
>
> The fruit of the plant
> encased in the husk
> It closes itself
> we call it dusk.

The florets within
are arranged in a spiral.
Golden angles my kin
will prove it's not viral.

Nature has perfect math,
but Fibonnacci we adore!
God has eternal symbols,
but heliotropism is a bore?

DNA you call it
So, *you've* discovered the link?
There is no junk,
The code is not what you think.

The man, the bull,
the serpent, the lion
Don't you believe
in their sick Zion.

The first verse was repeated many times, and the poem had
numerous pages, but these were the ones she remembered.
She could see the bright colors on the pages of his book. This
brought a warm feeling to her. She drew a sunflower with her
colored pencils and hung it with tape on the steel wall. She then
read her next assignment:

"In time it will be essential to learn the various Hebrew,
Greek, and Aramaic words to understand the translations. For
now, one Hebrew word to learn is *Ruach*. It means the breath of
the Holy Spirit coming through you. It can also mean inspiration breathed into one and/or a whirlwind. As you read through
the Bible and have questions, pray that the truth will be 'ruach-
ed' into you, and you will find answers you never thought possible because, as promised, you 'knock' and He will answer."

She thought on this for a while, looked at her beautiful picture, and felt a little happy, an odd sensation, considering the circumstances. She thought about drawing and playing more but then decided to pray for this *Ruach* and for understanding.

She contemplated more on the strange verse of Amos 5:21. She was dumbfounded. What could this mean? Had she been worshiping feasts and participating in solemn assemblies after God had clearly said He would not tolerate this? The words overwhelmed her.

Now she was tired and upset. She had not slept in over twenty-eight hours. She thought about how horrified the Church would be to discover her reading the Bible. Despite all the lovely nuns she had known, all she could think about was how unforgiving Mother Superior would be if she knew that Sister Thérèse was *not* keeping the *rule*.

Despite this, she forced herself to focus on good thoughts. She took the last sip of tea, took another long look at her sunflowers, enjoyed some bites of chocolate, and lay down on the mattress. She thought fondly of the beautiful French countryside she had been taken from and managed to fall asleep.

chapter
21

Autopilot: "A device for controlling an aircraft or other vehicle without constant human intervention."

Encyclopedia Britannica, 2008

he ride through the country is glorious, and I'm enjoying the sun glaring down on us. It beats the chill of the convent, and I feel free and happy to be alive. The Alps are as glorious as I remembered them from past trips to Jausiers and the southern shores of France. But I'm extremely relieved we don't have to go through them because as a passenger, I'm a wimp when going

along the edge of the cliffs. I've no problem with heights when skiing, but something about being in the car makes me anxious.

We drive directly to the airport. Another, even larger, plane is ready to go. I'm adding up pieces in my head, trying to think if I've missed anything from the nun's room at the convent. I excuse myself from the front of the plane and a somber Dr. Janus and say I'm going to get online, send some e-mails, and do some more work on the first and second pictures. I'm anxious to see if my Jewish scholar friend has gotten back to me yet.

The French pilot comes out to let us know beds have been set up in the back of the plane and we will be departing shortly. He's handsome in his uniform but nowhere near as dreamy as my first captain. His actual words, while looking at me, are, in poor English, "Your bed with me is set up in back." *Cute.* I smile politely and thank him. Dr. Janus flashes a grin. Getting a sense of humor, *finally!*

After a few hours of work, I take a break. No news from the scholar, and no new ideas on the first picture, except I've determined that the center picture is definitely a relief in the Temple of Enrah in Egypt and refers to the zodiac in some form. I have no idea about the number of stars in each quadrant. I know the oroborous symbol, but I really need the Hebrew translations to figure out its significance. I have managed to guess the center is a compass, and the reason for the sphinx and the three pyramids is that they are pointing due east. I confirm on the Internet that the sphinx near the pyramids at Giza in Egypt does actually face east. The directions in the drawing seem purposeful, so I need to look deeper. From there, I'm stumped. I want to look at the second clue more deeply, but given everything that has just transpired at the convent, I feel an odd compulsion to check on Dr. Janus.

I walk back to the front of the plane and ask how he's doing. He says he's fine and seems somehow more relaxed, so I ask, "When we get back, we're having dinner with James to go over security for the house, correct?"

"Yes. Not sure how that will help my sister, but whatever he recommends."

"If the kidnappers have your phone number, they know where you live!" I blurt out. "Besides, James feels he'd like to get extra security in, and I trust his judgment."

"I agree."

"And then on Monday, we have the gala."

"Yes, your dress should be waiting for you to try on when we get back."

I can't imagine what he's picked out for me, but at the moment it's not my top priority. "And then the next night is dinner with ... Sal?"

"Saul," he corrects. "S-a-u-l."

"Oh, Saul. Can you tell me more about him?"

"Sure. We have known him since we were kids. His parents sent him over from Italy in the 1960s because they wanted him to get an American education. His aunt cared for him and is also close friends of the family. Dad took him under his wing, and he is a brilliant scientist. They worked hand in hand until my father's death, and then we sort of lost contact. Other than brief get-togethers here and there, we don't see much of each other. Tess was smitten with him, as girls at that age often are. She was fifteen, and he was twenty-one; her entrance into the convent broke that off. Besides, my father would never have gone for it."

"Why is that?"

"My father was old-fashioned, old school. He used to joke, 'I named you after a virgin and a saint, and that you shall be the rest of your life!' He sort of meant it. My mother would then joke back, 'But dear, how will you have grandchildren?'

"'Immaculately, of course!' he'd say, and they would both laugh."

I smiled. It was a sweet story. I asked, "Have you come up with any ideas on why the gala?"

"No, not really. I mean, we're patrons of art museums and the Met, so you don't need to kidnap my sister to get me to donate $100,000 a ticket."

That amount still amazed me. Tickets for the three of us, $300,000—ten years' salary for me!

"And have you come up with any new theories on the artwork the kidnapper sent?"

"Not yet, but I do have some e-mails out, and by the time we get back to the house, I hope to have the words translated at least."

Suddenly, I realize that tiredness has crept up on me. "If you don't mind, I'm going to the back to get some more sleep. I guess the pilot won't 'bed' me," I say, trying to be witty and failing miserably.

He smiles. "I suppose someone should fly the plane."

"Isn't that what the autopilot is for?" I joke.

He laughs. "Sleep well."

I do. Hours slip away with vivid dreams and crazy imagery, and I get to visit with my first captain again. I awake flushed. If only that dream could come true!

chapter
22

*And God said, "Let there be lights in the firmament of the
heaven to divide the day from the night; and let them be
for signs (Heb. 'oth=things to come) and seasons
(Heb. moed=appointed times), and for days and years."*

Genesis 1:14, KJV

e land, and faithful James is there to pick
us up, looking spiffy as usual. He's hand-
some in his own way. Formal as ever, he
opens the doors and lets us into the perfectly clean limo. Not a spot on it. I guess
as the son of a barber, he keeps everything
clean, orderly, and disinfected. He used to tell stories about his
dad and the cleanliness issues at the house, sounded like OCD
(obsessive compulsive disorder) to me. His father seemed like
quite the character, and James was very close to him.

James updates Dr. Janus about the outside grounds and says, "Cameras are being installed around the fence at the property lines so we have better views of the acreage. I'd like to add some staff inside but wanted you here before we rummage through the house."

Dr. Janus's eyebrow lifts a little. "Good move, James."

I wonder if there's something inside Dr. Janus still wants to keep secret.

When I get out of the limo this time and look up, I notice above the door of the mansion the wording, "The Granite House." I hadn't seen it before.

Dr. Janus then says while getting out, "Mags, when you get settled back in, since we have been so cooped up, have Ana show you to the fitness area and pool if you like, and take some time to stretch out a little. I have some business I must attend to, a phone conference that serves as a board meeting for Columbia University donors. We can get together to review other details at dinner. Will this work?"

Nothing sounds better at the moment. I'm shocked to hear there's a pool. This house must go on and on. I feel like I'm at a retreat, not on a kidnapping job with clues I'm failing miserably to uncover and, of course, the only reason I'm here.

I go upstairs, unpack some things, set my computer up, and then take Dr. Janus up on his offer to stretch out. I soon discover that the pool and fitness area is in a gazebo and conservatory of its own, about one mile away. Ana has us walk around to the side of the house where, to my astonishment, golf carts are parked.

"There's a golf course on this lot?" I ask in amazement.

"Nine holes, *Si*, but we use-*a* cart-*a* for to get around-*a* property."

"Cool!"

We each get on a cart, and Ana points the way to the pool, showing me turns I'm not to take for fear I'll get lost. She then drops me off, gives me a walkie-talkie, and says if I get lost, I'm

to call them! Things are just getting better and better; if only I could find the nun, life would be perfect.

Walking in the gazebo, I see there's a section that reads "Visitors," and sure enough, there are new swimsuits of all sizes for guests. I had wondered what I was going to swim in, so had a tank top and little shorts in case, or may even have braved it in the buff, if no one was around. This dilemma solved, I pick a Speedo and get changed. The swim is glorious, and I feel refreshed. One hundred laps, an Olympic size pool, a great workout indeed. I'm amazed because the pool doesn't seem to have a drop of chlorine in it. I'll have to ask how that's done.

I enjoy every minute, dry off, throw on some clothes, and get back in the golf cart. I find my way back with only one wrong turn that leads me to what looks like a gardener's storage shed that has a sign on it that reads:

Beneath the ground, where seeds are planted.
Is God's perfect plan for those remanded.
Ready to grow? Your needs supplanted.
Secret fields, crops' healings recanted?
Ready to sow, the seed has been implanted.
Claim your stake, your kingdom is granted.

T. Janus sure loved his riddles! I turn back and get on course, park the cart, and head up to the office to check e-mails.

Finally, an e-mail has come in from my Jewish colleague, a recognized biblical scholar. One of the questions I'd asked was if he had ever heard of the word *Zoad* and what it meant. The only thing I had come up with was some form or path that refers to the zodiac, and this is loosely using a Hebrew translation. His e-mail stated that it's an individual path, a *destiny* or way, so to speak. Then he wrote I could call him anytime, he would fill me in on the rest. He is most intrigued.

I think about the zodiac and how I had learned in Hebrew that the word for these constellations and "the twelve signs" is *Mazzor-ath.* This is not to be confused with the list of thirty-two passages in the Massorah, written hundreds of years before Christ, known as "A Fence to the Scriptures" because it locks in the words and helps dispel all the man-made errors of translations through the years. It's been described as the true mind-to-mind transfer of God's Word, without human error. Instead, the zodiac, the degrees which mark the sun's path through the heavens, is the Mazzorath and is quite fascinating. If there's a God and He wanted to speak to His people with all nationalities and languages simultaneously throughout the universe, why not put pictures in the sky? Symbols and pictures are a universal language that span across all time. They cannot be manipulated or corrupted by man. But what exactly do they mean? This has always gotten my attention.

Surprised I have reception all the way out here, I dial my cell phone to call my Jewish scholar and can't help smiling just thinking about him. He's not the stereotypical Hassidic man in a black robe with a long beard and a yarmulke. Not my Jewish scholar. He's an African American man in his late sixties. I just love these little ironies in life!

He picks up the phone by the third ring and obviously with caller ID knows who it is. "And how is my Dr. Magdalena today?"

We catch up on all the niceties, and I say a client has received these pictures as gifts and is paying me to figure out their significance. He reiterates how intriguing they are and starts with his explanations.

"As I said in my e-mail, the main word *Zoad* means an individual path or destiny. Often this word is used to signify a full circle, like the zodiac being completed and finding one's life purpose or meaning. The Hebrew underneath is from the Torah;

they're verses from Genesis, the first book," he clarifies. I know that Genesis is the first book in the Bible, but that's where my knowledge pretty much ends.

"The first phrase is Genesis 1:14–19, where the Creator states He put the stars in the heavens 'for signs and for seasons and days and years.' Few realize that God did put the stars in the heavens and named them, and, according to Psalm 97, they are to convey a message that could be read by all civilizations throughout the world. This is why the signs of the zodiac have been passed down through the ages. The amazing thing is all cultures break the signs into twelve groupings, some name them by animals, some by constellations, and some by pictures with no words. In the United States, we usually go by the solar calendar and constellations, while the Chinese use a *lunar* calendar and further break it down with a binary ying-yang cycle with yang, symbolized by the dragon, and yin, symbolized by the snake.

"All the major themes of the *solar* zodiac are God's blueprint of God's purpose and are told in the stars, starting from the beginning of time to this earth age's birth of Christ through a virgin, to the eventual rule of the *lion*—Judah's tribe—when Christ returns to earth and we move into the third age or final earth and heaven age. Even many Christians have forgotten that He put the stars there to warn and to teach us. No one pays attention to them any more. Most don't even know if they are following solar or lunar patterns and what that may mean."

I agree with him. Few people I know pay attention to the stars, and in some cities, it's now even harder to see the stars due to pollution. Besides that, we're so tied to our electronics that keep us focused downward, who thinks of what's going on above?

"To the Jews and many religions today, more than one deity is utter nonsense, but nonetheless, some historians are trying to get us to believe that 'Son' is a spelling error and should be 'Sun' and that the story being told, even in the Bible, is nothing more than the physical sun making its path through the twelve houses of the zodiac, or the constellations, to complete a full circle in the period of one year. This is *pagan*-speak.

"This corruption of the truth started even before the time of the building of the tower of Babel. Babel, translated from the Hebrew, means *confusion*. In early Egypt around 5000 BC, there are recorded drawings depicting crop irrigation in Egypt and what appeared to be the worship of one God. That continued to at least 2000 BC, but it appears that changes occurred in the number of gods worshipped, and by 1800 BC, the Babylonian times, the corruption really picks up speed.

"The Babylonians were masterminds at creating new rituals as a deceitful act of taking control away from one God and placing it in the hands of the rulers. These rituals served the rulers needs because they brought a lot of money and gifts to those in control. So, the meaning of God's signs became corrupted, and instead of His story, *history* changed it to create deities to honor those in power. Just as those rulers planned, people began to worship the sun, the moon, the planets, and the stars and idolized them, giving sacrifices to the gods versus God. Oh those Pagans, encouraging thoughts that there never was anything more than the 'sun,' thereby converting those close to coming to Christ, the true son, into followers of false teaching."

The disappointment in his voice was unmistakable. I'm confused. I thought Jewish people didn't believe that the Christ had come yet, and the way he phrased his sentences made it sound like he believed Christ had actually come to earth and had died. I didn't want to interrupt now because Judaism is all a blur to me.

He continues, clearing his throat. "From Babel, various forms of astrology were created. Most who do astrology look at the twelve signs, but in biblical language, the start and the end varies from both astronomy and astrology. In astronomy, Aries is presented at the vernal equinox 0 degrees at the top of a chart, but in an astrological chart, Aries is positioned at nine o'clock. Since the heavenly Bible starts with the Virgin, I believe this is why your artist chose the sphinx. It's a reminder, a sign to us not to fall into the ways of the world, the darkness of moon worship and the lower heavens, but to remember it all started with Virgo—the Virgin signified by the head of a woman—and will end with Leo, the lion signified by the tail."

Oh, the virgin! The nun. That struck a chord. Could this have to do with her, and if so, what did it mean? Why had I never heard this explanation before? The head of a woman and the tail of a lion: the sphinx? I had studied mythology and Egyptian cultures for years and had never even put those two together. But the thought that lingers in my mind is that Egyptians didn't believe in Christ, or did some of them?

He continues. "The more we ignore symbols and put actual words or language to things, the more defective, non-enlightened we become. That's why Chinese is so brilliant because that language still works in symbols. It has one sign that means both crisis and opportunity. To my mind, this is clever because it's often crises that can force us to change and can become an opportunity if we let them come to fruition, in His time."

I interrupt him, excited that I'm understanding, "Wow, that's powerful, and I definitely know my work with the unconscious has repeatedly proven that." I'm getting a lesson on culture and religion, and his theory of a universe created by God, one God, is clear.

Making sure I really get it, he adds, "So if you take a look at the degrees or steps that mark the stages of the sun's path through the heavens to the corresponding twelve months and trace back its origin, it begins before all the deities are worshiped, when, even in early Egypt, people believed in one deity. Mind you, this was even centuries before Ra, or the later regional merges of Amen-Ra, was worshipped monotheistically, which by the way was a political move to unify Egypt under one pharaoh and not a religious avowal."

He continues, "I think that's why the picture is a reproduction of the one in the Temple of Esneh from Egypt, which is a relief depicting the signs of the zodiac and clearly portrays the first sign as the Virgin, seen on the right, and the last as the lion, depicted on the left. To most, this would seem unusual, again, because people associate Egyptians with worshiping many gods, like the Greeks, but in the earlier centuries this was not true. The theme of where the zodiac needs to *begin* is repeated in your artwork, and thus you know the artist is making a point and trying to be understood."

He is correct. My Jewish scholar also knows how psychologists analyze drawings because whenever a client either repeats a theme or writes words on the piece of paper to clarify the drawing, it's an indication of them needing to be clear and to be heard. This, then, is an indication that the individual felt misunderstood in life. Some psychologists use the term *labeling* for this behavior.

"This theory, although in line with the *Mazzorath*, the Hebrew term for constellations, also dates back to the Far East over four thousand years ago. The figure is holding a sheaf of corn, denoting fertility or motherhood, clarifying she's a woman and not a man. I'm not sure why there are five stars in the one area and six in the next. But note the next incredible fact: the serpent at the heels of the woman in the relief engraving in the temple. This further clarifies the knowledge the Egyptians had about biblical truths.

"So the first phrase lets us know God put the stars there for 'signs' and 'appointed times,' and this leads to the second Hebrew line, from Genesis 3:15, which says, 'And I'll put enmity between thee and woman, and between thy seed and her seed; it

shall bruise thy head, and thou shalt bruise His heel.' Neat isn't it?" he adds.

"I'm certainly fascinated!"

"In general, Mags, we stopped paying attention to the signs and symbols years ago as we got programmed by the government, education, religion, and language. We stopped thinking and feeling for ourselves. Language is a corrupter and is why there is power in the true meaning of the Hebrew letters *YHVH* or Yahovah. But *that's* a discussion for another day!"

I agree, although I'm curious about his brief social commentary and want to hear more of his thoughts on government control. Another day though. And then to my surprise, the "biblical" scholar continues to help me understand more about astronomy and astrology.

He explains the concept of constellations and how each age lasts about 2,200 years. "We are currently in Pisces, and in 2050 we move into Aquarius. It, therefore, takes about 25,800 years for the pole star to make a complete circuit of the sky; astronomers call that the precession of the equinoxes, and astrologers call it the completion of the zodiac 'age.' It's fascinating because what we now call Polaris, or the North Star, has not always been and won't always be our due North. The earth tilts gradually and changes due to the gravitational pull of the sun and moon. That final magnetic shift will happen, after 25,800 years of waiting, on December 21, 2012. Imagine being alive to experience this? And guess who charted this to the day, thousands of years ago?" He's getting really excited.

"The Mayans?"

"Correct!"

At least I know something.

His scholarly voice continues. "As for astrology, there are two ways of reading the stars. One is the sidereal zodiac. *Sidus* from Latin means star, and it's physically made up of visible and fixed stars, which refers to the twelve constellations. The other is the tropical zodiac. The tropical is the 'apparent' path of the sun or the ecliptic, and it's neatly divided into 360 invisible degrees with the twelve signs within each thirty degrees.

"In India, they use sidereal astrology as a tool for self-realization through philosophical and practical application, and their zodiac begins in Regulus, the bright star of Leo, not the astronomical equinox of 0 degrees of Aries, nor the start of the biblical calendar in Virgo. Tropical astrology starts with the Spring Equinox, around March 21, so Aries is displayed at nine o'clock, Capricorn is at twelve o'clock, or straight up, Libra is at three o'clock, and Cancer is at six o'clock."

I needed a tape recorder and am jotting notes as quickly as I can, but I honestly don't get it quite yet. I'll have to study it at some point if it becomes relevant.

As if I'm not confused enough, he clarifies, "In around the third or fourth century AD, 'Anno Domini,' the year of our Lord, the zodiacs coincided, and today there's a gap of about twenty-four degrees, which means while a tropical astrologer says that the moon is in Aries ten degrees, it occupies a point in the constellation of Pisces of sixteen degrees. A general rule of thumb for easy conversion is adding six degrees to tropical longitudes and then subtracting a sign."

Okay, I think, *this is now* way *over my head!*

I must have sighed or been silent too long because he finishes with, "Last but not least, in our Bible, we start in Virgo and end in Leo. Some people even try to convince us Ezekiel's wheel within a wheel is the zodiac. They will have quite an awakening one day!"

I'm now so lost, I just do my best to sound appreciative.

"Enough on the zodiac," he says, "and now let me point out a couple of things I noticed in the second picture called Divine Providence."

He pauses, collecting his thoughts while I grab more paper to make notes.

"It's obviously depicting the scales of justice and representing the symbol of Libra. So, the zodiac theme resurfaces. The center part has a caduceus in the middle, which is the serpent wrapped around the rod. This has a fascinating history of its own, which anyone can read about and most people are familiar with, but what most people don't know is the good and evil factor, which I think is what this artist is trying to say. The person obviously feels we are currently over-weighted with evil. *Symbol* translated from Greek is *sym-Bolos*, which means to move or throw apart, in essence to separate, and an interesting antonym is *dia-Bolos*, which translated to English means *devil*. A great way to explain this is to think of a zipper. If you pull it down and it separates, then it's of the devil, if it joins and heals the split through wisdom and knowledge, then it's of the Creator or good. That's how the caduceus works symbolically."

"I'm confused about some of the symbols that appear to be good but are on the evil side."

"Well," he says, obviously pleased he has cracked this one for me too. "The left side of the scale is heavy and defined with the word 'evil' and 'mortis,' which means death. If you follow the three symbols in the circle to the left of the scale, the upper one is alchemy and means white arsenic, but ironically it is also a symbol used for the pope. To the right on the good side, the libertas or freedom side, is the sign of the dove or holy spirit. Then, again on the right, there is the sign that has the three lines across, which is clever because three equal signs horizontally over one vertical line means poison in botany. In the ancient Hebrew, it represents the letter *S* and means support, and for some reason it is placed on the good or right hand side, but look carefully because three lines with two shorter on either horizontal end on the left means the cross of the pope! Two of these words on the left hand or evil side denote things to do with the pope!"

His excitement is contagious, and I jump in, "Wow, so this person seems to be making a judgment call on religion, inferring that the poison in botany is less dangerous than the pope in Rome?"

I pause for a couple seconds then speak aloud, "You want to know something funny? That sign on the left, the pope's cross sign, also means checkmate in chess." I look at the third sign and say, "And finally, the evil side has the sign for money and the opposite symbol on the right stands for strychnine. Is the artist telling us to beware of the evil of money, it's worse than poison? Could this be what it means? It's all so clever. "

My scholar fills in, "But the really clever thing is the right and left side mirror each other. In the upper portion of the drawing, the ladder is drawn as moving down on the left and up on the right. That's a pretty traditional statement of joining heaven to earth through ascension or descension. But look at the uppermost reflection carefully. It's not a perfect reflection, although very clever. What do you see?"

I look, and at first glance, it appears as a reflection, like the others. I see the ladder, and I see the lettering, but then on the left, it finally hits me. "It says Zion on the left, and on the right it says 2012. That *is* clever!"

"Good work. So it appears that the ultimate time when divine justice or providence will reveal itself is 2012, and those against it have something to do with Zion. This I can't answer for you because Zionists are traditionally Christian, so I'm not sure what this person is getting at."

Excitedly I add, "Oh, then look down, to top it off there is an hourglass on the left, which probably means time is running out, and on the right there is the scientific drawing symbolizing

the ecliptic. So with the 2012 date and the ecliptic, this person believes in this *doomsday prophecy?*"

"Perhaps, but look carefully at the caduceus. What do you see?"

It takes me a couple of minutes. I'd been staring right at the center and not getting it.

"What is odd, what is different?" He gives me time.

"Oh I see, there are two serpents to the good side and only one to the evil side, and in medicine, there's only one on each side."

"Correct again."

"What does it mean?"

"Did you not take biology, my dear?"

What an appropriate time to ask that question! "I did, and may I say I nearly flunked!"

"If you look closely at the curves of the snakes, you will see nothing other than a DNA strand!"

I'm blown away. He's right! Now I'm getting really excited, not because I know where the nun is, but because this is the most fascinating thing I've seen in a long time. "What does it mean?" I can't contain myself.

"I don't know; that's where my biology ends and another scholar's job begins. But two 'heads' are better than one!" And he's a comedian too. We both laugh.

He continues, "Seriously, though, in the Trinity we have the Father, the Son, and the Holy Spirit. So maybe there will be more spiritual gifting when the poles change in 2012, or perhaps there will be a lessening of the hold evil has on us, or perhaps we'll finally realize evil does exist and that people really worship it. Perhaps we'll take the initiative and regain power over it, as God has promised. Or, perhaps, that's just my projection of what it all means."

"Good one!" He's familiar with my past profession's tools and lingo.

I quickly get back to business. Time is ticking away and I ask, "What do you personally believe about 2012 and the world potentially coming to an end?"

"Ludicrous. Yes, there's all this talk about Doomsday December 21, 2012, which is fear mongering in my mind."

"Well, why did the Mayan calendar end there?" I'm hoping he'll have an answer to a long-debated question.

"They were charting the earth's movement, and that's when an axis change will occur. We weren't always as stupid as we are now! Look, any time the earth's axis changes, a lot happens in the physical world. Earthquakes, tornadoes, changes in weather. You name it. So I do believe a drastic physical change to our earth and the unseen magnetic grids on earth will come. With this, should we chose God, a spiritual shift is going to move us closer to the consciousness and care of the earth and our fellow men, and there may even be physical changes in humans. If you read the Bible translated from Hebrew, without all the false interjections in the many new replications of what people call the Bible, God promises us, the faithful and undeceived ones, regenesis, or regeneration. He tells us specifically, He will *never* destroy the earth. He promised He won't even destroy mankind as He did during the flood, but instead He will bring back the rejuvenation of the earth if we as his children chose Him, not Satan. If we finish the mission or purpose we each came here to do, which, mind you, most of us have forgotten because of the distractions in the material world, He will come back for his chosen ones and live in a time some refer to as the Golden Age."

"Is this a Jewish belief?"

"Oh my, no. They'd have a field day with me. It's just what I believe, but what would an old Jewish black man like me know?" We laugh again.

"What don't you know?" I reiterate back. I start to review the key points as I ask him to hold on a minute while I review my notes. Stars, twelve constellations, appointed times, Zion, 2012, Caduceus, good/evil, pope, botany, and possible DNA changes.

"All right, I think my notes are in order, although I'm still not sure if I get it all!"

"Rome wasn't built in a day, my dear!"

"You are so right!"

We catch up on personal things for a couple more minutes, and then I sign off, saying I'll touch base soon. He is always such an inspiration to me. I hope that one day I'll attain his level of understanding of the universe and spiritual things.

I put all the pieces he told me about together and label each set. I run downstairs to show the symbolism to Dr. Janus, and the excitement of this, dealing with a Virgin, makes me think of the reference to the nun. Dr. Janus doesn't seem quite as excited as I am.

"Well, what does it mean?" His tone is accusatory.

"It means someone is setting a path, a story, maybe your life, the nun's life, your family's life. It's a clue as to what the artist feels is wrong in the world. You said your mom was into herbs"—I point out the symbols—"your dad was into biology. Look at this center part of the scales, Dr. Janus; does it remind you of anything?"

Without missing a beat, "As a matter of fact, it looks like DNA!"

"B-I-N-G-O."

"You said your dad had been working on DNA since the fifties. Maybe there are answers in this."

He tenses up and then says, "But what would that have to do with my sister? No one has ever really taken an interest in her religious endeavors, or my mother's herbs, and my father and she have been dead for years now."

Unwilling to budge, I say, "Someone cares about all of this, and I'm going to find out who."

I feel a little hurt. He isn't as enthusiastic as I thought he'd be. I convince myself he's under stress, excuse myself, and go back to the computer and clues to work through these new interpretations. I make notes. The person who did this must: 1) know sister is a nun, a virgin; 2) be familiar with signs/symbols/ zodiac; 3) understand Egyptian mythology and even biblical prophecy if it's saying Virgo is the true starting point and Leo the ending point; 4) understand the "appointed times," whatever or whenever they are; 5) be weighing good versus evil and trying to convince us evil is winning; and, 6) be showing us a possible positive change in the future with a date of 2012 or a negative impact with Zion, again, whatever that means.

But with all that, Dr. Janus is accurate. I've no idea where his sister is or exactly why she's been kidnapped, and even worse, my keen intuition is not letting me know if she is dead or alive, as it usually does.

chapter

23

Let your conversation be without covetousness; and be content with such things as ye have: for He hath said, "I will never leave thee, nor forsake thee." (5) So that we may bodily say, "The Lord is my Helper, and I will not fear what man shall do unto me." (6)

Hebrews 13:5–6, KJV

 he awoke assuming it was next morning, with bits of chocolate still in her mouth. After praying in her dreams to false idols and saints she had never heard of, she started rethinking. If this Bible was the Word of God and not some sick translation, what did it really say about her relationship as a nun to her Holy Father?

She used the sophisticated remote control and punched in breakfast. She had no idea how it happened, but suddenly through the door came hard-boiled eggs, hot coffee, and a note. It was the answer as to how people are to pray. She was pleased she had already found this, but the verses seemed to have even more power to them this time:

> And when thou prayest, thou shalt not be as the hypocrites *are:* for they love to pray standing in the synagogues and in the corners of the streets, that they may be seen of men. Verily I say unto you, They have their reward. But *thou,* when thou prayest, enter into thy closet, and when thou hast shut thy door, pray to the Father Which is in secret; and thy Father, Which seeth in secret shall reward thee openly. But when ye pray, use not vain repetitions, as the heathen *do;* for they think that they shall be heard for their much speaking.
>
> Matthew 6:5–7

And his note below the verses read, "Remember: God tells us that whatever we ask for in Jesus's name will be granted. Be careful that you ask for what is God's will and the best for you because people do get what they ask for, not realizing that it may not even be what they want or need. Ask God because He knows better than anyone how to please you, and with faith like the proverbial mustard seed, He will give you more than you ever imagined. Never forget Hebrews, first from the Annotated Bible and then the *KJV:*

> Hebrews 11:1: Now faith is the assurance (the confirmation, the title deed) of the things [we] hope for, being the proof of things [we] do not see *and* the conviction of their real-

ity [faith perceiving as real fact what is not revealed to the senses].

Now faith is the substance of things hoped for, the evidence of things not seen.

And in the KJV, it is the word we translate as "evidence" that comes from the Greek word *elenchos,* which means "proof." So it is important to see that it is through faith, picturing the belief first in our minds and *believing* that it has already been *granted,* that the belief then becomes a reality and is manifested on earth through the power of the Holy Spirit working through you. Enjoy the meal.

She did. She ate exuberantly, both of the food and of the Word. Feeling quite satisfied, unlike after her breakfasts at the convent, she went to work on the first question. She had faith, she knew that, but this concept of directing faith with a purpose and then believing it would be granted was a new way of thinking. She haphazardly prayed, "I have faith I will get out of this alive." But did she really believe that?

Question #1: Are you saved through grace or works?

Read Ephesians 2:8–9.

"Oh, this is an easy one," slipped out aloud. She knew it was through good works that people got to heaven. She could hear the bishop explaining it. To be honest, she was never really clear on how many of those good works it needed to be, but she knew that was the answer.

For it is by free grace (God's unmerited favor) that you are saved (delivered from judgment *and* made partakers of Christ's salvation) through [your] faith. And this [salvation] is not of yourselves (of your own doing, it came not through your own striving), but it is the gift of God; (9) Not because of works (not the fulfillment of the Law's demands), lest any man should boast. (It is not the result of what anyone can possibly do, so no one can pride himself in it or take glory to himself.)

What? She read it again. *Could it really be saying that it is through our belief, through our faith, that God sends us grace as a gift, that it is not from how many good works we do?* How could that be? Then that final part about "lest any man should boast." If great acts were done, if miracles happened and men claimed they had done them, they would be liars. Therefore, to stop man from pretending to take credit, He levels us all out with grace. The difference is that only those with faith can access it. That could make sense. God loves all his children who seek truth. If this is the truth, then it is not how many works you do. It is purely that the works you do are done by the path He has prepared for you, by the purpose he has assigned you for your journey on earth. Interesting. *Couldn't buy into it quite yet, but interesting.*

Then the strangest thought emerged. *What would be the purpose of all the Masses because isn't justification* not *of* faith *but of sacraments?* Justification of the Catholic individual is progressive, being regenerated by baptism, being purified by confession and penance, growing in grace and holiness through the reception of the other sacraments so that one is holy enough to make it to Purgatory! That means that as a Catholic, one is becoming justified not by grace but by the number of sacraments or works done? *Could that be wrong?*

The question made her then wonder why people paid money for Mass cards when someone died. Simply put, if the above were true, one could not buy enough cards or pray enough to get another person into heaven. She had always wondered why the pope allowed the merchandising of such cards. Intercessory prayer could help but could not do it alone, and what benefit would it really serve after death? As a matter of fact, sacraments

during one's life could not do it either! If it were not the number of times one did these things but instead for the grace given by God, she had been badly misled.

Was this why the Roman Catholic Church did not want its people to read the Bible? She began to second-guess what she had been taught about Purgatory and all the Masses. She was taught that Masses relieved souls from their sufferings, but now she could not find where this was in the Bible, which instead seemed rather to expose this as a false teaching.

It also made her question this place called Purgatory, that intermediate holding spot where one added up one's sins for an indeterminable amount of time to see if one could even make it to heaven.

But she noted that when she read about the crucifixion of Christ in the New Testament, which she had done the other day when she had departed from the syllabus, she had realized that Jesus said to the thief being killed on a cross next to him, "This day thou shalt be with me in Paradise." He did not say, "In the next century after you have been judged and put into Purgatory and spent years adding up the number of masses you did or did not attend"; He said on *this* day.

She was really thinking now and not sure she liked herself for it.

Question #2: How many times must one repent to be properly forgiven? To whom should one repent and why?

Read Hebrews 10:14.

"For by a single offering He has forever completely cleansed *and* perfected those who are consecrated *and* made holy."

The word *single* struck her. *According to those words, it seems like God is saying that if you repent honestly and ask one time for forgiveness, He will grant it and then forget about it. Could this be? Would He really never bring it up again?*

That was such a strange thought since she could think of numerous times she had asked for forgiveness from the priest for the same thing and repeated numerous infractions over and over. From the above verse, it did not seem as though this was what He wanted.

Imagine asking one time for forgiveness and it being granted. She had never looked at Christ's crucifixion in such a way. How could this have eluded her? She started to think about the repetition in Mass, and it suddenly hit her as absurd. Confession was repetition too, and what was the purpose of a priest hearing the same words over and over again? This made her feel like she was a hamster caught on the wheel, unable to stop the next thoughts. *Could forgiveness really be this easy? Could I finally feel forgiven for my deed?*

She flipped to the pages in the Bible and read what led up to this verse.

> Furthermore, every [human] priest stands [at his altar of service] ministering daily, offering the same sacrifices over and over again, which never are able to strip [from every side of us] the sins [that envelop us] *and* take them away– (12) Whereas the One [Christ], after He had offered a single sacrifice for our sins [that shall avail] for all time, sat down at the right hand of God, (13) Then to wait until His enemies should be made a stool beneath His feet.
>
> Psalm 110:1

Wait, what is this saying? The priest really cannot strip our sins away, only Christ can? She had never seen those words before. If that was true, that Christ was the only mediator to God, then what had she been doing? *This Bible seems to be saying to cut out*

the middle person. It is as if God's saying, "Why would I ever ask you to go to confession or to a priest? I sent my only begotten Son so by confession and belief in Him you could be saved. Therefore no intermediary can forgive you. Only I can." Her stomach ached. Her eyes fluttered involuntarily. She had always gone to confession. What would this mean to her now, if this was even true?

And then she read the next recommended verses:

And so each of us shall give an account of himself [give an answer in reference to judgment] to God.

Romans 14:12

For there [is only] one God, and [only] one Mediator between God and men, the Man Christ Jesus.

1 Timothy 2:5–6

And there it was. This summed it up. We are accountable to Christ only. So why had Pope Pius the XII proclaimed Mary as the Mediatrix of all? Did this mean Mary or the saints were not to be prayed to after all? What had she been doing all of these years?

She pounded the side of the mattress. She thought of using the glass from the vase to kill herself but was too afraid. How could she live with her world and her lifelong beliefs falling down around her?

She would go to sleep, she told herself. She would sleep until the perpetrator arrived, and then she would just let him kill her. Her life was over anyway. Nothing would ever be the same. She lived with the devil now, and she knew it. This book was obviously a divided brethren trick to get her to change religions.

Despite how she felt, she could not give up. Something deep in her soul was stirred and driving her to know more. She hungered for answers. She couldn't let a few verses destroy the very beliefs she had been taught for over thirty years and the rules she had followed daily. Or should she call them rituals? But she needed more answers before she would believe completely. It was her desire for proof, for evidence, that was a part of her, ingrained in her. She would eventually need to find a verse to back up what she was learning.

Question #3: Where does it say it is a good thing to take religious vows of poverty, chastity, and obedience versus just caring for the poor and meek and the downtrodden? Where does it say to never marry?

Good question, she thought. She hoped there was guidance on this one.

> Now the Spirit speaketh expressly, that in the latter times some shall depart from the faith, giving heed to seducing spirits, and doctrines of devils; Speaking lies and hypocrisy; having their conscience seared with a hot iron; Forbidding to marry, and commanding to abstain from meats, which God hath created to be received with thanksgiving of them which believe and know the truth.
>
> 1 Timothy 4:1–3

Now she was angry because something in her heart had shifted like never before. The verses said that those would come in later times demanding that people not marry and to abstain from eating meat. Was that not the perfect description of a Catholic? A nun didn't marry, and Lent was most definitely about abstaining from meat! Could it be that what she had been following in the Catholic religion was more related to the devil? Was this what God or the church wanted? Could she have been wrong twice in her life?

She was raging and hurting. Bubbling over, she could not hold it in any longer. She yelled at the top of her lungs a piecing and painful cry. The screech unnerved even the rhythms of the earth. "I am a mother! I had a child. A sin. Out of wedlock. This is why I was forced to disappear."

She crumbled to the floor crying for the child she had given up, for the freedom she had lost. Through sobs she gasped, "Why am I just learning this information now? I could have been a good mother, raised a child, and married the man I loved. So what if I was young? Why could I not have worshiped my Lord that way? Why God, why, if this is the truth, did You not just show me years ago? I am old now; what could possibly be recouped in my life?"

Her hand automatically moved to the missing rosary to pray. But then, as if an electrical current went through her, she began to think that her rosary had never really answered any of her prayers. She began to wonder if it really had answered prayers for others, or perhaps they were controlled by the same fear that she was. What kind of church could elicit such control?

Tess sobbed harder as her fists hit the hard ground. She cried out in terrible pain for hours until she was so numb, so unable to focus, unable to think, that she finally stopped dead. *You, God, You have forsaken me.* She shoved her head on the pillow and fell asleep, exhausted.

chapter
24

In 1917, Oscar Callaway entered in the US Congressional Record, "JP Morgan hired twelve major newscasters to find out how many people it would take to generally control the policy of the daily press of the US." He later noted in this record how unhappy he was that the policy was actually adopted and that an editor was placed at the head of each group to make sure the press was in line with the new policy.

Note: Same year the Code of Canon Law is credited.

hile waiting to have one of those special meals in the dining room planned by Ana, I'm getting more frustrated that my unconscious, my intuition, and my extrasensory abilities are not helping me more. My finely tuned unconscious, the connection I felt proud to teach others how to use, was just not cutting it. I usually pick up when people are hurting or dying. Why is this not working for me now?

Regardless, I'm looking forward to catching up with James at dinner to see if he's made any progress. I change out of sweats and into my black khakis, which I'm sure Dr. Janus is now tired of seeing. I put on a fresh shirt. I might need to get some clothes if I'll be staying too much longer. I go downstairs, and there are three settings, one on each side of where Dr. Janus sits. Dr. Janus is there alone and has his Scotch in hand.

He starts, "I apologize for not being more enthusiastic earlier. I could sense I hurt your feelings."

"No, you're right; technically I'm no closer to knowing where your sister is. However, it's a start."

James enters, says a quick hello, followed by, "Well, no fingerprints were found, so I'm returning these. I recommend you keep these in your safe."

"That's too bad," I say as Ana comes in, telling us to "Sit *y mange!*"

It's Sunday, homemade pasta day, and she's not kidding. There are raviolis with spinach and cheese in an olive oil, garlic, and basil dressing, manicottis, tortellinis, and a huge plate of antipasto, various salads all lined up for us to chose what we want. I guess Sunday is self-service day. Each bite is better than the next!

We catch up on security issues, and part way through the meal, Dr. Janus pulls a note from his pocket and says, "Here is a list of groups and organizations I'm part of."

They are broken down into numerous categories: Heads of universities and associations such as the AMA, ACS, NCI; CEOs, CFOs, and COOs of major pharmaceutical companies; senators and other politicians; biology magazines and pharmacological articles he'd worked on; people he defined as leading researchers and what they'd researched related to AIDS, DNA, data typing, fingerprinting, chips, and satellites; international contacts related mostly to medicine; some real estate moguls; his mom and dad's priest; a lady friend of his mom's who came and tended to the garden sporadically; and a sadly small number of personal friends and or acquaintances, plus, of course, Saul, Ana, James, a few staff members, and a few biotech friends he said he heard from occasionally, usually either to show off their newfound wealth or to ask for money because they had handled it so poorly before the Internet and biotech crashes and are already broke. He had no relatives to speak of since his parents were dead and had not been in contact with family from their European ancestry. The Janus's were the lucky ones who had come to America and made it.

That's his entire life on a page of paper. Not one girlfriend or significant other mentioned. Could he really live such an isolated life?

Sad, I think, but then I realize that if I were to put my life on a piece of paper, my list would be even shorter since I'd invested everything with the families and students I'd worked with and only kept one or two close friends. I had always hoped that one day, coming from such a small family, I'd get married and have a dozen kids of my own. That day is nowhere near. I'm a failure in the relationship area because I just can't find someone my age secure enough in themselves. Men have no problem wanting to give me a ring. So, like jobs, I've left numerous broken-hearted suitors in the wings, with *Gone with the Wind* in my mind and just another chapter of my life marked "closed."

James reviews plans with Dr. Janus on security and how we are to handle the gala. It sounds a little scary to me, but James seems to have it together. Dr. Janus is barely listening and asks if we mind if he heads to bed, saying he thinks all this is catching up with him. We agree.

"Try to sleep," I urge supportively. "I'll see you in the morning."

After he leaves, James and I look at each other.

"Are you thinking what I'm thinking?" he asks.

"He's hiding something."

"Well, ye-ah!"

"But what?" I ask.

"I've no idea-r!" He had been so formal with Dr. Janus, I welcome this. He continues. "Have you asked him what his current pet project is?"

"No, I keep meaning to, and then I get sidetracked. All I know is that it's going to 'revolutionize the pharmaceutical industry' and that it's secret."

"Well, we need to find out."

"You're right. I'll ask at breakfast."

I walk James to the door and lock up. I go to the kitchen to thank Ana for another incredible meal, but no one is around. I wonder if I should clean up the dinner plates. I decide against it, as it may offend her. I go upstairs and bring the computer into the bedroom. It's already close to midnight. I wonder what research Dr. Janus is working on, and I also fear that there might be some condemnable act whereby twelve large groups are getting together behind the scenes to control the American public, just like they did with the broadcasting companies years ago. Then the number twelve hits me. Twelve signs of the Zodiac, twelve tribes, twelve apostles, twelve—is someone trying to tell us something more profound by using twelve "large" groups, or is it a corruption of the blessed number proving that the minds of U.S. people could be swayed by any made-up story? What a crazy mind I have.

I decide to play some music I'd downloaded onto the computer to help the circling thoughts stop. It relaxes me, and I fall asleep before the third song.

chapter
25

Sapphire: The independent investigation of truth.
The color of faith, inspiration, loyalty, and truth.

 he next morning to my great annoyance, there's no Dr. Janus for breakfast. I'm beginning to wonder what he's really up to. Finally lunchtime arrives, and Dr. Janus rushes in. "I know you have a bunch of questions, but I had to head out this morning to try to get some paperwork completed, in case the banking transaction has to go through. I left early because my advisor wanted to meet with me and I didn't want to be there with his other clients."

That makes sense. I start right in with, "All right, since we won't have time to chat tonight, you need to tell me more about what work you do for the pharmaceutical companies."

"It's really simple. I take the pharmaceuticals the companies have researched and, following the same old scientific research method, work through all phases of the project with their information and their results. I don't redo the testing myself. I review the steps to see if anything has been missed. So, as you may remember from class, it starts with the research questions and goes through hypotheses, experimental design, which includes variables, control, observations, collecting of data, journaling, reviewing charts and graphs, then it moves through to procedure, results, conclusions, applications, and resources used." He looks at me as I nod my head. I actually remember this from his class. I can even imagine the Roman numerals highlighting each title.

"I slowly and methodically review each step. My only job is to make sure it appears accurate so as to not raise concerns for any party or consumer involved. I review all the documentation and help with a significant amount of rewriting and proofreading of the materials. I do present the data in the best possible light, but I don't change the data. The scientists within the pharmaceutical company do the lengthy research. I am, in a sense, simply an outside advisor, a consultant, making sure the technical research and conclusions drawn make sense. It's common knowledge this is done to cover the pharmaceutical company with the FDA regulators and other groups. I could not possibly be seen as a threat because I simply take existing data and look for nonobvious errors," he repeats himself for clarity.

I must have looked baffled because he clarifies again, "I do not define the illness, treatment, or even scope and efficacy of the medicine. I analyze the data to make sure, as a biochemist, professional scientist, and professor reading it, that there are no blatant discrepancies. For example, I once reviewed research on a sickle-cell anemia treatment, and if you got down into the actual numbers, which everyone else seemed to miss, I found out some subjects were labeled as Caucasian. Well, white people don't get sickle-cell anemia! Therefore, the data could not have been accurate. It had been fudged in some way, or simply overlooked, perhaps, so the hospital or doctor could get the recognition of another published work. As you know, Magdalena, if you are in a teaching hospital or university setting and looking for tenure, you need to publish as much as possible, as quickly as possible. This leaves a lot of room for error."

Room for error, I think to myself. *That's an understatement!*

He readjusts himself in the seat. He knows I'm not buying it. Carefully, while watching every expression on my face, he continues. "Despite my advice, that article was published with the drug *and* the error. It may still be used today. I did my due diligence. I advised against it; no one took my advice. I got paid for my work, and I've never heard another thing about it."

I don't respond, so he again elaborates, "An error resolved like this can save a pharmaceutical company billions of dollars in erroneous research, humiliation, and possible lawsuits if the medication has side effects that weren't listed appropriately or if it's discovered that the core research is faulty. So many new drugs now have minute molecular changes just to get a new name and get quickly patented. This makes the process easier for the drug companies to get information approved and disseminated. They just bulk the old research with the new changes, file the paperwork, and a newer and better drug is introduced to the public. So, although I point out issues and concerns, or recommend changes, they control the choice to determine whether the error is important enough or not. In this case, they ignored it. I have not heard of any backlash since."

"Important enough? What do you mean? Blatant errors can be published, and no one does anything about it?"

"Exactly."

"But how is that possible? How is that *ethical?*"

"I do not determine if it's ethical or not. I determine if it's scientifically plausible."

I'm in utter shock. I want to throw something but try to contain my anger and appear as though I'm listening. What I'm thinking is, *What if one person loses their life because of bad reporting? Wouldn't that be important enough? Perhaps that one person is an impoverished "non-Caucasian" person on welfare who in some people's minds doesn't aid in the growth of the nation.* I could just see some sick, educated, politically driven, power-hungry person making this statement as if his/her bigoted whiteness is any better than any other person.

Trying to act calm, I return the conversation to the topic I need answers about. "So tell me what you've found out so far about the one you're working on."

"Not much really. The research seems valid. They have only sampled about three thousand people, which is a very small sample, so I'm amazed they can progress so quickly and move on it, but from what I can tell so far, there are no glaring errors." He then adds, "Mags, this is not a moral-, emotional-, positive-, or negative-type decision. Facts are presented to me, and I help determine if they make scientific sense, if they are presented according to the 'scientific model'; if they do not, I give suggestions. I don't ever even see the finished product. I get paid for my recommendations, not judgments. Purely scientific analysis."

Now I can no longer control myself about this huge over-rationalization. "Thus keeping your hands and conscience clean?" I wince as I say it but just can't keep my mouth shut.

"Somewhat harsh, Mags. Not everyone operates on your emotional realm or has your level of need to uphold morals and ethics. Some of us can just live with the status quo. I have never claimed to be anything different."

I wonder for a split second if this is how he's looking at his sister's kidnapping. He has emotionally cut himself off by working through the steps as a scientific equation. I then whimper a bit with, "But in classes you always had us search for the truth."

"The truth of the scientific equation, yes, not the ultimate quintessential life truth. Who could possibly know that?"

"I don't know," I say, clearly exasperated, "I guess we need to change the scientific model then. But don't you ever just know deep in your heart and get a gut feeling something is just plain wrong?"

"I'm not like you, Mags. I don't really operate in the emotional mode."

"I hear you. I'm sorry for being so curt, especially with everything you're going through. But what if those lies, or rather omissions, are the reason for your sister missing, or if someone dies because of it, wouldn't that make you think differently?"

"I don't know, Mags. I truly don't know. Part of me cannot feel responsible for what I cannot control, and a new part of me is feeling levels of guilt and disgust in myself I have never felt. I'm just being honest."

"I do appreciate that. I do, and I know this isn't easy." I back down a little and then ask, "Have any of the drugs you researched over the years killed anyone?"

"Well, I am sure all drugs have some deaths associated in some form or another, but no one would know I wrote or reviewed the data, as it's all kept confidential. From the twenty-five to thirty drugs I have reviewed, I have only been called in to one closed case hearing, and I can get you the names of those involved if absolutely necessary. I would, of course, be breaking every confidentiality law in creation and could be jailed for such exposure. But, there wasn't enough evidence for the case to be pursued, so the pharmaceutical company got a slap on the wrist, fined for about $22 million, settled out of court, and nothing was publicized. The fine is always just part of their operating expenses, the cost of doing business."

"*The cost of doing business?* $22 million? We could feed a poor nation with that amount. We could feed *our* American poor and middle class for that amount!" Trying to keep it together, I think, *Where did everyone's sense of responsibility and morals go?* Kill some to save the masses, or so we're taught to believe. But what if that one death doesn't even help the many but is a slow poisoning? I don't know if I like this detached part of Dr. Janus. And on the flip side, maybe this is a good thing. I've been on the verge of thinking he's perfect, and no person can live up to that.

Just then, as if conjured up to get Dr. Janus out of the conversation, the tailor, a short plump man, with combed-over, dark, greased hair and oval spectacles, runs in, moving his arms and hands in big gestures. *Must be Italian,* I muse. "Tonight-*a?*" he cries, looking frantically at Dr. Janus. "The dress needs to be tried on and altered by tonight-*a?* What-*a* you think, I'm-*a God?* O Mia solo …" under his breath, then much louder, "A lowly tailor, I am. I have hands-*a, mani,* not wings!"

Dr. Janus calmly smiles and says, "Roberto, good to see you. I think once she tries it on, you will be pleased with how little it will need to be tailored. I am not expecting a miracle, but in this case, I don't think we will need one. Do your best, and thank you for coming on such short notice."

The tailor already has his hands on me as if measuring and is pushing me out of the room. Forcing him back, I say, "Oh, by the way, before I go up, what exactly is it you're doing the write up on?"

"A new type of vaccine," he says nonchalantly. "It's all hush hush, and I have signed a confidentiality agreement the size of Mount Olympus, but we can talk about that later."

"A vaccine?" I know the word originated from vax in Latin and later became vache in French and meant cow. Biased as I am, I think, *Yeah, that's what we the public are, cows to experiment on.* "Vaccine?" I repeat in dismay, as the tailor is pushing me, now impatiently.

Dr. Janus says reassuringly, "We'll talk about it later. I promise."

We head up the stairs, but my mind is long gone.

I'm getting dressed, turning as I'm told, but I'm barely focused on the dress because I'm thinking about the vaccination issue. I've never been much for the concept of vaccinations because, with the little medical and biological knowledge I have, it has never made sense to me. I also know this is one crusade my parents instilled in me and, ironically, is a condition of my adoption, as if I came with a warning label, "No Vaccinations Allowed!"

During one of my "stints" (a lifetime career choice at that point) as a Child Play Therapist and Early Education Teacher in hospitals, I worked at one of the leading hospitals north of New York City for developmentally and physically challenged children. My time there was an incredible and humbling experience. I was horrified to see the increasing number of children being enrolled with severe forms of autism, ADD (Attention Deficit Disorder), ADHD (Attention Deficit Hyperactivity Disorder––a later addition to the DSM-IV, that "omniscient" fourth diagnostic and statistical manual), and all of the neurological disorders that severely affect the IQ and the child's ability to function, to say nothing about adding a needless and alarming increase in allergies to the equation. The situation left me overwhelmed. I knew something was wrong and had an inkling it was vaccines,

but I had only made it through basic research I had done for a paper in an undergraduate class.

I remember reading some shocking articles, such as one written in "Science," dated March 4, 1977. Jonas and Darrell Salk warned, "Live virus vaccines against influenza or poliomyelitis may in each instance produce the disease it intended to prevent ... the live virus against measles and or mumps may produce such side effects as encephalitis," which means brain damage. They also claimed it's dangerous with the added Thimerisol (which contains ethyl mercury and has been proven to have adverse effects in humans exposed to it) and the heavy metal aluminum which produces neurotoxic effects. Several childhood vaccines have this metal in them, such as: DTaP, Pediarix (DTaP-Hepatitis B-Polio combination), Pentacel (DTaP-HIB-Polio combination), Hepatitis A, Hepatitis B, Haemophilus influenzae B (HIB), Human Papilloma Virus (HPV), and Pneumococcal vaccines. To top it off, they contain formaldehyde, which, in itself, is acknowledged as a brain cell killer. With these chemicals in the vaccinations, they will no doubt cause more ADD, ADHD, autism, developmental and neurological delays, all the problems I saw at the hospital. Looking at this epidemic today, it only seems to me that things are getting worse, not better. One in six children are suffering from these illnesses, and there are dramatic increases in allergies, asthma, ulcerative colitis, inflammatory bowel diseases, all at earlier ages, and even an increase in deadly degenerative diseases, such as lupus, rheumatoid arthritis, juvenile diabetes, and cancer.

Even before the article by Dr. Jonas and his son, Darrell Salk, there was a fascinating study done by Dr. Sandier at the U.S. Veteran's Administration in North Carolina. In 1948, he exposed that the overconsumption of heavily sugared drinks, refined sugar products, ice cream, candy, and other sweets consumed by children during the hot summer months is the reason polio became epidemic in 1948. By simply warning the public and parents, there was a 90-percent decrease in polio in his state that year. By 1949 there were only 229 cases versus the almost 2,500 the year before. That was astounding and certainly proved beyond any shadow of a doubt the correlation between consumption and illness. Not surprisingly, when Dr. Sandier's study affected the deep pockets of the soft drink manufacturers and candy distributors—such that their sales began to drop—the study disappeared. Just two years after the study was published, in 1950, the soda companies launched a free sample and promotional campaign to boost sales. The result: polio increased well above the 2,500 person mark again. It sickens me to think how wrong this is on so many levels. Could Dr. Janus inadvertently be caught up in some sick promotional campaign that could negatively impact people?

My research at that time had led me to read that, even in 1955, the Surgeon General of the United States, Leonard Scheele, stated at the AMA (American Medical Association) convention, "No batch of vaccine can be proven safe before it's given to children," and James R. Shannon of the NIH (National Institutes of Health) declared, "The only safe vaccine is a vaccine that is 'never' used." What did this mean for Dr. Janus and his research? How could he even morally consider working on a vaccine? Perhaps someone had finally realized his involvement, connecting past illicit work of allowing these research projects to get published, and was now seeking revenge?

Dr. William Koch declared, "The injection of any serum, vaccine, or even penicillin has shown a marked increase in the incidence of polio, at least by 400 percent." Shockingly, twenty-two years later in 1999, the American Academy of Pediatrics (AAP) was able to say that we should get thimerosal-containing vaccines reduced or eliminated, and although from 1999–2003 they started the reduction, there are still old batches left. They couldn't possibly throw out the old batches; that would mean losses of millions of dollars of profits to the pharmaceutical companies. So what if a couple more kids got sick? People wouldn't know it was from a thimerosal batch. Vaccinations are required today; who would ever suspect they're from an older batch that contained the poison, or from a newer batch? No one would even know to question this.

As I feel the sharp pinch of a tailor's pin on my ankle, I recall the children and babies who are now getting the flu vaccine along with their routine ones. Despite all the warnings, the Vaccination Committee of the American Academy of Pediatricians also had the audacity to lower the age from twenty-four to eighteen months. It seemed to me insane to give this to a being who hadn't even had a chance to grow its own complete immune system yet. We're born to adapt and survive even being exposed to some poisons and some toxins. But is this really the way to start a healthy life in the world, or are we setting our children up for long-term chronic and terminal illnesses?

The tailor is explaining words in Italian. Eventually, from his body movements, I get the idea he wants me to lean over because if the strap around the neck is too tight, it will pull up the dress or possibly snap if I bend over too far. I do as he commands, and he loosens the strap just half an inch. Smart idea. The evening won't need any extra spice to it; that I'm sure of! Then I'm lost in thought again.

I recall my days after the hospital, when I began to understand monetary and fiscal policy and saw the billions of dollars of profit. When I understood the drug industry, it disgusted me. It's mostly about money. I become concerned that the plane I rode here in, the luxuries I'm enjoying, the tailor at my feet, are paid for by these industries, which horrifies me. Is Dr. Janus securing their testing and their results so they can stand confidently behind their "findings" and claim ignorance? Is he part of allowing vaccinations, cleverly disguised as saving the population from these terrible illnesses and saving the American population from itself, when all that really matters to him is the bottom line? Is he really like them, or even worse, in on it with them?

This issue of compulsory vaccination makes me even angrier because what better way can there be for a pharmaceutical company to generate guaranteed income in the future? Groups such as the CDC (Centers for Disease Control), HEW (Health, Education Welfare), USPHS (United States Public Health Service), FDA (Food and Drug Administration), AMA (American Medical Association), and WHO (World Health Organization) know all about it; therefore, they're allowing it and participating, no matter how coy they are, no matter how strongly they deny or refute this knowledge.

I thought about the parents who had told me heartbreaking stories of their children being born healthy, who then suddenly got sick after visits to the doctors for shots. Other children showed a slow progression and waxing and waning of symptoms. No one would admit the vaccine itself was the culprit. Parents are on to it but are so tired from the strain, it's all they can do to run a household and get the children in for special education programs. They don't have the time, the energy, or the money to go up against the corporate giants or government agencies. I watched as parents got divorced, families broke up, and, all the while, the pharmaceutical companies continued to get richer. You don't have to be a brain surgeon to understand that if the children were born healthy with no symptoms, the chronic illnesses and neurological toxicity effects could only have developed from exposure to something introduced to their system. It's sad to think that these poor parents are trying to protect their beloved children from illness, yet, by allowing the

injection of a foreign substance that no one really understands, may be doing the exact opposite.

The tailor instructs me to take the dress off and wait while he sews what he's just pinned together. I put a robe on over my slip and sit on the bed. I watch the happy little cherubs smiling down at me and pray for their help. I pray I won't discover that Dr. Janus is actually helping to perpetuate that demented medical requirement. I especially pray that it's not that one unmentioned vaccine in particular that I fear the most. The tailor's needle and thread are moving at a pace that amazes me. I don't think a sewing machine could have worked as quickly as he did. I feel sad.

My mind then goes off on yet another tangent. I recently heard about actors pushing for "green" vaccines. I've great respect for their diligence in helping to educate the public on ADD, autism, and the other illnesses. My deepest fear is half-truths. I struggle with how a portion of some vaccines can be okay and others not. Can it be that vaccines are either all good or all bad? Hearkening back to the zodiac sign, Libra, shown as the scales of justice on the artwork, I can see the evil side weighted down. Can I even appreciate the other side of the story, their benefit, or am I too jaded? My gut rarely fails me, and in this case, I have backed it up with research. Will I ever be able to prove it without real medical or biological knowledge?

Some of the most ethical and knowledgeable physicians still swear by some childhood vaccines. Are they wrong? Medical schools still teach they are "safe." University professors claim that people not only need not worry about the aluminum, etc., contained in the vaccination; they also need not worry about the vaccination, period. They distort the information and make it sound safe with statements like, "The virus is not 'alive' because there's no separate functioning respiratory system, digestive system, or, for that fact, nucleus. A vaccine is specifically a protein waste in a solvent solution." Because we don't understand what they're talking about, we believe this means it's safe.

As I've learned from experience, not everything presented in school is true. I was taught that out-of-body experiences don't exist yet knew they existed. I was preprogrammed and brainwashed in the highest level of my courses. Perhaps we all are, and in our best intentions to be "healers," we're doing things without all the information on hand. I mean, if Dr. Janus could have found the "Caucasian" error after numerous scientists reviewed and missed the information, can we also not be missing vital facts and therefore jumping to the wrong conclusions? I still shudder to think that by parents not having all the information, kids are getting up to fifty vaccinations before the age of eleven. How can that possibly be healthy?

Lost in my own thoughts, time disappears. I want to be back in nature with the calm of the trees gently whispering through my soul, summoning me to know it's going to be okay. I want to escape to the ocean and hear the waves as they speak to the universe and reset our personal biological clocks. I want to be somewhere else less painful, protected by the nature I have ignored.

As if a queen, I'm summoned back to the tailor as he presents me with the dress. I put it on. I can't see what it looks like because I'm no longer by the full-length mirror. He has me in the hallway walking up and down to watch the movement of the skirt. He's obviously overjoyed. He claps his hands, laughs, more like a tense, vibrating woodpecker laughs, and keeps repeating, "Bella, Bella, Bella!" And then as quickly as he came, he runs, grabs his bag of sewing tools, and disappears down the stairs as the echo of "Ciao" trails behind him.

I take off the dress without looking in the mirror because I'm in no mood at the moment. I know I need to shower and do my hair. I place the dress on the bed, careful not to wrinkle it, and head for a much-needed shower. As I let the clean water flow

over my face, I think about how honorable my parents had been following my adoption "instructions."

They would justify their decision regarding vaccinations by recommending people go back to the history of polio, swine flu, and regular flu vaccinations; then they would take them down the paths of "history" to explain what most people have long forgotten has transpired in the "evolution" of vaccines. To pull the hard-nosed critics in, they would start by asking the following pointed question: "What happened to the 1909 Bill No. 8 introduced by the Senate of the Commonwealth of Massachusetts entitled, 'An Act To Prohibit Compulsory Vaccine?'" They would elaborate, "It shall be unlawful for any board of education, board of health, or any public board acting in this state, under political regulations or otherwise, to compel by resolution, order or proceedings of any kind, the vaccination of any child or person of any age, by making vaccination a condition precedent to the attending of any public or private school, either as pupil or teacher."

Oddly enough, this bill was buried in 1909, which leads me right back to my thoughts on the fifty large, controlling families and the Rockefellers, who learned how to work through the legislature by creating their own council in Chicago, overseeing state governments that dictated what the legislature was, and is, to this day, to follow.

However, sticking to my family situation, trying not to force anyone to contend with the number of facts that hit my brain at one time, like bugs hitting windshields, my parents were extremely informed about the things going on when I was just a few months old in 1976. They were advised by numerous people not to adopt me with such a "ridiculous conditional clause," or just to ignore it. The "good people," in other words, "busy bodies," said this was a death sentence and I could end up in social services if I didn't get proper medical treatment. My parents got an earful on things most of us today have long forgotten, or perhaps more precisely, since it doesn't affect us directly, we never really pay attention to. They had to pay attention. They always honor their word. They did their research and thought I was worth the risk.

My parents then kept notes on some related issues so should anyone come after them, like a "caring" governmental agency that doesn't have enough workers to do what it needs to do, they had their ducks in a row. It was around 1976, and a national vaccination campaign was launched. At the time, President Gerald Ford was pushing for it. In my parents' opinion, it was a $135 million scam for the major drug firm that was claiming a swine flu cure. Farmers saw their pigs drop dead instantly from the vaccine itself and wanted nothing to do with it. But, hey, if it doesn't work on pigs, why not try people?

Gerald Ford and the cherished, most trusted, television news anchor, Walter Cronkite, went on national TV to scare Americans into getting the vaccine while there "is still time" and before there's a national pandemic. There was no education about how the vaccine worked and why, no scientific analysis and help so each person could make their own informed choice, no information on the many toxic poisons in it, including alien viral protein particles, formaldehyde, residues of chicken and egg embryo substances, sucrose, thimerosal, polysorbate, and some eighty other substances. I've always wondered if the alarming increase in the number of egg allergies is a result of the components of those injections. I don't believe any one else has made this correlation, even today. But, just like the present, even as agencies warn us that artificial sweeteners can kill or maim, manufacturers are still putting them in food and vaccines.

To add fuel to the fire, if that swine flu vaccine was so essential, did the government pay for it? No way. Instead, my parents would explain. "On April 15, 1976, good old Congress passed Public Law 94–266, which provided $135 million of taxpayers' funds to pay for a national swine flu inoculation campaign." Many fearful Americans took the advice to save themselves, and within a couple of months, over $13 billion in claims had been filed by those who were permanently damaged or even died due to it. It wasn't bad enough that it was being forced on us, but in times when people were feeling economic constraints, they were putting out money for something they didn't need that could possibly kill them.

While in the shower, attempting to let the water wash away my pain, I take a deep sniff of an almond mint scent. It's lovely, but I go back to my eucalyptus spearmint. Partially a creature of habit, partially I just feel invigorated by its refreshing smell. I hear my mother's voice, "If it isn't from God's green earth, it should not be put in or on the body!" This part of my parent's personalities made them look more like hippies than respectable, knowledgeable Princeton Ph.D.s!

My mind then skips to what it's like as a child not having been vaccinated in this world and what a feat it can be to convince yourself you won't die of all these horrible illnesses because you've never had the vaccine. I was not allowed admittance to a couple of schools. For travel, we sometimes had to go to lengthy measures because I didn't have the appropriate paperwork. At times I felt like a dog with the wrong tags. So traveling abroad could be a nightmare, but there are ways around it; the Geneva Convention papers guarantee it.

I also sometimes think that's the reason for my good health. Rarely have I gotten a cold, and when the flu shots came out, I warned as many people as I could to stay away from them. I had seen horrifying reactions to the actual shot. Even people who bragged about their perfect immune systems, touting that illness is all in the head, started to blame the shot itself. Elderly people who died after the flu vaccine had their deaths reported as due to cardiac arrest, old age, or some other reason. Physicians seemed to have some unspoken code and would not report the link to the vaccine.

My understanding of the dangers of vaccines was amplified when I discovered research that smallpox was going away on its own, and the vaccine was killing more people than it was curing. Of course, this was after the United States made it compulsory for our service men and women to be vaccinated. In late 1976, forty-nine soldiers died in one month, not from being in a war, but from the vaccine intended to help should they go to war! Many more people died after that. Do we hear about these stories now? Just like the 1949 study that disappeared when it affected the soda and candy companies.

Rather than confess to the damaging results of the swine flu vaccination, the brilliant medical, news, and presidential monopolies invented a new label, a new epidemic of something called "Guillain-Barre Syndrome" to make most of the side effects look unrelated to the vaccine. Pharmaceutical companies still use the Guillain-Barre term to refer to it as a separate illness when they pitch new drugs in commercials without explaining that the illness is most likely a result of some previous vaccination or a side effect of the exact one they are selling. I must admit it's pretty effective. It threw the American public off base, along with most physicians. Many of the children at the hospital for the developmentally delayed had this "new illness" and were paralyzed from it. It scared me because it's debilitating, if not deadly, and is such a quick acting, quick spreading disease that leaves the children paralyzed. To the rest of the world not confined to the hospitals, we seemed to do what we do best: "Out of sight, out of mind."

Not only had I wondered about ADD and the alarming amount of neurological illnesses at the developmentally delayed hospital, but I had also heard rumblings of a future cure for cancer through a vaccine. At this, I nearly flipped. No detailed medical explanations were given as to how this would work, and as much as I could let some vaccines slip through, the ones that would cure cancer just don't cut it for me. If this is what Dr. Janus is into, I won't be able to look him in the eye.

The hazard of working in a hospital is that you read too much and see too much, and I've become leery. When you think of America, the land of the free, you sure don't think of the government controlling what viruses are being injected into us as *freedom*. It's sad, but as my eyes have been opened over the years, my perspective has changed.

As for the conspiracy theorists, some say the AIDS epidemic is a viral variation of the swine flu vaccination. Others say it's engineered by human scientists and was given to the gay population in the 1980s in New York City for depopulation. I haven't done enough research to form an opinion on that one yet!

I marvel at the fact that with all the hype about the necessity of the vaccination for the swine flu epidemic in the Ford era, still 1976, Dr. J. Anthony Morris, the Director of the Virus Bureau at the Food and Drug Administration (FDA), declared there could be no authentic swine flu vaccine because there had never been any cases of swine flu on which they could test it. He went public with his statement, and his exact words were, "At no point are the swine flu vaccines effective." He was promptly fired, all his research burned, and the three-year study and all the animals destroyed.

Years later, the Washington Post of January 26, 1988, announced at a national conference held in Washington that *all* cases of polio since 1979 had been caused by the polio vaccine. They quoted, "In fact, all the cases in America come from the vaccine. The naturally occurring (or wild type) polio virus has not been shown to cause a single case of polio in the United States since 1979."

I get out of the shower and dry off. While brushing my hair, I notice some beautiful sapphire and diamond earrings and matching combs on the counter, which I know I'll have to incorporate into my outfit. I think again about my parents and about our lively family discussions.

I remember at one of those dinners when we discussed history, they warned me that the issues with vaccinations would repeat again if people didn't take charge and stop the lies. And then I'd ask, "What? How could the pharmaceutical companies and government get away with this? The president and Cronkite actually scaring the American population into getting the swine flu vaccine while there's still time? Is taxpayer money really wasted, and are people dead and sick because of it? Could it really happen ten or twenty years down the road since no one is putting two plus two together any more? Would people really let the past be buried?" My typical fire stream of questions.

My father would calmly answer, "Not only did they get away with it, but think, years later when it was announced in 1988 that all cases of polio had been caused by the polio vaccine, no one fought back!"

"Why?" That beautiful two-year-old question emerged from my mouth.

My father ignored the whine in my question. "Well, suppose that while this was published, the government cleverly made another issue seem of the utmost importance to get Americans off its back and fearful about something else so we had no time to pay attention to what had just been announced."

"Really? No!" I said, shaking my head at my naivety in thinking this didn't happen.

"You wait; you watch; you will see!" And we would move on to the next topic.

It's scary to think that history repeats itself. I presume that even with a more educated public today, we aren't immune, or else the spin put on the information being disseminated is so good that we actually fall for the same lies again.

Some politicians and industrialists who have slyly admitted to the overuse of both vaccinations and antibiotics have sloughed it off with the excuse that the income they generate through our large corporations is what keeps the stock market afloat and America rich. If we lose all that money, we'll lose jobs and our stocks will tank and the richest country *per capita* in the world will tumble.

I suppose it depends on how the public defines rich. When we're listed in 2007 as number twenty-nine in the world as far as overall healthiness and we're in the "civilized" world, there's something wrong with the equation.

I know Dr. Janus is a bright man. He couldn't possibly think any cover-ups, overuse of medicines, introductions to processed foods, and an overexposure to vaccines at a young age could follow the principles his parents seemed to believe in, could he? He couldn't be so detached as to really not feel morally obliged to stop this, could he?

I walk back to the bedroom, thumping the brush on my palm, just wanting to make my points to him. I need to get my hair done, though, as it's getting late. So lying down on the bed on my back, I slide my neck over the side, I get my hair to fall behind me, and go to work on it. Tonight I wanted something up, almost Egyptian, with bands of braids. I twist pieces of the braids up, add bobby pins, and put the gorgeous combs in for security and *élan*. I finish putting on my lipgloss and stand to adjust my magnificently tailored dress. I run to the full-length mirror for the complete effect. I'm shocked. I look good! *Huh*, I think, *what money can do!*

The color of the dress is awe-inspiring, a dark sapphire-blue velvet that compliments the color of my hair. A full-length gown with Swarovski crystals shining like diamonds, creating a *V* down my back, with a silky draping over the shoulders. It's heavenly. The color pleases me since sapphire is referred to as the color of faith, inspiration, loyalty, and truth. It also purportedly means the "independent" investigation of truth and is the perfect color to wear at this precise moment. I'll be a truth renegade for the evening.

Despite the doubts that are in my mind now about Dr. Janus's morals, another person's life is at stake; and while needles aren't involved in Tess's case, I hope, it scares me to think that this mystery could be all about vaccinations. Something is going on, and I want to get to the bottom of it, no matter what, or so I think at that moment.

chapter

26

⬤⏐⏐⛎⊏⊏⛎⅂⛎⏐⏐⏐⊐⛔⛎⊐⏐⏐⬤

t 5:30 p.m., I head downstairs. Cocktails and hors d'oeuvre will be served at the gala. No sign of Dr. Janus. I head down the stairs feeling like royalty, and sure enough there's James, looking as hunky as ever in his tux.

Whistle, clap, and the noise from James causes Ana to come running in and stop dead in her tracks. "*Que bella. Que bella,* a princess!"

And I feel like one. Slowly, aware of each step, I make my way down. I don't want ostrich legs this evening. The crystals on my dress reflect the sun from the skylight, lighting the entire place up, offering a colorful laser show. At the bottom of the stairs, James stands waiting with a package in hand.

"For you," he says, bowing low, "from Dr. J."

"Where is he?"

"His meeting ran late, and he's going into the city from there. He'll ride home with us."

"Is he avoiding me? He told me he was working on a vaccine, and I knew from the look on his face and the way he hustled me out with the tailor that he didn't want to get into it, and I don't think it's just an issue of confidentiality."

"I don't know," says James, "but at the moment, all the thinking and freaking and worrying won't make any answers from him come more quickly. This is an evening few ever get to experience, so why don't you try to relax and enjoy it. Ya know my motto: The time to be happy is now."

"You're right! It's just so hard for me!"

"I know."

"But I do have this incredible gift in front of me; can't wait to see what is in it."

"Well, open it!"

So I ravage the paper, bow, and tape, the card flying to the floor to get to what's inside a dark-blue velvet case. When I open it, it's the most unique, most beautiful necklace I have ever seen: all gold—probably twenty-four carat rose gold—about two inches wide and six inches long and has some strange letters. I can't tell if they're Hebrew or hieroglyphics. "This is stunning!"

⚫ⅠⅠⅣⅭⅭⅣ⅂Ⅳ ⅠⅠⅠ⅂ⅣⅣ⅂ⅠⅠ⚫

James looks at it, not sure if he agrees. "It's … well … different."

I laugh. "Always honest!"

"Let me put it on for you."

"Absolutely." It fits perfectly around my neck, the letters sitting gently on my collarbone, the gold links wrapping around to the hook in the back, all elegantly framed in sapphires and diamonds, matching the dress. It's a sensational completion to my already perfect gown.

James leans down and picks up the card. "Don't you think you should open the card?"

"Oh, yes! I know … I'm impulsive!"

The card reads, "Dearest Mags: My mother used to wear this to big events. It will be beautiful with the dress and your red hair. Forgive me for my absence. Despite what you think, I am not avoiding you. Yours truly, Dr. J. See you tonight."

"Well, isn't that nice?" A little sarcasm inadvertently escapes.

Looking at his watch, James says, "You ready? Because we should be on our way."

"I believe so. Let me see, purse, ID, phone, cash, a credit card, lipstick … I think I'm all set."

Ana is pushing us off. "*Andiamo! Una buona notte.*"

"We will have a good night. Thank you, Ana!"

chapter
27

Though we travel the world over to find the beautiful,
we must carry it with us or find it not.

Ralph Waldo Emerson

here's surprisingly little traffic, and James and I arrive easily at the event, where he lets me out in front of the stairs. It's all so exciting to be back in New York City and have a chance to do it the "wealthy" way for once. It's a perfect temperature outside, not the least bit muggy for a warm July day, and despite the construction and numerous people coming and going, I spot Dr. Janus immediately. His face looks a little sullen, and the bow

tie of the tux seems to be holding him up, but he's still debonair. I always wondered why he never married. My heart melts. How could I've been so angry at him?

"You look beautiful, Magdalena. Turn around; let me see the whole picture. Unbelievable. Unbelievable."

"You look dashing yourself," I say.

"Still mad at me?"

"Nope. Thank you for letting me wear the necklace. It's beautiful. Any idea what it means?"

"I knew you were going to ask, but I didn't have time today to try to figure it out when I pulled it out of the safety deposit box with the 'other' things."

"Too funny. I guess you know me well!"

"Are you ready to go in?

"Absolutely."

We immediately start meeting all sorts of people. I get so many looks, I almost feel like royalty. The color of my dress stands out, since most of the women are in black dresses or black and white, all elegant, but mine is definitely unique. People are wandering up and commenting on my outfit. I'm certainly not falling under the radar this evening. When we come to the stairs, I hold on to Dr. Janus's arm for support since it's been so long since I've worn 3.5-inch heels. I tower over most of the people there. I feel like quite the oddity and am wondering if putting my hair up so high was a good idea because it probably makes me look six foot three inches since I seem to be as tall as Dr. Janus. I'm sure I hear people whispering about the "nature" of our relationship. It's that *gossip* that I never miss hearing any more and keep myself away from as much as possible.

When we get to the main level one staircase up, I look down and around. The Met is just as fabulous as I'd remembered it. The tall entrance, the incredible chandelier, the staircases winding down from each side.

The impeccably dressed mingle, sipping their champagne in crystal flutes versus the normal plastic ones people pay $10.00 to have sparkling wine in. We mix and talk and smile and do what I suppose the rich do. We have about fifteen minutes before we're to be at our seats, in the orchestra section no less, and I ask Dr. Janus if he minds if I take a brief tour from the top of the Met to the bottom. I used to get the discount tickets while in college and just wanted to remember what it's like to see what the poor starving artist had to put up with.

Dr. Janus continues to socialize, and many people seem to know who he is. The women are swooning. They look so pretentious to me. *Am I jealous?* I take the elevators on the right up to the top floor and walk around. I peek into the Family Circle and standing room only section and think how great it is that New York City makes sure the arts are accessible to all—it's a little high up, but wonderful, nonetheless. The sound has always been perfect in this hall; it doesn't matter where one sits or stands. It's even better than I remembered.

I step out and look over the rails. I check out the chandeliers from this angle and try to enjoy every second. It's a spectacular view from the top floor. My eye then catches a memorial plaque, and if I hadn't taken an actual picture of it, I would never have believed it. My newly developing conspiracy mind is hard at work.

It reads: "The Family Circle donated by Harold S. Vanderbilt in appreciation of the continued interest in Rockefeller Family and Foundation in Vanderbilt University. It would've been impossible for this to have occurred naturally." The bronze was completely worn in the word *appreciation* and the only three letters one could easily read were *C-I-A*. The hairs on my arms stood up. It couldn't be that any of these rumors were true about the listed families controlling the CIA, could it?

The bell rang, so I knew I had to get to my seat. I took the elevator down and tried not to trip. My heart was fluttering. Could I be seeing things?

I get to the main level and step over numerous people in our row to reach Dr. Janus, who helps me settle in. We don't speak because the lights are starting to dim and the chandeliers are starting to rise. I'm here. I'm really at the Met! It's so exciting to be the third row in, smack in the center! I've loved the Opera ever since I saw live shows with my family in Italy. There, however, the outdoor amphitheaters were so large, horses and people could enter and exit, and hundreds of people from all walks of life could enjoy the show.

The first musical selection is my favorite one from the *Magic Flute*, "Queen of the Night." I have chills the entire time. The number of notes that woman can hit are beyond human. The second selection is a humorous piece from *The Marriage of Figaro*. It shocks me how relationship issues have not changed, even hundreds of years later! And last is the grave scene from *Don Giovanni*. I am simultaneously in tears and smiling. Only Mozart can stir my soul like this. I feel so privileged to be in the audience. I'm even able to get lost and forget the reason why we're here. I glance at Dr. Janus, who seems as moved as I am.

It feels like only minutes have passed, but it's already time for the Intermission. Dr. Janus and I head to the main area, where food and champagne are being handed out everywhere by a professional staff. Everyone's raving about the performance. I can still hear "Queen of the Night" in my head.

Then out of the blue, a waiter who has been eying me approaches. Dr. Janus sees him staring and nudges me, laughing that the server has the audacity to flirt with me at an event he's working. The waiter comes up, stands directly in front of me with nothing in his hand but a Playbill, grabs my hand, places the Playbill in it, and says, "A gift for a lovely woman, a signed Playbill."

"Oh, how nice! Thank you."

Then he leans up to my left ear, the one away from Dr. Janus, and says, "You're being followed, and your life is in danger; make a scene, and then get out of here quickly. Pretend you're flirting with me and let me walk away." His hand grasps mine painfully. He's serious. It happens so quickly I don't even realize my heart is playing staccato. I laugh and flirt as commanded, but all I can hear is the loudest laughter, my own, echoing back at me through the high ceiling built for excellent acoustics. I then do what I've been asked, as a finale, and what Dr. Janus, James, and I had planned to do if anything were to go wrong. I look him in the eyes one last time, trying to take note of his features, and then arms flailing out and up as if I'm about to faint in the most royal manner possible, I accidentally hit an entire tray of champagne glasses and collapse to the ground. While things are spilling and crashing everywhere, my entire body sprawls upon the floor in the least feminine way possible, and he's able to disappear.

There are "oohs" and "oh mys," and while some waiters make people move away from gawking, as if I'm the only entertainment around, others try to make space. Appearing out of nowhere, in a split second, I see James has gotten his cue to get the limo, and he again vanishes.

Medical doctors come running, practically every third invitee, and I think if I can keep a straight face and act as if I've fainted, it will be a miracle. People take my wrists for a pulse, others demand my head be raised, some fan me, and finally I hear Dr. Janus pronounce, "I am a doctor, and she is with me. Move out of the way. She is with me." At that, I pretend to weakly open my eyes, try to catch a breath, and say, whispering and confused, "What happened?"

"I think you fainted, my dear."

"Me faint? I don't think so."

He says, taking my pulse, "Your breathing is normal; you have color back in your face. I knew I should have made you eat something earlier. All the excitement." We did this for a couple more minutes, and then he says, "Can you stand?"

"I think so," I say bravely. Getting up from the floor in stilettos and a tight gown isn't a gracious move. I'm very relieved the tailor had given extra room in the straps of the gown. Had he not, there would have been a peep show at this performance!

Managers say they'll get an ambulance, but Dr. Janus hands them his card and says that won't be at all necessary.

I pump it for all it's worth, and Dr. Janus is pretty believable himself. We know the managers are afraid of lawsuits, but we assure them I'd just not eaten that day due to all the excitement. They start announcing everything is fine to the onlookers, who then go back to enjoying their evening.

We both look around a little anxiously as we make our exit; once out of the building, we practically run to the limo.

Next thing you know, it's a whirlwind. James drives fiercely, and we're moving in and out of traffic. "We're being followed!" he yells. There are clothes in the back under the seats. "Take off your outfits and change. Leave the evening wear there." We're moving so fast, but I can just make out a section near Grand Central Station. James announces, "We're going into the tunnels now. We'll stop in about a minute and a half. Jump out, let the two look-a-likes in, and ask the taxi driver standing there if he's Emmanuel. If he says, 'No, but do you need a taxi?' you say 'Yes,' and he'll take you home. I know all of these people. If he says he is Emmanuel, get out of there as soon as you can and call for the police. Do you understand?"

We're changing quickly, getting our clothes off, both Dr. Janus and I trying to look in the opposite direction so as not to embarrass the other. With certain quick turns, it's impossible for us not to rub elbows. I've just slipped the sweats on, and my high heels are totally out of place, but the only choice I have. James yells, "Now!" He pulls to the side, we jump out, two people jump in, and the cab driver is there ready to go. He says he's not Emmanuel, and we're off.

Dr. Janus and I just sit there stunned. Neither one of us knows what to say, so we just pray we're being taken home safely. I'm impressed with James's skills but nervous that it has come to this.

The only thing the taxi driver says is, "We're going the long way home and will meet up with James at the train station so he can take you the rest of the way home. He'll call me if anything changes."

I've no idea what to do, what to say, and I remain silent. So unlike me.

I start flipping through the Playbill and sure enough, it had been autographed. This will be a neat memento. Then, carefully folded up in the section where there's an envelope to make donations, is the next piece of artwork.

I nudge Dr. Janus and point. He shakes his head, motioning for me not to look at it now. I agree.

We get to the Dobbs Ferry train station, which feels oddly déjà vu, and James is waiting for us. No look-a-likes to be seen, we get into the back of the limo, opening the doors ourselves.

"Good work, guys."

Then Dr. Janus and James look at me and say in unison, "What happened back there?"

I explain everything about the waiter and the playbill, and we unfold the clue to look at it further. It's not anything concrete.

Then James starts joking with me. "Well, I guess when we ask you to make a scene, you sure know how to follow through!"

"Slightly," I say, laughing. "I had no intention of hitting the poor waiter in the face and bringing down the entire tray of champagne glasses. I was afraid I was going to laugh."

"We thought we would too," says Dr. Janus; then he turns serious. "What do you make of all this, James? Were we really in danger, or was the man a set up?"

"I don't know. I want both of you to make note of what the waiter looked like in case we need to try to sketch him. But, I truly don't know. What would be the point of going out into public to get the next clue when they could have just delivered it?"

We silently shake our heads.

James starts the limo and gets us safely home. I'm exhausted from the event.

I have so many questions for Dr. Janus and feel as though I haven't learned a thing. All that money in one room that could feed twenty starving nations. Some seemed nice, some dutiful, and most were just playing the game, acting the part. Just like I had. I smile to myself thinking about the scene I'd made.

Some interesting conversations had occurred that evening, nature versus nurture, but most were discussions on getting old and the drug upon drug people are taking, issues of depression and fatigue, blah, blah, blah, each one bragging about how well their medicine works and how others should switch. With so many doctors there, I wondered how many of them were on drugs themselves.

But had we learned anything? Did we speak to the right people? Was the waiter a setup from the beginning? What is all this about? It makes no sense.

"We're going into the study for a drink. Would you like to join us, Mags?" says Dr. Janus as he enters through the foyer.

"Not tonight," abruptly comes out.

I had been dressed up, had feigned fainting, been lied to, had my life allegedly put in danger, been part of a car chase, swapped cars in an underground tunnel, and was now back safe and sound. This is no game. I have the next clue but feel too worked up to even look over it any further.

They head to the study. I head toward the first step of the stairs and am so tired that, without realizing what's happening, my foot gets stuck, and I trip out of one of my heels. I manage to grab the banister before really hurting myself. I look down and see to my surprise that my heel is in an indent in the floor. "Oh great, now I've ruined the beautiful mosaic floor," comes out with no one to hear it. I bend down and see that it's stuck right in the center of the serpent's eye. Ironic, since I'm not intuitively "seeing" anything. At closer glance as I pull the heel out, it appears as though the indentation is purposeful.

Relieved and thinking nothing much more of it, I head up to bed. I manage to get the sweats off and put my head to the pillow. I think about how fortunate I've been to have experienced such an artistic evening and survive. The note progressions fill my head as I think of the queen arising from the depths of the underworld at the Met. I fall asleep with my under garments on, not even making it all the way under the covers. The last thought I have is, *What am I doing here, and again, why me?*

chapter
28

Man can hardly recognize the devils of his own creation.

Albert Schweitzer

ays were flying by for Tess, and she wished she had a calendar to let her know how long she had been a captive. She had been diligent in her reading, and this day she began to think on all the circumstances that had transpired at the convent. She needed to ask for forgiveness one time from Christ. She wanted her sins to be erased from the Book of Life. There were so many terrible things like penances for mealtime infractions. There

were simple reprimands given for bad behavior, like having to kneel through dinner versus sitting, and there were cruel ones, like having to lie on the floor at the entrance for the other sisters to step over and to kiss the feet of the Mother Superior. *That was humiliation,* she thought, *not the teaching of humility.* She felt sick at having followed some of those rules.

She thought of the sisters who had sent letters home that never "arrived." Weddings, funerals, and special events missed because leave was not granted. She thought about a situation that made her run away for a couple of weeks. One of her sisters had suffered terribly through an illness, but no physician was called in because all were made to believe she was being non-virtuous by seeking attention. They were told no money was available for her to be cared for, so she died. Tess knew it was an unnecessary death. She was so sure about it that she wrote to the pope for a letter of release, but all she got back was a letter of denial—"No grounds for such a request"—and from the Cardinal came a letter reminding her that correcting her own wrongs in her own way would only lead to more penance, more humiliation in front of others, and, worst of all, admonition to the entire convent. A letter was then sent to everyone, reminding them it was a mortal sin to leave the church after the vows had been taken.

An evil thought came into her mind that this convent probably didn't want her to leave because of her trust fund. Of course, she had to live daily with the fact the Mother Superior *never* forgave her for that reprimanding attention from the Cardinal. Mother Superior even went so far as to make her an example and claim she had been seduced by evil spirits and needed to be cleansed of her ill thinking by the monsignor. The other nuns felt terrible for Tess that she had been so weak as to let the devil enter her. They were all relieved when the monsignor was successful in the exorcism.

The disillusionment, the hypocrisy, the real lack of life started to weigh heavy on her heart. Her thoughts were cycling and anger was building when suddenly she heard the voice. No hello, no quick idle chatter, but an immediate lecture pursued.

"First, you were taught about papal supremacy and their infallibility and that, according to the Catholics, Christ made Peter the first pope to head the church on earth with this infallible authority. The pope, as Christ's representative on earth, guided all people, Catholic or not, into all truth. This is according to the Vatican Council 1, 1870.

"Then you were taught that any Christian, meaning specifically someone who believes in Christ, who is not a Catholic, is a separated brethren. They are lesser people because they have not learned the ways of the Catholic Church. This is a judgment call, but we ignore we were told not to judge. God very clearly told Job not to judge because where were we when He created the earth? Are we able to loose the bands of Orion or create the Pleiades? No. Therefore God is the final judge, not us.

"Some Catholics are even told that the Protestant churches are corruptions of the Catholic Church. Remember, for every truth one is told, an answer is in the Bible to prove it, and your heart, where God implanted all truths, will confirm this, if you seek the truth and not just the convenient truth.

"God has promised to be the same, yesterday, today, and forever. He never changes. Therefore His Word, if interpreted correctly, never changes. Beware because Scripture is often taken out of context. That is why you must go out and read and learn and get the answers yourself. The Word must infiltrate your core.

He continued without even a pause, "Now as for religion, beware; there is one line in the Bible that the Catholic Church is built upon and that line is taken out of context. It says ... the one true church founded on Saint Peter as quoted from the gospel,

'That thou are Peter and upon this I will build my church; and the gates of hell shall not prevail against it.' That is found in Matthew 16:18. But no explanation is given to you as to how this is taken out of context. I will leave this up to you to research so as not to influence your final thoughts.

"If you are going to read the Bible, you need to get the words in order, the definitions in order, and read it verse by verse to follow the subject all the way through, or you will believe the lies."

Tess was now sitting at the edge of the mattress, ready to take notes.

"So how is it that what the pope declares as infallible can change through the years? It is because, unlike God's Word, man is fallible. Could you imagine how awful it must be for God to hear anyone claim that Christ and His infallible Word needs an interpreter at a higher level, such as a pope? God wants to speak to all his children.

"Look into how the various popes changed their minds through the cultural, social, financial, and political pressures of the world. In May of 2008, it was announced that Catholics could finally believe 'aliens' might exist. That seems so odd, since there are numerous religious paintings that depict UFOs, dating from the sixteenth century. Those are quietly packed away though. We try not to talk about or look at those in public!

"First the popes said that nuns must wear habits, but now that isn't necessary. They said that nuns addressed a higher calling, but now it is the responsibility of all Catholics. For some time, it was okay for self-mutilation to occur, but now it is not. To my mind, a truth is 100-percent truth, or it is not truth. It will never change. People may try to reinterpret or misinterpret religion, but follow it back to the source and the inspired work, and truth can never be defamed. 'And ye shall know the truth, and the truth shall make you free.'

"If one knows history at all, the Council of Trent declared in 1545 that the church tradition was equal in authority to that of the Bible. It clearly was not until after Vatican II, the Second Vatican Council, that it became acceptable for people, priests, and nuns to study the actual gospel."

She interrupted. "I didn't even realize that rule was changed and that women can now study it." She should have been taught this at the convent. This *simple* change had been conveniently neglected in her strict setting. She was annoyed.

Without missing a beat he said, "God does not want us to suffer, to be deceived here on earth. He meant it when He said the truth would set us free. He wants us to lie down in green pastures for Him to restore our souls. Not because we are physically dead and are having Psalm 23 read to us at the grave site, but because we walk on earth among the spiritually dead, and He promises that if we ask, He will remove all fear and walk with us in beauty on this earth, despite the deception and poverty, and He will restore us to more than we could have ever imagined if we just have that 'unseen' thing called faith. This does not mean stupidity.

"That is why the Lord's Prayer in Matthew 6:9–13 says, 'Thy Kingdom come, thy Will be done on earth as it is in Heaven.' It is not for the day when we are dead, but it is for now, to manifest His strength, claim our childhood right, our blood heritage through Christ's death, and enjoy it on earth now.

"But we don't bother to learn that we have been foretold all things, so we keep seeking new answers through all sorts of sick, man-made professions and practices. We think we need psychics and soothsayers because we don't understand our purpose. The destruction caused because of this is so great and so scary, I think it is even too much to tell you about now."

Tess blinked for a moment, and her old spunk came back. She mumbled, "Oh really, too much to tell me about now? You've opened my eyes and shattered my entire life and way of thinking, and *now* it's too much to tell me?" But he was talking so fast, he didn't hear.

"So instead, let us look at how honorably, both socially and morally, our Roman Catholic Church has responded in history. Few pay attention to this, or they shuffle it under the carpet since it is too uncomfortable to hear. The death of Pope John Paul I in 1978 could have opened all of our eyes, but did it? The pope wanted to return the church to its rightful spiritual purpose, so he refused to wear the priceless jeweled tiara or even to ride in the papal sedan. He wrote his own speeches, not wanting his thoughts and beliefs changed by anyone. This did not please the Curia, so in retaliation they stopped printing his words and speeches in the Roman Catholic daily newspapers. I believe in the U.S. we would call this censorship and a violation of our first amendment rights, but how many people remember him and his plight now? How many people even realized they had stopped printing his words?

"Does it remind you of any situations in the United States, such as with our presidents? John F. Kennedy was pushing against a system, not playing by the big boys' rules, and some alleged he was ready to spill the beans about the presidency and *bang;* he was dead. This was not some lone shooter, and anyone stupid enough to think it was is deceived or has blinders on. In my opinion, our own agencies took him down. He was a risk to those in power behind the scenes, or so some claim. But remember, all but one of the numerous theories and explanations are false. It's just unclear which one is true."

Tess stood up, shocked at what she had just heard. *Inside job? What on earth could he mean?* Her parents adored J.F.K. Could this be true? This man had to be psycho. "How dare you cut down my church and a man like Kennedy, whose heart was truly devoted to the American people, and accuse our government of

such terrible things?" She even surprised herself with the anger that emerged.

"I'm sorry," he said. "There's too much to teach you, but for now I need to stay focused on the church history. The underhanded manipulation and outright deceit did not just start in the 1970s. If one traces history back to the nineteenth century and the time of the Italian revolution, one discovers that the Roman Catholic Church was stripped of its power, but somehow, miraculously, Pope Pius XI (1922–1939), through a Lateran Treaty in 1929, was able to have the papacy's temporal sovereignty restored at the Vatican. But, before we get too far into this, what year was the stock market crash in the United States? Surprise, surprise, 1929. Were they tied together somehow? No one has even bothered to make that connection."

Tess could not even imagine how these two things could be related. She was dazed for a second but knew she didn't have a clue about the stock market so opted just to write down a note about it. She would have to get someone more knowledgeable to answer that question one day.

"However, back to the point. How did this 'pius' pope do it? He handed over the Italian nation to the demented warmonger Mussolini and allowed a national battle with much bloodshed in return for eighty million dollars. Today that is equal to about five hundred million dollars."

He paused, took what sounded like a sip of a beverage, and said, "So I suppose in the pope's ideology, it was fine to destroy a nation with Roman Catholics included as long as the Catholic Church got its power back and lots of money to go with it. What is even scarier is what he did with the money. His first move was to set up the Vatican Bank, which was created with rules and regulations only it had to follow. This has continued through the years.

"Pope Paul VI, who served in the Vatican State Department from 1922–1954 and was pope from 1963 to his death in 1978, was another great example of one who was involved in every sick scheme in existence to move the wealth, grow the wealth, and take charge of international banking. His main connection was a banker, Michele Sindona from Sicily, who worked with Lucio Gelli. Lucio was a well-known member of the Illuminati who headed the P2 Masonic Secret society. It had ties at the time with the Mafia and the Gambino family. They dealt with drugs, mostly heroin, but nothing was out of reach. Tax evasion, money laundering, and sordid deeds that left a trail of assassinations and bribes, all in the name of amassing and controlling Italian and international banks as part of shell corporations created by the mob, done to keep the Vatican looking clean."

Tess was fascinated but couldn't help thinking how strange it was to be kidnapped and then preached to.

"The most amazing thing was that the Vatican was even able to pull off creating a law so the Vatican did not have to report the massive wealth it had scammed, thus bypassing the need to pay taxes. That way the Roman Catholics and Italian people could never learn how much money had been swindled into the Vatican. Imagine having to tell the world that the income on interest owed to the Italian people was millions, if not billions, of dollars and was being withheld totally from the little people who were still suffering to pay taxes, many even living in poverty."

Her heart broke to hear this about the poor. She became a nun to help the poor and the sick, not to make their lives worse. Could the Catholic Church have really done some of these things? Surely, if this happened, this has all been repaired by now. She was about to comment, but the voice wouldn't stop.

"Did you ever ask why John Paul I, who met with Cardinal Villot and said he was going to expose all of this on September

28, 1978, after succeeding Pope Paul VI, reigned for only thirty-three days?" The voice paused and said, as if telling her something she might not understand, "Thirty-three is a sick joke on Christ's age when crucified, the number for the pope was in days, not years, when he died at 4:30 a.m., sitting up in bed clutching documents, with a low blood pressure medicine on the stand next to him? Who found him? Villot, of course, who covered up the entire situation and passed it off as a heart attack. This wasn't so hard since through embalming, draining the blood and removing certain organs, within twelve hours, even though the canon law says it can't be done sooner than twenty-four hours, he could get away with it. How are they able to break these laws, kill their own popes, and still live with themselves? Easy. Money. Con the population, sell millions of dollars of trinkets, Mass cards, Rosaries, merchandise. Appear as though you are good and working for God, and you can get away with anything."

He paused and then fired up again. "How can you honor a system based on fraud and lies like that? Why is it that, to this day, the Vatican will not disclose their fortunes and where they are all held? Why are at least fifty miles of books/documents hidden under the Vatican that teach many secret and hidden things that go as deep as witchcraft, incantations, spells, aliens, and other such things? Where are the 'real' set of accounting books and systems in the church and not the cooked books? Why are priests able to do exorcisms and others not able to, or so we are told?

"This deception and control is happening here in the United States too, not just in Italy. Look into the Illuminati, the controlling families such as the Rockefellers and the Rothschilds, and more and more you will see how strong the entire ambidextrous plan runs. The closed-off areas of prominent museums; the heroin and drugs held at Fort Knox; the viruses and vaccines from the supposed swine flu, polio, avian flu, etc.; the gold of which no one even knows how much is in there; the hidden files on the assassination of Kennedy, the proof of alien visitors, and the list goes on.

"When things are secret and hidden, there is danger. When fear can be put into people because the pope is made to look as if he is the savior and can rescue a community and nations praying to him, because he is a man of faith, what is really going on? Or when the president is expected to solve the woes of the world behind layers of corruption so thick each move is thwarted, and the people are no longer being honored or listened to, that is when we are in serious trouble.

"Not only do we accept this, but we give the church accolades, veneration, and honor, so aren't we part of the problem? I understand the separation of church and state, but this is absurd. Just like you, Tess, the people can't live in isolation and lies any more, or we the people are part of the problem.

Tess stopped for a minute and looked up to the speaker where the electronic voice resonated. *He has to be American,* she thought. *He said, "We the people."* She was ready to confront him, but thought he was on such a roll he might let more slip, yet at the same time she felt like she had been physically attacked.

He had worked himself up so had no choice but to slow down, pulling into the station at last, she hoped. "Now you understand why we are warned that we suffer from lack of knowledge and need to be wise like the serpent. The evil ones that are doing this to us, the wolves in lamb's clothing, are truly worshiping the greatest deceiver of all, Lucifer."

A heavy sigh could be heard behind the electronics again. "How do I know? I was part of the evil group with their sick perversions and initiations. The privileged one laughing at the masses, until I realized I was set up just like everyone else;

now, as a liability, when I finish their dirty work and get them the info they need from your father and brother, we will all be exterminated."

Tess knew the word *exterminated* should make her lose it, but she just couldn't muster up any more energy to respond. She wanted to lash out, to say how wrong it was, but her voice had gotten lost. It had been buried years before and still could not make it to the surface to attack what he was telling her. The most she could get out was, "All this history is overwhelming. I am so sorry, but my head is whirling. I don't know how much more I can take."

And to her utter amazement, he said, with what sounded like compassion, "I understand. I'll try not to attack you any more for now, but unfortunately, I do need to ask you some more questions."

He eventually started again, softly. "Did you remember anything at all about the house, the books, your dad's research?"

She responded, trying to be helpful, "It sounds so obscure, but the only thing I could remember was his poem about the sunflowers." She repeated it.

"Where did he keep this?"

"Upstairs in the 'open room' to the right."

He did not question this. *Odd,* Tess thought. *He didn't ask where that is. He must know. Could it really be someone close to our family?*

She wanted the conversation to turn personal. She now wanted to confess her secret. Her kidnapper had to know quite a bit about her because of the sunflowers. Tess was going to share to see if she could drag out who it was and what this was all about.

And then, as if it had read her mind, the voice asked, "What brought you to the Roman Catholic faith in the first place? I mean, did you question the faith, or did you just go?"

"I guess I just went because my family was Roman Catholic and I assumed that is what one did. As a young child, I went to catechism, enjoyed services, prayed on my own, felt I was a good Catholic, and by being a good Catholic, after I had repented for sins I suffered for, it brought me to a life I wanted. To only be married to God, to do good for Him was all that mattered. The natural choice was going to a convent," she responded. "Also, there was always a veil of secrecy over my family, excuse the pun, so much alone time, so the veil of Christ at the convent made some sense."

"So this was all of your own choice," he pried, pushing for more, as if knowing there was more behind it.

She hesitated, and then taken over with not wanting to lie, she said, "Well, there was a situation that forced me to need to leave home, so it was agreed upon, mostly by my father, but we all decided it would be best in the end."

"But this was a cloistered convent in the 1970s, after nuns had been given some freedoms by Vatican II. You could have gone to a community and been part of society, but you chose solitude, why?"

"Circumstances," she said slowly. "Circumstances outside of my control made it necessary for me to be away." She carefully phrased every word, trying not to place blame. Thinking now to herself how it was odd that her father was so persistent about this convent. She offered, thinking aloud, "But I, I chose to keep my name."

"If you were being hidden due to this 'circumstance,' wasn't it a bit risky keeping your consecrated name as Thérèse?"

"I never really thought about it that way," she said. "I loved my name. I loved the Saint Thérèse, and so, with Mother Superior's approval, I kept it."

"And how often did you see your family after that?"

"It was five years before both my parents came to visit. My dad had come on his own a couple times before that for brief 'business' trips. It was a strict order that only allowed you to go home if someone who was saved by the Catholic Church was dying. My parents both died so suddenly that I wasn't even able to make it for that."

"And your brother, how did he feel about you not coming home?"

"I don't truly know. I never asked him. He is my older brother and has always been in charge. This is the rule of the church, and so we follow it. He thinks the entire choice of going to the convent was mine."

"So then you are saying it wasn't."

Tess second-guessed her desire to speak and wondered if she had said way too much. She walked over to her sunflowers. She stared at the perfect center for a few minutes and then said, "I can't discuss it. What does this have to do with why I am being held captive here anyway?"

"All in due time."

Then she heard a strange sound through the electronic speaker as if a phone was ringing. He forgot to turn the speaker off, and she heard, "No, not now, it is too soon. I need more time."

Without thinking, the voice came on and said, "Tessie, I have to go, unexpectedly. There is still much that needs to be answered and discussed."

And at that exact moment, sunflower in hand, hearing, "Tessie," from the voice, she knew who it was.

chapter

29

Behold, I give you the power to tread on serpents
and scorpions, and over all the power of the enemy,
and nothing shall by any means hurt you.

Luke 10:19, KJV

ime is slipping away, but this morning
I awaken early, and by 6:00 a.m. I'm
already deeply entrenched in the clues.
I'm starting to catch on. I know I'll be
meeting with the boys at 7:30 a.m. so
want to get as much done as possible to
be prepared. I still need to get into something more comfortable,
brush my teeth, and get the mob of hair back in order. I throw
on my sweats and a T-shirt and then take the art piece with me

to the office to scan. I'll relinquish it to James in hopes of finding some fingerprints.

I'm beginning to see the themes of the zodiac, of the individual way, and this is obviously Sagittarius holding the bow aimed at the scorpion's stinger. I immediately send over the artwork to my friend to see what they mean. I run down briefly to look at the constellations in the entrance to remember how all the months and the signs are lined up. I smile when I see Leo and then Virgo, just as the scholar had said. Then at the door or six o'clock is Libra, Scorpio, then Sagittarius. So far we've gone from the lion to the virgin, Leo/Virgo, to the scales of Libra, to the archer of Sagittarius. I don't know if that's significant but make note of it.

I run back upstairs and find an e-mail explaining that although this appears to be the sign of Sagittarius, the way it is drawn with the scorpion's stinger and constellations brought to mind some verses in the Bible and 'biblical truths' he thought I should be aware of, after he clarified for me that the Hebrew name for the constellation Ophiuchus is "Akrab," which means Scorpion. The e-mail reads:

From the New Testament...
"Behold, I give unto you power to *tread on serpents and scorpions,* and over all the power of the enemy: and nothing shall by any means hurt you." (Luke 10:19)
and from Revelation...
"And they had tails like unto scorpions, and there were stings in their tails: and their power *was* to hurt men five months." (Revelation 9:10)
It helps to know Hebrew because the word for 'subdue' is *kabash,* which means to tread down as is used in the first verse listed above. It can also mean to conquer, to subjugate, and to bring into bondage. In the garden of

Eden, in the beginning, there's no illness, no sorrow, no limitation, and "sin" had not yet been introduced. Original sin did not enter until Satan seduced Eve, and we are not talking in that ridiculous story of a serpent handing Eve an apple. There's never an apple in the garden of Eden! How people can still teach this in Sunday school is crazy. Satan had sex with Eve when she was "betrothed" to Adam. She committed adultery, and, in this act, she was pregnant with fraternal twins, one from Satan and one from Adam: Cain and Abel.

I gasp as I read this. I've never heard such a bizarre story. I did know, however, that, though it's rare, twins can have two different fathers.

The scholar's familiar words reverberate in my head, "Too much to get into now because you'll never believe me."

His e-mail continues.

So what God is saying is that, despite this deception and Eve's error, mankind does not have to pay for the sin of disobeying God any more since Christ died on the cross, and if you accept Jesus, you can be saved for all but the "unforgivable sin." This will take too long to explain. The top line "hamartia," as on the artwork, is Greek and means the *art of archery,* and the translation for sin is "missing the mark!" Isn't that beautiful?

Skipping over the entire apple, twin, and Satan sex thing, I quickly type, "Can I call you? Where can I reach you?" As I wait for a response from the e-mail, I wonder what the "unforgivable sin" is and then assume it's suicide.

In a matter of moments, he replies, I pick up my cell phone, and, rushing through the niceties, get right to the point. "You

mean this horrible thing of sin we hear about in strict churches God really means as missing the mark, like in archery, and not some damnation type act?"

"What do you think of that?"

"It makes sense. I like that definition."

"Our Creator knows that when we're off our path, things don't work well for us. He wants us to sail through life and prosper, but this can only be done if we get in proper alignment and hit the mark. You know when you're there because you feel peace and understanding you never thought existed. The world could be falling apart around you, and you feel free."

I'm getting another new interpretation from the Jewish man.

As if hearing my thoughts, he says, "No, this isn't a Jewish or Christian thought." He returns to the picture. "See the tail of the scorpion on the right? The stinger? That's called the *hypodermic* aculeus, or venom-injecting barb. Then look to the opposite side of the picture, and if we pull through the artist's fondness for putting evil to the left, a *hypodermic* needle, with some form of fluid, is depicted. Of course, it helps to read Hebrew because the lettering to the left reads Satan, and to the right it reads Ehyeh Asheh Ehyeh, which is the sole response given to Moses when he asks God what He would like to be called, and His response means 'I am that I am.'

"Following along a Hebrew train of thought, Lesaith, noted as a constellation to the lower right, is fascinating because in Hebrew the sting is called 'lesath,' which means 'the perverse,' like Satan. Now look above Lesaith to Ophiuchus, the other constellation noted in the picture. Ophiuchus is inspiring in its own right. It is often depicted as a man holding a snake and his heel is holding down the scorpion with the stinger at his heel. In Greek mythology Ophiuchus was one of the gods held in the highest esteem for being a medical healer, the physician, or 'the one who brings the cure.' It is actually the symbol of the snake wrapped around him that is used in medicine today, the caduceus. However, this is just another sick perversion because the truth depicted in the constellations from the beginning of this universe is that Christ would come and overcome the serpent, thereby becoming the true universal healer or physician.

"Also, Ophiuchus is located around the celestial equator and, translated from Greek, means the snake-holder. Interestingly, it is a zodiacal constellation, one that the sun passes through yearly, but oddly enough, it has never been named as an astrological sign. It's located opposite of Orion—" and then he cuts himself off. "Anyway," this time he skips the phrase about how long it would take to explain, "in the real constellations the arrow is aimed at the heart of Scorpio and is mentioned in Psalm 64:7–9 when it talks about God shooting an arrow and wounding the enemies, but in this artwork, where does the arrow go to hit its mark? What's that a picture of?" He pauses.

I look carefully at the artwork I'm clutching in my hand, and honestly, I can't really tell. It looks kind of like an alien form, and I say so!

He laughs. "No, nothing that sinister! It's a depiction of the human brain."

"Oh my, you're right, I know what that is! It's the pineal gland. I remember it from neuropsych class as the place where dreams come from and where we have access to our 'third eye' or unconscious, God-connected visions. I can't believe I couldn't see it."

"That's your area of expertise, not mine. What I can leave you with, though, is that our Creator is clear when He tells us our carnal mind is full of deadly venom, and the only place we can be controlled by evil forces is in the mind. There are many evil spirits that roam the earth, and they are not the Holy Spirit.

They exist and can be seen by some people in ethereal type visions, but as God said, they can only control us if we don't take power over them in Christ's name."

He had lost me again, and he knew it. "Don't worry about that now. My recommendation to you is to get to the bottom of what this person is teaching you. The scales of evil are tipped, something in that vial is deadly, and somehow he thinks the person he gifted these drawings to can make a change. That's a tall order, but, my dear, you are a tall woman, and I have faith you'll get to the bottom of it."

His humor. "If only I thought that was true."

We finish our conversation, and as usual, he's been a huge help. I want to get online and refamiliarize myself with the pineal gland but know I have to get downstairs to report on the latest artwork.

Once downstairs, James takes the third piece of artwork to have it fingerprinted. There's no new news from the kidnappers. We're really no further along. I wonder what else the artist is trying to tell us. My carnal mind's getting the best of me. I'm failing. I try telling myself to have faith, but these are empty words.

chapter
30

There is something fascinating about science. One gets such whole-sale returns of conjecture out of such a trifling investment of fact.

Mark Twain

 uesday arrives, and we're having company for dinner. I'm not the least bit interested but know I have to be astute and charming. I've asked Ana if there are any pants or skirts around I may borrow because I've run out of clean clothes. She directs me to some closets near the maids' quarters, and I'm able to find a couple of skirts that look like they'd been Tess's. They're almost long enough, and with the elastic bands around the waist,

they've a one-size fits all look. The shirts are easy. To my surprise, we seem to have the same broad shoulders. I head upstairs to change.

Coming back down, I enter the dining room to see Dr. Janus standing with a quirky-looking character by the chairs near the fireplace. Tall, very white or fair skinned, early fifties, gleaming gray-blue eyes, the piercing kind that remind you of wolf's eyes, and a sort of roughness, roguishness under a shy, unassuming exterior. I have clearly walked in as they are greeting each other.

"Saul, it's so good to see you." Dr. Janus in a full suit. This time a red necktie with a dark square design that gives him a more powerful air. He has such a perfect build; six foot four, about two hundred pounds and toned, not the least bit scrawny. His olive skin under the beard and perfectly trimmed hair, eyebrows, and ears makes him almost glow with health and vitality.

"It's been too long, Peter." This is the first time I hear someone refer to him by his first name since Sophia at the convent.

"It has. We all get busy, I suppose," he responds in a resigned manner; then he picks up a beat and says, "Well, we are here now, let us enjoy. Let me introduce you to a current colleague of mine, Dr. Magdalena LaSige. Magdalena, Saul was the assistant to my father while we were growing up. His other son."

"It's a pleasure." Saul sticks out his almost hairless, white-skinned arm to shake my hand. Blue veins are visible. His hand is warmer than I expect, as it looks lifeless.

I respond with a firm handshake and a, "Mine as well."

Moving from the fireplace, Dr. Janus motions for us to sit, again one on each side of him, and Saul sits in the chair where James had sat.

"What have you been up to, Saul?" And the conversation begins.

"Much of the same. Busying myself in the lab, working on patents and new pharmaceuticals and such. It's becoming a little too run of the mill for me. I miss having your father to spice things up."

"I miss them both too."

Ana comes in on cue, and the meal commences. My first shot at venison is a huge success. It's tender, melts in the mouth, and has absolutely no gamy flavor to it. The sauce is sweet but with a kick to it that takes a couple seconds to catch up. I would have never guessed it was some combination of Bourbon and Root Beer! I'll have to ask for the recipe.

As good as the food and service is, the high-class treatment is starting to lose its appeal. All the kidnapping, clues, secrecy, and the pressure of not knowing where Tess is or if she's even alive hangs so heavily on my heart. I want to get to the bottom of what Dr. Janus is doing because I've heard, from watching too many detective shows, that the longer kidnapping victims are held, the less chance there is of finding them alive and unharmed.

Dr. Janus catches up with Saul as if all was well with Tess and handles it with a perfect poker face. Saul asks me about my job and relationship to Dr. Janus, who explains that I had been his student. Saul remarks on how few visitors have come to this house, explaining that most had been invited to the other one, but how Theodore "Teddy" Janus had put so much work into constructing every detail of this place. "The observatory," he says, "is a masterpiece that needs to be experienced. Your father loved his constellations and the riddles of life."

"I will have to show her," Dr. Janus agrees.

"The stars are radiant this time of year. The only constellation that can't be fully appreciated from the Northern Hemisphere is The Scorpion, or Scorpio," he elucidates.

This catches my ear. "Scorpio? Really? Can't be seen completely; I never knew that!"

"Why," he says inquisitively, "does that mean something to you?"

"Not really," I did my best to cover, but I'd just realized that that was the missing constellation. We had Virgo, Libra, no Scorpio, and then Sagittarius. "I am just always fascinated by the thing that is the odd one out, doesn't match or follow a pattern."

"Hmm," he says, "you must be a scientist at heart."

Dr. Janus and I both burst out laughing, and I say, "With that, you could not be further from the truth!"

"Really?" he says, looking intrigued.

"Well, I almost failed all my biochemical, physics, and pharmacological classes, and I've Dr. Janus to attest to it." I pause, then fill in, "As if it's a badge of honor!"

"She's not really exaggerating," Dr. Janus gently emphasizes. "But she tried hard, worked hard, and always made it through the classes."

"A for effort," Saul says.

"C," I pipe in, "for 'Credit,' just get the credit and get out! There's no preferential treatment in Dr. Janus's class!"

We all chuckle and, as if in sync, take sips of our wine together.

"Science, however, isn't only about what one learns in the classroom," Saul continues. "It's about wanting to get to the bottom, the truth of things, and relooking at the facts we've been given. Analyzing them thousands of times over to find out if any basis, any starting point, is even true."

"That's an interesting way to put it," I say and mean it.

Saul continues. "Like Napoleon said, 'History is a set of lies agreed upon,' well, science is a set of 'facts' agreed upon, but often even the basic assumptions of these so-called facts are wrong. Look at the arguments over the start of life on earth, the Big Bang theory, evolution versus creation theory. They all slant their 'science' to fit their preconceived notion of the answer. Some even unconsciously."

I couldn't help but comment, "That's an interesting statement from a scientist, but you know, I've heard about that unconscious slant before. For example, in psychology, a study was done of people who were told to play with nine-month-old children in a video- and audio-taped environment. The children were picked at this age because the subjects couldn't really tell if they were a boy or a girl. So the researchers would take a girl, put her in a blue outfit, and give her to the subject, who was told simply to play and to bond with the child. Ninety percent of the time, the adult subjects played with trucks and picked male-dominant toys when the child had a blue hat on and picked dolls when the child had a pink hat on. This experiment went on for years, and although I can't remember the exact details, it has proven that even the people most sensitive to gender issues unconsciously repeat the same behavior. It's the same presupposition as only men being the income earners or the 'learned ones' in a family. It's why I always smile when people assume Dr. LaSige is a man. I must admit I've made the same *faux-pas* at times myself, and I should know better!"

Saul raises his eyebrows and takes another sip of the wine. He wipes his mouth with the napkin and starts to nervously wring it. "Well, the same goes for science, Magdalena. We're often given a set of rules to work from, but if the basic premise is wrong, how could the answer or outcome possibly be right or accurate? We operate daily under false assumptions, and it has gone so deep that not one of us even knows—we are being conned. I learned this from Peter's father, a brilliant man. Imagine, for example, in DNA, they say we have sixty-four chromosomes and some are junk. I tell you there's no junk DNA, my friends, none. I can't wait to see the expressions on scientists' faces when they start to get this fact! Don't you agree, Peter?"

"Well," Dr. Janus says, hedging, "it has been so long since I've had to think about the actual structure of DNA that I couldn't even form an opinion."

"Well, what do you teach in your courses?"

"Good point. We only spend a couple of hours on the basics of DNA and its structure. You are correct; we do mention the word, but never explain it much further. It isn't the purpose of the courses I teach."

"I see," Saul rebuts. "It isn't the purpose of your courses to teach the truth."

Now *this* is getting interesting! I want to jump up and hug Saul, while feeling sorry for Dr. Janus having to think this hard with all the other things going on his life. *Too bad, though,* I think, *I want to know his answer!*

"No," Dr. Janus carefully explains, while, unaware, loudly jabbing his venison, "it's not about getting to the bottom of truth, I suppose, but one must start somewhere in a course to get to the meat of the matter and teach the necessary lessons for the course." To my surprise, I notice that each man is holding a knife. It's a beautifully unconscious movement that makes the duel real. Neither has a clue he's giving himself away.

"And these courses, lessons, are essential for what exact purpose in life? And how can you get to the meat if the basic premise is a lie?"

"Well, it's not a *lie;* it's just unknown or unnecessary…junk per se. Anyway, I don't get paid to teach how people arrived at this 'fact.' I simply teach where we are to go with it now." A speck of meat flicks off the knife and onto the table. Dr. Janus carefully wipes it away with his napkin.

"But," says Saul, "you know those textbooks are old, outdated, and missing large amounts of information that those in charge don't want you teaching or haven't even learned themselves."

"I think that is an overgeneralization," Dr. Janus responds. "Ivy League colleges often have the best information available."

"They may have access to it, but they aren't necessarily allowed to use it," Saul rebuts him.

I want to butt in but don't want to distract Saul from his interesting perspective. I agree with it! The fencing picks up speed.

"Let's skip Ivy League for the moment and go back to elementary school. We teach that Christopher Columbus was the first one to discover America and arrive here when there's written documentation the Chinese had discovered it well before the 1400s and have maps to prove it! But we still teach it in our crazy school system! I often wonder if it's because we're afraid to give China credit and a Spaniard, or 'Frenchman paid for by Spain,' is more politically to our liking. Ridiculous, no?"

Saul continues, eying Dr. Janus, "Look at all the things we do in the name of science. It's not science, it's pseudo-science, politicized, jump-on-the-bandwagon type science with no real proof. People have long forgotten eugenics, where the lesser people were to be 'exterminated.' We even forget great men like F.D.R. and H. G. Wells supported this concept. This was crazy. No one even really knew what a gene was then, but it became the rage for some time. This concept of building a better gene base in mating was as crazy as thinking the earth was flat. However, everyone somehow started to think that if we got rid of the people who were 'useless,' the Down syndromes and the ill and the poor and the colored, we could rise above and create a better nation. How sick, how elitist, how Ku Klux Klan.

"It scares me when I see the papal wardrobes of the highest level and they have the same design as the KKK robes. It makes me wonder what they're really trying to tell us. I used to think in some of the same perverted ways and am now ashamed I looked down and judged other valuable people in such a way."

Dr. Janus eventually puts down the knife and says compassionately, "Saul, when did you become such a crusader? You were always so rational, so detail-oriented, so non-involved and quiet."

"Time, my dear Peter, I suppose time has both awakened and hardened me. I'm sorry, no more difficult talk; let's just enjoy our time together."

"Sounds good." Dr. Janus quickly moves to change the direction of the conversation with, "How about more wine. I've found the most delightful…" and a knowledgeable conversation pursues, but I'm only half-listening. It tastes wonderful. I have a warm sensation and am just so intrigued by this man Saul. Hours go by like minutes until Dr. Janus announces out of the blue that it's 10:00 p.m. and since it had been a long day he would like to retire for the evening. "But don't let me interrupt your evening. You both seem to have much in common. Enjoy the fireplace, have a night cap, and don't rush."

"Are you up for more, Magdalena?"

"Sure."

Saul looks to Dr. Janus, "It has been a most delightful evening," he asserts. We all stand.

Dr. Janus walks toward him, saying, "You know what, Saul, it was nice. I suppose I've missed family conversations these past few years. We will have to do it again, sooner rather than later." There's a genuine sincerity in his voice and a deep look of caring in his eye. "I've missed having you around."

"You too, my brother, you too." They clasp hands heartily, as if they were saying good-bye forever.

chapter

31

History is a set of lies agreed upon.

Napoleon Bonaparte

aul and I move over to the comfy seats by the fireplace, and he has already gotten us brandy. He sits a little tentatively and then starts with "So you are a psychologist, Magdalena?"

"Was. I *was* a psychologist. I actually gave that profession up mostly due to social and financial injustices," and I launched into the canned speech I had given Dr. Janus on the way to France, adding, "To me, this was a political game, and as long as I was ethical and making that 'honest living for a hard day's work,' I would be okay. This meant two jobs, full-time courses as a student, and never having enough money to do fun things, all with the false belief that when I got my degree, my life would be perfect and fall in place. Well, my life didn't just fall in place, nor did most others' I knew, but the debt sure piled up, just like clockwork! So who had time to worry about whether or not there was any truth to all this? Bills needed to be paid." I realize I'm speaking more to myself than to him.

Saul seems intrigued anyway and just watches and listens as I motor mouth my way through.

His head gently tilts and a smile forms, and when I finish the canned speech part, I say, "You know, Saul, the sad thing is I used to be a great therapist. It's too bad being able to make a living came in the way of it," I babble on. "It was my fear of being able to survive and pay *my* taxes, combined with changes in insurance practices and managed-care issues causing my salary to take a nose dive, that eventually got the best of me. I went from earning $30,000 per annum at the hospital as a Ph.D. psychologist with the possibility of only ever being allotted 4 percent raises for the rest of my career there, to $150,000 in private practice, back down to $40,000 when managed care took over. Forty thousand seems reasonable until you subtract business expenses, small business fees, health, disability, and life insurance out of your own pocket. I was netting less than $8,000 per year, working ninety hours a week, minimally, and was a living example of doing all the right things and ending up living below the Federal poverty level, even with three degrees and numerous awards.

"Today, the poverty level is $10,400 per individual and $14,000 per couple. Back then, it was still $8,500 per American family per year. This was a confusing and devastating lesson to me, especially when I found out what salary I could make as a sales representative or even a level II secretary or clerk at a major pharmaceutical company, which nearly gave me a heart attack. I'm not degrading or devaluing any person's position, but one doesn't spend ten-plus years broke, studying, working, and denying themselves a life after high school to make less and less as one's professional abilities grow.

"I'm not the only person to whom this has ever happened, and I won't be the last! Some incredible psychologists and almost tenured professors, brilliantly published, have sold out in a second to pharmaceutical companies. In one career move, they made four times more in income, plus bonuses, travel, meals paid for, entertainment perks, and a lot less pressure. How could that be a healthy or balanced system? Who could refuse wanting to live a more comfortable life with less stress? So what if you didn't really believe in what you were pitching; or worse yet, you did really believe in what you were pitching, you just didn't realize the final product would be changed or used for different purposes when it was finally marketed. You had kids to pay for, a house, a car, debt, and you had to keep up to look the part, and by the time your work was implemented, you had no control to change it anyway." I finally suck in a deep breath and let it out in a frustrated growl. Turning my attention back to Saul, I see his attentive expression and smile sheepishly. "Oh, poor you, listen to me ramble."

"I'm enjoying it. And, I am sure you would be great at whatever you put your mind to."

I think about that for a couple of minutes then say, "Sure, as long as some 'professional' association isn't behind me pulling the strings. That's why I like the consulting business. I like the quick jobs; the learning about symbols and what they mean to other people. I'm also fascinated by what draws people to certain religions and how they come to believe what they believe. I mean

I believe in God, in Christ, in the spiritual things in the world, and I just wish others had a chance to learn about their options.

"Don't get me wrong, Saul, I'm not some religious God-freak out to change anyone, following some crazy, man-made religious cult, visiting church every Sunday like another controlled ant marching to its pesticidal ant house, going out of obligation like it was the only social event in town, hearing the same thing week in/week out.

"I'm just mesmerized by the workings of the universe, the earth, the human body, the mind, the stars; in awe that every snowflake, every fingerprint, and every DNA is just a little different; in awe of the signs and wonders of the world that we have either long forgotten or don't bother to look at any longer, since the history, politics, and lies we were force-fed have now become our 'truths.'"

Saul nodded, a man in full agreement. "Well, I hear you on that. I don't normally repeat myself; however, as I said at dinner, Napoleon Bonaparte said, 'History is a set of lies agreed upon.' I would have never believed this until recently, and now I think he could not have been more accurate."

My intuition perks up a bit, first at the fact he repeated a quote, which psychologically means he needs to be completely understood, and second at the "until recently" comment. I peer closer at my companion as I feel myself smiling in understanding at the familiar quotation and at him. "I so agree, Saul, and love that saying. You know history, what we know, how it repeats, how there is truly nothing new under the sun, should instill a sense of awe in everyone. That I respect; that I want more of. Perhaps that's why I keep seeking answers and clues to the meaning of life. That, combined with my eternal fascination with what makes each person tick. Speaking of which, tell me more about you. I have consumed this entire conversation."

My head cocks to the side, a quirk I've had since I was little. Any time my interest is captured, my head takes on the mannerisms of fowl.

"A conversation I have found much more enjoyable than most and much more interesting than my boring scientific life," he affirms.

I feel my face flush. It could have been the brandy, but I bet not.

"Oh," and then, interrupting even my own thoughts, not letting him have a chance to even share his story, I throw in, "You know, it's so weird being back in this area." Now I'm laughing at myself for not allowing him to get a word in, and he has a full grin on his face and finally some color in his cheeks.

"Go on," he graciously interjects.

"I used to live in Dobbs Ferry, and I'd heard conspiracy theories to a degree through the years, but never really paid much attention to them. Things like, the government is suppressing cures for cancer and has let AIDS flourish for profit, that there are secret agendas and the controlling groups such as the Federal Reserve Board, the FDA, and other groups are just a front for more greed, money, and power. I had heard stories of the Illuminati, the ties to the Trilateral Commission, Skull and Bones Society, the Council on Foreign Relations, the Bilderbergers, the Rothchilds, the Rockefellers, and the list goes on, but other than some basic interest in religious secret societies, I'd never really become that involved. Saul, you seem upfront, what do you think?"

His enthrallment is obvious. He leans forward and almost giddily whispers, "Which conspiracy theories? I've followed most of them."

I now can't wait to hear his response. I feel like a little kid about to get good gossip. The gossip I normally try to avoid, but

tonight I can't seem to control myself. "Oh, like the Rockefellers and the Bilderberg meetings."

He leans in even further and with an eerie expression, that makes his eyes look even more wolflike, he says, after glancing around for privacy, "They're real; they happened and are still happening. And we swindled Americans sit back and let them occur right before our eyes. We're still so naïve we believe the Federal Reserve is a Federal agency and don't even know it was secretly swapped into private hands at secret meetings of the Bilderbergers and others as early as November 23, 1913. There are many things going on under the radar in our country, the question is, which one does a person tackle and how does one start to make change?"

He's so intense he makes me a little nervous. So because I'm not sure what he meant by the Fed, I move to the second part of his statement about how one goes about choosing one's battles and try to lighten the conversation, "That's my everlasting question. I think it starts with choosing to get educated on certain topics and then not allowing society or government to dictate what to believe or how to live. Treat thy neighbor like thyself. That's why I want to be rich, though, so I can help educate people, show them the lies we've been fed."

"Be careful what you ask for, Magdalena, because the world is not what it seems and you might just get what you want, not fully realizing that what you asked for is not going to flow with those in control and may not be for your highest and best good as an individual. Unfortunately," he said with a huge sigh, "I learned that lesson too late."

"Don't be ridiculous, you're only in your fifties!"

A small smile curved at his lips. "Fifty-six, actually, but sometimes you just know when your time is up."

Concerned, I look at him and say softly, "Why, are you sick?"

He sits back and laughs nervously. "No, I've just been dealt a joker that I never saw coming."

I jump in, "Well hand it back and turn it into a King!"

He cocks his head, and I note how amazing it is that when we are in conversations and relating to people we often mimic the other person's behaviors. "Oh, to be young. Anyway, it's too late, maybe in my next lifetime."

"It's never too late," comes out robotically because I feel like I've just been passed along a warning of some sort.

"I used to believe that." He lets out another long sigh that shows he's not ready to share. "However, speaking of late, I should be a gentleman and dismiss myself. It has been an intriguing and enjoyable evening."

"I apologize for gabbing so much, I must have needed to vent."

"No apologies necessary."

As he stands he puts the empty glass on the table and I do the same. We head down the hallway, and when we get to the main entrance, Saul looks up and exclaims, "Oh my, I had forgotten how the stars glimmer down on the mosaic floor, highlighting each letter with the changing of the seasons and days."

I take a closer look and excitedly agree, "You're right! I'd never noticed that before," and catching myself before explaining too much and getting myself in trouble, I say, "Lovely to have met you," while then glancing back up to the stream of light.

"Lovely to have met you too! I look forward to meeting again soon."

"It will be my pleasure."

He then looks me directly in my eyes, long and hard, and says, "There's an uncanny resemblance of your face to someone I've met, but I just can't place who it is."

"Oh, everyone does that!" I say, laughing. "A couple days ago someone thought I was a nun!" Oops, too much information. But hey, he wouldn't know. The wine and then the brandy. I knew better. It made me a confessor of all!

He smiles. "Have a good night. Oh and by the way, I'm glad to hear you enjoyed the Met. I see you still have the necklace on!"

"Oh, the necklace," I reach up. "I'd totally forgotten about it."

"It's lovely. Mrs. Janus used to wear it to special events."

"Were you there?"

"As a matter of fact, I was. A charming evening but with just a little too much social gossip for my liking. I left at the first intermission. I do love those alchemical operas though."

Not sure what he means, but thinking some of his thoughts are as strange as mine, I say, "Probably a good thing, I mean leaving early; the second half of the show was nowhere near as good as the first." I'm lying. I have no idea how the second part ended. I hadn't wanted him to have seen any of my drama, and apparently he hadn't.

"Saul, do you know what the necklace says? I mean, is it some form of writing?"

"Yes, as a matter of fact, it is. It's the old Templar language, and it says, '*I Oppose Deception.*'"

"I oppose deception. I *love* that!"

"So did Mrs. Janus, so did she," repeating himself and rubbing his boney hands together. "Well, goodnight then."

"Goodnight," I say as I impulsively reach over and give him a hug. It's awkward, though, and I feel funny.

He blushes slightly and turns to leave. "Oh, by the way, there's an envelope sent through me with the request to give it to Dr. Janus. I think he left it in the dining room, so will you remind him?"

"An envelope?" I try to act nonchalant. "No problem."

Saul exits. I close the door, run to the dining room. It's still there on the chair by the fireplace. I open it, and it's yet another piece of artwork. This time it says, "Beware of the Scorpion's Sting." I get a chill, but I don't have time to look too closely because I have to get back to the entrance to see the reflections. My gut tells me I'm on to something.

I get back, and the way the light reflects is astonishing. How had I not noticed that before? I then spot a ray that hits a letter on the floor in the mosaic and notice for the first time some letters are larger than others. I follow the saying,

Bless Those Who Enter,

For Within All People Unveil Their

True Nature, And All Things Have

Been Foretold. Beware Of The…

and one by one, because of the reflection, I notice the larger letters start to spell S-E-R-P and realize all spelled out it says, "Beware of the … Serpent."

I know that "serpent" has so many meanings attached to it from various myths and religions. Its interpretations and unconscious meanings are endless. But it strikes me at this moment that there's more to the floor, to the constellations, and I dive onto the ground and start feeling around. I yell down the hall, "Dr. Janus, call James! Call him now. I need the drawings to the house and yards. I'm on to something. I'm sure of it."

I run upstairs to grab the other pieces of artwork and am down before he returns. "This is it!" I yell. "I'm getting it. Dr. Janus are you asleep … I'm getting it!"

Dr. Janus is coming down the stairs in a robe. "What is all the commotion? Are you okay?"

"Yes, yes, but I need you to call James." I'm on the floor feeling the ground.

"I see you got the artwork sent via Saul," Dr. Janus clarifies.

I hurriedly demand, "Grab a couple of pieces of paper for me … please! I can't believe I never noticed this."

Dr. Janus does as he's told and comes back looking quite confused. He hands me the pieces of paper and proclaims, "James will be here in five minutes; for some reason he was already on his way."

chapter
32

(1) My God, My God, why hast thou forsaken me? Why art
thou so far from helping me, and the words of my roaring?
(30) A seed shall serve him; it shall be accounted to the Lord for
a generation. (31) They shall come, and shall declare his
righteousness unto a people that shall be born, that he hath done this.

Psalm 22: 1, 30–31, KJV

 he name "Tessie" reverberated in her head. "Tessie." *It has to be,* she thought.

There was only one person *ever* in her life that called her Tessie, and that was her "puppy love," Saul. But how could he be caught up in this? Should she let him know she was on to him? Since when had he become such an advocate of the *truth* yet participating in such evil? He was a close-mouthed, shy, scientist type. Perhaps hiding behind the

facade, the voice made it easier for him to speak. She decided she would stay silent for now.

"I don't have any more time to talk with you now. I need to know where your dad kept his research on DNA. Please, you have to help me, you, your brother."

"But, I truly don't know. I am telling you the 100-percent truth."

"Okay, I will be back, but maybe not for another week. I have reprogrammed the system, which is now set to let you free in seven days if I have not returned. At that time, there will be directions as to what you need to do next and where you need to go. You will only have a thirty-minute window of time to escape, and then all evidence here will be blown up. I am sorry, truly sorry for everything."

She stood there silent, trying to take it all in, and had an eerie feeling, a sweet feeling combined with nostalgia. She then managed to stammer, "But I thought we could...," but he was not listening as he interrupted her thoughts.

"Oh, I have some more gifts for you so you won't feel alone. And remember, no matter what, the crazier the lies people have told you, the more they may appear to be the truth, so beware." With that, he sent in this little less-than-palm-sized thing that looked like a cigarette lighter and then more flowers. She put the flowers in their vase and looked at this curious black item. She was grateful the machine had instructions with it. "MP3" it read. *What on earth could this little thing be?*

She was thankful it came with those instructions, and she managed to get it to work. She had the music playing and loved the new technology that made listening through a tiny earpiece easy. How much she had to learn about the outside world. At about the ninth song in was a beautiful woman's voice saying that she had put Psalm 22 to music some years ago and was now just ready to share it. Tess listened attentively to the sad and melancholy song, and she was so impressed it prompted her to turn the music off and read the Psalm aloud to understand it better. A portion of it read:

(1) My God, My God, why hast thou forsaken me? Why art thou so far from helping me, and the words of my roaring? (30) A seed shall serve him; it shall be accounted to the Lord for a generation. (31) They shall come, and shall declare his righteousness unto a people that shall be born, that he hath done this.

What does this mean exactly?

She read the entire Psalm through again. *For that matter is that Psalm talking about the crucifixion of Christ?*

chapter
33

The only safe vaccine is a vaccine that is "never" used.

James R. Shannon of the National Institute of Health

'm on my hands and knees in the foyer crawling over the snake etched on the floor, like a cat scoping out prospective prey, desperately looking for answers. The only thing I can hear in my head is, *The cost of doing business.* Dr. Janus had said, "So the pharmaceutical company got a slap on the wrist, fined for about $22 million, settled out of court, and nothing was publicized. The fine is always just part of their operating

expenses, the cost of doing business." $22 million! It rings over and over again like an alarm that won't turn off. I'm trying to keep my thoughts on the task, but *The cost of doing business* won't leave me alone. I can't get it out of my gut either. It feels so incredibly wrong.

Could the issue of vaccines possibly have anything to do with the kidnapping? Questions, in no particular order, are popping up like kernels exploding in a popcorn popper. Could someone else be as against vaccinations as my undisclosed birth mother? Is someone sending clues to warn against groups that might have a hidden agenda, groups that appear to be saving lives when in reality they're taking lives? Is this an odd way to get Dr. Janus to pay attention and to report an error in the concept of a vaccination? Could the premise of vaccines really be all wrong? A few more kernels burst, and I swear, I could feel my ears pop. Why would someone threaten his only living relative and ask for that much money? Is it even "La Compagnia"—whoever they are—and how could these clues possibly benefit companies that make millions on innocent children? The scales of justice were heavily weighted toward evil, so no company would want this advertised.

Ever since the opera last night, I have repeated the same thoughts over and over, contemplating vaccines, ethics. Where does one draw the line? I enjoyed the interruption of dinner with Saul and admired his apparent crusade for the truth. It proved to me I'm not the only one offended by Dr. Janus's non-commitment to things, his non-attachment to the drugs he was reviewing. Saul is unusually concerned about the issue of ethics and scientific premises. I like this about him. I also like that he knew what the necklace said. "I oppose deception." *So do I. So do I!*

With this thought, I'm pouring over every mosaic on the floor with new determination, but I'm unable to remove the surfacing feelings of rage. With each tile I grope, another bubble of anger surfaces. If a person could erupt, this would be the time I would. Imagine Dr. Janus having to pick up little pieces of me. He would never be able to put them back in order. This is how impossible finding his sister is feeling, and I hate the feeling of failure. *How can someone be so removed and claim it's just science while the heads of corporations are making millions? What is the "secret" vaccine Dr. Janus is working on, and where has he been sneaking off to while calling it business?*

I reach for the pieces of paper Dr. Janus dropped off before excusing himself too quickly. I had gotten up only long enough to run upstairs, turn on some extra lights and grab the scanned copies of the other artwork and a sketch I'd done of the entrance. I have the new one Saul dropped off. I read it again, "Beware of the Scorpion's Sting." I look carefully at the details.

The part I notice immediately is that the outer constellations on the artwork are exactly opposite to how they're set up in the entrance. The astronomical signs go counterclockwise; in the actual entrance, they go clockwise. Mirror writing, or works done in reverse, is one the favorite things of alchemists and secret societies. *So what does this mean? And thinking of alchemy, what did Saul mean when he said we had seen an "alchemical" opera at the Met?* I knew alchemy was the ancient mixing of metals and that some believed gold could be made from base metals if one knew the tightly guarded secret. I had heard this referred to as the Philosopher's Stone, but no one practices alchemy any more, do they?

Looking back to the first clue of Zoad, or "the way," it hits me. The serpent around the mosaic matches the serpent on the drawing. Obvious now, but I missed it! I line the pictures up and look through each one carefully. On the bottom of "The Scorpion's Sting" artwork it reads, "Behold () have foretold you all things." It's an eye, not an "I." I remember getting my heel stuck the night of the gala, so I crawl back to that spot in the eye. I finger the area to feel or see if there's something more. My heart is racing. I feel a specific indent with a small square shape.

Looking back from the floor to "The Scorpion's Sting" artwork, in the center is a silhouette of a redheaded woman who has astrological signs all along her body. I look closely at the head, which starts with Aries and moves down the body. Next is Taurus, and this time each sign corresponds in the same order as the entrance. What does this mean?

Little by little, as my eyes move slowly down the redhead's body, I repeat aloud, Aries at the head, Taurus at the neck, Gemini on the shoulders, and when I get down past the stomach to the reproductive area, sure enough, what do I see? A scorpion! I jump up with the pictures in hand, but drop all the pages as a chill runs down my spine, causing my entire body to shake.

I get it. This has to be a warning for some medicine or vaccine related to the reproductive organs. Why else would the other warning in the artwork that symbolized Sagittarius express the hypodermic was evil and that the arrow, I believe mankind, is missing the mark? Could this needle and stinger, like a scorpion, warn that only a small percentage of people really die and the rest are just hurt for a period of time, like those injected with the venom of a real scorpion? This couldn't be that crazy "depopulation" conspiracy theory, could it? I had to think more about this, but I still couldn't buy into it.

Shaking with the newness of the realization, I go to collect the pages that only seconds ago had fallen to the outer parts of the circle. Then, like a little spasm, one paper looks as if it flutters. Now fully confident I'm imagining this, I figure my small body movements have created a breeze, so I stay perfectly still. And yet, it flutters again. I look around to see if anyone is moving, but I'm definitely alone. I get spooked again, expecting to see a ghost or hear a voice like I did in Tess's room when I heard, "You kneel amidst a multitude of holy angels."

Slowly, trying not to create any wind, I move to the paper. I pick it up and shove it in the outer circle line. Nothing happens. The paper simply bends. I move to the inner circle. Now the paper slips easily down into a crack. This is not just an entrance to the mansion. I shiver. There's something beneath this house. *Secret tunnels?* Now I'm completely spooked. I've gotten myself into something much bigger than I can handle. I get down, sprawl out on the floor, and while completely lost in thought, I hear a voice, "Well that's a new position!" and I jump.

"James!" I hop to my feet as if I'm guilty of something.

"Just jivin'. You look like you've seen a not so friendly Casper. Did you lose something?"

"I'm fine," I lie. "I'm just deep in thought!"

"Dr. J. called and wanted me to come right away with the plans, so here I am, at the door, quicker than a gazelle at a lion's mouth!"

Thinking a moment and having that odd stomach feeling, I decide to keep what I know to myself. "Let's go to the open room upstairs across from my bedroom," I say as if now I own the place, "and set it out on the table there."

The evening hours are ticking away. James follows dutifully, plans in hand.

On the way up the stairs, I look up at the ceiling, analyzing the stars and the light reflections more intently. I'm being told something, but I'm not getting it yet. Paying so much attention to the ceiling, I inevitably trip up the stairs, grab the railing, slide to the right, and sit with a thud on one step.

"Well, well," James says. "Head in the clouds, missing feet on the floor!"

"Ugh, James," I say in frustration, "will I ever get used to my own feet? I'm not really that awkward, am I?"

"Awkward, no!" James says sweetly. "Preoccupied, yes!"

I stand up, rearrange myself, and start back up to the top without further event. I lead James down the hallway to the right, past the grandfather clock, and through the door. Lights on. To the desk.

chapter
34

Success is not a doorway, it's a staircase.

Dottie Walters

e spread the plans out. I look intently. "There are the grounds, 144 acres, surrounded by a fence. What kind of fence, James, penetrable or not?"

"Easily, but thickly forested, and someone would need to know the way."

"Okay, grounds..." I look at the areas, marking each with my finger. "Back of kitchen, herb garden, flowers, veggies, fountain, golf carts, gazebo, pool, and then all these monuments, Mother

Mary, sphinx, obelisk, etc. There are winding roads through the property, a nine-hole golf course. Such an odd set of objects. The property appears to be a perfect square, but everything seems to flow in a circular motion to the fountain with a fig tree smack in the center of it. Who would build something like this?" I try to line up the circle with the angles in the picture because I notice the obelisk is in one direction and the sphinx is facing due east, as the real one does in Egypt. I'm hoping that where the Virgin Mary statue is placed will be something to do with Virgo and a clue. I then realize it might need to be the opposite, as in mirror writing. I have no answers yet. James stands at attention, and I mutter.

I notice that the house is in the lower quadrant of the property. I again try to line up the columns I had drawn with the constellations from the entrance. Nothing is working. Then looking at the house sketch and outline, it clicks. I say aloud, "Ah ha! The granite house is set up in the shape of 'The Granite House.' James, look, look at this, the way it goes, just in reverse ..."

"What do you mean, *the granite house?*"

"I mean the inner chamber of the pyramid in Giza ... just flipped in reverse." I get another chill. "I had better not find out this is some secret society sexual ritual house. I couldn't bear that."

James raises his eyebrows and says, "What does it mean?"

"I don't know yet, but I can't imagine this just happened by accident. Dr. Janus said his father designed every part of this house. And look here. Look how the observatory falls here and the conservatory is here. Take off the balconies, and you have the inner chamber."

I try to clarify, "Most people don't have a clue, but there are no bodies; no mummies have ever been found in the sarcophagus in Egypt. The tombs are not to bury the bodies of the pharaohs and kings. The pyramids were made as measurements, timepieces of the earth in relation to the universe. When the

light shone directly from the sarcophagus of the King's Chamber up with the positioning of the earth where it was in that century, one could see straight to Orion. These huge pyramids and, believe it or not, one single light could flow from the star to the sarcophagus in perfect alignment. This was an amazing architectural feat during more primitive times!"

He cocks his head and winces apologetically. "I'm totally lost," he says.

"Look, the house tells us, in the entrance,

BLES𝐒 THOSE WHO 𝐄NTER,

FOR WITHIN ALL 𝐏EOPL𝐄 UNVEIL THEIR

TRUE 𝐍ATURE, AND ALL 𝐓HINGS HAVE

BEEN FORETOLD. BEWARE OF THE…"

"Yeah, I always wondered what to beware of, kind of strange."

"The serpent," I say, nonplussed.

"What do you mean, the serpent?"

"Well, when the light shines down at certain angles, it highlights certain letters. I realized that this evening when Saul pointed out the light from the stars, and I connected that with the thrill I had when I realized what the pyramids were really about. Imagine huge blocks perfectly aligned so that one ray from another sphere can pick a point in the depths of the pyramids. So I looked more closely at where the rays struck the floor, and I noticed there are some letters slightly larger than others that reflect better at night. The larger letters cleverly spell *serpent*, but I don't know the full extent of what it means. Serpent has been used in so many cultures and has so much significance to it, it would take days to explain."

"But it's a start," James says, trying to be a cheerleader.

"Yes, a start, but certainly no answer as to where Tess is yet. Listen, I need to scan this in the other room and do some mathematical measurements because their father, who set up this house and yard, was exacting and he has to be telling us more."

Just then Dr. Janus walks in. "I wondered what had happened to you two," he says.

"And we you," I retort.

"Find anything out?"

"You said your dad put the plans on the house together. Do you have any idea why?"

"Not really," he says, almost nonchalantly. I want to slap him.

"All right, if that's true …"

He looks at me quizzically, seeing my underlying anger. "It is."

"Then he has left us clues in the house and on the grounds. There's a mix of Egyptian mythology and architecture, Roman Catholic statues, unusual symbology, signs of the stars and constellations, and I'm sure we're going to find some sacred geometry when we start to take apart the house and the property." I stare intently at Dr. Janus. "How much do you know about ancient Egyptian mythology and culture?"

"Pretty much nil, Mags. I'm a scientist; it never interested me."

"Well, it interested your dad. Do you know what the Granite House is?"

"The sign on the front of our house?"

Ugh, he cannot be that dumb. Crisply I say, "No, the real one."

"I'm afraid I don't."

"Well, it's in the King's Chamber in the pyramid at Giza in Egypt. Everyone keeps digging, hoping to find a mummy of a king—they never will. The sarcophagus was found empty because it's not a burial site for the king; it's much more."

"Interesting." He hesitates, then asks, "But what does that have to do with Tess's kidnapping?"

"I'm getting there but will absolutely go no further on this until you start telling me the truth. You're sneaking out, lying to me, and if you don't answer some questions, I'm going to think you have set me up and put this whole sordid affair together for some sick reason that at the moment is beyond me."

Surprise and then silence from Dr. Janus.

"Well, I'm waiting," I say, feeling my neck and face turn red and shaking a bit at defying a man I thought I respected.

Nothing. Turning abruptly to James, I grind out through clenched teeth, "I'm outta here. James, will you get the car. I'm going to need a lift to the airport."

"Sure things, Mags," James says with a lingering question to the statement, not really moving toward the door and certainly looking apologetically at Dr. Janus, his boss.

Dr. Janus holds up his hand to halt, and his face is drawn, almost white. "All right, hold up a minute you two; wait. I'm not sure what to say."

I jump in, "You can start by telling me exactly what vaccine you're working on. And drop the 'proprietary info' bull. I've had enough niceties to last me a lifetime!"

chapter
35

"He that overcometh shall inherit all things, and I will be
His God and he shall be my son. But the fearful, and
unbelieving and the abominable, and murderers, and
whoremongers, and sorcerers, and idolaters and all liars, shall have
their part in the lake which burneth with fire and brimstone."

Sorcerer translated from the Greek word pharmakeus
means witchcraft and those who have commerce
with evil spirits, as modern "spiritists."

Revelation 21:7–8, KJV

r. Janus takes his time, putting his hand
to his forehead as if wiping the sweat
from it, shakes his head with what looks
like true concern, and says, "It is not that
simple, Mags. I have worked on antibiotics, vaccines, chemotherapy agents, and
numerous other pharmacological medicines. There continue to
be drug resistant strains of microbes causing diseases that are
spreading more quickly and generating genetic variations that

are growing at unheard of rates, such that they can do in minutes what used to take years. In some ways, this has been caused by the misuse or perhaps a better term, *overuse,* of antibiotics. It has therefore been essential to get new antibiotics out, to look deeper into vaccinations as well as altering DNA to change this so we can win the war on disease, and on cancer, specifically."

"In English, Dr. Janus, English. You know how poor my biology is."

Slowly, he sits in a chair, looks down at his feet, sighs, and says, "Are you familiar with HPV?"

"HPV! Of course I am." I'm beside myself. I don't know whether to stay around and listen or to get out that second. I point an index finger at him and James as if they've been bad dogs and command, "Sit. Stay."

I run across to the bedroom, and neither James nor Dr. Janus dares move an inch. I need to breathe. I know about HPV. Through the years after the hospital, the one thing I continue to do is mentor young teen girls and women. I tackle anything from unwanted pregnancies to abstinence to abuse, etc. Sex is not an easy topic to discuss with any teen, especially those that are now defined as "naughty" or "bad.' It's my way to give back to those who could not afford the help otherwise.

The information on HPV is coming to mind quickly, and I'm trying to figure out the best way to spell out all the facts to Dr. Janus. I'm emotional, I'm upset, and when that happens my ability to spout information off the top of my head is not quite as razor sharp.

I decide to print out some notes and information I'd gathered in the past to help girls and moms determine why they should not accept the HPV vaccine. Most information on HPV is from pharmaceutical companies, which always makes me leery. I've learned through experience that they always have enough money to get their slant out without outright lying. Their motto: Get enough info to the public to get consumers on board as quickly as possible. They wash hands with the government and are often funded through research institutes headed by those top fifty families. Then there are the ridiculous "can't sue me" disclaimers that say "more studies need to be done." So how can something in this early stage where more research needs to be done become a compulsory requirement in some states? Not good.

I'm printing and flipping through pages as quickly as possible, wondering if Dr. Janus and James are staying put. I come upon the one study in the *New England Journal of Medicine* dated November 21, 2002. November 21 has always bothered me as the actual date when John F. Kennedy gave his speech about the nation trusting its people, the day before he died. Was that synchronicity, irony, or again some sick way to hide the truth in plain sight? I've never really believed all the crazy conspiracy theories about pyramids on dollar bills, the Statue of Liberty, Isis or Ishtar, as a sick play on people's passions when it represented the ruler of death, but strange things like the new "day after abortion pill" being called RU-486, which, if you spell it out, asks "Are you for 86ing these babies?" and then goes ahead and does it, makes my skin crawl. And now there's this HPV vaccine, another medical hoax? I know in this case no one is sharing the fact that up to 90 percent of these cases go away on their own and don't ever need treatment.

Then the fact that the pharmaceutical companies are giving the vaccine in large quantities, three doses, even when the research admitted the exact dosage needed was unknown, seems ludicrous. Another monetary scam, three shots means guaranteed ROI; ironically, *roi* means "king" in the French, but it means "return on investment" in the financial world. For those who are covered and have insurance, it's a no-brainer, but for those who

don't and have to pay out of pocket $120 a dose for three doses, it's a more difficult situation: Do they buy food for the family or pay for the drug? No matter what, it's a moneymaker for the pharmaceutical company.

My mind's racing and in such a negative place that even I'm shocked by my thoughts: $360 to possibly hurt your own child. Seems cheap enough to me. Maybe the $600 economic stimulus check is to encourage us to use it for this purpose. Now let's just convince the U.S. public the vaccination needs to be repeated every five years, with millions of kids in the country renewing at the ages of nine, fourteen, nineteen, twenty-four, with some companies now discussing infancy, this is not a bad influx of money! Gee, with this brilliance, why don't they just make it for boys too; then they can double their billions of dollars of profits and get them into the trillions! And if we're lucky, people will die at an earlier age so it won't matter if the Social Security system exists. No one would ever be able to prove the vaccine did this.

Even with the pressure of time, I take a breath and look out the office window at the plants below and try to think more rationally. I know the cervical cancer vaccine is part of the routine childhood vaccines schedule and whether or not it's a requirement is decided on a state-by-state basis, with the lie, of course, that the more girls who receive it, the better the benefit that will be seen. The state of Texas by-passed people's rights and own choice through an executive order that mandated girls must get the HPV vaccine. It's actually required to come from a specific pharmaceutical company! Is anyone talking about this?

I tell people to do the research themselves. Check out how the company receiving the financial rewards from the executive order has donated millions to specific politicians who make the rules. It's a sick cycle and doesn't only happen in Texas with one company, but happens all over.

Lobbyists are often politicians who end up in the pharmaceutical companies after their political careers are over and make much more money than they ever did before. By encouraging executive orders be put into place, they can move from the government lobbyist position into the pharmaceutical employee position. I'd watched past editions of *60 Minutes* programs, documenting individuals who have moved swiftly from their low-paying lobbyist job into million-dollar pharmaceutical jobs. This should be illegal.

My mind is racing and not on track. The worst part, as with the swine flu, is that no one is telling the stories of the girls who died from the injections, the ones paralyzed, the ones who are losing vision, who have terrible new rheumatic problems and fatigue. These are vague symptoms that no one can target, but there are over three hundred side effects reported so far, and they're not mild. Who is getting this information out?

Turning away from the window with my feet stuck to the floor as if in cement boots, I try to put an argument together for Dr. Janus. Fear is the motive behind the pharmaceutical ads, "It is your child who can be saved from cancer with this shot." Nothing is further from the truth, but it leaves people begging for the injection. It takes the responsibility off of the pharmaceutical company and doctor because the patient or mom *asked* for it. Is this not the deepest level of deceit? Is this not a sick form of sorcery? The Greek word for witchcraft is *pharmakeus.* Don't tell me the "pharmaceutical" companies were not playing on this wording as their name was created. They knew what they were up to and still do. I have a sinking feeling Dr. Janus does too.

I'm standing in the office debating with myself while Dr. Janus and James are waiting, but I can't seem to pull away from the thoughts. How can a state mandate a vaccine that a law already says is illegal? That's the beauty of an executive order; it can override whatever it wants, whenever it wants. And where are the doctors who should be reporting the adverse effects of vaccines, according to the Federal National Childhood Vaccine Injury Act of 1986? I know these adverse effects are not being reported, just as I also know at this time that there are no repercussions for failing to report them, so few doctors get involved.

Do I blame all the doctors? Probably not, as I have seen some phenomenal, care-based, and ethical physicians along the way. But even they are so busy, so overloaded with information, so rushed around in unhealthy environments, how can they sort out the truth? They often work with the information given to them by the same pharmaceutical representatives who bring them samples. I assure you, those write-ups are good! They convinced me for the longest time when it came to anti-depressants and anti-psychotics, until I figured out what was really going on. Their discussions on how serotonin worked, how neurotransmitters were blocked, etc., had me convinced for years. Perhaps this is what's happening with the HPV vaccine and it's just taking people awhile to see the truth, like it had taken me.

I calm myself down and realize I'm lumping all psychiatrists, all doctors, and all pharmaceuticals together, and I know this isn't right. I know great scientists who are really searching for the truth. I know physicians whose skills and love for their patients blow me away. I even know there are times when emergency medicine is necessary. I mean, I don't want to be one of those people in an accident who doesn't get a great anesthesiologist and surgeon when I need an operation! There's a need for specific drugs, and, yes, even anti-depressants and anti-psychotics can be necessary and beneficial. And, not all my children with cancer died, so some chemo must work. I don't want to be a total extremist. However, if the pharmaceutical industry comes knocking to tell me there's a vaccine to stop the depression gene, I'll tell them where to shove it!

My biggest fear is how to sort out fact from fiction. Pharmaceutical companies have a right to amass huge fortunes, if it actually benefits the world and their research is based on fact. However, the trend is going in the wrong direction. The HPV vaccine today, a vaccine for AIDS tomorrow, a vaccine for psychosis next year, then a vaccine for bird flu! Then just start going back in history and reintroducing the ones we have forgotten, like polio, swine flu, etc. Create another new scare tactic that will keep people running for a while. Pull out the old vaccinations from the "vaults" and administer the mercury, aluminum, and other left over vials. Why not? We wouldn't want those to be wasted.

Some physicians are having second thoughts because there's no proof of the HPV vaccination doing one beneficial thing. As a matter of fact, some research proves that having the vaccination increases your risk for cancer by 44.6 percent. The medical groups admit it themselves. Even the Journal of the American Medical Association (JAMA) has clearly stated there's no evidence that any phases of the vaccination can be proven effective and provides the details.

Some hard-core, ethical scientists who are fervent in their protests when pharmaceutical companies do wrong have been discredited and had their research taken from them. This is not freedom of inquiry. This is about the bottom line. The pharmaceutical companies have had cases brought against them for price fixing, deaths, paralysis, and other side effects, yet they're getting away with payoffs or burying evidence about the drugs. Some are working with the Food and Drug Administration, "conspiring" with them on what some are now calling "biospiracy."

How can they get away with this? I, however, don't mean that we should throw out the entire industry for the few bad apples. We shouldn't have denounced *all* chiropractors and alternative healing methods in the 1980s, but somehow the government and drug companies were able to wipe them out for many years. This was seriously unethical, so in retaliation should the holistic practitioners side with the government and do this to the pharmaceutical industry? No. There has to be an ethical, workable compromise. We have to go back to the premise and get a more reasonable and honest review of this vaccine and get it tested for many more years before its use continues.

My thoughts are still ping ponging back and forth, I know it's my gut speaking, and if Dr. Janus was really going to push for this as a valid vaccine, I'll need to call some scientist friends of mine to help debunk the premise.

I'm trying to figure how to calmly get back into the room to hear the rest from the horse's mouth. I've been here before with the kids with cancer, with some of the treatment modules, the experimental drugs given well before they should have been ready. People who got special treatment because of money and which hospital they went to, others who lived because they left for alternative treatments, but in the meantime social services tried to take those children away because the "unfit" parents pulled them from traditional care.

When I left the hospital setting, I cited my reason for leaving as political and salary-related, but I knew it was more than that. I knew part of me felt we were hurting some of the kids, but I also hadn't taken the time or interest to find a cure that worked. I was a psychologist after all, not a *real doctor,* as some have said. My recollections of the families and their losses broke my heart, and if I had let them sense my fear, it would have devastated them in an already impossible situation. So like most of the rest of the world, I kept silent.

I compose myself with proof in hand. *Act a little more rationally,* I tell myself as I walk back into the room. No one has moved. "Sorry about that. I'm familiar with HPV. Go on."

As if I had never exited, Dr. Janus continues. "Well, what I am working on is similar to that. It is a new, not-yet-released vaccine for males. It's similar to the one for HPV for girls that's to be administered to all boys over the age of nine so that if they have sexual encounters with girls, they don't pass the virus to the girls and increase their partner's risk of ovarian cancer."

"That's insane!" Looking at him in utter disbelief, I say, "This is my worst nightmare coming to life before my very eyes. You can't really believe this crap? How can you do this when you know in your heart of hearts there's no vaccine that can cure cancer, nor will there ever be one, and the American people are all being lied to for the money and greed of pharmaceutical companies, insurance companies, and the government?"

"It's not that simple, Mags," he says calmly as I stand over him waving my papers, as if he'd know what I have in my hand.

"Again, I only *review* the materials I'm sent. I don't do the testing. I simply determine, with the information provided, could it be plausible and are there any missing links that would make the companies look stupid? I am an independent researcher. So far I haven't found any glaring problems."

"No glaring problems? Excuse me? What about the crazy study of 2,392 women ages sixteen to twenty-three who were followed for seventeen months after having received the three shots over a six-month period, and the researchers admitted that 859 of the group were removed because some had HPV-16 infections already or other cervical abnormalities. How can actual vaccines be given to the masses when in the end only 1,533 girls were initially studied? Don't you need years of research and more conclusive evidence? Wouldn't this be part of your review job, Dr. Janus? Wouldn't it be your job to point out the basic errors in deductive reasoning and scientific test and measure samples?" My pitch is getting higher, and if I'm not careful, I'll sound like Mozart's queen of the night!

"It might if that was the information I had been given for this research study," he says too coy for my liking.

Skipping over that statement, I say, "What about the most important piece hidden in the literature, that the pharmaceutical company admits to, which is that just because a female tests positive for HPV once does not mean she is likely to get cervical cancer. She would need to test positive many times, over many years, and even then only 50 percent of cervical cancers are linked to HPV-16, the one the pharmaceutical company believes *might* cause cancer. The research admits the vaccine doesn't even stop current infections from becoming cancerous."

Glancing at my paper, calming down a bit, the drama unfolds, and I feel like I am in a play as the leading actress spouting off phrases I had memorized like the back of my hand. I fire away with, "Do you know that in the study of the remaining 1,533 women, the forty-one subjects who developed HPV-16 were all in the placebo group? Nine of these forty-one with HPV-16 developed precancerous lesions. Twenty-two of the women from the placebo group also developed pre-cancerous lesions, but these were *not* associated with HPV-16. So for nine people with not even full-blown cancer, we are freaking out moms, telling them to save their children, doing national ad campaigns for billions of dollars; and the commercials lead you to think it's an epidemic. I have numerous friends who are parents of girls who are at their wit's end about this. They don't know what to do.

"I've worked with this disease, and if I thought in a second this was true, I'd be out there pitching the cure. Cervical cancer is not good. I remember one beautiful, thirty-year-old woman with two young children who died from it. But the bottom line is that of about 15,000 women a year who get ovarian cancer, around 4,100 die from it. Of this 4,100, it's less than .5 percent who even have the HPV-16 virus; even the researchers can't prove the precancerous lesions were what led to the full-blown cancer.

"Are these enough cases to create a vaccine and make it compulsory?" Now I am glaring at him and up in his face.

He's starting to go red. "I have nothing to do with what is compulsory or not."

"Oh, I beg to differ, if you review these drugs with a positive catch phrase and let them go to market then you are part of the problem. Do you know that some scientists and physicians who are not anti-vaccine completely, even clearly, state we are weakening our girl's immune systems so they will be more likely to get cancer of some form from the overuse of drugs. Even the pharmaceutical companies themselves admit the vaccine blocks HPV 6,11,16 and 18, but only if you have been exposed to that particular type. Listen to this craziness and what one explanation says:

> The cervical cancer vaccine is recommended for girls ages 11 to 12, although it may be used in girls as young as age 9. This allows a girl's immune system to be activated before she's likely to encounter HPV. Vaccinating at this age also allows for the highest antibody levels. The higher the antibody levels, the greater the protection.

"Dr. Janus," I say so loudly I'm waiting for the vases in the room to crack, "Even the FDA doesn't believe that HPV causes cervical cancer. I don't care what they are telling the public. Way back on March 31, 2003, the FDA released a statement that spoke about HPV itself, saying, "Most infections are short-lived and not associated with cervical cancer … and … Most women who become infected with HPV are about to eradicate the virus and suffer no apparent long-term consequences to their health." To prove the FDA's continued knowledge that HPV does not cause cervical cancer, in March of 2007, a company filed an HPV PCR (polymerase chain reaction) test reclassification petition with the FDA, which essentially is a laboratory test that can amplify the amount of DNA from a tiny sample to a large amount within hours by theoretically taking one molecule and producing measurable amounts of identical DNA for DNA fingerprinting and sequencing. The FDA agreed to reclassify, which proves 100 percent that the FDA knows and acknowledges HPV is not linked to cervical cancer and does not directly cause cervical cancer. This being the case, how can it be sold as such? How can our federal Food and Drug Administration, which is supposed to ensure the public receives accurate information about health-related matters, let this continue? Who is out there protecting the human rights and health of our girls?"

Tears are welling up in my eyes, but I start to back down because for the first time, I see some genuine questioning in Dr. Janus's eyes. It may be over me and have nothing to do with the vaccine, but more quietly I say, "And finally, what about the plausibility, the fact that not one part of the basis of this research is on how the human body really works and what vaccines really do?"

"Again, that's not what I am paid to do." But this time his tone is weaker and almost defeated.

It gets me revved up again. James has still not moved.

"Well, mister…" slips out, surprising myself, this time as if reprimanding a rebellious teenager, "someone has caught on to you and others like you and is making an example of you by attacking your money and your sister, and you still aren't listening."

I angrily pull the Scorpion's Sting picture Saul delivered from behind the architectural plans of the house, point to the organs, and start aggressively jabbing at them on the desk. "See this! And this?" They both come over and are looking at me like I have two heads, and I'm acting like it!

Totally frustrated, I bark, "Genitals, reproductive organs, sting-needle, arrow, missing the mark, see?"

"I'm trying, but I'm not getting it," says Dr. Janus.

"To be honest, me neither, Mags," pipes in James as I throw him a glare so strong he takes a physical step back.

Trying to calm me down, Dr. Janus says, "I'm trying. I'm listening, more than you know, Mags. I am listening. You're telling me someone wants me to look deeper at this research, but I am not doing anything different than any other scientist hired in my role would do, so why target me?"

"Who cares about the other scientists? I'm talking about the life of your sister. I also care about the fact you're letting a drug that's going to kill and maim young children, potentially cause birth defects and paralysis and other things, slip through your fingers while you do nothing about it but sit back in your comfy home drinking Scotch! That's what I'm talking about."

Blank stare.

"You could be using your money for good, for educating people. What is keeping you tied to these companies anyway? What do they have on you?"

"Nothing. They don't have anything on *me*."

"Then what is it?"

"I'm not sure, Mags. It could only be related to my dad or my sister. I made some calls. Not sneaking around so much as you think, but to some old acquaintances of my dad I had forgotten about and had been asked never to contact or let their names get out to *anyone* unless it was an emergency. I did not tell them why I was calling, and although they were close-mouthed, each one agreed dad was working on something to do with DNA. He had cracked something so profound that it would put medicine and drugs as we know them out of business for good. No company or government would want this to get out. It would bring down our economy. Maybe Dad or Mom didn't die naturally. Maybe someone or some group was on to him. I truly don't know." His

hand goes to wipe small beads of sweat from his forehead. He looks visibly distraught.

Backing down a little, I murmur, "Okay, we'll start with that idea." And then as an afterthought, "And your sister, what do they have on your sister?"

"Mags, I can't tell you that."

"You must."

"I am sorry. I just can't, not right now."

"James, the car please—"

"Oh, you *can* be infuriating!" Dr. Janus is intense. "All right, I recently, as an utter shock, found out—"

And then comes the fateful sound. *Dring*...

chapter
36

Then his wife said to him, Do you still hold fast your blame-
less uprightness? Renounce God and die! (9) But he said to
her, you speak as one of the impious and foolish women would
speak. What? Shall we accept [only] good at the hand of God
and shall we not accept [also]misfortune and what is of bad
nature? In [spite] of all this, Job did not sin with his lips.

Job 2:9–10; when even his beloved spouse did
not believe or have faith in him or God

 *ring.* "The phone now? Who could it be at midnight!" The phone's interrupting the most important conversation I'll probably ever have in my life.

I ask, "James, can you get it?" while hoping to pry out more information.

"Janus residence. The what? French police? One moment, please."

We look at each other nervously. Dr. Janus barely moves. If it had been me, I'd be running, but step by step, as if on his way to an execution, he walks methodically to the phone.

"Dr. Peter Janus speaking. Yes? I see, Yes. No! Oh no, no ... ," as he looks ahead in shock. "Yes, I'm here. No, I understand. You didn't want to lie to me. I'll be there."

In a trance, he hangs up the phone. I stand there, afraid for the worst.

"Well, I suppose it's all over now. She is dead." Then, repeating the words as if they would make sense a second time, "My sister is dead." I gasp. He fills in. "The French Police have asked if I would come to claim the body."

Silence. All but my pounding heart. My mom's words, which I dare not speak aloud, *You need to take the good with the bad, Mags, the good with the bad. That's life!*

The final kernel in the popper explodes in my head. It's all over.

chapter

37

*Success seems to be largely a matter of
hanging on after others have let go.*

William Feather

he worst news always transpires when revelation is about to occur. I want to yell at Dr. Janus and shake him and tell him we should have called the police and hug him and hold him and tell him it will be all right. I can't do any of those things. I'm paralyzed.

Dr. Janus's flat voice and empty face remotely manages to mumble instructions.

"James, prepare the limo. Mags, it's over now; your work is done."

"Please, Dr. Janus, let me go. I want to see this to the end, if you're okay with that." Now feeling such guilt for having attacked him only five minutes ago. And then, as if commanding him, "No way. I'm coming with you; you need someone there. I need to go. We don't even know who did this or why."

"It doesn't matter now, Mags. She was all I had left."

"Please, Dr. Janus, don't compartmentalize this. She can't have died for no reason."

"Do as you wish." He leaves the room.

I'm stunned, head reeling, nauseous. Overwhelming doubt consumes me. What was I thinking to have even wanted to help? Who am I, playing God and failing miserably? The burden of her death is mine and will be for the rest of my life. I have failed, big time.

I look to James. "What do you think? Is he staying quiet because he is part of this, responsible for it? Help me out here."

"I don't know, but men, when they've lost a loved one, don't react the same as women."

"I know, I know. I'm the stupid psychologist here," I say, getting defensive, "but come on; something serious enough to kill for to get his attention is happening; we can't just ignore it. This is not a game. Someone is making an example out of him and his sister."

I'm verging on tears of frustration. I bite my lip hard enough to bring blood to the surface. I suck it in.

"I agree," says James, tenderly moving in front of me, taking me in his arms. "I know this is terrible. I'm so sorry you have to be part of this."

I stay there for a couple minutes trying to get myself together and then kiss James on the cheek, thank him, and say I'd better go pack. I feel so safe, so secure, I have to move so I don't weaken.

James senses this and directs, "I'll see you out front."

We go through the motions, get into the limo, and finally Dr. Janus says, "The call explained my sister has been found bludgeoned to death in her bed at the convent. It's quite gruesome. She was left disemboweled. You may not want to see it."

"I wondered what happened, but this is terrible. I'm so sorry for your loss. I'm so sorry for everything."

"I know, Mags. It's not your fault. We are all sorry."

I know that's supposed to make me feel better. It doesn't. Failure is not sitting well with me.

chapter
38

*A human being is a part of the whole, called by us
"Universe," a part limited in time and space. He experiences
himself, his thoughts and feelings as something separated from
the rest, a kind of optical delusion of his consciousness. This
delusion is a kind of prison for us, restricting us to our
personal desires and to affection for a few persons nearest to us.
Our task must be to free ourselves from this prison by widening
our circle of compassion to embrace all living creatures and the
whole of nature in its beauty. Nobody is able to achieve this
completely, but the striving for such achievement is in itself a
part of the liberation and a foundation for inner security.*

Albert Einstein

o many days passed for Tess that she began to worry about her perpetrator. She was beginning to understand the psychology behind why those kidnapped often fell in love with their perpetrators. The Stockholm Syndrome, she thought it was called. *What if he doesn't come back, and what if it is Saul?* She *owed* this man who had brought her to Christ in a new way. *What if the machine doesn't open as it is supposed to? What if I can*

never get out of here and am left to rot? This was similar to the way she had felt when she was first placed at the convent and had given up her beautiful baby. She had forgotten that terrible fear. Thoughts had plagued her as to what a disappointment she must have been to God for having a child out of wedlock and how she would spend the rest of her days on earth atoning for it.

What if, what if... And then she heard, as if in her head, a shockingly loud, angry sound, maybe even out loud, "I brought you to Jesus, and I will give you a kingdom of your own." It was so strong she fell to her knees. She looked up to the speaker-phone to see if there was any more to the phrase, but the author-itative voice she heard was gone.

She began to think, still genuflecting, *But what on earth could that phrase mean?* She was shaking inside but was also a little excited. Was this God? Had she actually, finally after all these years, heard from God himself? And the irony of it happening here and not at the convent. Suddenly, she knew for the first time what Ruach meant. It was as if the Word had penetrated her, and she was feeling a connection, a guidance. God had breathed life into her, and she could feel communion with Him! Then she realized, *He would not have pulled me out of the wilderness to let me die now.* Somehow in her heart this she knew!

Then while digesting the information, she heard the elec-tronic "voice," not a voice in her head or heart!

"Hello?"

"You made it? You made it!" She was so thrilled to have him back.

"I am here, but the time has come. The plan is falling apart, everything has gone wrong, and I am afraid I am going to kill you now."

"Me?" she yelped. "After all this, you can't kill me."

"I must," he said. "I have no choice."

Maybe she was wrong; maybe she didn't know who it was. She was afraid for a split second, but then felt the force of God behind her.

"Everyone has a choice," she reiterated. "You taught me that."

Banter went on for minutes as she pleaded for her life and finally, she blurted out, "I know it is you, Saul. I figured it out. The sunflowers and your slip of 'Tessie' made me realize it."

There was no response.

Then slowly, "I wondered if you might have. A very, very stupid moment on my part. It was just all so familiar, and I was enjoying our exchange so much, like when we were young."

"Or perhaps unconsciously you wanted me to know it was you?"

"Perhaps."

"Saul, let me out. Let us talk in person. If you need to kill me after, so be it, but at least let me know what this is all about."

"I can't do that," he said.

"Saul, I have a confession to make, something you need to know."

"I'm listening."

"Please, I need to tell you in person."

"I can't do that."

"You have to Saul, what I have to tell you involves both of us and our past," she cried as she pressed her forehead against the door, practically hugging it for human contact.

"Saul, I did go to the convent for a reason, as you know, but not the reason you think. After our encounter, I was pregnant, but I did not go to the convent after having an abortion as you were led to believe. I went there and had the child. Saul, you are a father. We are parents."

There was a loud clank, and doors were being opened as if a bank vault time had come and the bolted locks were being unclinked. The entire left wall with slots moved and were rolling open. The right came inward as the left went outward, and he stood in the opening.

"A baby?"

She saw him. She saw his pale, beautiful face; he was as handsome as ever to her. His blue eyes were slightly reddened and welling with tears. He looked so much as she remembered him. He had aged a little, but his skin was as smooth and pure as she had envisioned.

"Come here, Saul."

He walked over to her slowly, sunken shoulders, sullen face. She took him in her arms. "A baby?" he said again in disbelief.

"Yes," she said, "a baby. A beautiful baby girl."

"A girl! How can you even look at me after what I did to you? You don't hate me? You don't want to kill me? I violated you."

"Well, in my mind, I wanted to share an intimate moment with you. I loved you. It didn't turn out the way I had hoped when I was young and afraid, and the first time is difficult under any circumstance. I never blamed you, Saul. I never once hated you. I loved you!"

He wept in her arms as if all the years had disappeared and he was once again back with her. "You were my only love, Tessie. I never again had a relationship. If I had known, I would have married you, helped raise the child with you. Our lives would be so different now."

"That is true, but somehow fate has brought us back together again. We can figure a way out of this. I know we can."

"But we can't. You don't get it Tess; we can't."

"Saul, I beg of you, you must tell me what all of this is about."

"It is your father's work they are after. He has the keys, the truths, and the proofs, documentation to many of the questions I have been asking you to look at and much more. I was going to steal them, run away, sell them, and get rich. I was angry at

him that he kept secrets; perhaps I was angriest that he took you away from me."

With a huge sigh, he continued. "But they will just kill me anyway, and in the end, I could not break the codes he has them hidden under. I think only you and your brother can."

He took a deep breath, wiped some tears from his eyes, and continued. "He was working mostly in the observatory before his death, a death that I feel was in no means natural, neither was your mom's. He had holographic programs and was able to store them on chips the size of a dot or period. I could never get him to divulge what it was or how he was doing it. That offended me and made me bitter. I was his assistant, closer than his son, his brightest star; he should have shared them with me. He trusted no one, and his only statement to me was, 'In time, my friend, in due time.' I hated those words. He said the right person would come along who would understand the clues and take the time to learn what they meant. In the meantime, he kept them in riddles and symbols so that no one would discover what he was working on."

"So you think now someone has gotten on to this research and is after us because of it."

"I don't think so. I know so because I am the one who let it out that he had such materials. When I started this, I had no qualms about getting the materials by any and all means possible. I was even willing to kill for it."

"And now?"

"Well now, I don't have a choice."

"Saul, why didn't you just tell me how you felt about me? Why didn't you track me down and tell me?"

"I couldn't. I knew that how you became pregnant was wrong. I committed a horrible act of evil by being intimate with you before I married you and while you were a minor."

Her heart actually hurt for him in a strange way. He was not completely to blame for the interaction, nor did she feel he wanted to hurt her. She knew he wanted to show his love.

"Your dad, despite respecting my scientific abilities, hated me on a deeper level for having done this to you. He could have had charges filed against me for statutory rape. Instead, he told me you had had an abortion and that he put you in a nunnery. My world ended at that moment, thinking of the pain you must have felt killing a child, our child. He paid me a million dollars to keep my mouth shut and perhaps kept me on as his assistant so he could keep an eye on me. 'Keep your friends close and your enemies closer.' When he died, the only thing left was his research. I found his work. I found scattered notes, odd diagrams, and fascinating machines. I knew the codes had to have something to do with his love of science, biology, the constellations, and nature. I knew his love for his family was the only key to breaking it. But no matter how hard I worked, I could not break the codes. I became more frustrated, more left out, more set up. I wanted one thing. Revenge.

"So then a group I had never heard of, 'La Compagnia,' with roots in France, Italy, and New York approached me and told me how much money they would give to get parts of his research to them. I knew then I had to devise a plan to get Peter, good ol' Dr. Janus, to pay attention. He had no real interest in anything but his current life and research, so I forced him to look more closely by touching the only thing I could think of that would hurt him. Not money, but his sister."

Tess knew he was right. Despite the distance and sparse contact, she knew her brother loved her deeply, as she did him.

Resignedly, Saul wrung his right hand around the back of his neck and let his spine snap from the tension. His piercing eyes were so strong that Tess stepped back, becoming fearful of what

else was about to be disclosed, wondering if she really knew the man at all. It had been years since she had last seen him, after all.

"You see, Tessie, people don't change if they're comfortable, only if they are forced to. At first the plan seemed to be working perfectly. Peter was starting to understand the kidnapping was real. He had made some calls to organizations your father belonged to and met with people who came out of the woodwork. He kept all of this silent. The only person he pulled in was a girl, a beautiful girl, I must add, with striking red hair who had been his student at Columbia. Her parents are professors. He pulled her in to see if she could decode the symbols of some artwork your father created and I anonymously sent. Then I added a few clues and hints to push her along because I needed her to get to the bottom of the DNA information so I could claim it as my discovery for the world to know, for my name to live on forever, and so I could sell it for a fortune."

With each word, he spoke more rapidly until the sentences seemed to merge together as one thought, and Tess started to separate her mind from her body, as she used to do at the church when too much difficult information came to her at one time. She was sure she looked blank. She felt numb.

"It was going along perfectly until I happened upon something that shocked me. I came upon writings of your dad's, and this time, instead of being encrypted, they were blatant statements about how the American people were being lied to by pharmaceutical companies, governments, educational institutions, and even the news media and publishing houses. Groups listed were posing as our protectors but were really sabotaging us secretly, behind the scenes. It then suddenly dawned on me that I was their pawn as well. I kept that info in my house, but, of course, it was broken into, and most of it was stolen. The only pieces saved are the ones I sneaked into your safe room at the Granite House.

I was surprised your dad still let my fingerprints open that door. Anyway, the group who stole the items left a note saying, 'Don't betray us again. Next time it is your life.' Once they had that info, I knew they would never let me go. I had been set up from the beginning. Then one thing after another started happening. Money started disappearing from my accounts, my cat was killed, my car was tampered with, and I was being watched."

He stepped back but then changed his mind, walking right up to Tess, putting his hands to her head, and touching her little growing lockets of red hair. Tess felt as though she snapped back into her body and into the situation, but her emotions were so confused she wasn't sure if that was what she really felt. The touch weakened her while the words angered her. *Have I really been this disconnected from my emotions since learning the rules in the convent?* She was only partially listening as he rambled on, raw emotion driving the words.

"I knew it was over for me. Then as you and I spoke more, I fell in love with you all over again. I don't want and didn't want to kill you, but the thought of you cooped up in that convent, potentially being lied to, drove me crazy. Something inside of me went wild that we are all living under such lies for the love of money, greed, and power, and so I lost it. I did something I can never be forgiven for, so truly my life is over. You, however, can be saved, can make change. You must, Tessie, you must."

Something fit, something snapped her back to her purpose. Maybe he was right. Maybe she did need to live to get into the world and discover her purpose. But what about him; what about Saul, and what about the man he had become? She couldn't believe that her first and only love could be evil.

"But you are not a murderer," Tess managed to speak gently.

He turned to her intensely. "I was not then, but I am now."

"But you haven't killed me yet."

"You don't get it, Tessie; you just don't get it."

There was a ring on a walkie-talkie, and Saul quickly held up his finger to his mouth, motioning silence. "Stay put," he whispered and left through the door.

She heard his response as he spoke into the machine. "I will be there in one hour."

He came back in looking intense yet resolved to finish what had spun completely out of control. He approached Tess so quickly she jumped back, afraid that that was her time. "No, no, Saul, don't hurt me. Don't kill me, please." She ran for the vase, ready to crack him over his head if he got any closer.

Saul was shocked by her reaction and her fortitude and backed off, trying to look calmer and nicer. "No, no, Tess, I won't, not now. I'm sorry, I didn't mean to scare you."

Her hand lowered but she still looked at him, confused.

More gently, he said, "I have to go now. I need you to stay here for a couple more days to see if I can figure any way out of this. This is truly the only safe place for you at the moment."

"Where is here, Saul?" escaped from Tess in a frustrated tone. The thought of being in that prison when so much needed to be accomplished upset her.

He smiled slyly. "You are in the underground tunnel section below your family's Granite House."

"Really!" It was such an odd and unexpected answer. But somehow she felt relieved to be home. In some sick way, if she died now, she would be amidst her family and their holy angels. "How odd, I never knew there were tunnels under the house."

"There are a lot of things you don't know about this house and its grounds. I must run. Stay away from the door as I shut it, and I will reprogram the system for meals, etc."

She put the vase down and ran toward him now, not ready to let him go. "Saul, please, please let me go. Let's go to Peter; let's beg him to disappear with us. He has the money, the connections.

We can all run away together. Then you and I can pick up our lives where we left off." She grabbed him and held him tightly. She remembered his sweet smell. She couldn't lose him again.

"If only it could be so." He forced her hands from him, turned, and walked away.

The door closed slowly, but this time she was already starting to feel lonely. The fact that she was under the house was startling. She smiled.

She knew she should be clawing at the door, yelling for her brother, hoping someone in the house could hear her, but an unexpected sense of serenity overcame her and all fear was gone. It had something to do with how clever her father had been and how anomalous it was to be back "home." It was so like him to create underground tunnels and hide pieces of artwork.

But just as quickly as the feeling came, the smile faded because she felt once again like she had lost a loved one. What if she really never got out? Would she ever see her brother, the house, Saul again? The peace she had briefly felt was now infiltrated with doubt. Not knowing what else to do, she cried aloud from the depths of her heart, "My God, My God, Why hast thou forsaken me?" Feeling lost and abandoned by her Father, not even understanding the true meaning of these words, she shook from head to toe.

She was not used to experiencing such quick and uncontrolled mood swings. Calming herself down, she actually began to think through the words she had just said and how strange it was that God would have left Jesus on the cross when He said He would never leave or forsake His children. Had she read the verse wrong? Had she somehow misinterpreted the words said on the cross?

Then it hit her like lightening. Why would Jesus have said these precise words on the cross when He already knew He was to be sacrificed? Jesus had told his disciples all about his coming death and resurrection as He had been told by His Father. His fate was sealed, so why would He feel His Father had forsaken Him, and why announce it to the doubting public watching Him being crucified? Why would He not shout words of encouragement to the onlookers? This made no sense at all.

She was back in the Bible reading, and, as if by some miracle, her pain started to dissipate again as she worked diligently to find an answer to what those words really meant. She went back to Matthew 27:46, KJV and re-read:

"And about the ninth hour Jesus cried with a loud voice, saying 'Eli, Eli lama sabachthani?' that is to say, 'My God, My God, why has Thou forsaken Me?'"

It took her back to the first day she had been kidnapped, when she cried out in pain at having been abandoned by her Father. But finally an incredible revelation came to her: the beautiful Psalm 22, which she had recently read, answered the question. Jesus was never crying out in pain to the Father why have You forsaken me? He was repeating a phrase a thousand years old, telling the people that his death had all been foretold in Psalm 22 and his destiny had been supernaturally pre-ordained. He had accepted and known his fate, well before coming to earth as Immanuel—God with us—and in believing and understanding this, one can begin to put confidence in the fact that all things have been foretold and therefore fearlessly perform our duty on earth by learning and understanding the signs left for us.

The odd mix of liberation and imprisonment engulfed her. She had unwittingly cracked one of the phrases that confused her. She had the live Word breathed into her. She repeated aloud with new pride of understanding, "Eli, Eli, lama sabachthani!"

Then without warning, a strange phrase came to mind and she wrote it down, "Sometimes the only prison that exists is the one in our own mind."

chapter

39

Make failure your teacher not your undertaker.

Zig Zigler

e arrive at the convent. My stomach is a mess, but I'm being strong for Dr. Janus. I know this feeling well. I went through it every time one of my children died and I was there to support the parents. I always managed to keep it together while in front of them, but it was never easy. It was only when I was away from people that I allowed myself to grieve, to cry, to throw up, whatever was necessary.

By the time we arrive in France and get to the convent, we're breaking visitor protocol. The Mother Superior meets us at the main entrance and states that the gendarmes are in Tess's room waiting for us. The body has been there for hours. She escorts us to the room, repeating, "This is such a terrible thing. We have never had such horror happen in our own convent. I do hope you do not hold the church responsible. Who could be behind such monstrous acts? Lord, protect us from the evil going on in the world." The Mother Superior's demeanor hasn't changed a bit, and I feel offended for Dr. Janus.

My cynical side thinks she doesn't want to be held responsible because the nun's money needs to keep flowing in.

She makes a sign of the cross and leaves. Dr. Janus turns. "You can go in if you want to subject yourself to such goriness."

"Thank you, but I didn't come this far to wimp out now."

A gendarme, a perfectly dressed French policeman, comes out and introduces himself. "My name is Inspector Montaillue, and I will be overse-*eing* this investi*ga-t-ion*." The real Parisian accent. "I must tell you this is not a pretty scene, so beware. You are Dr. Janus, *Oui?*"

He nods.

"I am deeply regretful for your loss." The *R* rolls perfectly from his tongue. "Please, follow me, and take your time."

I've heard about that salty smell of blood and death, but it's unimaginable until you're in a room with a corpse that's hours old. I'm overwhelmed and almost in shock. I had seen dead bodies. I had seen people die, children die, but I had never seen anything like this. A few policemen wander around taking pictures, measuring, and looking closely at the body. The face was covered with an entire scalp of red hair, hiding the actual face. I belt out, making others jump. "I didn't know she had red hair!"

Everyone looks at me, and I look at Dr. Janus, who calmly says, "I guess you have only ever seen black and white photos of her in her habit." I look closer and see that it looks as though the locks have been scalped and placed over the face, which seems odd to me, as I think most nuns keep their hair short or shaved. The hair intrigues me because it looks awfully similar to mine and to that crazy scalped thing in the relics room. The body is lying there in the habit with the midsection carved out. Dried blood is everywhere. It's as if someone has mutilated the nun's midsection and removed it from the body, leaving the rest of the habit untouched.

"*Mauvais, mauvais.* Who would do such a brutal and strange thing to a sister and why?" The inspector asks Dr. Janus, who has no words coming out of his mouth. I step closer to Dr. Janus in case he needs support.

The inspector starts talking about the body. "We do autopsy and announce the findings. We must figure this out. *Regardez-La, Docteur,* look to the *stomach-e.*"

I had no interest in getting that close to see details and didn't remember enough anatomy and physiology to have known the inside of a body anyway. I step back. The police and Dr. Janus hover closer over the body like flies, and I start to look around the room in hopes of getting some kind of clue and to refocus my mind so I won't puke. Sweating profusely, I see nothing has been moved.

As the inspector describes the physical findings around the stomach area, he says to his worker, "*Qu'est-que c'est?*" The coroner jumps in closer and admits it looks like something is lodged in her and says, "Humph, looks as if we have been left a note."

The inspector fidgets with his holster, moves it to the side so he can bend over further, and slowly repeats, "A note?" *Donne-moi.*" The inspector puts on gloves and takes it. It's rolled up like a scroll, about four inches long. He unrolls it and reads aloud:

An eye for an eye
A tooth for a tooth
Poison tongues
are hiding the truth.

Needles of fear
are mostly to blame.
"Harmless spear"?
Cancer? Shame, shame.

Then the coroner comments, looking at the body while pondering the sick poem, "This is the strangest thing I have ever seen. It is only the reproductive organs that have carefully been removed. She technically has not been disemboweled. All the rest of her remains! How odd."

Turning back toward the body but keeping my distance, I'm about to speak, but Dr. Janus gives me a look, and I know for some reason I'm to be quiet. I obey. Something is not right.

The inspector turns back to the body and asks Dr. Janus, "Are you ready to identify the body by viewing her face?"

"I suppose."

I say that I'll wait outside. I want to give him some room. Instead of asking about the poem, the inspector goes on to explain that the face is bloated and gray, that perhaps some poison had been administered.

Standing outside the door, I hear Dr. Janus gasp, deep and uncontrolled from his throat, and then whisper, "That is my beloved Tess." I start to cry but regain my composure as I've learned to do. He composes himself. I peek in to see that the inspector has his arm on Dr. Janus's shoulder for support. I decide not to go back in.

Dr. Janus discusses business. "When can I get my sister's body?"

The inspector explains they'll do a basic autopsy, get pictures, a chem screen for poisons, and that, depending on the depth of investigation, it could be his within a few days.

"That long?" asks Dr. Janus.

"Well, things need to be done correctly if we want to catch who did this to your sister."

"Of course, but I would like to get my sister cremated as soon as possible, as those were her wishes."

"A nun who wishes to be cremated," the inspector says in an accusatory French tone that even takes me aback. "I didn't know Catholics allowed that." The inspector continues almost to himself yet aloud, "Rituals and customs are strange things," then turns to Dr. Janus and says matter-of-factly, "I am not Catholic myself, but on every third Sunday in September, people arrive, and a lot of them too, they take relics enclosed in a casket under the reliquary for an annual procession in Lisieux. It seems amazing that every year pilgrims go to the Chapel of St. Thérèse to venerate and honor the remains. Some of the Sister's actual body parts have been inserted into the statuesque figure, which represents St. Thérèse on the deathbed. Above the reliquary is a statue of the Virgin Mary, which is the same statue that cured Thérèse on May 13, 1883 in her home."

Then he mumbles to himself, "Strange customs. Strange rituals. *Oh c'est un monde étrange.* This murder is strange. Could it be some sick religious sexual crime to say nuns should never have children? *Non, ça n'est pas possible.* Is it some sick person collecting organs? I have never seen this before." He finally stops as if catching himself, realizing his monologue is in fact in the presence of an audience.

"It was her wish to be cremated," Dr. Janus says tersely.

"*Mais Oui, Monsieur,* of course. We do as the nun wishes," he agrees quickly, as if suddenly embarrassed by what he has said.

"May I go now?" Dr. Janus asks curtly, turning his back on the policeman and moving toward the door.

"Of course. I again am sorry for your loss. Leave your information with the policeman out front guarding the door."

"Oh," Dr. Janus says as an after thought turning on his heels, "may I please take her rosary?"

"Her rosary?" says the Frenchman quizzically.

"Yes, you can't miss it; it is large and was a gift from my father. She never went anywhere without it."

The coroner moves the habit cloth and says, "There does not appear to be one, and I looked on both sides, just in case."

The inspector's brows lift as he comments, "Her rosary missing, how odd. This was certainly not thought of as a robbery. Was it valuable?"

"Only sentimental."

"Perhaps the Mother Superior has it," he offers consolingly.

"Perhaps," says Dr. Janus.

"Do you see anything else missing?" asks the inspector.

"Nothing I can tell." Dr. Janus solemnly turns to walk out, verifies basic information with the policeman, and says we can find our way out. He motions to me, and we head down the hall. When out of earshot, he turns to me and says, "None of this makes sense."

I start to say how sorry I am, and he interrupts me with, "Where could her rosary have gotten to? It was a gift from my father. She would never have left without it. It was so unique, no nun had one like it; at first, the Mother Superior didn't want her to keep it because it was large and jeweled and not the simple Carmelite one. It set Tess apart from the other nuns, but my father insisted she wear it; I think the church agreed, for fear of losing funding."

"Jeweled?" I say, jumping. "Jeweled as in three on each side and one big jewel in the middle, hanging from a huge chunk of gold, jeweled?" I'm so excited I can barely get the words out.

"Yes?" Dr. Janus looks confused.

"Come quick. I think I might have seen it when you were signing us in upon our first visit. I came upon a sign that said 'Relics Room.' I had no idea what it was, but the door was slightly ajar, and I sneaked in. To my shock it was a saint's hair, robe, shoes, shovel, and all these other things that must have belonged to her. It grossed me out a bit, but I remember thinking, on top of the fact that that could be my scalp with the way the red hair fell, that the rosary seemed regal for such a simple convent. I thought, wow how things had changed from pictures I had seen of nuns and the ones I had met in Italy." I look at him. "You don't suppose the rosary could be hers, the real thing, do you?"

"Show me." We walk briskly, trying not to draw attention, and I almost take my shoes off because all that can be heard is the *click* of my steps vibrating through the halls. I try to step on the balls of my feet, which helps a little, but so far we're alone.

I get him to the courtyard, look around to reacquaint myself and trying to look nonchalant, I say under my breath, "This way."

The courtyard is empty because the nuns are in vespers and no attention is being paid to us. The relics room's door is slightly open as it had been that previous day, and I point in excitement to the rosary hanging below the simple wooden cross on the wall.

"That's it," Dr. Janus says, utterly shocked and looking at me strangely. "Good memory," he says calmly, as if he has not just found out his sister is dead.

There's only an arms length of rope keeping us from touching the rosary. "What do we do?" I ask. "Perhaps you should go to Mother Superior and point out it is Tess's and you would like to take it home."

"But what if she doesn't agree? What would we do then?"

"I don't know." I pause and think, knowing I'm about to commit a Ten Commandments sin. "Do we just steal it? I mean it is hers, so technically it wouldn't be stealing, I suppose."

I realize there's not much time. This is a murder though. If we take it, we could be accused of tampering with evidence. Or is that only in the room where the crime is committed? I have no idea. People have lawyers for such things. I quickly motion to him to go stand by the door. "Is anyone coming?"

He looks around and shakes his head no. As if expecting to get electrocuted, I jump over the rope, grab the rosary, stick it in my pants, and pretend nothing has happened.

Casually, we both head back through the courtyard. I'm acting as if I'm comforting him for his horrible loss, which is true. We get to the limo, and he orders the driver to leave immediately.

My heart is palpitating. For a second I wonder if I'll go to hell for stealing from a convent. It's pretty much the only commandment other than coveting another man's wife I remember, oh, and of course, murder. Having no real knowledge of religion, I decide I'll think about it later. My hands are now shaking, a delayed response, like after one recovers from an accident, as I hold the precious last article belonging to Tess in my hands and look at it closely.

"What do you know about this rosary, and why did your dad give it to her?"

"He made it. Each piece of gold was melted from other jewelry from the family and each stone placed by his hand."

"It's stunning."

"Yes. He used to tease Tess by saying 'Your savior or your death.'"

All of a sudden we both look at each other, stunned. "Your savior or your death? That was the first note," I yelp.

"Yes, it was! How could I have forgotten?"

And now it is too late, I think. My head is spinning. You could see some excitement for the first time back in Dr. Janus's eyes. "Mags, I have something…" and he cuts himself off. "Later, never mind," and he looks forward to the limo driver. "Can we pick up the speed a little today?"

"*Oui, Monsieur.*"

The ride seems to take much longer, and I want my computer to work on this new clue. I can see most of the artwork in my head, but not all of it. *This changes everything. Why would his father refer to the rosary as such?*

Then the sadness of Tess's death starts to sink in. There's gloom and heaviness in the car. All of a sudden I have to go to the bathroom really, really badly. "How far are we from the plane?"

"Oh, about forty-five minutes," the driver states.

"Forty-five minutes. Hmm…" Then a couple of minutes later, "Would there happen to be any rest areas along the way?"

"*Non, ma Cherie,* is all until *l' aéroport.*" I look at Dr. Janus embarrassed and say, "I'm afraid I'll never make it that far. Not to be rude, but I have to pee so badly that if we hit one more bump, I can't promise what will happen."

He looks at me and laughs endearingly, in the way he had done at the table when the chairs were too big for me. "Driver, pull over please, our Mademoiselle must 'pee,' as she so delicately informed me."

The driver pulls over speedily on demand. Dr. Janus pulls some napkins from the bar and gives them to me, grinning widely. "Enjoy the scenery! We'll look the other way!"

"Promise?" I say, laughing, welcoming a moment of lightness amongst the gloom.

"Promise."

I exit the limo, walk around to the side, see absolutely no place to hide behind a tree. The landscape is perfectly flat, so I lean up against the limo wondering if the limo driver will be

angry, and well, quite frankly, I squat. Despite the humiliation, I'll now be able to think again.

I get into the limo to see Dr. Janus still smiling. "Did everything meet your expectations?" he inquires, still with a good sense of humor.

"Most certainly," I reply. "I do apologize, sir," to the limo driver.

He laughs. "Only you Americans would be so tied up. We French, we love every part of the human body and respect its nature!"

I knew he meant "uptight," but I was in no position to correct him.

"Onward, James," Dr. Janus mocks, using the universal name for a limo driver, an international joke. The limo driver smiles, and we're back on our way to the plane.

chapter

40

Roman de clef

French word that means blueprint

n the plane, I run to my computer, pull up the first scanned clue, write the new rosary information: "Your Savior or Your Death." I have to figure this out even though Tess is dead. The gruesome scene makes me run to the bathroom to wash off. I swear I can still smell the stench of death from the room, worse than cheap perfume.

After we're in the air for a while, Dr. Janus comes over to me and says, "Mags, look at me. Don't look away. Don't feel bad, and listen to every word I have to say."

I look at him tentatively, as I assume I'm about to hear a confession of his involvement in this case. "Okay…"

He leans over to me, grabs my hands, put his eyes down and then back up, and looks directly into my eyes. "Magdalena…"

"Yes?" My heart is jumping out of my skin.

"I could not say anything while we were there, please understand me."

"Yes?" By the tone in his voice, I know something is wrong, and all the fear that had been replaced with excitement now comes flooding back, and I think I'll cry. "What?" I squeak out.

Very slowly and methodically, as if in a rhythm, "That (*beat, beat*) … was not (*beat, beat*) … my sister."

"*What?*" I jump up from the seat, almost losing my balance. He recoils as I start pacing with my hands grasped over my mouth. "Are you sure?" I shoot him a look like a dagger.

He sits calmly, leaning back into the seat. "Positive."

"What do you mean? Wait, when did you know?"

"When they removed the hair from her face, I realized it was Sister Sophia Marguerite, whom we met when we were there last. Their resemblance was uncanny."

Still in shock and letting it sink in. "Sister Sophia Marguerite?"

"Yes."

"You're sure?"

"Yes."

"Well, why didn't you say something?" I'm utterly baffled.

"Mags, there may still be a chance to save Tess. If people think she is dead and the police are involved, maybe the perpetrators will give up."

"Oh, I see, I see!" I pace for a few more minutes, not really seeing. "Whew!" A big moan emerges. I'm relieved and then angry again. "You let me think it was her? You waited until now to tell me?"

"I didn't know who I trusted. I almost told you in the limo. I didn't want you to suffer any more, but who knows who the driver is and if he can be trusted."

My bobble head is going full speed, as if this helps register the information. "I don't know whether to hit you or hug you! She's alive. I mean she may not be dead yet, I mean this may not be over?" Overwhelming excitement hits. *Some psychologist,* I think, *exhibiting manic behavior like that.* Up and down, up and down, but the situation warranted it, so I wasn't going to be too hard on myself.

"It's not over?" I look to him for confirmation.

"It is not over."

"That's great!"

"Yes, it is great."

I jump into his arms and give him a huge hug. "Thank God!"

"Yes, Mags." He smiles. "Thank God and thank you."

"Oh, I was feeling so guilty as if I had killed her myself and so angry at you."

"I know, Mags. I was having those feelings about myself. I heard what you said to me, every word. What I'll do about it, I don't know, but these people mean business, and I can't ignore that any longer. It will not be acceptable if I do nothing."

"Good, let's get back to work!" I settle into the seat.

We review every clue and are coming to the same conclusion. The person sending them is fervently against the pharmaceutical companies and feels Dr. Janus can do something about it. Dr. Janus had talked about how nature- and herb-oriented his parents were, but he couldn't imagine they were this anti-pharm too. They lived in a civilized world. They had seen people from the old country die due to poor sanitary conditions and poverty.

After a while, I offer, "Dr. Janus, do you think the killer meant to leave us a clue at the convent and hide it in plain sight? He or she didn't kill Tess, somehow, and for some reason the kidnapper may be protecting her. Perhaps *he*, for simplicity of the conversation, is helping us get to the bottom of this but can't be too obvious. Who would know you and your family well enough to do such a thing? This is an intimate issue."

"Well, Ana, not really James, Saul, my parents are dead, me, and Tess. I can't think of anyone else who knows Tess that well or would even know about the house."

We are quiet, and I'm fidgeting with the seatbelt when I see the sign to fasten is lit. I expect turbulence and breathe in deeply.

Then, as if I'd been injected with a clue, I break the silence. "That's it, Dr. Janus, that's it. It has to be. There's only one common denominator to Tess and this information, *if* we rule out the fact you have not set this entire thing up yourself, and that's Saul."

"Saul? Saul would never hurt Tess." His face was contorted; I'd never heard such a high pitch from his voice.

"That's my point. But what is larger, more powerful than him that would force him to make these moves and still try to save her? What would he gain? That's assuming he has her best interests in mind."

We both think, and then I ask, "Was he mad at you, your family?"

"Well, when dad died, he was out of work, but we still provided for him, so I can't imagine it would be about money."

"Think, Dr. Janus, think. I have a sinking feeling time is running out."

An odd look came to Dr. Janus's face. He looked green as if he had realized something but couldn't get it out.

"What? You're green."

"Nothing. I think the relief of knowing Tess might not be dead has just caught up with me."

I wonder if that's really what he's thinking. Then I hear words in my head, *Roman de clef.* I know the words means blueprint, but what was a blueprint? Why did these words come to mind now? Then I wondered if it was Roman "de" clef or Roman "a" clef that popped up. Irony creeps in again because I've been told "Roman a clef" means a novel that depicts (usually famous) real people and events under the guise of fiction. And that is what my life was beginning to feel like, fiction! So was it a blueprint or the crazy story of my life I was being warned about?

chapter
41

Nature does not hurry, yet everything is accomplished.

Lao Tzu

ess had spent days thinking about Saul, her daughter, and what her life would have been like should they have been a family. She loved this man despite what had happened and now hoped that somehow she could get out of here, find her child, and perhaps the three of them could be a family.

One day she finally heard to her relief, "Good morning, Tessie," in Saul's real voice, no longer manipulated by the electronic machine.

He went in to lie next to her. He held on to her for dear life, and she reciprocated.

"You're safe now, Tess. You can live."

She didn't want to ask more at that moment.

Much later, after the solitude, he moved to sit up and face Tess with a serious look. "Tess, there are some things you still need to know. You'll have to hide for life, but you can't stop working on what your father started. He meant it when he used to tell you, 'Your Savior or Your Death,' and it wasn't about religion. It was about the manipulation of the DNA system, cloning, genetically modified food, new drugs, chemical sweetening agents, pesticides, antibiotics, and all; combined, they're killing the population. Your dad figured out the real links and keys to DNA and healing, and now they want all his material destroyed.

"Listen, from what I can tell, the key is in the DNA double helix concept. If your dad was right, there is no *junk* DNA and all the answers are right in front of us. Our DNA is still evolving. I know it's hard to understand if you're not a scientist, but mankind continues to evolve. Not in the crazy Darwinian-evolution-lie-we-come-from-apes sort of way versus creationism, but in a more electro-energetics way. Our systems are so incredibly sensitive, and we respond to light, sound, other people's energies, the list goes on, but our ability to flourish is totally being killed from the core. We are being 'dumbed down,' disenlightened, and damaged with vaccines, cancer treatments, food, chemicals in the air, and that list goes on.

"For a while, seeing how brilliant your dad was, I became jealous and wanted the accolades, to receive the patents and get the info out, but no matter what I did, I kept missing pieces and could not match his level of intelligence. Some of his ideas were really 'out there.'"

He paused for effect and said with a great gesture of his hands, "Like his crazy notion we were living in a two-dimensional world because we've been restricted by the evil doers with a double helix DNA. He claimed to have found a way to remove the veil and open up the other helixes so we can have our systems programmed the way they're supposed to be.

"Your father asserted that in this non-dumbed-down state, illness and rapid aging is greatly decreased, if not eliminated. We can return to the state of living 120 years as we were intended to. Look back to the long-lived patriarchs in the Old Testament for how life is supposed to be. In the current double helix state, we are lied to and forced to believe medicine is necessary. Your father took information from the Bible, translated it more properly with the help of scholars and bio-geneticists who had given up the 'system' and started figuring out how this worked. Peter did finally contact some of the people from your father's past when he realized the kidnapping probably had to do with his work on DNA. They're all underground at the moment until their time of glory arises."

He stopped, proud, and pointed at Tess, which caused her to smile like a schoolchild.

"Your father used to always tease that we should take the gospel—'God's pill'—and throw out some of the medicine, 'med-is-sin!' The deceivers are the men and spirits in this world that affect and ruin the will of man. The serpents and the scorpions are the creeping things symbolizing the emotions of people, the mind-control of people. We have been misled by religion, by media so we no longer remember truth. God tells us if we believe and ask in Jesus's name, we have control over *all* these things.

"This is where you'll need to come in. One day your father explained a fascinating part of Genesis to me and almost made me a believer in the 'factualness' in the Bible when it is translated properly. He joked it was the 'Genes-is good part from

His story,' plays on words for Genesis and history!'" He said the words slowly for emphasis as Tess silently nodded her head in understanding.

"Your father explained that after all the races were made, God created Adam on the eighth day. 'Adam,' translated from Hebrew, simply means a man with white skin, such that blood can be seen in his face when he blushes."

He looked at Tess to see her reaction, and she was just listening. He continued. "Therefore, first, all the other races were made, and God said they were good. Then he created Caucasians. This means all these years of races fighting is 100 percent against the Word of God. He loves all his people who love Him and not evil. We should never have judged a race. But that's not even the interesting part."

He looked to Tess eagerly for her expression. "The interesting part is where God used the rib of Adam to create Eve. Now what kind of psycho story is that, since there's no person on earth who is born with a missing rib? When you get to the proper translation and realize there's *no* lie in the Bible, just misinterpretations, you see things you've never seen before. The singular word *rib* occurs in the Bible once and only in Genesis. Why? Translated it means 'curve.' God took the curved substance of which Adam was made and created Eve. God took Adam's—what looks like a curve or helix—" he paused for effect, and his eyes became bluer, "DNA and made Eve!

"Your dad diligently worked through every Scripture and found all the hidden answers to how we as humans work, why we are here, and our ultimate purpose in life. He shared a lot with me and taught me what I know, but he withheld the final pieces. He knew this information would change the world, but he started getting death threats and feared for your family's lives. He trusted me to a degree and set up the Granite House. Every

part has a new clue. He didn't want his work taken over and destroyed, nor did he want it changed into other lies."

He leaned close to Tess, "I have left some information for you in the safe room. You'll need to look it over at some point. You must open your *eyes* and help others do so too."

He inadvertently rubbed his eyes.

"Your father said it all in the entrance of your house, where it tells you all things are foretold, beware of the ..." He looks at her for an answer.

"I always wondered what was after that."

Saul continued proudly, "Serpent. You'll see the lettering in plain sight now that you know what it says. It's the serpent, the deceiver of all, which most do not even believe exists, which is why it's so easy to control all of us. I had gotten this far, but I needed help with some information on the zodiac and signs, so I sent the actual artwork of your father's, which you've never seen, as clues to Peter, inserting a couple of weak ones I made up on my own to make some clues more obvious. What I really wanted to know was what they meant. The girl working with Dr. Janus has them. She seems pretty smart, quite an archetypal genius and some kind of symbol researcher. She was making headway, but I'm afraid we've run out of time."

He paused, paced, and then knelt at her feet. Tess looked down lovingly.

"I'm sorry for having to kidnap you, but you know as well as I that had I come to the convent to discuss this and told you of such things, you would have thought I was possessed by the devil. You would never have believed me. I would never have gotten Peter's attention either."

"I suppose ..." Tess reached out and put her hand to his cheek.

"Besides, I thought you hated me for what I had done to you."

"I see."

She stroked the furrow in his brow gently, and after a moment he grabbed her hands in his. "Do you? Psychologically, Tessie, you have had such a trust and attachment to Holy Mother Church that you stopped seeing the truth years ago. You can no longer trust that two plus two equals four. It could be a deception, a lie. You need to re-examine all the premises again and search for the real truth, not the lies and hooks of man sent to put you off course and make them bow down to the hierarchy of the day, but to the *true* thing that gives you life and peace in the midst of pain and suffering."

He stood, saying, "God wants the scales to be lifted from your eyes, so let them be. Look into the hierarchy; Council of 13, The Grand Druid Council that takes orders from the Rothschilds; Council of 33, the highest thirty-three masons in the world, who some believe Billy Graham is on this level; Council of 500, the wealthiest people in the world, most outside the U.S. Groups involved include Scientology, Unity, and are the main platforms for witches. People in these congregations do not even know."

Tess looked perplexed but he continued on, "The Roman Catholic Church is by far the richest and most powerful, but in God's eyes, all false teaching makes them poor. The cathedrals with the pagan symbols of the obelisk, the phallic symbol, the vagina, Isis—all on the front lawn of the Vatican City and Washington, D.C., for that matter, because these rulers worship pagan and perverted sexual gods. We should tear them down and put up God's true desire. One nation truly under God ruled by the people, for the people. Not the deceived ones paying taxes.

"So the Roman Catholic Church, with its cathedrals and pillars and domes and basilicas and convents and monasteries and banks and coins and merchandise for the church and selling vendor items, is all one big money-making scheme. How is it that miles of books can be kept secret from the public, that the most priceless

art and paintings can't be shared but are kept underground? How else can you secretly trade things the public doesn't know about for monetary or political power? If we, the people, don't know it exists, how can we accuse them of selling it? Clever, isn't it?"

He paused for a quick breath and to read her eyes, and then continued, "Tess, I don't have the answers to so many things, and it's now out of my control to resolve them. But you have a chance to answer questions and build an army, a true army for the Lord the way He would want it. You can help people find real truth by removing the veil of deception. I know there are documented healings at Lourdes and that Evangelicals heal people, but how does it work? Is it mass hypnosis, hysteria, a belief that controls the mind? Is Lourdes an apparition summoned by the devil to control and presents itself as the Virgin because Mary would not have lied, would she? Or is it a real supernatural healing from God, which I now have proof occurs. But for some, these healings are an elaborate hoax of the devil to pull you in further, show you some neat things, and then have you worship evil."

He seemed to stop mid-sentence and then walked around the cell looking at the walls as Tess attentively watched him pace. "What is it Saul, what are you thinking? What are you afraid to ask me?" she asked, knowing intuitively something was going on inside him.

He turned and studied her attentively. "Yes, I need to know some things from you, please, do you know anything about our baby girl?"

She thought before replying, going back in her mind over all the choices that had brought her here today, then spoke. "Yes, from what I have heard, she is beautiful, tall, and really quite brilliant. Dad helped place the baby with an incredible, loving family. The parents did not want to have children of their own."

"Is she evil like me?"

She looked Saul in the eyes, wondering what his life had been like after she left. "No, from what I have heard, she is loving and kind and good and is, in a sense, her own form of crusader for truth and justice."

"Did you ever name our daughter?"

Tess smiled so proudly. "Oh, yes, Saul, I gave her a beautiful name. Nature made her perfect, so I named her after a saint, the Saint de' Pazzi, who was also a Carmelite nun and whose feast is kept on May 27 of every year.

"She was sainted sixty-two years after her death due to innumerable miracles that had followed her death. I chose her because of raptures that seized her whole body, forcing her to move toward sacred objects, and she would utter maxims of divine love, the perfection of souls, and is said to be quoted even more than St. Thérèse. In ecstasy, she could embroider and paint perfectly composed paintings. Saint Mary Magdalen de' Pazzi. Our daughter's name is Magdalena." Tess had such pride on her face and was bursting with excitement.

"Magdalena? What? Oh dear Lord, I couldn't have!" Pure terror crossed his face. He ran toward the door.

Tess was suddenly terrified. "What? What is wrong?"

"We have to go. We have to go *now*."

chapter

42

And I say also unto thee, That thou art Peter; and upon this rock I will build My church; and the gates of hell shall not prevail against it. And I will give unto the keys of the kingdom of heaven; and whatsoever though shalt bind on earth shall be bound in heaven; and whatsoever thou shalt loose on earth shall be loosed in heaven. Then charged He His disciples that they should tell no man the he was Jesus the Christ.

Matthew 16:18

 return to the empty house the next day, back from the 'staged' funeral. The staff has been given the week off to mourn the loss of Tess and allow Dr. Janus his privacy. I'm fidgety. I've kept Tess's rosary and start looking more closely at it. I pull the cross up to my eyes and fiddle with it to take a closer look. I push a little too hard on one section on the back, and a whole piece of the arm snaps down.

Having a conversation with myself, I freak. "I broke it. Oh no, I broke it." Then it dawns on me it is purposeful. By playing with it like a puzzle piece, I'm able to unhinge some things, and, to my amazement, it falls into a perfectly formed pyramid with the center top diamond or stone looking as if it were the clear capstone.

"Cool! Just like the pyramids in Egypt, but this one has a capstone."

This is the oddest shaped diamond or crystal I have ever seen. Carl Jung was accurate; my hand has just solved something my brain could not. It's incredible. I turn it around in my hands a couple of times. I jiggle a couple more parts, the stone falls out, and under it I see a gold clasp. I flip it up, and I finally realize what a portion of Dr. Janus's "secrecy" has been all about.

I look at this precious little baby's picture in the locket part of the rosary. I now know this is why Tess was sent to the convent. Poor Tess. What it must have been like to have a child at such a young age. Family secrets.

I hate lies. Tess has to be alive, and that's all that matters. I get back to the eerily quiet house and head to the gardens. James and Dr. Janus will be at the service longer.

I've been having this nagging reminder of the sign at the gardener's shed, and I want to check it out. Something feels incomplete. I also want to learn more about what's under the house. I still haven't told anyone. I need to walk off some tension, so I opt to leave the golf cart and use my own legs.

My head, as usual, is partially in the clouds, but I find my way to the shed and hear some rustling. No one's supposed to be around. *Who is it?* I wonder. And then, catching me totally off guard, a man jumps out from the side of the shed, pulls a gun, aims, and at that exact moment, in perfect Magdalena fashion, I trip over a stone in the path and fall to my knees as the bullet whizzes past me.

I look up, and in a split second the gunman is closer. I see his perfect aim at my head, and in a flash, I see a man appear from nowhere behind him, the sun blocks the view of his face, and as a shovel hits the marksman's head, I feel a sting so sharp everything goes blank.

chapter
43

Who looks outside, dreams; who looks within, awakes.

Carl Jung

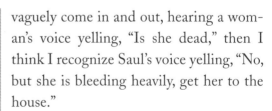vaguely come in and out, hearing a woman's voice yelling, "Is she dead," then I think I recognize Saul's voice yelling, "No, but she is bleeding heavily, get her to the house."

It makes no sense, why would Saul be in the garden? All goes blank for seconds until I realize that I am bouncing up and down...blank...a bump...blank...a bump...*Where am I?*

I try to look around. . . . a lady is yelling, "Help!" at the top of her lungs. I realize I am in a wheelbarrow. *Am I hallucinating? Am I dying?*

I open my eyes long enough to see Dr. Janus and James running toward me. James is taking me in his arms and yelling, "No time for re-acquaintances now. Get to the kitchen and get me some boiling water and clean towels."

I smile weakly at my beautiful James. He looks at me firmly, "You're gonna be okay, Mags, hang in there. You've been shot."

"Shot?" I say weakly. "Like in the movies, shot?"

A tiny smile creeps to his face. "Yes, like in the movies," he says in a soft and loving tone. I then hear such a loud explosion, the earth tremors, and James stops for a second. "What on earth?"

Then a woman screams in terrible pain at the top of her lungs, "Oh my beloved Saul!"

Blank.

chapter
44

Woe betide any book or author that falls outside the official guidelines. Foundation support is not there. Publishers get cold feet. Distribution is hit and miss, or non-existent.

Anthony C. Sutton

fter Saul had put his daughter in the wheelbarrow and knew Tess would be safe, he dragged the body of the dazed assassin through the entrance to the tunnel into the shed, which had been covered by a tool closet, locked the door from the inside, heading down to his grave.

"Forgive me, Father, for I have sinned. I do take Jesus as my Savior but know it is too late." He then adds, "I'll call the final chapter of my life 'The Scorpion's Sting,' just like the artwork. A scorpion can kill a creature larger than itself, and for now I have paralyzed La Compagnia. I'll never have to worry if any foundation, pharmaceutical company, medical community, organization, media enterprise, or publishing company ever believes me because I'll be dead. My time on earth has ended."

He tried to keep calm, knowing that the underground holding cells had been set to explode and at any moment he'd be engulfed by flames. But then his thoughts rested on the scorpion once more, maniacal laughter wracked his pale body. There was a well-known fallacy that when a scorpion is cornered by fire, it commits suicide.

He repeated to himself as a way of trying not to focus on his looming death, "Scorpion. Kingdom: Animalia; Phylum: Arthropoda; Sub phylum: Chelicerata; Class: Arachnida; Sub class: Dromopoda; Order: Scorpiones. The scorpion is an arthropod with eight legs; its tail has six segments, with the last one bearing the stinger called the telson, at the end of which is the hypodermic aculeus or venom-injecting barb. Oh, the irony of the hypodermic, the irony of the scorpion's sting. The irony of my life! I have a daughter." More hysterical laughter unexpectedly erupted. The assassin never stirred.

He continued thinking, *The scorpion has armor—too bad I no longer do. The scorpion's outer hyaline layer makes them fluorescent green under the ultraviolet light…*

And suddenly he got it.

Twenty years of missing the most significant clue, and now he finally got it? The laughter exploded as he held his belly.

"How could I have been so stupid? Could it really end this way?"

But it was out of his control now.

His gaze was filled with flames, and then … nothing.

chapter
45

Only he who can see the invisible can do the impossible.

Frank Gaines (1897–1977)

he next thing I remember is waking to terrible piercing pain, trying to piece together the events that had transpired. I have no idea what day it is. Despite the throbbing, a nagging thought of what's under the entrance of the Granite House pulls me out of bed as I find my voice, stronger than my body feels, I yell, "Dr. Janus, meet me in the entrance!" As I do so, I realize Tess's rosary is hanging around my neck. *How sweet*, I think.

As I'm making my way to the foyer, not only does Dr. Janus come running, but so does a woman. I'm stunned and confused. Dr. Janus exclaims, "Are you okay? What's wrong?" My eyes don't leave the gorgeous female. My heart drops for a second, thinking he actually does have a lover.

It takes some time to regroup as my mental acuity has not completely returned, and Dr. Janus realizes I must not remember anything. "Magdalena, this is Tess, my sister, safe and sound and alive because of you!"

They both come closer dotingly and fill me in on what I had obviously blocked out. I grab Tess's hand. "I'm so glad you are safe, I thought my inexperience had killed you at one point!"

"No, my dear, you saved my life and I shall be forever grateful."

Then, as if this incredible reunion didn't just happen, I'm back to business telling them that there's no time at the moment to catch up. I'm on to something and we need to get to it "emimitly." They look at me like I've lost my mind.

"Oh, it's what I used to say to my mom as a child when I wanted her to change something impossible, like the color of my red hair, and wanted it done immediately. Never mind." Perhaps I was looped up on some drug. I deliver this explanation from all fours, or rather threes, on the ground, rubbing the floor, as I suddenly realize they aren't yet privy to the new ideas in my mind and that I've caused a mild panic.

I explain I'm really fine, and as if on cue, James lets himself in, glances down at me, and without missing a beat, says, "Back in that position again I see!"

"James!"

"How's it hangin'?" James asks in his unique accent.

"Not bad." I stand up rather clumsily since I can't use the full strength of my arm to assist me. "I'm vaguely remembering you asking for hot water, did you operate on me?"

"I did."

"Am I scarred for life?" I ask jokingly, but he looks hurt.

"I..."

"I'm kidding. Thanks, hero," I say, and I lean up to kiss him on the cheek.

"Aw, gee shucks!" He blushes under the dark tones of his skin, and his eyes twinkle.

Dr. Janus pipes in, the most jovial I've seen him since this all began. "Mags clearly has a new idea, so we are indulging her."

I get back on the floor and take the rosary from my neck, just then realizing I'm not even totally dressed. I notice I have on a pair of shorts and what looks like a man's jean T-shirt covering me. I play with the back of the rosary, fold down the arms, shape it as the pyramid so I can extract the diamond-type crystal, feel on the floor with my one working arm, and head for the next location.

Tess and Dr. Janus had obviously never discovered this about the rosary. I tell everyone to stand in the center, then I go to where my heel had previously been caught in the floor, jam the stone into the eye of the serpent with the point tipped to the skies, and, to everyone's shock, the floor starts to slowly move in a counterclockwise direction.

"What is it? What's happening?" they ask in unison. We're all slightly off balance with the moving of the floor. The mechanism that makes the floor move whines and squeals from years of neglect. Over the sounds, I half shout, "If I'm right, there's a whole section under the house and this is how you get to it."

"Could that be?" they echo.

I'm a little nervous, but at this point, having survived a bullet, what's the worst that can happen?

"The light from the stone reflects into the sky dome and constellations in some way such that its light beam hits a trigger and the floor moves. I'm no mechanic, but when I got the words,

All things foretold and then saw how S-E-R-P-E-N-T lit up when in a certain light, I knew it was a clue." I have everyone's rapt attention. "I was convinced something manmade was under here when I saw a piece of paper flutter—clearly air was coming from somewhere. I still didn't know how to get to it until I realized 'The Scorpion's Sting' clue said 'Behold (),' as in eye, not 'I' have foretold you all things. Thinking back to mythology and the 'eye' of Horus, the all-seeing eye, which is the capstone or cornerstone above the pyramid and on the American dollar bill, I knew there had to be a connection. It wasn't until a diamond-shaped stone that could fold into a pyramid fell out of the rosary that I realized the stone was about the size of my heel, and why else would the mosaic floor be missing only one piece? Always look for the odd one out.

"If I'm correct, we'll slowly descend until the spot of Scorpio hits Taurus. I have no idea how this works, but if you've ever been to a theatrical show or opera, like the Met, you know how incredible the stage is underneath and what goes into these huge productions. If I hadn't seen the Queen of the Night ascend from the depths to the main stage at the Met, I would never have realized this could be done. All you need to have is a switch, and in essence, I found the switch!"

We have now slowly descended about five feet, and sure enough, we stop where Scorpio hits Taurus. Conveniently placed is a curved, steel staircase directing us further into the depths of the house. There's enough light to see a huge lab with all sorts of machines, books, and microscopes with very little dust on the actual machines, considering almost twenty-five years must have passed since anyone has been here.

I had imagined the impossible and had been correct.

chapter
46

For we are not wrestling with flesh and blood (contending only with physical opponents), but against the depotisms, against the powers, against (the master spirits who are), the world rulers of this present darkness, against the spirit forces of wickedness in the heavenly (supernatural) sphere.

Ephesians 6:12, Amplified Bible

ith just enough light to get down the stairs, at the bottom there is a box to flip on an overhead light that completely illuminates the place. It's a lab, all right. Dr. Janus and Tess are shocked.

I'm immediately drawn to the middle of the room where there's an odd-looking machine. It's like an old movie projector, and encased above it is a three-foot-by-three-foot glass cover with an odd reflection to it. It has a power

button, and as I analyze it, I see a shape for the insert. "This isn't just an ordinary machine," I say. "This needs an insert, like a punch card but larger. What could this be?" I turn the power on, but nothing happens.

James says, looking around, "There seems to be every type of microscope and updated machine available."

A shocked Dr. Janus says, "It's as if our father advanced them himself."

Enthralled, as I look to the sides of the same projector machine, it dawns on me. "I think I know what fits in here. I'll be right back." I run past a bewildered Tess, a puzzled Dr. Janus, and a curious James, and with new energy, take the stairs two at a time disappearing up to the foyer.

"Careful, Mags!" they yell in unison, knowing my proclivity for falling on stairs!

When I come galloping back yelling, "I got it, I got it!" I see Dr. Janus exploring the room, hands behind his back, broad shoulders hunched over this bit of machinery. "This is fascinating," says Dr. Janus, deeply enthralled by this machine with numerous holes and vials and tubes and a circular type insert. "I don't ever remember Dad having access to blood analyses and what looks like advanced DNA testing!"

Tess and James look over at him and seem just as intrigued so that they neglect to respond to my excitement. Then Dr. Janus points to the right of the microscope where there is a huge, wooden shelving unit, with glass inserts and cubicles. "Look, in each place there are little apothecary squares perfectly labeled. The top of the drawers reads *Energetique Magnifica Du Monde*. Each sample is named. There are flowers and herbs, species, blood, and then there are musical notes and language words and all these other things. How odd!"

"Hey guys," I say again, "I've got it!"

"Got what?" Now I have their full attention.

"Why, that's one of our wall hangings on the way up to the second floor," Dr. Janus proclaims.

"That it is," I say with pride. "And I think I know what it's for."

Tess walks toward me and adds, "I believe Dad said they were molecular structures, although he used to call them the crop circles coming in the fields to help us uncover our true selves and take away the lies of the world. We used to laugh."

"Laugh, but Tess, what if he was right? What if some of these have occurred on earth and they're correct? What if the only ones lying are the guys who tried to copy the crop circles—miserably—and got a government payoff to lead the public astray?"

"But you couldn't possibly believe in UFOs, aliens, or crop circles, could you?"

We gather around the lab table, and I respond as I get ready to insert the article, "I don't think so, but at this moment, I don't want to rule anything out."

Tess looks at me and says, "You've reminded me of something Saul said. He said even the Roman Catholic Church now allows people to believe aliens exist. Is there something the government is hiding? Is there something that has been going on that Dad knew about and it was just too risky to expose? Is this what it's all about?"

I take one last look at the first piece of metal I grabbed, hoping I'm not wrong. Then I move around to the side of the machine, lean down, and slip the glistening metal into a slot. I had grabbed the first one on the stairwell, and it seems to fit.

James heads toward the stairs. "I'm heading back up to check on things. Something doesn't feel right to me."

We barely acknowledge him while waiting a minute, wondering if anything will happen with the machine. We look cautiously at each other, and then smoke suddenly starts coming out

of everywhere. We back away and then toward each other as we realize we could be engulfed in poison. Nervously I say, "I think I've overheated or ruined the machine." Then an image comes from the puffs of smoke, like a holograph, and, to our surprise, a beautiful female voice speaks.

"Welcome back, Teddy. It has been twenty-two years since our last conversation. We are happy you remembered us. You have been dearly missed."

No one speaks, and then I brilliantly announce, "It's not Teddy, this is Mags, and I'm with his son and daughter. Unfortunately, Teddy is deceased."

No answer.

Tess turns to me in a sweet way. "Do you really think it can hear, dear, or perhaps it only speaks."

A little embarrassed, I blurt out, "At this point, Tess, I could believe almost anything!"

"Point taken," says Dr. Janus, his voice taking on an authoritative tone.

The ethereal voice speaks again. "You must now enter the password to continue."

We look at each other as the smoke in the hologram appears to gesture to a panel that has alphabets, numbers, and symbols on it. I ask them, "Do you guys have any idea what the password is?"

They shake their heads no. *Great*, I think. I certainly have no idea where to start.

"You have not responded yet; have you forgotten?" the voice prods just as sweetly.

"Yes," I blurt out. "Yes." I don't care if it can hear me.

Snapping into action, Dr. Janus turns and says, "Tess, look around to see if there are any books with codes or anything you can think of that would have the answer."

Tess moves to obey but throws up her hands as she heads to the nearest bookshelf, saying, "I don't think Dad would leave it out for anyone to see. He had an excellent memory, so he wouldn't really need to write it down."

Stopping Tess in her tracks and calling Dr. Janus back to attention, the machine speaks. "This is not like you, Teddy; perhaps this is the day you spoke of when you would no longer be around and hoped your children would have the scales removed enough to want to seek the truth."

The machine continues, immune to our quizzical looks and utter confusion. "The code is four letters and one sign. You have only three tries and five minutes before the system shuts down," and then, pausing as if for effect, "permanently."

"What? Five minutes and three tries?" I grab a paper and pen from another table and start writing their names and fooling with letters, asking them for clues. They start listing four letters, "Tess, Pete …" but are stumped.

"What else in your life? Come on, what else, what would also have a symbol?" Then it dawns on me. "Oh, wait a second, the machine said, the children would have the scales removed … scales …" I pause and think a few more seconds.

"When I saw you in the study, Dr. Janus, you were listening to a record that you said was made by your Dad from his favorite music. The lady's voice on the machine said hopefully 'they would have the *scales* removed.' She could have used many other words but didn't. You said your Dad loved music and was fascinated by harmonics and vibrations and genius composers."

The seconds were ticking away, and we hadn't punched anything in yet.

"Who or what could it be that has four letters?" I say, as if my panicked prodding will get them to think quicker. Tess puts her hands together as if folded under the scapular, perhaps hoping it

will help her think. Dr. Janus looks up at the machine hoping it will trigger a thought on the code.

"And don't forget a symbol," Tess adds, somewhat tentatively, "as if we don't have enough to come up with."

Dr. Janus starts with the composers on the tape, Mozart, Debussy, Wagner, Bach, Beethoven ..."

"No, no go back, Bach. That's got to be it. In secret societies, they used to take notes and chords and translate them into a secret language," I continue thinking aloud, "but in harmonics, well, there are only eight notes in a scale and if you play them, they're ABcDEFG ... and then back to A, but then there are the flats and Bach spelled in musical terms is Bac-h, which is B flat! Look, look there are sharps and flats on the symbol keyboard. Bach is spelled B-A-C-B flat. That would be four letters and a symbol!"

"You have thirty seconds remaining; please enter the code."

"Go ahead, Mags; we have no other ideas."

"Let's try it." My voice of excitement defies my inner nervousness.

Controlling my shaking fingers, I lick my lips and concentrate as I carefully punch in B-A-C-B flat and hold my breath.

To my utter amazement, we hear, "Welcome Teddy's children, we are pleased to meet you at last." Every hair on my body stands on edge, a mix between excitement and anticipation or fear. It's astounding. Truly amazing. Tess sighs with great relief, and Dr. Janus puts an approving arm on my good shoulder as we all turn our attention to the voice and the holograph.

"Let us introduce ourselves. We are called the 'Light Bringers.' We have been watching over your planet for centuries, but we are not allowed to enter your atmosphere unless you are about to cause permanent damage to the beautiful creation, earth, or you specifically call on us for help. We have been around almost from the beginning of time. We do not inhabit an earth body like yours but, like you, are made in His image."

We all eye each other as if to check we're hearing the same thing and are in fact really standing in some secret room below a foyer watching a holograph.

The voice continues. "We have been through the first earth age with many of you. We saw the fallen angels mate with humans in the second earth age and create the giants called geber and hybrid ones. This was against God's plan, so he sent the great flood to recleanse the earth. He had Noah bring one *pair* of each untainted race, animal, and plant. Their essence, or DNA, contained in the Energetique Magnifica du Monde of each living being in existence, was brought on the ark, as directed by God.

"We have seen all the trials and tribulations of *humans* and watched their pain. We work on many levels of light and in more dimensions than you could understand. We know Michael and the other archangels that some of you refer to but that *many* humans believe are just myths. The angels, the story of creation, and the tribulations on earth are not myths."

The voice continues from the smoke, and in the depths is the most beautiful pinkish woman in a flowing gown moving from the reflections. We are spellbound. "In this second earth age, there is a huge war going on around planet earth. Not just the physical ones of Afghanistan, Israel, and Iraq, but a spiritual war. Few people are willing to see this spiritual war that dominates your world. You are being taught false religions, run by corrupt politics and governments who are only after their own power and greed. You are being taught false histories while being poisoned with your own foods and chemicals in the atmosphere and poisons you call medicines. It has been this way for centuries, but instead of waking up to it, you have become the most

deceived nation in the world because you accept this false information freely."

It's amazing. Is the hologram an angel, a species in a time warp? How could it have kept up with knowing what had happened in the past twenty-two years? My mind is racing, but I can't think with the voice continuing.

"You are not worshipping the light, but rather are in a constant state of mind control and manipulation. The dark ones make you act in unhealthy ways and try to convince you of royal bloodlines and other lies. You are their slaves. Remember loved ones, after the death of Jesus, all who claim Christ can be part of the resurrection. Your one main purpose and reason for being sent here is for revelation, which means to re-remember your calling and past. You are given freewill to choose whether you want to worship good or evil. Most of you chose evil simply by non-action, 'fence sitting,' being comfortable, and being deceived.

"It's time to wake up, to make change. The universe is moving quickly, and if you choose to become an enlightened one, you need to start acting now. You have heard talk of Doomsday, December 21, 2012, and the end of calendars, such as the Mayans, etc., and although much of this is exaggerated, there is some truth to it.

"Doomsday is not a good term because, done right with positive intention, it could be the start of peace and harmony. At that time, the earth will change its axis, which will cause huge magnetic shifts in the poles. This will cause tornadoes and hurricanes and other things, but God promised after the destruction from the flood and the ice age that He would never permanently destroy the earth. With more prayer and more people moving to the good side, you have a chance of moving into 'paradise' versus the hell on earth in which you are living."

Tess moves backwards and leans against the unit that holds the earthly vials. She looks pale, I assume from being bombarded with information. Dr. Janus stands firmly, not removing his eyes from the source of the voice. The smoke continues but is dissipating quickly and not sticking in the room. Somehow, despite this, the image is still there.

She continues. "As these shifts are happening, the lines and differentiation between the physical and spiritual are loosening. People are being born with abilities to speak to the Father more easily. All can speak to Him now, directly, as was promised when Christ said, 'You can do all these things and more.' Animal sacrifice or high priests are not needed to intervene with your Father. Pray, as He asks, for the things unseen, for He will make them manifest, if you have the substance called faith.

"There are those who believe Christ's crucifixion was a 'nice story,' yet these people still label themselves Christians. Because they claim to be good people doing good acts, these types of 'nominal' Christians can be more dangerous than those who imprison others. This is not entirely their fault, as so many of them are stopped from hearing the truth either from God or from seeking it, by interference of frequencies from TV's, radios, satellites, computers, angry music, and all the other distractions of the earth."

My mind is wandering briefly. *Is this a mirage? Can this be evil? How was this technology created over twenty-two years ago? What if we haven't found the right code? What if this is the evil side of information and we are being brainwashed. Will all this profound information be lost once it stopped talking?*

The voice gently cuts into my thoughts. "Discernment needs to happen. As the layers of deceit lift, more spiritual understanding will arise and the people who hunger for the truth will find it in the Word. Not the misrepresented church pronouncements, but the Ruach, the Holy Spirit speaking through earth people and being understood. Not just in forms of speaking in tongues, but in languages that will be understood by the dialect and time-frame one is in. God wants you to know and to hear His voice; He sends His Spirit to inspire and have those who listen write it down for the lost and deceived to read or to hear."

Now my head is starting to spin; I hope it's not the stress to my body from the gunshot wound.

For the first time, the voice pauses. "But that understanding is for a later lesson. It would be difficult for you to believe this with the way you think now."

As I stand there next to Dr. Janus, I wonder if the "you" is for him, for me, or for mankind in general.

Finally, I need to sit. This is all so much. I look for a chair, and intuitively Tess gets me one. I sit, and she stands by my side.

Tess sighs and has an odd expression of recognition on her face. I wonder if Saul had told her this strange tale.

"God is not the author of confusion, of Babel. If you are hurting, broken, addicted, and have given up, we assure you, you live in Satan's realm. Most do not even believe there is a *Satan*, a devil. They laugh. Do not laugh, my loved ones. Lucifer fell *eons* ago, and although being held by Michael in the heavens now with one-third of the fallen angels, he has free reign of the earth, and his method is to blind you to his presence so he and the government can control you.

When even one soul breaks through the veils of deceit to the truth, like your father and mother, our rejoicing is heard through all the heavens!"

She continues. "Beware of the Serpent. The Hebrew term for 'serpent' is Nachash, which has a primitive root meaning 'to hiss or to whisper.' It also means to search and scrutinize closely, to find out by experiment, to practice divination, augury, incan-

the scorpion's sting

tation, or enchantment. The serpent is therefore an enchanter, a magician, and diviner whose sole source of control now can be exercised in man's mind. He and his followers rejoice in things that are deceitful, cunning, sly, deadly, perverted, corrupt, delusional, and distorted; he plays gloriously with emotions and hallucinations, changes reality to benefit him and have you bow down to his needs."

Tess's voice breaks through as she utters slowly, "Every day I seem to learn more and more about how naïve I've been in the world. To think I may have been worshiping a false God, one set up by man, a church that may have other motives behind it. How oddly symbolic that after removing my veil and the scapular, I'm seeing more than I've ever seen before. What do we do now?" The machine sputters as if emphasizing her point.

There is silence until Dr. Janus turns in our direction and says, with a profound sadness in his eyes, "You have an excuse, but what about me actually living in the outside world and never seeing it?"

The sputtering stops and the lady's voice continues. "You must now pay attention to your misdirected, man-made notions and false history. You are taught to believe there are pharaohs buried in the three major pyramids at Giza and they are monuments to the dead! It is sad, children, for us to see how wrong you are to believe such tall tales. Tell me what pharaoh was found there?"

The Hebrew scholar rushes to my mind. I think about what he had told me about the pyramids and the constellations. The voice goes on. "You are in possession of one of the finest timekeeping pieces in existence that lines up and matches the three pyramids on Mars, but no one at NASA lets you talk about it. They have all the information; they just don't choose to share it! You don't look outside of your immediate perimeter, but children, you need to start to look. Look to the constellations to see us.

God said only He could loosen the belt of Orion and the bands of the Pleiades, your seven sisters. Look to the stars. Look to the stars in Draco, of which there are about eighty, with a *special* one called Thuban. Translated from Hebrew, *Thuban* means 'the subtle.' Scientists know today that 4,600 years ago, Thuban was as bright as Polaris in its time and is the one star that, during the time of the pharaohs in Egypt, it shone through the downward sloping passage of the Great Pyramid of Giza to the bottom of the foundation. In recent years, famous people have paid to experience sleeping in the sarcophagus of the King's Chamber; however they could never get the full experience because during the time of the pharaohs, it was perfectly aligned to the *true north*. How could this be possible unless the pyramid was perfectly built, no errors, and to a specific degree? Do you really think slaves pulled up these blocks and placed them in perfect order?

"The pyramid tells us everything, the circumference of the earth, the weight of the earth, the location of the nearest planets. It explains mathematics, such as pi (3.1416 ...), the mathematical equation to use; it is a sundial of the years, months, days; it shows the universe and its density. Its knowledge is endless. These three pyramids are the configuration of those in the belt of Orion. Sadly, no one teaches you this information. If you opened your eyes, you would see even more mathematical equations to explain man's life on earth by looking inside *the pyramids*. What do the distances in the passageways tell us? People are forever digging, when the truth has nothing to do with some crazy archaeological find but is all about the geometry. Geometry is defined as 'geo'—geophysical, 'metry'—measurements of the earth and its relation to the universe. How misleading when new media arises that is still trying to convince you these are coffins. They are encouraging misinformation. You have been told all things; you just don't see the messages because you are too busy to take the time.

"There are many lessons to be learned, and Teddy has been diligent so as not to get them into the wrong hands. You are our earthly renegades and lovers of light. Spread the news, unloosen the bonds and shackles of deceit; a more harmonious time is coming."

Then bluntly and quite mechanically, we hear, "Please move on to the next lesson on DNA." The sweet voice returns. "May we entice you with the thought there is no junk DNA and children with triple helixes are on planet earth now? We send our love and our enlightenment to those who ask and remember that God promises, 'If ye seek, the door shall be opened and ye shall find.' We send our love and blessings. The Light Bringers."

At that moment a loud siren breaks the silence with a sound more horrid than even the worst phone ring. A mechanical voice comes on, commanding, "Intruders coming. Go to safe room."

We all look at each other, coming out of the haze of information we've just been given, and then another voice, though not mechanical, comes down from the top of the stairs. "Get out of there now. Tess and Mags, get to the safe room. Dr. Janus, there are a series of black cars and SUV's approaching. You and I need to be present to answer their questions, see what they want, especially if for some reason they have a warrant." Not hearing movement, he commands, "Do you hear me?"

We start rushing up the stairs, letting James know we have heard.

I turn around because I need to pull the metal piece from the machine. I need to get it back in place so it doesn't appear as though anything is missing. I get on the stairs and hit a switch from the bottom to ascend. If only this had been built for speed! Not waiting for the floors to even out, we jump up from the rotating floor. Tess has moved away toward the dining room, and Dr. Janus joins James behind the front door. He has a broom and dustpan in hand and is working on getting the dust off the floor so as not to give the area away. I pull the crystal, and the floor finishes closing itself. I take the stairs two at a time and quickly hang the picture back on the wall, standing back briefly to make sure it's somewhat straight.

"They're entering the driveway!" James yells.

I come back down to the main floor, heading in Tess's direction, glancing back long enough to see the backs of Dr. Janus and James at attention at the door. I must have lingered too long because Tess grabs my healthy arm and leads me through the kitchen to the safe room. Just another room I never knew existed! She moves a glass jar, and behind it is a box in which she places her thumb. *Biometrics, even back then,* I think. *How James Bond.* We wait as the shelves that hold the kitchen canning material move to the left; then a small opening becomes visible. We go down some wooden stairs, and there's one more steel door. The area is illuminated by a faint, yellowish safety light. There's another keypad. This time she enters something, and the shelves close behind me while the steel door opens in front. Hearing tires come to a sudden stop on the gravel outside of the house, we don't wait for the space to open fully. Following Tess's lead, I turn to the side and squeeze along after her, careful not to bang my arm against the steel door.

Entering a room, she pushes another button after making sure I'm in, and the door bolts shut. We're locked in. The thickness of the door itself reminds me of a bank vault. I hope there's oxygen. A light inside that had been triggered by the door opening was bright enough to cancel out the safety light, and the room becomes visible. We hear the final knock on the door as the vault closes, and now we can hear nothing.

Tess had moved with such efficiency, as if she had been through this drill a hundred times. She moves to the back wall, pressing button after button, illuminating screens that show different angles of the house. On one screen we see the front door with Dr. Janus's and James's backs to us. On another we see a long shot of the driveway, showing five to seven assorted black cars and SUVs. On yet another, we see the heads of three men approaching the front door. From the angle, it's hard to tell their age or their business.

Except for my "Ugh," when she had grabbed me, neither of us has spoken since hearing James's command. We stand there looking at the black and white screens, silence surrounding us, unable to hear any voices. It's not cold in the room, but I get a chill, a fear of the unknown for James and Dr. Janus that engulfs me. If only this were just a bad black and white movie.

chapter
47

But take ye heed; behold I have foretold you all things.

Mark 13:23, KJV

n the safe room, Tess and I watch the screens for minutes until all goes blank. "So much for technology," I say and Tess can see my fear.

"Look, let's keep our minds occupied. Saul said he left a knapsack for me of materials I need to review."

I see a bed and go directly to it, carefully adjusting myself, muttering, "We still need to find the common denominators to cornerstone or capstone, pyramid, zodiac, sacred geometry, astrology, astronomy, nature, scorpions, the oroborous symbol, the Bible."

"And sunflowers!" Tess fills in. She has found the knapsack.

I go through the list again, slowly repeating each one to show how many there are. "The closest I'm coming is they're timepieces and have something to do with sacred geometry," I mumble as I watch Tess feverishly rummaging through the bag.

She calls each item aloud as she pulls them out, "A Companion Bible; a Strong's Concordance, and a bunch of handwritten notes and some pages that look like they are my father's scribbles. One is titled: *Electro-astromedicine* and has all these garbled sayings. Listen to this Magdalena!" She reads carefully:

> The Greek Sorcerer or Pharmacia
> put the Kabash on health
> enticing or electing death
> through sordid means
> killing innocent children
> and their future kings ...
>
> Politics, government
> And education alike
> Are ploys to dumb you down
> creating nothing but worry and strife
> The four cardinal directions
> are deeper than you think
> I sai I
> Go back to the link.

There's Taurus the Bull, Scorpio the Eagle,
Leo the Lion, Aquarius the human face.
What does it mean when they spin around?
Is it only tall tales or is something more in space?

Look to Ezekiel 1:10
and Revelation 4:6–7, the same
See the amber wheels that came
The things your government shall defame

Remember DNA
Remember Sine Wave
Remember self-correcting
and evolving codes will save.

Tess shakes her head and almost laughs, "I have no idea what my dad means, but these words do remind me of all the crazy children's books my father wrote, like *The Sunflower Song, There Is a Mole in My House,* a little French ditty about *l'Horologe,* another one about the grandfather clock with French words about grand-père and so many others."

"Oh I saw those in the open room, just never had a chance to read them, and I'm as baffled as you are, Tess."

"Look and here's an actual letter from my father with the heading: Behold, I have foretold you all things."

Tess excitedly but carefully reads the letter:

Dear children,

I miss and love you dearly, and if you are reading this, I believe your eyes have finally been opened, but you need to push your mind beyond what can be seen. We are on this earth but not of this earth. Think of Orion as the central threshold and the Pleiades as the measurement for all time clocks and temples of measurement. These time clocks are all located on magnetic grids and focus into the Great Pyramid at Giza. There are twelve energy spokes all interconnected at parts of the earth's star field; these are all working for the power of good and the Christ consciousness. There are fallen angels, nephilium, and aliens living from chemical waste and ugly to look at, but there are those who are here to help, who have higher abilities to move matter, which walk among us. While you think of Egypt as the mathematical and astronomical base of information, you need to think of Israel as the spiritual base, the new JerUSAlem that is coming. There will be people fighting for Israel, God's promised land, who will distort the truth. They will hide under the name of Zionists, but they're playing both sides against the middle and are not who they appear to be. They are not of 'Zion.' You need to learn about them.

You should have learned by now the pyramids are not tombs. The Great Pyramid is built on a point where the magnetic field under the earth crosses with those on the celestial fields so that the fields of alignment are direct. There may be war over who owns the pyramid or attempts to stop who can access it, but this will serve no purpose because owning the pyramid can't control owning the magnetic points of the world.

The Sphinx was not placed there with a face of a pharaoh. It's the head of a woman and the tail of a lion. In other words, from Virgo to Leo, the constellations, a mathematical time piece! It's telling you of the precession of equinoxes, the time changes, and the upcoming date of December 21, 2012 when we move into the next zone of life. This is when the earth's axis will tip and a new true north will be set. Magnetic points will be opened in New York, Tennessee, Texas, Oregon, and other specific points. Look to the dove for more answers.

But always beware of your dates because they were miscalculated early on. You may be six or seven years off in calendar years. No one knows the exact time the final confrontation will happen; God, however, has told you every sign so you will know when it is here, thereby foretelling you all things, despite purposefully leaving the day out so man does not distort the concept of time.

Look to the *Keys of Enoch* and refer to the quotes below. This is not an evil book as some say; it is an awakening with Christ at the core. "The Pleiades and Orion give the mathematics for every chemical sacrifice required in life from Genesis to Revelation." The Bible needs to be decoded, but in the end, this book says those who "carry the image of the Lamb will be separated from those who carry the image of the Bear (Urs Major) and the Dragon (Alpha Draconis), the fallen spiritual powers controlling the old linear astronomy of the Babylonian sciences, forcing man to do homage to the lower heavens.

"Those who worship the Beast through their astronomy and the astrology of the lower heavens and by their mathematical graven images of light are returned to begin their consciousness program once again. The beast, the physical force fields of 666, controls the minds of those on earth and makes them pay homage to money, spiritualists, power, greed, etc. You need to move from the Mazzorath, the lower powers of the heavens of the zodiac, to the Mazaloth, the distant galaxies within the visible spectrum that feed higher consciousness and love you have never known, without the trappings of the world.

And so you know, our central North Star does not appear to revolve in a circle as does every other star. At the time the constellations were mapped, about seven thousand years ago, the Dragon Star (Alpha Draconis) was the Pole Star that marked the central gate or hinge of the earth's motion. The gradual recession of the Dragon star makes it now far away from the Pole.

"Beware as Revelation 21:8 warns. Get out of the slander, the idle gossip, and "godless chatter," and hear the true word. We are living in the biggest perversion of all time when the healer is the physician. You don't even know it. There are fabulous surgeons and doctors, diligently cutting and prescribing drugs and giving chemo, all to save men.

There are times when one breaks an arm, needs emergency help, and these gifts of people from God are your best friends. And there are times, because you are not doing the basic work you need to do yourself, that you are relying on them when it is humanly impossible for them to cure you of what ails you. Some of you have stronger immune systems and look at others as being weak, but there are the enlightened ones who fight the system because only they have hurt so badly to know that "medicine," other than quick care, is not the ultimate answer. You laugh at their weakness and illness, but one day you will wish you'd been as strong as they had been in pain and so close to death.

You need to learn to care for your own body and not trust what they tell you on TV or even what some doctors say as they hand out too much medicine. You need to see the beauty of the human instrument and learn to tune it like a violin. When you vibrate at the right note, you will be well.

Remember, this is only the tip of the information out there. You have years to find what these walls and 144 acres have in store for you within, but what is done before 2012 and given to our people before then will make all the difference in the world. Your goal is to look beyond everything you have ever been taught to believe from the sciences, religion, politics, and history and to reshape a new and higher truth that is being hidden from you. Let go of outdated ideas and concepts, especially if your entire life's work was based on them. Think anew.

Those whom I threatened are the evil ones because I wanted to expose the truth. Since you are reading this, you have probably arrived at the darkest of times where even future children to be conceived by children are being poisoned. The genital organs ruled by *Scorpio* are being destroyed by the evilest and most deceitful lie. In sparing children of so-called cancer, they will start hurting innocent people, and most don't even realize they're doing this.

You can stop this. You can finish the DNA work and get the information out.

There is nothing new *under* the sun. Above it and beyond, however, is a whole new world. Don't fall for the changing and manipulation of DNA; let the helixes change as they're supposed to. Anything else will keep you trapped in the lower heavens. Search for the answer to the riddle of the fig tree. Get to know the groups who are out to hurt you. Learn about the return of the dove. Think beyond all you have been taught and always go in peace and in love. Remember, it has been said, "the first casualty of war is truth." Until we meet again, my love forever, Dad.

chapter
48

*Secrecy is the freedom zealots dream of: no watchman
to check the door, no accountant to check the books,
no judge to check the law. The secret government has no
constitution. The rules it follows are the rules it makes us.*

Bill Moyers

ith all the noise in my head as thoughts collide against each other, I struggle to make sense of all that Tess has just read. I consider myself well educated, but after this I feel like I am clueless. I'd seen hidden underground labs, holograms, and safe rooms all in a few short hours and hadn't even regained my complete memory since the bullet shot. My head is spinning; and I stare at Tess, just so amazed that she is alive. As I'm

just about to try to rest my eyes, a buzzer goes off and I jump. I remember James and Dr. Janus.

Finally this is a sound of welcome interruption. Although I have enjoyed getting to be with Tess, and I really want to know more about who she is, I'm concerned about what happened upstairs. Dr. Janus and James beep into the safe room to let us know all is "safe," four hours after we entered.

Dr. Janus fills us in.

"They asked a lot of questions, had a warrant, but found nothing other than some 'fancy astronomy stuff,' a lot of colorful artwork and some 'harmless children's books.' With the people James knows, they won't be able to get a new warrant for another six to twelve months, so we now have time. They believe Tess is dead, asked no questions about you, Mags, and think the house is just a house. I am sure they will keep an eye from a distance, but we are all safe for now." We stare at each other for minutes as if unsure what to do next.

chapter
49

*Great spirits have always encountered
opposition from mediocre minds.*

Albert Einstein

hese few hours later, to what had seemed like the longest day of my life, we are standing in the foyer where it all began. James finally turns to me, saying, "I'd love to stay longer, but I promised my mom I'd visit her. Today is July 27, and tomorrow is the anniversary of my dad's death. Will you leave tomorrow, Mags?"

I look to Tess and Dr. Janus and say, "If it's all right with you, I'd like to."

"Absolutely," says Dr. Janus.

James comes close to me, "Good trip. Better seeing you than a day at Mardi Gras with all the free alcohol you can drink. It's been fun!"

"Well, fun may be pushing it, but it's been great seeing you too." His bear hug engulfs me, and I yelp.

"Oh, the shoulder, sorry." he says.

"I'll survive."

"Don't be an alien."

"Don't you either. Thank you, James, for everything."

"Just doin' my job. Just drivin' the limo and looking after the passengers!" he says, exiting with a gesture and a grimace, and we all have smiles on our faces.

I know I'll miss him. It's been like being home. The thought of leaving him, Dr. Janus, and Tess with all these issues unresolved about who's after them and with all the knowledge and truths they now have access to is almost more than I can bear. But it's not my home, not my life, and, therefore, I have no real right to the information.

Going up the stairs Dr. Janus mutters Einstein's phrase, "Great spirits have always encountered opposition from mediocre minds." I never realized *I* was the mediocre one! Exhausted, and barely able to muster the energy for proper good night wishes, we all head to bed.

chapter
50

*Just look at everything backwards, upside down—
doctors destroy life, lawyers take away justice, universities
destroy knowledge, major media destroy information
and religion destroys spirituality (Paraphrased).*

Michael Ellner

he next day comes quickly. Somewhat rested, although overwhelmed by all the new info, I pack and then longingly look at the beautiful sapphire dress I had worn to the Met. What an amazing few weeks. I decide to take one last glorious shower before leaving. I grab my towel and a plastic bag to put over the dressings of my "mummied" shoulder. The shower feels great, after I adjusted the nozzle choice with a lighter pressure. I

choose the rosemary mint scent and clean up. I take a final look at one M.L.S. towel and smile.

When done, I head to the kitchen that feels so empty without Ana and see Dr. Janus and Tess staring hopelessly at each other, leaving me with the impression they have no clue as to how to cook for themselves. I burst in, "Okay, Dr. Janus … What's with the M.L.S. towels?"

He looks at me in surprise. I take advantage of his momentary speechlessness to take in the siblings. Tess looks radiant in a bright lime green shirt with some hippie necklace and colorful bangle bracelets. "You look adorable, Tess," I say as I see Dr. Janus still trying to figure out the question.

She responds energetically, "I thought since I have dropped the habit, I should get some color and spunk back in my life!"

Dr. Janus says very delayed, but informally, "And a good morning to you, Mags." Then finally it registers with Dr. Janus, "Did you actually think I had the towels monogrammed for you?"

I'm thrown aback at his incredulous tone. "Well they are *my* initials."

"This is true, however, my mother's maiden name was La Scorvilla, and her first name was Maria. So they were actually made for her by my father, who wanted her to know that he would always remember who she was back in Italy before becoming a Janus."

"That's sweet." Then I say, "I'm starved, how about I make you an old fashioned, good ol' American breakfast with sausage and eggs and pancakes and the likes?"

"Really?" Dr. Janus looks quite surprised. "You like to cook?"

"I love to. How about it?"

"Be our guest."

Pulling chairs around the chopping table, we start talking. I get some coffee brewing and start pulling out pots and pans and food. I ask Tess to tell us more about what Saul said. Noticing tears well up briefly, I say how sorry I am that he died, but how much he must have loved her to have sacrificed himself like he did. "I really liked him," I say.

"I'm glad to hear that, Magdalena. I'm really glad to hear that. He was a good man. Always remember that." I look at Dr. Janus uneasily, not sure why she's addressing me. She then starts to fill us in on many of the things he had taught her.

"Oh Peter, I forgot to tell Magdalena yesterday about something Saul told me. I can't wait to get your impression on this!" We stop and focus on her as the bacon and sausage crackle in the background. She becomes more animated, less strained the longer she talks, and I start to feel more of a connection to her.

"First of all, Jesus was conceived, yes, the Holy Spirit came down and made the Virgin Mary pregnant on that special day, December 25. So if He was conceived on that day, does it not make sense that he was indeed born like other human beings nine months later around September 21? And although we talk about AD and BC and start the calendar at his year of birth, we even have that wrong. It should technically be AD 5 or 6 because the person, I believe a monk, doing the calculations forgot some years. So how can we celebrate his birthday and give presents out on December 25? We don't call our birthday the day Mom and Dad conceived us and celebrate it then; no, we celebrate on the day of our birth. God set the appointed times to feast and to honor Him, and Christmas is absolutely not one of them. Did you know that some churches continue this tradition because it is the time people feel the most generous and give the most donations?"

I jump in, "Now that you say that, Tess, it is interesting to realize how much money is made during the holidays on something that isn't even about Christ. In fact, do you know that advertisers have stripped the holy aspect of it further by keeping

us from saying Merry Christmas in favor of the more politically correct Happy Holidays?"

"No, are you serious? That is a travesty," she says with outrage, making her sound like the Mother Superior.

Tess looks back to Dr. Janus, "Do you remember our Christmases, Peter? We'd gather anxiously around the tree and our parents always had us make one gift by hand, and then after all the presents were opened, they would make us give our favorite gift away to a needy child. It was a beautiful act of charity, and our parents always made the loss up to us somehow. A lot of times we learned we didn't need or even want it as much as we thought."

Dr. Janus is smiling and agreeing. He looks so relaxed, it makes me feel warm.

Tess's wrists jingle with her movements. "We celebrated and honored Christmas on December 25th as well! Why would our intelligent parents never have discussed this discrepancy in dates? Our father would have known this. He would never have let a detail like this slide."

"You are absolutely correct, he would not have."

I walk over to turn the bacon and sausage, and Tess is rapidly moving on to the next points.

"Saul taught me that God was clear that there are three days for us to embrace yearly once Christ was crucified: Passover, Pentecost, and the Feast of Tabernacles. Do you know of any Christians that would know about these?"

We both shake our heads.

She continues, "The minute you mention Passover, people think you are Jewish. Think about how far we have gotten away from the true meaning of a holiday such as Easter."

"Easter?" I turn toward her after placing the bacon on paper towel to degrease.

"Eastre, spelled with an "re," was invented by the Saxons to worship their fertility and sexual goddess. It's a pagan holiday.

Saul told me the word Eastre is in the Bible once. One time! It is a mistranslation in Acts 12:4, and in the Strong's Concordance is the word number 3957, which is 'to pascha,' which means passover. Easter is a heathen term that was also used by the Syrians as Venus. In the Old Testament, it is referred to as Ashtoreth. What should be a holy day, one that honors God's only begotten Son, who sacrificed His life on the cross for us and is resurrected, has a much deeper and richer history than a fun day to put little children in new clothes, selling sugar candy, and hiding Easter eggs. Can you imagine how God must feel?"

Dr. Janus and I are listening attentively, but I'm also multitasking, getting our breakfast plated. With that I say, "Wow, it's all fascinating, but breakfast is served. Let's eat."

We eat in silence, pondering everything that has been said. Then, as it always happens, it is time to go.

"We could not have done this without you, Magdalena. I will be forever grateful to you," Dr. Janus says with a strange glint of pride.

As things are wrapping up, I say, "Well, if you find out the answer to the riddle of life, will you call me first? Because now I'm leaving even more confused than ever!"

They agree they will. Then Tess runs to get something. "Here is a gift for you. Perhaps some day we can look over them together and learn something."

"Oh, how nice," and I go to open it.

"Wait until you get home, okay?"

"Sure. It's heavy. Hmm ... a gift in hand, and I can't open it. You obviously don't know me well!"

Dr. Janus laughs. "I think I am beginning to!" He smiles. "It is getting late though, and we need to get you to the airstrip. The driver should be here in a couple of minutes.

We all stand in the entrance, and I take a longing look around. I mention to Dr. Janus, "With all the excitement, I never made it to the observatory."

"Oh my, you are correct." He looks at his watch, but we know there's no time. "A good excuse to come back sooner rather than later."

"I'd love that! You both feel like family to me!"

We say our good-byes, and the final pang in my heart thumps as I hug Dr. Janus. All is forgiven, and I have that strange feeling again. He grabs me and takes a final look, careful of my shoulder. I swear I see wetness in his eyes. To avoid a meltdown and as an afterthought, I say, "Oh, and don't forget to give Ana my love and thank her for everything. I don't think I've ever been so spoiled."

"We will."

Dr. Janus adds, "Love to your parents, Mags."

"Oh yeah, my parents! How am I going to explain a bullet wound to them?"

Tess comes over and hugs me, kisses me on each cheek, and says, "You have been an inspiration to me. Please stay in touch."

"Oh, I will. You can't get rid of me that easily!" We each sigh, and I bravely head out the huge front door where the limo awaits, and they wave gracefully to me from the stairs.

James has the day off, and the ride to the jet doesn't seem quite as special. I take a final glance at the house, and a big lump forms in my throat. I feel like I'm leaving my home, that somehow I really belong here. "If only," slips out aloud.

A single tear trickles down my face as I realize I'm being ridiculous, but my mind has already started its questions. *How can I go back to work, to my life? How can I interact in this delusional society? How can I pretend nothing has changed?* All questions I'll have to work on.

I try summarizing things. Dr. Janus has lost his "scientific system" and may need to start from a new hypothesis. Tess has lost religion but may have found faith in return. Tess's perpetrator, Saul, a long-time student of their dad, is dead. The group that hired him is still a mystery. Ana is Ana and will still be running a great house. Her knee-sock nylons hanging well below her skirt and the netting on her head for meals are ingrained in my memory for life. James is just James the limo driver, although he did surprise me with some of his medical skills and quick driving maneuvers. As for me, somewhere in here I'm still me, but I have to admit, I'm leaving more confused than ever.

The limo drops me off at the jet, and I board, deep in thought. The return flight is uneventful. My pilot has morphed into a woman and my stewardess into a sweet, elderly steward, and although the crystal still gleams, the insignia is still there, the food is still served, and any alcohol I wish for is available, none of it has the same excitement as before. Suddenly, it just doesn't seem important.

I stop when I remember I have a gift!

I grab the package from my carry-on case and rip through the paper; this time, there's no bow. I beam. Tess has given me a copy of the Strong's Concordance, the Companion Bible, and Saul's syllabuses. One day I'll have to look at them more closely. Then there's a note, "Testimony is the greatest witness of all!" and a check for $25,000 is enclosed. My hand flutters. This is extremely generous. At first, I think I should return some of it, and then I think, *You know what, in this case they can afford it and I'm worth it.* I snort out loud. *Some businesswoman,* I think. I'd totally forgotten about payment when I left. Perhaps I should be concerned about where the money came from, but at the moment don't have the energy to deal with any more conspiracy thoughts.

Holding the napkin in my hand, I smile at the ever-present T. J. I had seen the initials in so many places that I stopped paying attention to them. Then for the first time, as if being hit by a car, I see the letters in an entirely new way. *Wait a minute,* I think. *That's not a T, it's the sign for Pi. Pi.* The more I think about it, the more I realize that it's not an actual J either. I now remember where I've seen it before. It's a spiral with a square, which means it's the golden mean. *No, it can't be, can it? Am I seeing things, making things up?* I motion quickly for the steward. "Please, can you tell me if you have any pieces in this plane similar to the full wording on the outside of the plane?"

"You mean the T. Janus?"

"Exactly."

"Well, I don't know. Let me look around." He's puzzled, but still courteous. He's gone for what seems like an hour. I pull out my laptop and furiously try getting reception from the satellite to do some searching. It's not connecting, which annoys me to no end. I know I'm on to something. What was "Teddy" trying to tell us? Hiding things in plain sight was his specialty, and I'm realizing that nothing, *nothing* he did was by chance. That old flame in my heart starts to burn, and my head starts to *click, click,* or is that my fingers on the keys moving without me even realizing it? How will I ever be able to live in society now because, if my overactive mind hadn't been crazy enough before, how am I going to live with it now?

Finally, the steward returns. *Flight attendant,* I remind myself but think how ridiculous it is we've become so overly sensitive about labels.

"I believe this is what you are looking for, Dr. LaSige."

And there it is. I'm not imagining things at all. All the letters are spelled out. T. Janus with a spiral, each one now appearing more as a mathematical symbol than as a letter, but what does it mean? What exactly was he trying to say? I can't get my computer going, and I know that my lack of knowledge of secret numbers and geometrical shapes means I'll need to do more research. This may have to stay unsolved for today. The closest I can come up with is *pi, spiral, pyramid, aleph, upside down aleph, serpent.* "What does this mean, Teddy?" I say aloud, and the steward comes back over. "I'm sorry, bad habit. I'm talking to myself again! I'm fine." He quietly returns to work.

My mind is focusing and flashing on the insignia in the house, the wall hangings, the architecture, and the gardens as I busily write notes on the computer for future reference. Why does everything in this world seem so upside down?

Before I know it, we're landing—not as smoothly as my captain from heaven, but this pilot knows her job, no doubt about that. I wonder briefly why women are so critical of other women and if I had just made the same pathetic *faux pas.*

chapter
51

Though we can't always see it at the time,
if we look upon events with some perspective,
we see things always happen for our best interests.
We are always being guided in a way
better than we know ourselves.

Swami Satchidananda

 gather my things, thank both the pilot and the steward, and head carefully down the stairs with no distractions this time. No James to meet me, no limo to greet me. Oh well, I'm back, safe and sound.

Then, there it is, my own beautiful, little red Mazda Miata, parked exactly where I had left it. A sense of relief comes over me. "Oh, my car," I say aloud, as if it can hear. "Did you think I left you, abandoned you? How have your last few weeks been? Thank goodness there are some things that don't change and that no one is watching or listening!"

I look around and breathe in more deeply than I have in weeks. Dante said, "All of nature is God's art," and I feel it deep down. It's a beautiful day, warm and dry, just the way I like it. I snap the convertible top down and, using my good arm, throw my computer and bag in the passenger seat and get in. The car starts immediately, and we're off. No one will believe what's gone on in my life in just a few weeks. It'll be all right. Me and my little Miata. It doesn't matter what state, what place—in my car, I'm home.

The Scorpion's Sting has gotten to me. Has it poisoned me to want to give up, or am I hurt enough to want to do something about it? Am I permanently tainted, destined to consider every-thing and everyone untrustworthy for my entire life? Things are never exactly as they seem. I should know better because, as a therapist, one of the deadliest diseases of all is trying to fix some-thing when you don't know the truth behind why it is broken.

Has my life come full circle? Will part of me "die" to the lies of society and be reborn? I know I need to defrag. I know I've just gone through my own oroborous transformation, still the same person but soon to have an entirely new perspective. I have some of the puzzle pieces, but I'm concerned they'll never all fit together. Will I leave this earth without some answers? Will the "Compagnia" find me and, like an evil manufacturer, hide pieces from me? That scares me more than I want to think.

Coming down the hill, approaching the town of Newport, a sense of pressure lifts from me. The lake is visible and has not changed; it has not failed me today. From here I head to the Canadian border. I pass through customs without a problem. Upon arriving at the cabin, I see a note that the owners have gone to Montreal for the week. I'm alone, and that's fine. I can now go back to the nature no one is listening to and see if I can finally relax. For some reason JFK's speech comes to mind, and I wonder if we are really a nation that can trust our own people, or is this a lie? Will I be able to sort through all the disinformation to find the truth? The thought is daunting, and I leave it at that, giggling over his phrasing of "alien" philosophies.

The next morning, after a terrible dream, I get up in the dark at 4:00 a.m. because I want to reconnect with the Omniscient Artist's sunrise, and a new passion is burning in my heart, a new drive. It concerns me some, though, because I'm not sure how many professions we're really allotted in one lifetime! Perhaps, however, this might be *my* time, *my* season, just as Ecclesiastes promised.

I know I want to focus on the concept of breaking through the zodiac control of the Old, of the Mazzorath into the Mazaloth. I want to get a handle on the DNA riddle, on what's really going on with our bodies and medicine, and perhaps even open that thing called the Bible to study it more deeply. One thought had, however, popped up in the wee hours, and it stuck in my head. I'm grateful I have access to the Internet, even out in the middle of nowhere (such a dichotomy). There has to be more to "The Scorpion's Sting" than I'm getting. I don't think we really have that clue yet, or others, for that matter, but this one has stuck with me the most. I go online and look up information about the scorpion.

Scorpion. Kingdom: Animalia, Phylum: Arthropoda …

I read on about the scorpion being an arthropod with eight legs, a tail with six segments, the last one bearing the stinger called the telson, at the end of which is the *hypodermic aculeus* or venim-injecting barb. I think about my Hebrew scholar, the hypodermic needles, and the artwork. Then I see what I've been missing: "The scorpion's outer hyaline layer makes them fluorescent green under ultraviolet light."

And suddenly I get it. Those clues were only surface—yes, an idea that helped me get in touch with the Janus house, but they are by no means the answers. I know what this means. I know those three pictures, the artwork with the sayings, have an odd inkish look to them, but it never dawned on me to put them under a black light. I clumsily get up and do some form of jig. "I got, I got, I got it!" I make the long way over to pick up the phone and realize I can't be rude and call the Januses this early in the morning. On top of that, I want to sit in my glory with nature and try to just honor my intuitive gifts—a little late to hit that mark, but better than not at all!

Sitting back down in the Spitfire car seat on the deck of the boathouse, trying to relax, I break down, lean to the left, and look back through the window to see the time on the clock. It's now 5:15 a.m., and I know that at 5:35 a.m. the sun makes its grand entrance. I'm thrilled. It's as if I'm waiting for a long-anticipated movie and have secured the best seat in the world. The sun's movement over twenty days has only changed nineteen minutes, but my life in that same span of time will never be the same. How can nature's twenty-four hours be so consistent and human days be so obtuse?

The sunrise and nature, unlike man, don't disappoint me in the least. It's more awesome than I remember it. I am at last "listening."

I sit there for at least an hour melding. Settled in and happy the car seat can't go anywhere, I am once again enjoying the omnidirectional rays shedding over the resplendent Lake Memphremagog. Now the sun is so hot that my legs feel crazy-glued to the vinyl. I wonder if this is supposed to be comfortable. I'm glad to be back though. There are some things that don't change. I double-check. The mountains: The owl to the right; the elephant ahead. Everything seems intact. I suppose that's a good thing. For the first time in a long time, I know I've been guided in a way I would never have chosen for myself. I realize that synchronicity is at work and I'm in that single moment when all your life paths join and you know you're exactly where you're supposed to be.

I realize I have a huge smile on my face. No one is there to see it, but it feels good. It feels real. My life has changed by no choice of my own, but I have a sense that it's going to be okay.

I take in another deep breath, just enjoying the silence, when I hear *bam, bam, bam.* I jump out of the car seat, leaving my top layer of epidermis, look around, and realize to my utter dismay that it's pheasant hunting season on the island and the corporate killers are out trying to feel like real men, hunting birds whose wings have been clipped so they can't fly off. My perfect setting is being temporarily violated.

I manage to ignore the sound, sit back down, and start to relax and doze in the sun. A tan would be a good thing for this pale, freckled body. Peace is returning. The sun feels healing on my shoulder wound.

Waking up some minutes later, the sky has changed, and waves are starting to kick up. It's not yet clear if a storm is coming because no rain clouds have passed over, but the white caps fight with each other determining direction. I'm feeling agitated and unnerved, I think because of a bad dream I temporarily had, but then an eerie feeling comes upon me when ... that horrible sound ... the phone rings. Unnerved and frustrated, I have no interest in picking it up, but knowing what happened the last time someone tracked me down at this hour, I figure I'd better answer it. Reluctantly, I get out of my seat, trip again over the phone wire I know is there but have forgotten, pick up the phone, and groggily say, "*Oui, Allo?*"

"Mags, it's your mom calling. I don't know how to say this in any other way than to just give you the facts. Your father has just been diagnosed with cancer. It's terminal."

Dead silence.

Author's Note

The Order of the Carmelites exists and its rituals are real. Many nuns, not just Carmelites, were forced to burn their King James Version of the Bible before entering the convent. Since the 1960s the Roman Catholic Church has lost over 120,000 nuns, about 70 percent of which are directly as a result of broken promises that led to diminished roles from the Second Vatican Council. The remainder have died. As of August 2009, there were less than 59,000 nuns remaining in the United States, and most of them were over the age of seventy. If it had not been for Social Security agreeing to provide financial support, a large majority of them would live in complete poverty.

As for HPV and other questions, the reader is encouraged to visit the website at www.jdmasterson.com to participate in up-to-date information, which is being made available with the purpose of helping people make more informed decisions. A section is dedicated to voicing the reader's concerns. J. D. Masterson also can be found on Facebook.